P9-BIR-550

MASTERS OF SCIENCE FICTION PRAISE ONE OF THEIR OWN:

"R.A. Lafferty is one of the most original writers in science fiction. He bends or breaks normal story restrictions apparently at will, pokes fun at serious matters and breaks into a kind of folk-lyricism over grotesqueries. All this, plus the most unfettered imagination we've enjoyed in years."

—Terry Carr

"The Lafferty madness . . . is peppered with nightmare"
—Samuel R. Delany

". . . wild, subtle, demonic, angelic, hilarious, tragic, poetic, a thundering melodrama and a quest into the depths of the human spirit . . . R.A. Lafferty has always been uniquely his own man."

—Poul Anderson

"Lafferty's stories, like Philip K. Dick's, are not susceptible to being confused with the work of any other writer."

—Fred Saberhagen

"It is a minor miracle that a serious philosophical and speculative work should be written so colorfully and so lyrically."

—Judith Merril

"As with everything the man writes, the wind of imagination blows strongly . . . and we can settle back to appreciating the special magic proffered by the madman Lafferty."

—Harlan Ellison

stories by **R. A. LAFFERTY**

NINE HUNDRED HUNDRED GRAND- MOTHERS

WILDSIDE PRESS
Berkeley Heights, NJ ▼ 1999

Nine Hundred Grandmothers

Copyright © 1970 by R A Lafferty

All rights reserved. No part of this book may be reproduced in any form or by any means, except for the in-
clusion of brief quotations in a review, without permission
in writing from the publisher
All characters in this book are fictitious Any resem-
blance to actual persons, living or dead, is purely coin-
cidental

WILDSIDE PRESS
P.O. Box 45
Gillette, NJ 07933-0045

"Nine Hundred Grandmothers " Copyright © 1966 by Galaxy Publishing Corp From **If,** February 1966

"Land of the Great Horses " Copyright © 1967 by Harlan Ellison From **Dangerous Visions.**

"Ginny Wrapped in the Sun " Copyright © 1967 by Galaxy Publishing Corp From **Galaxy,** August, 1967

"The Six Fingers of Time " Copyright © 1960 by Galaxy Publishing Corp From **If,** September 1960

"Frog On the Mountain " Copyright © 1970 by R A Lafferty Published here for the first time anywhere by arrangement with the author

"All the People " Copyright © 1961 by Galaxy Publishing Corp From **Galaxy,** April, 1961

"Primary Education of the Camiroi " Copyright © 1966 by Galaxy Publishing Corp From **Galaxy,** December 1966

"Slow Tuesday Night " Copyright © 1965 by Galaxy Publishing Corp From **Galaxy,** April 1965

"Snuffles " Copyright © 1960 by Galaxy Publishing Corp From **Galaxy,** December 1960

"Thus We Frustrate Charlemagne " Copyright © 1967 by Galaxy Publishing Corp From **Galaxy,** February 1969

"Name of the Snake " Copyright © 1964 by Galaxy Publishing Corp From **Worlds of Tomorrow,** April 1964

"Narrow Valley " Copyright © 1966 by Mercury Press, Inc From **Fantasy and Science Fiction,** September 1966

"Polity and Custom of the Camiroi " Copyright © 1967 by Galaxy Publishing Corp From **Galaxy,** June 1967

"In Our Block " Copyright © 1965 by Galaxy Publishing Corp From **If,** July 1965

"Hog-Belly Honey " Copyright © 1965 by Mercury Press, Inc From **Fantasy and Science Fiction,** September 1965

"Seven Day Terror " Copyright © 1962 by Galaxy Publishing Corp From **If,** March 1962

"The Hole On the Corner " Copyright © 1967 by Damon Knight From **Orbit 2.**

"What's the Name of That Town?" Copyright © 1964 by Galaxy Publishing Corp From **Galaxy,** October 1964

"Through Other Eyes " Copyright © 1960 by Columbia Publications, Inc From **Future,** February 1960

"One at a Time " Copyright © 1969 by Damon Knight From **Orbit 4.**

"Guesting Time " Copyright © 1965 by Galaxy Publishing Corp From **If,** May 1965

TABLE OF CONTENTS

NINE HUNDRED GRANDMOTHERS

CERAN SWICEGOOD was a promising young Special Aspects Man. But, like all Special Aspects, he had one irritating habit. He was forever asking the question: How Did It All Begin?

They all had tough names except Ceran. Manbreaker Crag, Heave Huckle, Blast Berg, George Blood, Move Manion (when Move says "Move," you move), Trouble Trent. They were supposed to be tough, and they had taken tough names at the naming. Only Ceran kept his own—to the disgust of his commander, Manbreaker.

"Nobody can be a hero with a name like Ceran Swicegood!" Manbreaker would thunder. "Why don't you take Storm Shannon? That's good. Or Gutboy Barrelhouse or Slash Slagle or Nevel Knife? You barely glanced at the suggested list."

"I'll keep my own," Ceran always said, and that is where he made his mistake. A new name will sometimes bring out a new personality. It had done so for George Blood. Though the hair on George's chest was a graft job, yet that and his new name had turned him from a boy into a man. Had Ceran assumed the heroic name of Gutboy Barrelhouse he might have been capable of rousing endeavors and man-sized angers rather than his tittering indecisions and flouncy furies.

They were down on the big asteroid Proavitus—a sphere that almost tinkled with the potential profit that might be shaken out of it. And the tough men of the Expedition knew their business. They signed big contracts on the native velvet-like bark scrolls and on their own parallel tapes. They impressed, inveigled and somewhat cowed the slight people of Proavitus. Here

7

was a solid two-way market, enough to make 'them slaver. And there was a whole world of oddities that could lend themselves to the luxury trade.

"Everybody's hit it big but you," Manbreaker crackled in kindly thunder to Ceran after three days there. "But even Special Aspects is supposed to pay its way. Our charter compels us to carry one of your sort to give a cultural twist to the thing, but it needn't be restricted to that. What we go out for every time, Ceran, is to cut a big fat hog in the rump—we make no secret of that. But if the hog's tail can be shown to have a cultural twist to it, that will solve a requirement. And if that twist in the tail can turn us a profit, then we become mighty happy about the whole thing. Have you been able to find out anything about the living dolls, for instance? They might have both a cultural aspect and a market value."

"The living dolls seem a part of something much deeper," Ceran said. "There's a whole complex of things to be unraveled. The key may be the statement of the Proavitoi that they do not die."

"I think they die pretty young, Ceran. All those out and about are young, and those I have met who do not leave their houses are only middling old."

"Then where are their cemeteries?"

"Likely they cremate the old folks when they die."

"Where are the crematories?"

"They might just toss the ashes out or vaporize the entire remains. Probably they have no reverence for ancestors."

"Other evidence shows their entire culture to be based on an exaggerated reverence for ancestors."

"You find out, Ceran. You're Special Aspects Man."

Ceran talked to Nokoma, his Proavitoi counterpart as translator. Both were expert, and they could meet each other halfway in talk. Nokoma was likely feminine. There was a certain softness about both the sexes of the

8

Proavitoi, but the men of the Expedition believed that they had them straight now.

"Do you mind if I ask some straight questions?" Ceran greeted her today.

"Sure is not. How else I learn the talk well but by talking?"

"Some of the Proavitoi say that they do not die, Nokoma. Is this true?"

"How is not be true? If they die, they not be here to say they do not die. Oh, I joke, I joke. No, we do not die. It is a foolish alien custom which we see no reason to imitate. On Proavitus, only the low creatures die."

"None of you does?"

"Why, no. Why should one want to be an exception in this?"

"But what do you do when you get very old?"

"We do less and less then. We come to a deficiency of energy. Is it not the same with you?"

"Of course. But where do you go when you become exceedingly old?"

"Nowhere. We stay at home then. Travel is for the young and those of the active years."

"Let's try it from the other end," Ceran said. "Where are your father and mother, Nokoma?"

"Out and about. They aren't really old."

"And your grandfathers and grandmothers?"

"A few of them still get out. The older ones stay home."

"Let's try it this way. How many grandmothers do you have, Nokoma?"

"I think I have nine hundred grandmothers in my house. Oh, I know that isn't many, but we are the young branch of a family. Some of our clan have very great numbers of ancestors in their houses."

"And all these ancestors are alive?"

"What else? Who would keep things not alive? How would such be ancestors?"

Ceran began to hop around in his excitement.

"Could I see them?" he twittered.

"It might not be wise for you to see the older of them," Nokoma cautioned. "It could be an unsettling thing for strangers, and we guard it. A few tens of them you can see, of course."

Then it came to Ceran that he might be onto what he had looked for all his life. He went into a panic of expectation.

"Nokoma, it would be finding the key!" he fluted. "If none of you has ever died, then your entire race would still be alive!".

"Sure. Is like you count fruit. You take none away, you still have them all."

"But if the first of them are still alive, then they might know their origin! They would know how it began! Do they? Do you?"

"Oh, not I. I am too young for the Ritual."

"But who knows? Doesn't someone know?"

"Oh, yes, All the old ones know how it began."

"How old? How many generations back from you till they know?"

"Ten, no more. When I have ten generations of children, then I will also go to the Ritual."

"The Ritual, what is it?"

"Once a year, the old people go to the very old people. They wake them up and ask them how it all began. The very old people tell them the beginning. It is a high time. Oh, how they hottle and laugh! Then the very old people go back to sleep for another year. So it is passed down to the generations. That is the Ritual."

The Proavitoi were not humanoid. Still less were they "monkey-faces," though that name was now set in the explorers' lingo. They were upright and robed and swathed, and were assumed to be two-legged under their garments. Though, as Manbreaker said, "They might go on wheels, for all we know."

They had remarkable flowing hands that might be

called everywhere-digited. They could handle tools, or employ their hands as if they were the most intricate tools.

George Blood was of the opinion that the Proavitoi were always masked, and that the men of the Expedition had never seen their faces. He said that those apparent faces were ritual masks, and that no part of the Proavitoi had ever been seen by the men except for those remarkable hands, which perhaps were their real faces.

The men reacted with cruel hilarity when Ceran tried to explain to them just what a great discovery he was verging on.

"Little Ceran is still on the how-did-it-begin jag," Manbreaker jeered. "Ceran, will you never give off asking which came first, the chicken or the egg?"

"I will have that answer very soon," Ceran sang. "I have the unique opportunity. When I find how the Proavitoi began, I may have the clue to how everything began. All of the Proavitoi are still alive, the very first generation of them."

"It passes belief that you can be so simpleminded," Manbreaker moaned. "They say that one has finally mellowed when he can suffer fools gracefully. By God, I hope I never come to that."

But two days later, it was Manbreaker who sought out Ceran Swicegood on nearly the same subject. Manbreaker had been doing a little thinking and discovering of his own.

"You are Special Aspects Man, Ceran," he said, "and you have been running off after the wrong aspect."

"What is that?"

"It don't make a damn how it began. What is important is that it may not have to end."

"It is the beginning that I intend to discover," said Ceran.

"You fool, can't you understand anything? What do the Proavitoi possess so uniquely that we don't know

11

whether they have it by science or by their nature or by fool luck?"

"Ah, their chemistry, I suppose."

"Sure. Organic chemistry has come of age here. The Proavitoi have every kind of nexus and inhibitor and stimulant. They can grow and shrink and telescope and prolong what they will. These creatures seem stupid to me; it is as if they had these things by instinct. But they have them, that is what is important. With these things, we can become the patent medicine kings of the universes, for the Proavitoi do not travel or make many outside contacts. These things can do anything or undo anything. I suspect that the Proavitoi can shrink cells, and I suspect that they can do something else."

"No, they couldn't shrink cells. It is you who talk nonsense now, Manbreaker."

"Never mind. Their things already make nonsense of conventional chemistry. With the pharmacopoeia that one could pick up here, a man need never die. That's the stick horse you've been riding, isn't it? But you've been riding it backward with your head to the tail. The Proavitoi say that they never die."

"They seem pretty sure that they don't. If they did, they would be the first to know it, as Nokoma says."

"What? Have these creatures humor?"

"Some."

"But, Ceran, you don't understand how big this is."

"I'm the only one who understands it so far. It means that if the Proavitoi have always been immortal, as they maintain, then the oldest of them are still alive. From them I may be able to learn how their species—and perhaps every species—began."

Manbreaker went into his dying buffalo act then. He tore his hair and nearly pulled out his ears by the roots. He stomped and pawed and went off bull-bellowing: "It don't make a damn how it began, you fool! It might not have to end!" so loud that the hills echoed back: "It don't make a damn—you fool."

12

Ceran Swicegood went to the house of Nokoma, but not with her on her invitation. He went without her when he knew that she was away from home. It was a sneaky thing to do, but the men of the Expedition were trained in sneakery.

He would find out better without a mentor about the nine hundred grandmothers, about the rumored living dolls. He would find out what the old people did do if they didn't die, and find if they knew how they were first born. For his intrusion, he counted on the innate politeness of the Proavitoi.

The house of Nokoma, of all the people, was in the cluster on top of the large flat hill, the Acropolis of Proavitus. They were earthen houses, though finely done, and they had the appearance of growing out of and being a part of the hill itself.

Ceran went up the winding, ascending flagstone paths, and entered the house which Nokoma had once pointed out to him. He entered furtively, and encountered one of the nine hundred grandmothers—one with whom nobody need be furtive.

The grandmother was seated and small and smiling at him. They talked without real difficulty, though it was not as easy as with Nokoma, who could meet Ceran halfway in his own language. At her call, there came a grandfather who likewise smiled at Ceran. These two ancients were somewhat smaller than the Proavitoi of active years. They were kind and serene. There was an atmosphere about the scene that barely missed being an odor—not unpleasant, sleepy, reminiscent of something, almost sad.

"Are there those here older than you?" Ceran asked earnestly.

"So many, so many, who could know how many?" said the grandmother. She called in other grandmothers and grandfathers older and smaller than herself, these no more than half the size of the active Proavitoi—small, sleepy, smiling.

Ceran knew now that the Proavitoi were not masked. The older they were, the more character and interest there was in their faces. It was only of the immature active Proavitoi that there could have been a doubt. No masks could show such calm and smiling old age as this. The queer textured stuff was their real faces.

So old and friendly, so weak and sleepy, there must have been a dozen generations of them there back to the oldest and smallest.

"How old are the oldest?" Ceran asked the first grandmother.

"We say that all are the same age since all are perpetual," the grandmother told him. "It is not true that all are the same age, but it is indelicate to ask how old."

"You do not know what a lobster is," Ceran said to them, trembling, "but it is a creature that will boil happily if the water on him is heated slowly. He takes no alarm, for he does not know at what point the heat is dangerous. It is that gradual here with me. I slide from one degree to another with you and my credulity is not alarmed. I am in danger of believing anything about you if it comes in small doses, and it will. I believe that you are here and as you are for no other reason than that I see and touch you. Well, I'll be boiled for a lobster, then, before I turn back from it. Are there those here even older than the ones present?"

The first grandmother motioned Ceran to follow her. They went down a ramp through the floor into the older part of the house, which must have been under ground.

Living dolls! They were here in rows on the shelves, and sitting in small chairs in their niches. Doll-sized indeed, and several hundred of them.

Many had wakened at the intrusion. Others came awake when spoken to or touched. They were incredibly ancient, but they were cognizant in their glances and recognition. They smiled and stretched sleepily, not as humans would, but as very old puppies might. Ceran

14

spoke to them, and they understood each other surprisingly.

Lobster, lobster, said Ceran to himself, *the water has passed the danger point! And it hardly feels different. If you believe your senses in this, then you will be boiled alive in your credulity.*

He knew now that the living dolls were real and that they were the living ancestors of the Proavitoi.

Many of the little creatures began to fall asleep again. Their waking moments were short, but their sleeps seemed to be likewise. Several of the living mummies woke a second time while Ceran was still in the room, woke refreshed from very short sleeps and were anxious to talk again.

"You are incredible!" Ceran cried out, and all the small and smaller and still smaller creatures smiled and laughed their assent. Of course they were. All good creatures everywhere are incredible, and were there ever so many assembled in one place? But Ceran was greedy. A roomful of miracles wasn't enough.

"I have to take this back as far as it will go!" he cried avidly. "Where are the even older ones?"

"There are older ones and yet older and again older," said the first grandmother, "and thrice-over older ones, but perhaps it would be wise not to seek to be too wise. You have seen enough. The old people are sleepy. Let us go up again."

Go up again, out of this? Ceran would not. He saw passages and descending ramps, down into the heart of the great hill itself. There were whole worlds of rooms about him and under his feet. Ceran went on and down, and who was to stop him? Not dolls and creatures much smaller than dolls.

Manbreaker had once called himself an old pirate who reveled in the stream of his riches. But Ceran was the Young Alchemist who was about to find the Stone itself.

He walked down the ramps through centuries and

15

millennia. The atmosphere he had noticed on the upper levels was a clear odor now—sleepy, half-remembered, smiling, sad and quite strong. That is the way Time smells.

"Are there those here even older than you?" Ceran asked a small grandmother whom he held in the palm of his hand.

"So old and so small that I could hold in my hand," said the grandmother in what Ceran knew from Nokoma to be the older uncompounded form of the Proavitus language.

Smaller and older the creatures had been getting as Ceran went through the rooms. He was boiled lobster now for sure. He had to believe it all: he saw and felt it. The wren-sized grandmother talked and laughed and nodded that there were those far older than herself, and in doing so she nodded herself back to sleep. Ceran returned her to her niche in the hive-like wall where there were thousands of others, miniaturized generations.

Of course he was not in the house of Nokoma now. He was in the heart of the hill that underlay all the houses of Proavitus, and these were the ancestors of everybody on the asteroid.

"Are there those here even older than you?" Ceran asked a small grandmother whom he held on the tip of his finger.

"Older and smaller," she said, "but you come near the end."

She was asleep, and he put her back in her place. The older they were, the more they slept.

He was down to solid rock under the roots of the hill. He was into the passages that were cut out of that solid rock, but they could not be many or deep. He had a sudden fear that the creatures would become so small that he could not see them or talk to them, and so he would miss the secret of the beginning.

But had not Nokoma said that all the old people knew the secret? Of course. But he wanted to hear it from the oldest of them. He would have it now, one way or the other.

"Who is the oldest? Is this the end of it? Is this the beginning? Wake up! Wake up!" he called when he was sure he was in the lowest and oldest room.

"Is it Ritual?" asked some who woke up. Smaller than mice they were, no bigger than bees, maybe older than both.

"It is a special Ritual," Ceran told them. "Relate to me how it was in the beginning."

What was that sound—too slight, too scattered to be a noise? It was like a billion microbes laughing. It was the hilarity of little things waking up to a high time.

"Who is the oldest of all?" Ceran demanded, for their laughter bothered him. "Who is the oldest and first?"

"I am the oldest, the ultimate grandmother," one said gaily. "All the others are my children. Are you also of my children?"

"Of course," said Ceran, and the small laughter of unbelief flittered out from the whole multitude of them.

"Then you must be the ultimate child, for you are like no other. If you be, then it is as funny at the end as it was in the beginning."

"How was it in the beginning?" Ceran bleated. "You are the first. Do you know how you came to be?"

"Oh, yes, yes," laughed the ultimate grandmother, and the hilarity of the small things became a real noise now.

"How did it begin?" demanded Ceran, and he was hopping and skipping about in his excitement.

"Oh, it was so funny a joke the way things began that you would not believe it," chittered the grandmother. "A joke, a joke!"

"Tell me the joke, then. If a joke generated your species, then tell me that cosmic joke."

"Tell yourself," tinkled the grandmother. "You are a part of the joke if you are of my children. Oh, it is too funny to believe. How good to wake up and laugh and go to sleep again."

Blazing green frustration! To be so close and to be balked by a giggling bee!

"Don't go to sleep again! Tell me at once how it began!" Ceran shrilled, and he had the ultimate grandmother between thumb and finger.

"This is not Ritual," the grandmother protested. "Ritual is that you guess what it was for three days, and we laugh and say 'No, no, no, it was something nine times as wild as that. Guess some more.'"

"I will *not* guess for three days! Tell me at once or I will crush you," Ceran threatened in a quivering voice.

"I look at you, you look at me, I wonder if you will do it," the ultimate grandmother said calmly.

Any of the tough men of the Expedition would have done it—would have crushed her, and then another and another and another of the creatures till the secret was told. If Ceran had taken on a tough personality and a tough name he'd have done it. If he'd been Gutboy Barrelhouse he'd have done it without a qualm. But Ceran Swicegood couldn't do it.

"Tell me," he pleaded in agony. "All my life I've tried to find out how it began, how anything began. And you know!"

"We know. Oh, it was so funny how it began. So joke! So fool, so clown, so grotesque thing! Nobody could guess, nobody could believe."

"Tell me! Tell me!" Ceran was ashen and hysterical.

"No, no, you are no child of mine," chortled the ultimate grandmother. "Is too joke a joke to tell a stranger. We could not insult a stranger to tell so funny, so unbelieve. Strangers can die. Shall I have it on conscience that a stranger died laughing?"

"Tell me! Insult me! Let me die laughing!" But Ceran nearly died crying from the frustration that ate him up as a million bee-sized things laughed and hooted and giggled:

"Oh, it was so funny the way it began!"

And they laughed. And laughed. And went on laugh-

18

ing . . . until Ceran Swicegood wept and laughed together, and crept away, and returned to the ship still laughing. On his next voyage he changed his name to Blaze Bolt and ruled for ninety-seven days as king of a sweet sea island in M-81, but that is another and much more unpleasant story.

LAND OF THE GREAT HORSES

"They came and took our country away from us," the people had always said. But nobody understood them.

Two Englishmen, Richard Rockwell and Seruno Smith, were rolling in a terrain buggy over the Thar Desert. It was bleak, red country, more rock than sand. It looked as though the top had been stripped off it and the naked underland left uncovered.

They heard thunder and it puzzled them. They looked at each other, the blond Rockwell and the dark Smith. It never thundered in the whole country between New Delhi and Bahawalpur. What would this rainless north India desert have to thunder with?

"Let's ride the ridges here," Rockwell told Smith, and he sent the vehicle into a climb. "It never rains here, but once before I was caught in a draw in a country where it never rained. I nearly drowned."

It thundered again, heavy and rolling, as though to tell them that they were hearing right.

"This draw is named Kuti Tavdavi—Little River," Smith said darkly. "I wonder why."

Then he jerked back as though startled at himself.

"Rockwell, why did I say that? I never saw this draw before. How did a name like that pop into my mind? But it's the low draw that would be a little river if it ever rained in this country. This land can't have significant rain. There's no high place to tip whatever moisture goes over."

"I wonder about that every time I come," said Rockwell, and raised his hand toward the shimmering heights —the Land of the Great Horses, the famous mirage.

"If it were really there it would tip the moisture. It would make a lush savanna of all this."

They were mineral explorers doing ground minutiae on promising portions of an aerial survey. The trouble with the Thar was that it had everything—lead, zinc, antimony, copper, tin, bauxite—in barely submarginal amounts. Nowhere would the Thar pay off, but everywhere it would almost pay.

Now it was lightning about the heights of the mirage, and they had never seen that before. It had clouded and lowered. It was thundering in rolling waves, and there is no mirage of sound.

"There is either a very large and very busy bird up there or this is rain," Rockwell said.

And it had begun to rain, softly but steadily. It was pleasant as they chukkered along in the vehicle through the afternoon. Rain in the desert is always like a bonus.

Smith broke into a happy song in one of the northwest India tongues, a tune with a ribald swing to it, though Rockwell didn't understand the words. It was full of double rhymes and vowel-packed words such as a child might make up.

"How the devil do you know the tongues so well?" Rockwell asked "I find them difficult, and I have a good linguistic background." '

"I didn't have to learn them," Smith said, "I just had to remember them. They all cluster around the *boro jib* itself."

"Around the what? How many of the languages do you know?"

"All of them. The Seven Sisters, they're called: Punjabi, Kashmiri, Gujarati, Marathi, Sindhi, Hindi."

"Your Seven Sisters only number six," Rockwell jibed.

"There's a saying that the seventh sister ran off with a horse trader," Smith said. "But that seventh lass is still encountered here and there around the world."

Often they stopped to survey on foot. The very color of the new rivulets was significant to the mineral men,

21

and this was the first time they had ever seen water flow in that country. They continued on fitfully and slowly, and ate up a few muddy miles.

Rockwell gasped once and nearly fell off the vehicle. He had seen a total stranger riding beside him, and it shook him.

Then he saw that it was Smith as he had always been, and he was dumbfounded by the illusion. And, soon, by something else.

"Something is very wrong here," Rockwell said.

"Something is very right here," Smith answered him, and then broke into another song in an Indian tongue.

"We're lost," Rockwell worried out loud. "We can't see any distance for the rain, but there shouldn't be rising ground here. It isn't mapped."

"Of course it is," Smith sang. "It's the Jalo Char."

"The what? Where did you get a name like that? The map's a blank here, and the country should be."

"Then the map is defective. Man, it's the sweetest valley in the world! It will lead us all the way up. How could the map forget it? How could we all forget it for so long?"

"Smith! What's wrong? You're pie-eyed."

"Everything's right, I tell you. I was reborn just a minute ago. It's a coming home."

"Smith! We're riding through green grass."

"I love it. I could crop it like a horse."

"That cliff, Smith! It shouldn't be that close! It's part of the mir—"

"Why, sir, that is Lolo Trusul."

"But it's not real! It's not on any topography map!"

"Map, sir? I'm a poor *kalo* man who wouldn't know about things like that."

"Smith! You're a qualified cartographer!"

"Does seem that I followed a trade with a name like that. But the cliff is real enough. I climbed it in my boyhood—in my other boyhood. And that yonder, sir, is Drapengoro Rez—the Grassy Mountain. And the high

22

plateau ahead of us which we begin to climb is Diz Boro Grai—the Land of the Great Horses."

Rockwell stopped the terrain buggy and leaped off. Smith followed him in a happy daze.

"Smith, you're wide-eyed crazy!" Rockwell gasped. "And what am I? We're terribly lost somehow. Smith, look at the log chart and the bearings recorder!"

"Log chart, sir? I'm a poor *kalo* man who wouldn't know—"

"Damn you, Smith, you *made* these instruments. If they're correct we're seven hundred feet too high and have been climbing for ten miles into a highland that's supposed to be part of a mirage. These cliffs can't be here. We can't be here. Smith!"

But Seruno Smith had ambled off like a crazy man.

"Smith, where are you trotting off to? Can't you hear me?"

"You call to me, sir?" asked Smith. "And by such a name?"

"Are the two of us as crazy as the country?" Rockwell moaned. "I've worked with you for three years. Isn't your name Smith?"

"Why, yes, sir, I guess it might be englished as Horse-Smith or Black-Smith. But my name is Pettalangro and I'm going home."

And the man who had been Smith started on foot up to the Land of the Great Horses.

"Smith, I'm getting on the buggy and I'm going back," Rockwell shouted. "I'm scared liverless of this country that changes. When a mirage turns solid it's time to quit. Come along now! We'll be back in Bikaner by tomorrow morning. There's a doctor there, and a whiskey bar. We need one of them."

"Thank you, sir, but I must go up to my home," Smith sang out. "It was kind of you to give me a ride along the way."

"I'm leaving you, Smith. One crazy man is better than two."

23

"*Ashava, Sarishan,*" Smith called a parting.

"Smith, unriddle me one last thing." Rockwell called, trying to find a piece of sanity to hold to. "What is the name of the seventh sister?"

"Deep Romany," Smith sang, and he was gone up into the high plateau that had always been a mirage.

In an upper room on Olive Street in St. Louis, Missouri, a half-and-half couple were talking half-and-half.

"The *rez* has *riser'd*," the man said. "I can *sung* it like *brishindo*. Let's *jal*."

"All right," the wife said, "if you're *awa*."

"Hell, I bet I can *riker* plenty *bano* on the *beda* we got here. I'll have *kakko* come *kinna* it *saro*."

"With a little *bachi* we can be *jal'd* by *areat*," said the wife.

"*Nashiva,* woman, *nashiva!*"

"All right," the wife said, and she began to pack their suitcases.

In Camargo in the Chihuahua State of Mexico, a shade-tree mechanic sold his business for a hundred pesos and told his wife to pack up—they were leaving.

"To leave now when business is so good?" she asked.

"I only got one car to fix and I can't fix that," the man said.

"But if you keep it long enough, he will pay you to put it together again even if it isn't fixed. That's what he did last time. And you've a horse to shoe."

"I'm afraid of that horse. It has come back, though. Let's go."

"Are you sure we will be able to find it?"

"Of course I'm not sure. We will go in our wagon and our sick horse will pull it."

"Why will we go in the wagon, when we have a car, of sorts?"

"I don't know why. But we will go in the wagon, and

we will nail the old giant horseshoe up on the lintel board."

A carny in Nebraska lifted his head and smelled the air.

"It's come back," he said. "I always knew we'd know. Any other Romanies here?"

"I got a little *rart* in me," said one of his fellows. "This *narvelengero dives* is only a two-bit carnival anyhow. We'll tell the boss to shove it up his *chev* and we'll be gone."

In Tulsa, a used-car dealer named Gypsy Red announced the hottest sale on the row:

"Everything for nothing! I'm leaving. Pick up the papers and drive them off. Nine new heaps and thirty good ones. All free."

"You think we're crazy?" the people asked. "There's a catch."

Red put the papers for all the cars on the ground and put a brick on top of them. He got in the worst car on the lot and drove it off forever.

"All free," he sang out as he drove off. "Pick up the papers and drive the cars away."

They're still there. You think people are crazy to fall for something like that that probably has a catch to it?

In Galveston a barmaid named Margaret was asking merchant seamen how best to get passage to Karachi.

"Why Karachi?" one of them asked her.

"I thought it would be the nearest big port," she said. "It's come back, you know."

"I kind of felt this morning it had come back," he said. "I'm a *chal* myself. Sure, we'll find something going that way."

In thousands of places fawney-men and dukkerin-women, kakki-baskros and hegedusies, clowns and commission men, Counts of Condom and Dukes of Little Egypt *parɣel'd* in their chips and got ready to roll.

Men and families made sudden decisions in every country. *Athinganoi* gathered in the hills above Salonika in Greece and were joined by brothers from Serbia and Albania and the Rhodope Hills of Bulgaria. *Zingari* of north Italy gathered around Pavia and began to roll toward Genoa to take ship. *Boemios* of Portugal came down to Porto and Lisbon. *Gitanos* of Andalusia and all southern Spain came to Sanlúcar and Málaga. *Zigeuner* from Thuringia and Hanover thronged to Hamburg to find ocean passage. *Gioboga* and their mixed-blood *Shelta* cousins from every *cnoc* and *coill* of Ireland found boats at Dublin and Limerick and Bantry.

From deeper Europe, *Tsigani* began to travel overland eastward. The people were going from two hundred ports of every continent and over a thousand highroads—many of them long forgotten.

Balauros, Kalo, Manusch, Melelo, Tsigani, Moro, Romani, Flamenco, Sinto, Cicara, the many-named people was traveling in its thousands. The *Romani Rai* was moving.

Two million Gypsies of the world were going home.

At the Institute, Gregory Smirnov was talking to his friends and associates.

"You remember the thesis I presented several years ago," he said, "that, a little over a thousand years ago, Outer Visitors came down to Earth and took a sliver of our Earth away with them. All of you found the proposition comical, but I arrived at my conclusion by isostatic and eustatic analysis carried out minutely. There is no doubt that it happened."

"One of our slivers is missing," said Aloysius Shiplap. "You guessed the sliver taken at about ten thousand square miles in area and no more than a mile thick at its greatest. You said you thought they wanted to run this sliver from our Earth through their laboratories as a sample. Do you have something new on our missing sliver?"

"I'm closing the inquiry," Gregory said. "They've brought it back."

It was simple really, *jekvasteskero*, Gypsy-simple. It is the *gadjo*, the non-Gypsies of the world, who give complicated answers to simple things.

"They came and took our country away from us," the Gypsies had always said, and that is what had happened.

The Outer Visitors had run a slip under it, rocked it gently to rid it of nervous fauna, and then taken it away for study. For a marker, they left an immaterial simulacrum of that high country as we ourselves sometimes set name or picture tags to show where an object will be set later. This simulacrum was often seen by humans as a mirage.

The Outer Visitors also set simulacra in the minds of the superior fauna that fled from the moving land. This would be a homing instinct, inhibiting permanent settlement anywhere until the time should come for the resettlement; entwined with this instinct were certain premonitions, fortune-showings, and understandings.

Now the Visitors brought the slice of land back, and its old fauna homed in on it.

"What will the—ah—patronizing smile on my part—Outer Visitors do now, Gregory?" Aloysius Shiplap asked back at the Institute.

"Why, take another sliver of our Earth to study, I suppose, Aloysius," Gregory Smirnov said.

Low-intensity earthquakes rocked the Los Angeles area for three days. The entire area was evacuated of people. Then there was a great whistle blast from the sky as if to say, "All ashore that's going ashore."

Then the surface to some little depth and all its superstructure was taken away. It was gone. And then it was quickly forgotten.

LAND OF THE GREAT HORSES

From the *Twenty-second Century Comprehensive Encyclopedia*, Vol. 1, page 389:

ANGELENOS. (*See also* Automobile Gypsies and Prune Pickers.) A mixed ethnic group of unknown origin, much given to wandering in automobiles. It is predicted that they will be the last users of this vehicle, and several archaic chrome-burdened models are still produced for their market. These people are not beggars; many of them are of superior intelligence. They often set up in business, usually as real estate dealers, gamblers, confidence men, managers of mail-order diploma mills, and promoters of one sort or other. They seldom remain long in one location.

Their pastimes are curious. They drive for hours and days on old and seldom-used cloverleafs and freeways. It has been said that a majority of the Angelenos are narcotics users, but Harold Freelove (who lived for some months as an Angeleno) has proved this false. What they inhale at their frolics (smog-crocks) is a black smoke of carbon and petroleum waste laced with monoxide. Its purpose is not clear.

The religion of the Angelenos is a mixture of old cults with a very strong eschatological element. The Paradise Motif is represented by reference to a mystic "Sunset Boulevard." The language of the Angelenos is a colorful and racy argot. Their account of their origin is vague:

"They came and took our dizz away from us," they say.

GINNY WRAPPED IN THE SUN

"I'M GOING to read my paper tonight, Dismas." Dr. Minden said, "and they'll hoot me out of the hall. The thought of it almost makes the hair walk off my head."

"Oh well, serves you right, Minden. From the hints you've given me of it, you can't expect easy acceptance for the paper; but the gentlemen aren't so bad."

"Not bad? Hauser honks like a gander! That clattering laugh of Goldbeater! Snodden sniggers so loud that it echos! Cooper's boom is like barrels rolling downstairs, and your own—it'll shrivel me, Dismas. Imagine the weirdest cacophony ever— Oh no! I wasn't thinking of one so weird as that!"

—Musical screaming! Glorious gibbering with an undertone that could shatter rocks! Hooting of a resonance plainly too deep for so small an instrument! Yowling, hoodoo laughing, broken roaring, rhinoceros runting! And the child came tumbling out of the tall rocks of Doolen's Mountain, leaping down the flanks of the hill as though she was a waterfall. And both the men laughed.

"Your Ginny *is* the weirdest cacophony I can imagine, Dismas," Dr. Minden said. "It scares me, and I love it. Your daughter is the most remarkable creature in the world.

"Talk to us, Ginny! I wish I could fix it that you would be four years old forever."

"Oh, I've fixed it myself, Dr. Minden," Ginny sang as she came to them with a movement that had something of the breathless grace of a gazelle and something of the scuttering of a little wild pig. "I use a trick like the hoodoo woman did. She ate water-puppy eggs. She never got any older, you know."

"What happened to her, Gin?" Dr. Minden asked Ginny Dismas.

"Oh, after a while she got gray-headed and wrinkled. And after another while her teeth and hair fell out, and then she died. But she never did get any older. She had everybody fooled. I got everybody fooled too."

"I know that you have, Ginny, in very many ways. Well, have you eaten water-puppy eggs to get no older?"

"No. I can't find out where they lay them, Dr. Minden. I've got my own trick that's even better."

"Do you know, Ginny, that when you really cut loose you are the loudest little girl in the world?"

"I know it. I won it yesterday. Susanna Shonk said that she was the loudest. We hollered for an hour. Susanna's home with a sore throat today, but there isn't anything the matter with me. Hey, has that house ever been there before?"

"That house? But it's our own house, Ginny," her father, Dr. Dismas, said softly. "You've lived in it all your life. You're in and out of it a thousand times a day."

"Funny I never saw it before," Ginny said. "I better go see what it looks like on the inside." And Ginny hurtled into the house that she was in and out of a thousand times a day.

"I'll tell you a secret, Dismas," Dr. Minden said. "Your small daughter Ginny is not really beautiful."

"Everybody thinks that she is, Minden."

"I know. They all believe her the most beautiful child in the world. So did I till a moment ago. So will I again in another minute when I see her come out of the house. But her contemporary, my small son Krios, told me how to look at her; and I do so. For an instant, out of her incessant movement, I forced myself to see her as stopped cold, at rest. She is grotesque, Dismas. If ever she pauses, she is grotesque."

"No, she is like ultimate matter. Existence and motion are the same thing for her, and there cannot be the one without the other. But I've never seen her stopped, even in sleep. She's the liveliest sleeper anyone ever watched—a laughing and singing sleeper. Her mother calls her our beautiful goblin."

"Exactly, she's a goblin, a monkey, a kobald. She's even grown a little pot like one of them. Dismas, she has a monkey face and bandy legs and a goblin's own pot."

"No, she hasn't! There she goes! Out of the house and up into the rocks again, and she's so beautiful that it shakes me. Four years old—and she can still look at the world and say, 'Funny I never saw you before!' Yes, I've got a multidimensional daughter, Minden. Also a neighbor who is either deep or murky. You keep feeding me snatches of that paper of yours so I suppose that you want to excite my curiosity about it. And the title—*The Contingent Mutation.* What is? Who is?"

"We are, Dismas. We are contingent, conditional, temporary, makeshift and improbable in our species. Mine is a paper badly conceived and badly put together, and I shiver at the reception that it will get. But it is about man, who is also badly conceived and badly put together. The proposition of my paper is that man is descended, recently and by incredible mutation, from the most impossible of ancestors, Xauenanthropus of Xauen Man. The answer of that descent scares me."

"Minden, are you out of your mind? Where is the descent? Where is the mutation? The Xauens were already men. No descent and no mutation was required. The finds are all fifteen years old. One look at Xauen, and everybody saw instantly that the Neanderthals and Grimaldi and Cro-Magnon were all close cousins of the same species—ourselves. They were the template, the master key. They unriddled every riddle. We saw why the chin or lack of chin was only a racial characteristic. We saw it all. There is nothing to distinguish the Xauens from ourselves except that their adults were badly made ganglers, and probably unhealthy. The Xauens *are* mod-

31

ern men. They are ourselves. There is nothing revolutionary about stuttering out fifteen-year-old certainties, Minden. I thought your paper was to be a giant stride. But it is only stepping off a two-inch curb."

· "Yes, an abysmal step off a two-inch curb, Dismas, backward and around the world, and standing on one's head and turning into a howling monkey in the process. It isn't a simple step. If I am correct, Dismas, then our descent from the Xauens was by an incredible, sudden and single mutation; one that has been misunderstood both as to effect and direction."

"I've never been quite satisfied with Xauens myself. There is something misshapen about the whole business. Of course we know the Xauens only by the skeletons of ninety-six children, three adolescents, and two adults. We are bound to find more."

"If we do, we will find them in the same proportion. Oh, we will not recognize them at all. But does it not seem an odd proportion to you? How come there were so many kids? And how come—think about this a long, long time, will you?—that eighty-six of those kids were of the same size and apparently of the same age? The Xauen skeletons came out of nine digs, close together both in location and age. And of the total of one hundred and one skeletons, eighty-six of them are of four-year-old kids. Sure the Xauens are modern man! Sure they are ourselves chin to chin. But eighty-six four-year-old kids out of a hundred and one people is not a modern proportion."

"You explain it then, Minden. I suppose that your paper attempts to. Oh, scatter-boned ancestors! Here come the religious nuts!"

Drs. Dismas and Minden had been sitting in the open parkland in campesino chairs, in their own fine neighborhood between Doolen's Mountain and the lower brushland. Dr. Dismas drew a hog-nosed pistol from under his arm at the sight of the nuts who had shuffled up that way several times before.

"Be off!" Dismas barked as the nuts crowded and shuffled up closer from the lower brushland. "There's nothing around here you want. You've been here a dozen times with your silly questions."

"No, only three times," the nut leader said. He was clean-shaven and short-haired in the old manner still affected by fanatics, and he had fool written in every line of him. "It's a simple thing we seek," the leader sniffled. "We only want to find the woman and kill her. I believe that you could help us find the woman."

"There is no woman here except my wife!" Dr. Dismas said angrily. "You have said yourselves that she isn't the woman. Be gone now, and don't come back here again."

"But everything that we know tells us that the woman is somewhere near this place," the nut leader insisted. "She is the woman who will bear the weird seed."

"Oh, well, there are some who say that my daughter Ginny is a weird seed. Be off now."

"We know Ginny. She comes down sometimes to mock us. Ginny is not the seed, but there is something of it about her. Ginny is born and already four years old. The seed that we are seeking to kill is still in the womb. Are you sure that your wife—"

"Damnit, do you want a public pregnancy test? No, my wife is not!"

Dr. Dismas shot a couple of times around the feet of the nut leader, and the whole gaggle of the nuts shuffled off again. "It is only a little thing we seek, to find and kill the woman," they snuffled as they went.

"They may be right, Dismas," Dr. Minden said. "I've been expecting the weird seed myself. I believe that it may already have appeared several times, and such nuts have killed it several times. The contingent mutation *can* come unhinged at any time. It always could. And when it does, the human world can well pass away. But this time they won't be able to find the woman to kill her."

"This is fishier than Edward's Ichthyology, as we used to say in school. I begin to understand why you're afraid of the reception that your paper might get. And you, as well as I, seem to have developed a little weird seed lately."

"Yes, my young and my older son are both acting most peculiarly lately, particularly in their relation to the Dismas family. My son Dall has been jilted by your daughter Agar, or is it the other way around? Or have they both been jilted by your small daughter Ginny? As far as I can arrive at it, Ginny told them that that sort of stuff is out, no longer necessary, not even wanted on their parts. She is obsoleting them, she says.

"And my four-year-old son Krios is about out of his mind over your Ginny. He is so advanced in some ways and so retarded in others. It seems as though he grew unevenly and then stopped growing. I worry about him."

"Yes, Ginny has acquired several more small boy-friends now. She says that you break the fort with a big ram and you break the ram at the same time and throw it away. And then you find better tools to take it over. I don't know what she's talking about. But Krios is jealous as only a passionate four-year-old can be."

"Krios says that Ginny is bad and she made him bad. He says that he doesn't know the words for the way they were bad, but that he will go to Hell for it."

"I had no idea that children were still taught about Hell."

"They aren't. But they have either intuitive knowledge of the place, or a continuing childhood folk legend of it. Oh, here comes bad Ginny and her mother, and they both have that stubborn look on them. You have two strong women in your house, at least. I wish that Agar were; for my son Dall isn't, and one of them should be.

Ginny and her mother Sally came hand in hand with the air of something needing to be settled.

"I want to be fair about this, Father," Ginny called

34

solidly. "What I like about me is that I am always so fair."

"That's also what I like about you, Ginny," said Dr. Dismas, "and what is the argument?"

"All I asked of Mother is that she make me three thousand seven hundred and eighty peanut butter sandwiches. Isn't that a fair request?"

"I'm not sure that it is, Ginny," Dr. Dismas said. "It would take you a long time to eat that many."

"Of course it will, twelve hundred and sixty days. But that makes only three a day for the time I have to stay hidden in my nest up in the rocks. I figured that out by myself without paper. A lot of kids that have been to school already can't figure as well as I can."

"I know. A precocious daughter is a mixed blessing," her father said.

"Oh, Ginny, you're going to get a paddling," her mother said. "I made you three of them, and you said that you weren't even hungry for them."

"Father, who is this woman who talks to me so brusquely?" Ginny demanded.

"She is your mother, Ginny. You have been with her every day of your life and before. You have just come out of the house with her, and you still stand hand in hand with her."

"Funny I never saw her before," Ginny said. "I don't believe that this woman is my mother at all. Well, I will get my servants to make the sandwiches for me. Serpents kill you, woman!—Oh, no, no, nobody touches me like that!"

Musical screaming! Wailing of a resonance too deep for so small an instrument, as Ginny was dragged off by her mother to get paddled. Howling to high Heaven, and the plainting of wild hogs and damned goblins!

"She is in good voice," Dr. Minden said. "When she speaks of her servants, she means your daughter Agar and my son Dall. It scares me, for I almost know what she means. It is eerie that two compatible young people

35

say they will not marry because a four-year-old child
forbids them to do it. It scares me still more when I
begin to understand the mechanism at work."

"What is the mechanism, Minden?"

"The mutational inhibitions. It's quite a tangled affair. Do you remember the Screaming Monkeys of boondocks Rhodesia twenty years ago?"

"Vaguely. Bothersome little destructive monkeys that
had to be hunted down and killed—hunted down by a
sort of religious crusade, as I remember it. Yes, a mutation, I suppose. A sudden wildness appearing in a species. What is the connection?"

"Dismas, they were the first, the initial probe that
failed. Others are on the way, and one of them will not
fail. The story is that the religious crusaders said that no
human child could be born while the howling monkeys
flourished, for the monkeys themselves were human
children. Well, they were. Well, no they weren't children.
And they weren't human. But, in a way, they had been
both. Or at least—"

"Minden, do you know what you *do* mean?"

"I hardly do, Dismas. Here come the 'servants.' "

Dall Minden and Agar Dismas drove up in a little
roustabout car and stopped.

"What' is this nonsense I hear that you two are not
going to get married?" Dr. Dismas demanded.

"Not unless Ginny changes her mind, Father," Agar
said. "Oh, don't ask us to explain it. We don't understand
it either."

"You are a pair of damned useless drones," Dismas
growled.

"Don't say that, Dismas," Dr. Minden gasped. "Everything begins to scare me now. 'Drones' has a technical
meaning in this case."

"Ginny has just suffered an ignominy past bearing."
Agar grinned. She was a nice pleasant girl. "Now she
is sulking in her cave up in Doolen's Mountain and has
sent word for us to come at once."

"How has she sent word?" Dr. Dismas demanded. "You two have just driven up."

"Oh, don't ask us to explain, Father. She sends us word when she wants us. We don't understand it either. We'll go up on foot."

"Where is all this going to end?" Dr. Dismas asked when the two grinning young drones had left them and were ambling up the mountain.

"I don't know, Dismas," Minden told him. "But I believe it may as well begin with a verse:

Salamanders do it,
Tadpoles and newts do it.
Why can't me and you do it?

"It's a verse that the four-year-olds have been chanting, and you may not be tuned in on them. And the peculiar thing is that the salamanders and newts and tadpoles *are* doing it now, more than ever before. It's worldwide. See Higgleton's recent paper if you don't take my word for it."

"Oh, great blithering biologists! *What* are the squigglers doing more than ever before?"

"Engaging in neotic reproduction, of course. In many pocket areas, tadpoles have been reproducing as tadpoles for several years now, and the adult frog species is disappearing. There have always been cases of it, of course, but now it is becoming a pattern. The same is true of the newts and salamanders. And remember that all three are, like man, contingent mutations. But how do the four-year-old children know about it when it is still one of the best-kept secrets of the biologists? . . . Here comes my wife. Is it more family trouble, Clarinda?"

"Oh, Krios has locked himself in the bathroom, and he won't come out or answer. He's been acting abominable all morning. Have you that emergency key you made?"

"Here. Now get the boy out, whip him gently but painfully, then explain to him that we love him very much and that his troubles are our troubles. Then get dinner. This family here never eats, unless it is peanut butter sandwiches, and has not thought to ask me to dine with them. Get back next door and with it, Clarinda, and stop bubbling."

"There is something really bothering Krios," Clarinda Minden bubbled yet, but she got herself back next door.

"Where shall we take it up, Dismas?" Doctor Minden asked. "With the howling monkeys of boondocks Rhodesia who may once have been human children? But nobody believes that. With the neotic salamanders and newts and pollywogs? With the Xauens who were either our grandparents or our grandchildren? Or with ourselves?"

"Roost on the Xauens a while," Dr. Dismas said. "You didn't quite finish your screed on them."

"Humans descend from the Xauens. Australopithecus, no. Sinanthropus, no They were creatures of another line. But Neanderthal, Cro-Magnon, Grimaldi and ourselves are all of one species, and we descend from the Xauens. It is not true, however, that we have only one hundred and one skeletons of the Xauens. We have more than twenty thousand of them, but most of them are called Ouezzane monkeys."

"Minden, you're crazy."

"I am talking about the three-foot-tall, big-headed running monkeys who were mature and full grown at four years of age and very old at fourteen. They threw a few sports, steers and freemartins, who passed the puberty age without effect and continued to grow. They were gangling drones, servants of the active species, and of course sterile. They were the one in one hundred occurrence and of no importance. And one day they bred, set up a mutational inhibition against the normal; and mankind—the privileged mutation—was born.

"The Ouezzane monkeys, of whom the Xauens were

the transitional state, were the same as the howling monkeys of boondocks Rhodesia—going in the other direction. They had no speech, they had no fire, and they made no tools. Then one morning they were the Xauens, and the next morning they were humans. They passed all the highly developed apes in an instant. They were the privileged mutation, which is not, I believe, permanent.

"Dismas, the one hundred and one recognized Xauen skeletons that we possess are *not* of ninety-six children (eighty-six of them apparent four-year-olds), three adolescents and two adults. They are of ten infants and children, *eighty-six adults,* two mutants and three filial-twos.

"Let's take it from the flank. A few years ago, a biologist amused himself by making a table of heartbeat life lengths. All the mammals but one, he found, live about the same number of heartbeats, the longer-living species having correspondingly slower heartbeats. But one species, man, lives four or five times as long as he should by this criterion. I forget whether the biologist implied that this makes man a contingent species living on borrowed time. I do imply it. In any case, since the biologist was also involved in science fiction, his implications were not taken seriously.

"From the other flank. Even before Freud there were studies made of false puberty, the sudden hot interest and activity that appears about age four and then goes away for another ten years. It's been many times guessed that back in our ancestry our true puberty was at such an early age."

"Minden, no species can change noticeably in less than fifty thousand years."

"Dismas, it can change in between three and nine months, depending on the direction traveled. Here they come back! Well, drones, did you settle Ginny down? Where are you going now?"

Agar Dismas and Dall Minden had sauntered down from Doolen's Mountain.

"We're going to get four hundred and seventy-three loaves of bread and four hundred and seventy-three jars of peanut butter," Agar said rather nervously.

"Yes, Ginny says to use Crispy-Crusty bread," Dall Minden detailed. "She says it has sixteen slices to a loaf, so we can make eight sandwiches to a loaf and to a jar. There will be four sandwiches left over, and Ginny says we can have them for our work. She's going to stay in her cave for twelve hundred and sixty days. She says it will take that long to get her thing going good so nobody can bust it up. I think she's a numerologist at heart. This is going to take more than four hundred dollars. That's more than Agar and myself have saved up together. Ginny says to do it, though, even if we have to steal the money for it. And she says to be quick about it."

"Here come the religious nuts again," Doctor Dismas said. "I may have to kill one of the fools if they keep coming back."

"They won't come here this time," Agar said. "They'll prowl Doolen's Mountain from now on. They know it'll be there. But I don't think they'll kill Ginny. They don't understand what she is. They didn't understand the first time either; they didn't guess that it could possibly be one of the big ones. We are all hoping that they will kill me and be satisfied and think that they have done it. They will find me there where they think the woman should be, and that may fool them. Well, tootle! We have to hurry with everything or Ginny will be angry."

"No species can count itself secure that has not endured for ten million years," said Dr. Minden. "We still hear the old saying that evolution is irreversible. Hogwash! I have myself studied seven species of hogs washed away before one endured. The human race is so new that it has no stability. The majority of species do *not* survive, and we have lived only one tenth of the span that would tilt the odds for survival in our favor. Even the species that finally survive will commonly revert several times before acquiring stability. We could revert at any time."

"Revert to what?"

"To what we were, to what we still are basically, little three-foot-high, big-headed, howling monkeys, without tools, and with only a fifth of our present life span."

"Reversions are like cosmic disasters, Minden. They take a few thousand years to happen, and by that time we'll be gone."

"No, this can happen instantly, Dismas, by a single neotic conception. And then it becomes the norm by the mechanics of mutational inhibition. The reversion will inhibit the old normal. We have already seen that inhibition at work."

The very stones crying out like demented rooks! Bushes barking like coyotes! Green-colored yowling, and laughter that sang like a band-saw. And Ginny was in the middle of them again.

She was the howlingest kid ever pupped.

"I don't think that I will talk any more after today, Father," she said solemnly after she had cut off her other noises. "I think I'll just forget how. I'll just holler and hoot and carry on. That's more fun anyhow.

"Why aren't my servants back with my provisions? They've had almost time to get back if they did everything at breakneck speed and had good luck. They might have had to go to more than one place to get that much bread and peanut butter, though. I doubt if I'll eat it. I just want to have it if I need it, and I wanted to teach them obedience. I'll probably start to eat meadow mice and ground squirrels tomorrow.

"Here comes Mrs. Minden crying over that Krios. What's the good of that?"

There was a keening. Clarinda was running and crying, and Sally Dismas had rushed out of the house and met her.

"Clarinda, what in the world has happened?" Dr. Minden cried, rushing to his tearful wife.

"Our baby Krios has killed himself."

"I told him to," said Ginny. "I'd gotten everything I wanted from him. I'll find better ones for the other times."

"Ginny!" Her mother was horrified. "I'll whip—"

"Don't punish the child, Sally," Clarinda Minden sobbed. "She's beyond good and evil. Whatever was between her and my baby Krios, it's better that I never know."

"Did I say something wrong?" Ginny asked. "The last thing I ever say, and it should be wrong? Dr. Minden, you know about things like that. What are you creatures, anyhow?"

"People, Ginny," Dr. Minden said miserably.

"Funny I never saw any of you before. I sure don't intend to get involved with people."

Raucous rowling! Hound-dog hooting! Hissing of badgers, and the clattering giggle of geese! Shag-tooth shouting, and the roaring of baby bulls!

And a screaming monkey leaped and tumbled up the rocks like crazy water.

THE SIX FINGERS OF TIME

HE BEGAN by breaking things that morning. He broke
the glass of water on his night stand. He knocked it
crazily against the opposite wall and shattered it. Yet
it shattered slowly. This would have surprised him if he
had been fully awake, for he had only reached out weak-
ly for it.

Nor had he wakened regularly to his alarm; he had
wakened to a weird, slow, low booming, yet the clock
said six, time for the alarm. And the low boom, when
it came again, seemed to come from the clock.

He reached out and touched it gently, but it floated
off the stand at his touch and bounced around slowly on
the floor. And when he picked it up again it had
stopped, nor would shaking start it.

He checked the electric clock in the kitchen. This also
said six o'clock, but the sweep hand did not move. In
his living room the radio clock said six, but the second
hand seemed stationary.

"But the lights in both rooms work," said Vincent.
"How are the clocks both stopped? Are the receptacles
on a separate circuit?"

He went back to his bedroom and got his wristwatch.
It also said six; and its sweep hand did not sweep.

"Now this could get silly. What is it that would stop
both mechanical and electrical clocks?"

He went to the window and looked out at the ad-
vertising clock on the Mutual Insurance Building. It
said six o'clock, and the second hand did not move.

"Well, it is possible that the confusion is not limited
to myself. I heard once the fanciful theory that a cold
shower will clear the mind. For me it never has, but I
will try it. I can always use cleanliness for an excuse."

The shower didn't work. Yes, it did: the water came now, but not like water; like very slow syrup that hung in the air. He reached up to touch it hanging down there and stretching. And it shattered like glass when he touched it, and drifted in fantastic slow globs across the room. But it had the feel of water. It was wet and pleasantly cool. And in a quarter of a minute or so it was down over his shoulders and back, and he luxuriated in it. He let it soak on his noggin, and it cleared his wits at once.

"There is not a thing wrong with me. I am fine. It is not my fault that the water is slow this morning and other things are awry."

He reached for the towel and it tore to pieces in his hands like porous wet paper.

He now became very careful in the way he handled things. Slowly, tenderly and deftly he took them so that they would not break. He shaved himself without mishap in spite of the slow water in the lavatory also.

Then he dressed himself with the greatest caution and cunning, breaking nothing except his shoe laces, and that is likely to happen at any time.

"If there is nothing the matter with me, then I will check and see if there is anything seriously wrong with the world. The dawn was fairly along when I looked out, as it should have been. Approximately twenty minutes have passed; it is a clear morning: the sun should now have hit the top several stories of the Insurance Building."

But it had not. It was still a clear morning, but the dawn had not brightened at all in the twenty minutes. And that big clock still said six. It had not changed.

Yet it had changed, and he knew it with a queer feeling. He pictured it as it had been before. But the sweep second hand had moved. It had swept a third of the dial.

So he pulled up a chair at the window and watched it. He realized that, though he could not see it move, yet it did make progress. He watched it for perhaps five minutes. It moved through a space of perhaps five seconds.

"Well, that is not my problem. It is that of the clock maker, either a terrestrial or a celestial one."

But he left his rooms without a good breakfast, and he left them very early. How did he know that it was early since there was something wrong with the time? Well, it was early at least according to the sun and according to the clocks, neither of which institutions seemed to be working properly.

He left without a good breakfast because the coffee would not make and the bacon would not fry. And in plain point of fact the fire would not heat. The gas flame sprung up from the pilot like a slowly spreading stream or an unfolding flower. Then it burned far too steadily. The skillet remained cold when placed over it; nor would water even heat. It had taken at least five minutes to get the water out of the faucet in the first place.

He ate a few pieces of leftover bread and some scraps of meat.

In the street there was no motion, no real motion. A truck, first seeming at rest, moved very slowly. There was no gear in which it could move so slowly. And there was a taxi which crept along, but Charles Vincent had to look at it carefully for some time to be sure that it was in motion. Then he received a shock. He realized by the early morning light that the driver of it was dead. Dead with his eyes wide open!

Slow as it was going, and by whatever means it was moving, it should really be stopped. Vincent walked over to it, opened the door, and pulled on the brake. Then he looked into the eyes of that dead man. Was he really dead? It was hard to be sure. He felt warm. But, even as Vincent looked, the eyes of the dead man had begun to close. And close they did and open again in a matter of about twenty seconds.

This was weird. The slowly closing and opening eyes sent a chill through Vincent. And the dead man had begun to lean forward in his seat. Vincent put a hand in the middle of the man's chest to hold him upright, but he found the forward pressure to be as relentless as it was slow. He was unable to keep the dead man up.

So he let him go, watching curiously; and in a few seconds the driver's face was against the wheel. But it was almost as if it had no intention of stopping there. It pressed into the wheel with dogged force. The man would surely break his face. Vincent took several holds on the dead man and counteracted the pressure somewhat. Yet the face was being damaged, and if things were normal blood would have flowed.

The man had been dead so long however, that though he was still warm his blood must have congealed, for it was fully two minutes before it began to ooze.

"Whatever I have done, I have done enough damage," said Vincent. "And, in whatever nightmare I am in, I am likely to do further harm if I meddle more. I had better leave it alone."

He walked on down the street. Yet whatever vehicles he saw now were moving with an incredible slowness as though driven by some fantastic gear reduction. And there were people here and there frozen solid. It was a chilly morning, but it was not that cold. They were immobile in positions of motion, as though they were playing the children's game of Statues.

"How is it," said Charles Vincent, "that this young girl, who I believe works across the street from us, should have died standing up and in full stride? But, no. She is not dead. Or if so she died with a very alert expression. And, oh my God, she's doing it too!"

For he realized that the eyes of the girl were closing, and in a space of a few seconds they had completed their cycle and were open again. Also, and this was even stranger, she had moved, moved forward in full stride.

He would have timed her if he could. How could he time her when all the clocks in the world were crazy? Yet she must have been taking about two steps a minute.

Vincent went into the cafeteria. The early morning crowd that he had often watched through the window was there. The girl who made flapjacks in the window had just flipped one and it hung in the air. Then it floated over as though caught by a slight breeze, and sank slowly down as if settling in water.

The early morning breakfasters, like the people in the street, were all dead in this new way, moving with almost imperceptible motion. And all had apparently died in the act of drinking coffee, eating eggs, or munching toast. And if there was only time enough, there was an even chance that they would get the drinking, eating, and munching done with, for there was a shadow of movement in them all.

The cashier had the register drawer open and money in her hand, and the hand of the customer was outstretched for it. In time, somewhere in the new leisurely time, the hands would come together and the change be given. And so it happened. It may have been a minute and a half, or two minutes, or two and a half. It is always hard to judge time, and now it had become all but impossible.

"I am still hungry," said Charles Vincent, "but it would be foolhardy to wait on the service here. Should I help myself? They would not mind if they are dead. And, if they are not dead, in any case it seems that I am invisible to them."

He wolfed several rolls. He opened a bottle of milk and held it upside-down over his glass while he ate another roll. Liquids had all become so perversely slow.

But he felt better for his erratic breakfast. He would have paid for it, but how?

He left the cafeteria and walked about the town as it seemed still to be quite early, though one could depend on neither sun nor clock for the time any more.

The traffic lights were unchanging. He sat for a long time in a little park and watched the town and the big clock in the Commerce Building tower; but like all the clocks it was either stopped or the hand would creep too slowly to be seen.

It must have been just about an hour till the traffic lights changed, but change they did at last. By picking a point on the building across the street and watching what moved by it, he found that the traffic did indeed move. In a minute or so, the entire length of a car would pass a given point.

He had, he recalled, been very far behind in his work, and it had been worrying him. He decided to go to the office, early as it was or seemed to be.

He let himself in. Nobody else was there. He resolved not to look at the clock and to be very careful of the way he handled all objects because of his new propensity for breaking things. This considered, all seemed normal here. He had said the day before that he could hardly catch up on his work if he worked for two days solid. He now resolved at least to work steadily until something happened, whatever it was.

For hour after hour he worked on his tabulations and reports. Nobody else had arrived. Could something be wrong? Certainly something was wrong. But today was not a holiday. That was not it.

Just how long can a stubborn and mystified man work away at his task? It was hour after hour after hour. He did not become hungry nor particularly tired. And he did get through a lot of work.

"It must be half done. However it has happened, I have caught up at least a day's work. I will keep on."

He must have worked silently for another eight or ten hours.

He was caught up completely on his back work.

"Well, to some extent I can work into the future. I can head-up and carry over. I can put in everything but the figures of the field reports."

And he did so.

"It will be hard to bury me in work again. I could almost coast for a day. I don't even know what day it is, but I must have worked twenty hours straight through and nobody has arrived. Perhaps nobody ever will arrive. If they are moving with the speed of the people in the nightmare outside, it is no wonder they have not arrived."

He put his head down in his arms on the desk. The last thing he saw before he closed his eyes was the misshapen left thumb that had always been his and which he had always tried to conceal a little by the way he handled his hands.

"At least I know that I am still myself. I'd know myself anywhere by that."

Then he went to sleep at his desk.

Jenny came in with a quick click-click-click of high heels, and he wakened to the noise.

"What are you doing dozing at your desk, Mr. Vincent? Have you been here all night?"

"I don't know, Jenny. Honestly I don't."

"I was only teasing. Sometimes when I get here a little early I take a catnap myself."

The clock said six minutes till eight, and the second hand was sweeping normally. Time had returned to the world. Or to him. But had all that early morning of his been a dream? Then it had been a very efficient dream. He had accomplished work he could hardly have done in two days. And it was the same day that it was supposed to be.

He went to the water fountain. The water now behaved normally. He went to the window. The traffic was behaving as it should. Though sometimes slow and sometimes snarled, yet it was in the pace of the regular world.

The other workers arrived. They were not balls of fire,

but neither was it necessary to observe them for several minutes to be sure that they weren't dead.

"It did have its advantages," Charles Vincent said. "I would be afraid to live with it permanently, but it would be handy to go into the state for a few minutes a day and accomplish the business of hours. I may be a case for the doctor. But just how would I go about telling a doctor what was bothering me?"

Now it had surely been less than two hours from his first rising till the time that he wakened from his second sleep to the noise of Jenny. And how long that second sleep had been, or in which time enclave, he had no idea. But how account for it all? He had spent a long time in his own rooms, much longer than ordinary in his confusion. He had walked the city mile after mile in his puzzlement. And he had sat in the little park for hours and studied the situation. And he had sat and worked at his own desk for an outlandish long time.

Well, he would go to the doctor. A man is obliged to refrain from making a fool of himself to the world at large, but to his lawyer, his priest, or his doctor he will sometimes have to come as a fool. By their callings they are restrained from scoffing openly.

He went to the doctor at noon.

Dr. Mason was not particularly a friend. Charles Vincent realized with some unease that he did not have any particular friends, only acquaintances and associates. It was as though he were of a species slightly apart from his fellows. He wished a little now that he had a particular friend.

But Dr. Mason was an acquaintance of some years, had the reputation of being a good doctor, and besides, Vincent had now arrived at his office and been shown in. He would either have to—well, that was as good a beginning as any.

"Doctor, I am in a predicament. I will either have to invent some symptoms to account for my visit here, or to make an excuse and bolt, or tell you what is bothering me, even though you will think that I am a new sort of idiot."

"Vincent, every day people invent symptoms to cover their visits here, and I know that they have lost their nerve about their real reason for coming. And every day people do make excuses and bolt. But experience tells me that I will get a larger fee if you tackle the third alternative. And, Vincent, there is no new sort of idiot."

"It may not sound so silly if I tell it quickly," Vincent said. "I awoke this morning to some very puzzling incidents. It seemed that time itself had stopped, or that the whole world had gone into super-slow motion. The water would neither flow nor boil, and the fire would not heat food. The clocks, which I at first believed had stopped, crept along at perhaps a minute an hour. The people I met in the streets appeared dead, frozen in life-like attitudes. It was only by watching them for a very long time that I perceived that they did indeed have motion. One taxi I saw creeping slower than the most backward snail, and a dead man at the wheel of it. I went to it, opened the door, and put on the brake. I realized after a time that the man was not dead. But he bent forward and broke his face on the steering wheel. It must have taken a full minute for his head to travel no more than ten inches, yet I was unable to prevent him from hitting the wheel. I then did other bizarre things in a world that had died on its feet. I walked many miles through the city, and then I sat for countless hours in the park. I went to the office and let myself in. I accomplished work that must have taken me twenty hours. I then took a nap at my desk. When I awoke on the arrival of others it was six minutes till eight in the morning of the same day, today. Not two hours had passed from my rising, and time was back to normal. But there were things that happened in that time that could never be compressed into two hours."

"One question first, Vincent. Did you actually accomplish the work, the work of many hours?"

"I did. It was done and done in that time. It did not become undone on the return of time to normal."

"A second question: had you been worried about your work, about being behind in your work?"

"Yes. Emphatically."

"Then here is one explanation. You retired last night. But very shortly afterward you arose in a state of somnambulism. There are facets of sleep-walking which we do not at all understand. The time-out-of-focus interludes were parts of a walking dream of yours. You dressed and went to your office and worked all night. It is possible to do routine tasks while in a somnambulistic state, rapidly and even feverishly, to perform prodigies. You may have fallen into a normal sleep there when you had finished, or you may have been awakened directly from your somnambulistic trance on the arrival of your co-workers. There. That is a plausible and workable explanation. In the case of an apparently bizarre happening it is always well to have a rational explanation to fall back on. This will usually satisfy a patient and put his mind to rest. But often the explanation does not satisfy me."

"Your explanation very nearly satisfies me, Dr. Mason, and it does put my mind considerably at rest. I am sure that in short while I will be able to accept it completely. But why does it not satisfy you?"

"One reason is a man, a taxi-driver, whom I treated very early this morning. He had his face smashed, and he had seen—or almost seen—a ghost: a ghost of incredible swiftness that was more sensed than seen. The ghost opened the door of his car while it was going at full speed, jerked on the brake, and caused him to crack his head. This man was dazed and had a slight concussion. I have convinced him that he did not see any ghost at all, that he must have dozed at the wheel and run into something. As I say, I am harder to convince than my patients. But it may have been coincidence."

"I hope so. But you also seem to have another reservation as to my case."

"After quite a few years in practice, I seldom see or hear anything new. Twice before I have been told a happening or a dream on the line of what you experienced."

"Did you convince your other patients that they were only dreams?".

"I did. Both of them. That is, I convinced them the first few times it happened to them."

"Were they satisfied?"

"At first they were. Later not entirely. But they both died within a year of their coming to me."

"Of nothing violent, I hope."

"Both had the most gentle deaths. That of senility extreme."

"Oh. Well I'm too young for that."

"Vincent, I would like you to come back in a month or so."

"I will, if the delusion or the dream returns. Or if I do not feel well."

After this Charles Vincent began to forget about the incident. He only recalled it with humor sometimes when again he was behind in his work.

"Well, if it gets bad enough I may do another sleep-walking jag and catch up. But if there is another aspect of time and I could enter it at will, it might often be handy."

Charles Vincent never saw the man's face at all. It is very dark in some of those clubs and the Coq Bleu is like the inside of a tomb. Vincent went to the clubs only about once a month, sometimes after a show when he did not want to go home to bed, sometimes when he was just plain restless.

Citizens of the more fortunate states may not know of the mysteries of the clubs. In Vincent's the only bars are beer bars, and only in the clubs can a person get a drink, and only members are admitted. It is true that even such a small club as the Coq Bleu had thirty thousand members, and at a dollar a year this is a nice sideline. The little numbered membership cards cost a penny each for the printing, and the member wrote in his own name. But he was supposed to have a card or a dollar for a card to gain admittance.

But there could be no entertainment in the clubs. There was nothing there but the little bar room in the near darkness. The near darkness of the clubs was custom only but it had the force of the law.

The man was there, and then he was not, and then he was there again. And always where he sat it was too dark to see his face.

"I wonder," he said to Vincent (or to the bar at large, though there were no other customers and the bartender was asleep), "I wonder if you have read Zubarin on the relationship of extradigitalism to genius?"

"I have never heard of the work nor of the man," said Vincent. "Doubt if either exist."

"I am Zubarin," said the man.

Vincent instinctively hid his misshapen left thumb. Yet it could not have been noticed in that light, and he must have been crazy to believe that there was any connection between it and the man's remark. It was not truly a double thumb. He was not an extradigital, nor was he a genius.

"I refuse to become interested in you," said Vincent. "I am on the verge of leaving. I dislike waking the bartender, but I did want another drink."

"Sooner done than said."

"What is?"

"Your glass is full."

"It is? So it is. Is it a trick?"

"Trick is a name for anything either too frivolous or too mystifying for us to comprehend. But on one long early morning a month ago you also could have done the trick, and nearly as well."

"Could I have? How do you know about my long early morning—assuming there to have been such?"

"I watched you for a while. Few others have the equipment with which to watch you when you're in the aspect."

So they were silent for some time, and Vincent watched the clock and was ready to go.

"I wonder," said the man in the dark, "if you have read Schimmelpenninck on the sexagintal and the duodecimal in the Chaldee Mysteries."

"I have not, and I doubt if anyone else has. I would guess that you are also Schimmelpenninck, and that you have just made up the name on the spur of the moment."

"I am Schimm, it is true, but I made up the name on the spur of the moment many years ago."

"I am a little bored with you," said Vincent, "but I would appreciate it if you'd do your glass-filling trick once more."

"I have just done so again. And you are not bored; you are frightened."

"Of what?" asked Vincent, whose glass had in fact filled again.

"Of reentering a dream that you are not sure was a dream. But there are often advantages to being both invisible and inaudible."

"Can you be invisible?"

"Was I not so when I went behind the bar just now and fixed you a drink?"

"How?"

"A man in full stride goes at the rate of about five miles an hour. Multiply that by sixty, which is the number of time. When I leave my stool and go behind the bar I go at the rate of three hundred miles an hour. So I am invisible to you, particularly if I move while you blink."

"One thing does not match. You might have got around there and back. But you could not have poured."

"Shall I say that mastery over liquids and other objects is not given to beginners? But for us there are many ways to outwit the slowness of matter."

"I believe that you are a hoaxer. Do you know Dr. Mason?"

"I know of him, and that you went to see him. I know of his futile attempts to penetrate a certain mystery. But I have not talked to him of you."

"I still believe that you are a phony. Could you put me back into the state of my dream of a month. ago?"

"It was not a dream. But I could put you again into that state."

"Prove it."

"Watch the clock. Do you believe that I can point my finger at it and stop it for you? It is already stopped for me."

"No, I don't believe it. Yes, I guess I have to, since I see that you have just done it. But it may be another trick. I don't know where the clock is plugged in."

"Neither do I. Come to the door. Look at every clock you can see. Are they not all stopped?"

"Yes. Maybe the power has gone off all over town."

"You know it has not. There are still a few lighted windows in those buildings, though it is quite late."

"Why are you playing with me? I am neither on the inside nor the outside. Either tell me the secret or say that you will not tell me."

"The secret isn't a simple one. It can only be arrived at after all philosophy and learning has been assimilated."

"One man cannot arrive at that in one lifetime."

"Not in an ordinary lifetime. But the secret of the secret, if I may put it that way, is that one must use part of it as a tool in learning. You could not learn all in one lifetime but, by being permitted the first step, to be able to read, say, sixty books in the time it took you to read one, to pause for a minute in thought and use up only one second, to get the day's work accomplished in eight minutes and so have time for other things—by such ways one may make a beginning. I will warn you, though. Even for the most intelligent it is a race."

"A race? What race?"

"It is a race between success, which is life, and failure, which is death."

"Let's skip the melodrama. But how do I get into the state and out of it?"

"Oh, that is simple, so easy that it seems like a gadget. Here are two diagrams I will draw. Note them carefully. This first—invision it in your mind, and you are in the state. Now the second one—invision, and you are out of it."

"That easy?"

"That deceptively easy. The trick is to learn why it works—if you want to succeed, meaning to live."

So Charles Vincent left him and went home, walking the mile in a little less than fifteen seconds. But he still had not seen the face of the man.

There are advantages intellectual, monetary, and amorous in being able to enter the accelerated state at will. It is a fox game. One must be careful not to be caught at it, nor to break or harm that which is in the normal state.

Vincent could always find eight or ten minutes unobserved to accomplish the day's work. And a fifteen-minute coffee break could turn into a fifteen hour romp around the town.

There was this boyish pleasure in becoming a ghost: to appear and stand motionless in front of an onrushing train and to cause the scream of the whistle, and to be in no danger, being able to move five or ten times as fast as the train; to enter and to sit suddenly in the middle of a select group and see them stare, and then virtually to disappear from the middle of them; to interfere in sports and games, entering the prize ring and tripping, hampering, or slugging the unliked fighter; to blue-shot down the hockey ice, skating at fifteen hundred miles an hour and scoring dozens of goals at either end while the people only know that something odd is happening.

There was pleasure in being able to shatter windows by chanting little songs, for the voice (when in the state) will be to the world at sixty times its regular pitch, though normal to oneself. And for this reason also he was inaudible to others.

There was fun in petty thieving and tricks. He could take a wallet from a man's pocket and be two blocks away when the victim turned at the feel. He could come back and stuff it into the man's mouth as he bleated to a policeman.

He could come into the home of a lady writing a letter, snatch up the paper and write three lines on it and vanish before the scream got out of her throat.

He could take shoe and sock off a man's foot while he was in full stride. No human face since the beginning of time ever showed such a look of pure astonishment as that of the man to whom this first happened. Discovering oneself half barefoot of a sudden in a crowded street has no parallel in all experience.

Vincent could paint the eyeglasses of a man dark green, and this would somehow alter the man's whole personality. He'd gulp and wave his arms and develop new mannerisms. Or as a victim took the first puff of a cigarette Vincent would take it from his mouth, smoke it quickly down to the hot nub, and replace it.

He would take food off forks on the way to mouths, put baby turtles and live fish into bowls of soup between spoonfuls of the eater. And, as a cook cracked an egg over the griddle, he would scoop up the soft contents in midair, and set down a full-grown quacking duck to the discomfort of both cook and bird.

He would lash the hands of hand-shakers tightly together with stout cord, and tie together the shoe laces of dancing partners. Or he would remove the strings of guitars while they were being played, or steal the mouthpiece of a horn while the operator paused for breath. He unzippered persons of both sexes when they were at their most pompous, and it was on his account (probably) that Feldman was not elected mayor. This was something that happened on the public platform, and Feldman was completely undone.

This thing can remain a pleasant novelty for some time. There was, of course, the difficulty of moving large objects. Vincent always wanted to intrude a horse into the midst of a certain assembly. But a horse is too large to be moved in an accelerated time. Vincent drew out the diagram that the faceless man had given him, and presented it to the only horse he knew. But the horse did not get the idea. It would not go into the accelerated state.

"I will either have to find a smarter horse or a new method of moving heavy objects," said Charles Vincent.

Vincent would sometimes handcuff two strangers together as they stood waiting for a traffic light to change. He would lash leaners to lamp posts, and steal the the teeth from the mouths of those afflicted with dentures.

He would write cryptic and frightening messages in grease pencil on a plate just as a diner began to fill it. He changed cards from one player's hands to another's while play was in progress, and he interfered perversely with billard balls.

He removed golf balls from tees during the back swing, and left notes written large "YOU MISSED ME" pinned to the ground with the tee.

He stole baseballs from catchers' mitts at the instant if impact, and left instead small unfledged live sparrows. It was found that there is nothing in the rule book to cover this.

Or he shaved moustaches and heads. Returning repeatedly to one woman he disliked, he clipped her bald and gilded her pate.

With tellers counting their money he interfered outrageously and enriched himself. He snipped cigarettes in two with a scissors and blew out matches and lighters, so that one frustrated man actually broke down and cried at his inability to get a light.

He removed the weapons from the holsters of policemen and put cap pistols and water guns in their places. And he liked to rip off one sleeve only from the coat of a walking gentleman. There is something funnier about one sleeve missing than two.

He unclipped the leashes of dogs and substituted little toy dogs rolling on wheels. He put frogs in water glasses and left lighted firecrackers on bridge tables. He reset wristwatches on wrists; and played cruel tricks in mens' rooms, causing honest gentleman to wet themselves.

"I was always a boy at heart," said Charles Vincent.

Also during those first few days of the controlled new state, he established himself materially, acquiring wealth by devious ways, and opening bank accounts in various cities under various names, against a time of possible need.

Nor did he ever feel any shame for the tricks that he played on unaccelerated humanity. For the people, when he was in the state, were as statues to him, hardly living, barely moving, unseeing, unhearing. And it is no shame to show disrespect to such comical statues.

And also, and again because he was a boy at heart, he had fun with the girls.

"I am one mass of black and blue marks," said Jenny one day. "My lips are sore and my front teeth are loosened. I don't know what in the world is the matter with me."

Yet he had not meant to bruise or harm her. He was rather fond of her and he resolved to be much more careful. Yet it was fun, when he was in the state and so invisible to her because of his speed, to kiss her here and there in out-of-the-way places and show her other small marks of affection. She made a nice statue and it was good sport. And there were others.

"You look suddenly older," said one of his co-workers one day. "Are you taking care of yourself? Are you worried?"

"I am not," said Vincent. "I was never happier in my life."

But now there was time for so many things, in fact, everything. There was no reason why he could not master anything in the world, when he could take off for fifteen minutes and gain fifteen hours. Vincent was a rapid but careful reader. He could now read from a hundred and twenty to two hundred books in an evening and night; and he slept in an accelerated state and could get a full night's sleep in eight minutes.

He first acquired a knowledge of the languages. A quite extensive reading knowledge of a language can be acquired in three hundred hours of world time, or three hundred minutes (five hours) of accelerated time. And if one takes the tongues in order, from the most familiar to the most remote, there is no real difficulty. He acquired fifty for a starter, and could always add another any evening that he found he had a need for it.

And at the same time he began to assemble and consolidate knowledge. Of literature, properly speaking, there are no more than ten thousand books that are really worth reading and falling in love with. These were gone through with high pleasure, and two or three thousand of them were important enough to be reserved for future rereading.

History, however, is very uneven. It is necessary to read texts and sources that for form are not worth reading. And the same with philosophy. Mathematics and science, pure or physical, could not, of course, be covered with the same speed. Yet, with time available, all could be mastered. There is no concept ever expressed by any human mind that cannot be comprehended by any other normal human mind, if time is available, and if it is taken in the proper order and context and with the proper preparatory work.

And often, and now more often, Vincent felt that he was touching the fingers of the secret. And always, when he came near it, it had a little bit of the smell of the Pit.

For he had pegged out all the main points of the history of man; or rather most of the tenable, or at least possible, theories of the history of man. It was hard to hold the main line of it: that double road of rationality and revelation that should lead always to a fuller and fuller development, to an unfolding and growth and perfectability. Sometimes he felt that he was trespassing on the history of something other than man.

For the main line of the account was often obscure and all but obliterated, and traced through fog and miasma. Vincent had accepted the Fall of Man and the Redemption as the cardinal points of history. But he began to feel now that neither had happened only once, that both were of constant recurrence; that there was a hand reaching up from that old Pit with its shadow over man. And he had come to picture that hand in his dreams —for his dreams were especially vivid when in the state —as a six-digited monster reaching out. He began to realize that the thing he was caught in was dangerous and deadly.

Very dangerous.

Very deadly.

One of the weird books that he often returned to and which continually puzzled him was *The Relationship of Extradigitalism to Genius*, written by the man whose face he had never seen, in one of his manifestations.

It promised more than it delivered, and it intimated more than it said. Its theory was tedious and tenuous, bolstered with undigested mountains of doubtful data. It left Vincent unconvinced that persons of genius—even if it could be agreed who or what they were—had often the oddity of extra fingers or toes, or the vestiges of them. And it puzzled him what possible difference it could make.

Yet there were hints here of a Corsican who commonly kept a hand hidden; of an earlier and more bizarre commander who always wore a mailed glove; of another man with a glove between the two; hints that the multiplex adept, Leonardo himself, who sometimes drew the hands of men and more often those of monsters with six fingers, had had the touch. There was a comment on Caeser, not conclusive, to the same effect.

It is known that Alexander had a minor deformity. It is not known what it was. This man made it seem that this was it. And it was averred of Gregory and Augustine, of Benedict and Albert and Aquinas. Yet a man with a deformity could not enter the priesthood; if they had it, it must have been in vestigial form.

There were cases for Charles Magnus and Mahmud, for Saladin the horseman and for Akhnaton the king; for Homer—a Seleucid-Greek statuette shows him with six fingers strumming an unidentified instrument while reciting; cases for Pythagoras, for Buonottoti, Santi, Theotokopolous, van Rijn, Robusti. And going farther back in time, and less subject to proof, they became much more numerous.

Zurbarin cataloged eight thousand of them. He maintained that they were geniuses. And that they were extradigitals.

Charles Vincent grinned and looked down at his misshapen or double thumb.

"At least I am in good though monotonous company. But what in the name of triple time is he driving at?"

And it was not long afterward that Vincent was examining cuneiform tablets in State Museum. These were a broken and not continuous series on the theory of numbers, tolerably legible to the now encyclopedic Charles Vincent. And the series read in part:

On the divergence of the basis itself and the confusion caused by——for it is Five, or it is Six, or Ten or Twelve, or Sixty or One Hundred, or Three hundred and Sixty or the Double Hundred, the Thousand. The reason, not clearly understood by the People, is that Six and the Dozen are First, and Sixty is a compromise in condescending to the people.

For the Five, the Ten are late, and are no older than the People themselves. It is said, and credited, that the People began to count by Fives and Tens from the number of fingers on their hands. But before the People the——, for the reason that they had——, counted by Sixes and Twelves. But Sixty is the number of time, divisible by both, for both must live together in Time, though not on the same plane of time——

Much of the rest was scattered. It was while trying to set the hundreds of unordered clay tablets in proper sequence that Charles Vincent created the legend of the ghost in the museum.

For he spent his multi-hundred-hour nights there studying and classifying. Naturally he could not work without light, and naturally he could be seen when he sat still at his studies. But as the slow-moving guards attempted to close in on him, he would move to avoid them, and his speed made him invisible to them. They were a nuisance and had to be discouraged. He belabored them soundly and they became less eager to try to capture him.

His only fear was that they would sometime try to shoot him to see if he were ghost or human. He could avoid a seen shot which would come at no more than two and a half times his own greatest speed. But an unperceived shot could penetrate dangerously, even fatally, before he twisted away from it.

Vincent had fathered legends of other ghosts, that of

the Central Library, that of the University Library, that of the John Charles Underwood Jr. Technical Library. This plurality of ghosts tended to cancel out each other and bring believers into ridicule. Even those who had seen him as a ghost did not admit that they believed in ghosts.

Charles Vincent had gone back to Dr. Mason for his monthly checkup.

"You look terrible," said the doctor. "Whatever it is, you have changed. If you have the means you should take a long rest."

"I have the means," said Vincent, "and that is just what I will do. I'll take a rest for a year or two."

He had begun to begrudge the time that he must spend at the world's pace. From this time on he was regarded as a recluse. He was silent and unsociable, for he found it a nuisance to come back to the common state to engage in conversation, and in his special state the voices were too slow-pitched to intrude on his consciousness.

Except that of the man whose face he had never seen.

"You are making very tardy progress," said the man. Once more they were in a dark club. "Those who do not show more progress we cannot use. After all, you are only a vestigial. It is probable that you have very little of the ancient race in you. Fortunately those who do not progress destroy themselves. You had not imagined that there were only two phases of time, had you?"

"Lately I have come to suspect that there are many more," said Charles Vincent.

"And you understand that one step only cannot succeed?"

"I understand that the life that I have been living is in direct violation of all that we know of the laws of mass, momentum and acceleration, as well as those of conservation of energy, the potential of the human person, the moral compensation, the golden mean, and the capacity of human organs. I know that I cannot multiply energy and experience sixty times without increase of food intake, and yet I do it. I know that I cannot live on eight minutes of sleep in twenty-four hours, but I do that also. I know that I cannot reasonably crowd four thousand years of experience into one lifetime, yet unreasonably I do not see what will prevent it. But you say that I will destroy myself?"

"Those who take only the first step will destroy themselves."

"And how does one take the second step?"

"At the proper moment you will be given the choice."

"I have the most uncanny feeling that I will refuse the choice."

"Yes, from present indications you will refuse it. You are fastidious."

"You have a smell about you, Old Man without a Face. I know now what it is. It is the smell of the Pit."

"Are you so slow to learn that? But that is its name."

"It is the mud from the Pit, the same from which the clay tablets were formed, from the old land between the rivers. I've dreamed of the six-fingered hand reaching up from that Pit and overshadowing us all. From that slime!"

"Do not forget that according to another recension Another made the People from that same slime."

"And I have read, Old Man: 'The People first counted by Fives and Tens from the number of fingers on their hands. But before the People the——, for the reason that they had——, counted by Sixes and Twelves.' But time has left blanks on those tablets."

"Yes. Time, in one of its manifestations, has deftly and with a purpose left those blanks."

"I cannot discover the name of the thing that goes into one of those blanks. Can you?"

"I am part of the name that goes into one of those blanks."

"And you are the Man without a Face. But why is it that you overshadow and control people? And to what purpose?"

"It will be long before you know those answers."

"When the choice comes to me, it will bear very careful weighing. But tell me, Man without a Face who comes from the Pit, are not pits and men without faces very nineteenth-century Gothic?"

"There was a temper in that century that came very close to uncovering us."

After that a chill descended on the life of Charles Vincent, for all that he still possessed his exceptional powers. And now he seldom indulged in pranks.

Except with Jennifer Parkey.

It was unusual that he should be drawn to her. He knew her only slightly in the common world, and she was at least fifteen years his senior. But she now appealed to him for her youthful qualities, and all his pranks with her were gentle ones.

For one thing this spinster did not frighten, nor did she begin the precaution of locking her doors, never having bothered with such things before. He would come behind her and stroke her hair, and she would speak out calmly with that sort of quickening in her voice:

"Who are you? Why won't you let me see you? You are a friend, aren't you? Are you a man, or are you something else? If you can caress me why can't you talk to me? Please let me see you. I promise I won't hurt you."

It was as though she could not imagine that anything strange would hurt her. Or again when he hugged her or kissed her on the nape, she would call: "You must be a little boy, or very like a little boy, whoever you are. You are good not to break my things when you move about. Come here and let me hold you."

It is only very good people who have no fear at all of the unknown.

When Vincent met Jennifer in the regular world, as he now more often found occasion to do, she looked at him appraisingly, as though she guessed some sort of connection.

She said one day, "I know it is an impolite thing to say, but you do not look well at all. Have you been to a doctor?"

"Several times. But I think it is my doctor who should go to a doctor. He was always given to peculiar remarks, but now he is becoming a little unsettled."

"If I were your doctor, I believe that I would also become a little unsettled. But you should find out what is wrong. You look terrible."

He did not look terrible. He had lost his hair, it is true, but many men lose their hair by thirty, though not perhaps as suddenly as he had. He thought of attributing it to air resistance. After all, when he was in the state he did stride at some three hundred miles an hour. And enough of that is likely to blow the hair right off your head. And might that not also be the reason for his worsening complexion and the tireder look that appeared in his eyes? But he knew that this was nonsense. He felt no more air pressure when in his accelerated state than when in his normal state.

He had received his summons. He chose not to answer it. He did not want to be presented with the choice; he had no wish to be one with those in the Pit. But he had no intention of giving up the great advantage which he now held over nature.

"I will have it both ways," he said. "I am already a contradiction and an impossibility. 'You can't have your confection and eat it too.' The proverb was only the early statement of the law of moral compensation. 'You can't take more out of a basket than it holds.' But for a long time I have been in violation of the laws and the balances. 'There is no road without a turning,' 'Those who dance will have to pay the fiddler,' 'Everything that goes up comes down.' But are proverbs really universal laws? Certainly. A sound proverb has the force of universal law, is but another statement of it. But I have contradicted the universal laws. It remains to be seen whether I have contradicted them with impunity.

" 'Every action has its reaction.' If I refuse to deal with them, I will provoke a strong reaction. The Man without a Face said that it was always a race between full knowing and destruction. Very well, I will race them for it."

They began to persecute him then. He knew that they were in a state as accelerated from his as his was from the normal. To them he was the almost motionless statue, hardly to be told from a dead man. To him they were by their speed both invisible and inaudible. They hurt him and haunted him. But still he would not answer their summons.

When the meeting took place, it was they who had to come to him, and they materialized there in his room, men without faces.

"The choice," said one. "Well, you force us to be so clumsy as to have to voice it."

"I will have no part of you," said Charles Vincent. "You all smell of the Pit, of that old mud of the cuneiforms of the land between the rivers, of the people who were before the People."

"It has endured a long time," one of them said, "and we consider it as enduring forever. But the Garden, which was quite in the neighborhood—do you know how long the Garden lasted?"

"I don't know."

"Not even a day. It all happened in a single day, and before nightfall they were outside. You want to throw in with something more permanent, don't you?"

"No. I don't believe that I do."

"What have you to lose?"

"Only my hope of eternity."

"But you don't believe in that. No man has ever really believed in eternity."

"No man has ever either entirely believed or entirely disbelieved in it," said Charles Vincent.

"At least it can never be proved," said one of the faceless men. "Nothing is proved until it is over with. And in this case, if it is ever over with, then it is disproved. And all that time would one not be tempted to wonder 'What if, after all, it ends in the next minute?'"

"I imagine, if we survive the flesh, we will receive some sort of surety," said Vincent.

"But you are not sure either of surviving or receiving, nor could you accept the surety as sure. Now *we* have a very close approximation of eternity. When Time is multiplied by itself, and that repeated again and again, does that not approximate eternity?"

"I don't believe that it does. But I will not be of you. One of you has said that I am too fastidious. So now will you say that you'll destroy me?"

"No. We will only let you be destroyed. By yourself, you cannot win the race with destruction."

After that Charles Vincent somehow felt more mature. He knew he was not really meant to be a poltergeist or a six-fingered thing out of the Pit. He knew that in some way he would have to pay for every minute and hour that he had gained. But what he had gained he would use to the fullest. And whatever could be accomplished by sheer acquisition of human knowledge, he would try to accomplish.

And he now startled Dr. Mason by the medical knowledge he had picked up, the while the doctor amused him by the concern he showed for Vincent. For he felt fine. He was perhaps not as active as he had been, but that was only because he had become dubious of aimless activity. He was still the ghost of the libraries and museums, but was puzzled that the published reports intimated that an old ghost had replaced a young one.

He now paid his mystic visits to Jennifer Parkey less

often. For he was always dismayed to hear her exclaim to him in his ghostly form, "Your touch is so changed. You poor thing! Is there anything at all I can do to help you?"

He decided that somehow she was too immature to ever understand him, though he was still fond of her. He transferred his affections to Mrs. Milly Maltby, a widow at least thirty years his senior. Yet here it was a sort of girlishness in her that appealed to him. She was a woman of sharp wit and real affection, and she also accepted his visitations without fear, following a little initial panic.

They played games, writing games, for they communicated by writing. Milly would scribble a line, then hold the paper up in the air whence he would cause it to vanish into his sphere. He would return it in half a minute, or half a second of her time, with his retort. He had the advantage of her in time with greatly more opportunity to think up responses, but she had the advantage over him in natural wit and was hard to top.

They also played checkers, and he often had to retire apart and read a chapter of a book on the art between moves; and even so she often beat him. For natural talent is likely to be a match for accumulated lore and codified procedure.

But to Milly also he was unfaithful in his fashion, being now interested—he no longer became enamored or entranced—in a Mrs. Roberts, a great-grandmother who was his elder by at least fifty years. He had read all the data extant on the attraction of the old for the young, but he still could not explain his successive attachments. He decided that these three examples were enough to establish a universal law: that a woman is simply not afraid of a ghost, though he touches her and is invisible, and writes her notes without hands. It is possible that amorous spirits have known this for a long time, but Charles Vincent had made the discovery himself independently.

When enough knowledge is accumulated on any subject, the pattern will sometimes emerge suddenly, like
a form in a picture revealed where before it was not
seen. And when enough knowledge is accumulated on
all subjects, is there not a chance that a pattern govern-
ing all subjects will emerge?

Charles Vincent was caught up in his last enthusiasm.
On one long vigil, as he consulted source after source
and sorted them in his mind, it seemed that the pattern
was coming out clearly and simply, for all its amazing
complexity of detail.

"I know all that they know in the Pit," said Vincent,
"and I know a secret that they do not know. I have not
lost the race—I have won it. I can defeat them at the
point where they believe themselves invulnerable. If
controlled hereafter, we need at least not be controlled
by them. It is all falling together now. I have found the
final truth, and it is they who have lost the race. I hold
the key. I will now be able to enjoy the advantage without paying the ultimate price of defeat and destruction,
or of collaborating with them.

"Now I have only to implement my knowledge, to
publish the fact, and one shadow at least will be lifted
from mankind. I will do it at once. Well, nearly at once.
It is almost dawn in the normal world. I will sit here a
very little while and rest. Then I will go out and begin
to make contact with the proper persons for the dis-
position of this thing. But first I will sit here a little
while and rest."

And he died quietly in his chair as he sat there.

Dr. Mason made an entry in his private journal:

   Charles Vincent, a completely authenticated case
of premature aging, one of the most clear-cut in all
gerontology. This man was known to me for many
years, and I here aver that as of one year ago he
was of normal appearance and physical state, and

that his chronology is also correct, I having also known his father. I examined the subject during the period of his illness, and there is no question at all of his identity, which has also been established for the record by fingerprinting and other means. I aver that Charles Vincent at the age of thirty is dead of old age, having the appearance and organic state of a man of ninety.

Then the doctor began to make other notes: "As in two other cases of my own observation, the illness was accompanied by a certain delusion and series of dreams, so nearly identical in all three men as to be almost unbelievable. And for the record, and no doubt to the prejudice of my own reputation, I will set down the report of them here."

But when Dr. Mason had written that, he thought about it for a while.

"No, I will do no such thing," he said, and he struck out the last lines he had written. "It is best to let sleeping dragons lie."

And somewhere the faceless men with the smell of the Pit on them smiled to themselves in quiet irony.

FROG ON THE MOUNTAIN

HE WOKE TO mountains, as the poet says. Really, there is nothing like it. The oceans and the lowlands were made long ago, according to legend. But the mountains are made new every morning.

It took some doing. His name was Garamask, and he had done it.

"I hate space," Garamask had said when he decided on it, and the crewmen had been surprised.

"Why do you, Mr. Garamask?" the Captain had asked him. "You've logged more time in space than I have. You've been to many more regions. And you've made more money in the space business than anyone I know. I never saw a man so eager for voyages or for new worlds as you. You're so expansive a person that I thought you were in love with the expanse of space."

"I love movement and travel," Garamask said. "I love worlds! But in space, the feel of movement and the sense of travel is quickly lost. And space is *not* expansive. It is shriveling.

"I have, let us say, a passion for a certain unkempt and mountainous world, but space comes near to destroying that passion in me; for I have seen that world appear on the scope like a microbe, and I will watch it disappear like a microbe again. I have studied epic and towering things under the microscope. And when I put away the microscope, I know that the towering things are really too small to see. From the aspect of space, all the towering and wild worlds that I love are things too small to see or to believe in. I love a big world, and I hate space for spoiling that bigness."

"Paravata isn't so big a world, Mr. Garamask," the Captain told him.

74

"It is! It's big! It's huge!" Garamask insisted. "And I'll not have it spoiled. It is the largest possible world on the man-scale, and I will not let that scale suffer by comparison. It's a world as large as a man can get around on with ease, without becoming less than a man. It's half again Earth's gravity, so it calls out our strength. It has an atmosphere that keeps one on an oxygen binge, so it gives the strength something to draw on. It has mountains that rise ten thousand meters, the highest mountains anywhere that a man can climb in his proper body and without apparatus.

"And I won't have it spoiled for me! I'm rich enough that you can't regard me as a nuisance. I've given my instructions. So, follow them as regards me."

"Mr. Garamask, weren't you ever young?" the Captain asked him.

"I *am* young yet, Captain. I am physically the fittest man on this ship. And this is a very young and aspiring idea that I am effecting now."

"Ah, were you never something else, Mr. Garamask, not quite so young, and much more awkward?"

"I don't know what you mean, Captain, but I suspect that I never was. Follow my instructions."

The instructions of Garamask were that he be sent into a sustaining sleep, and that he be landed and lodged on Paravata of the Mountains while he slept. He did not know when Paravata was picked up microbe-sized, nor when it grew a hundred million times to the size of a pea. He did not see the planet grow to twice the size of Earth. He missed the landing.

He was taken from the ship at Paravata Landing and transported a hundred kilometers to the mountain lodge. He was installed there as befitted a man of means. He slept a determined number of hours, as he had planned it, and he woke in the very early morning. He woke to mountains.

He went out into the keen air of Paravata or Paravath, finding himself in the middle of the small town of Moun-

tain-Foot. He had a warrant for arrest and death in his
wallet; and he had a singing curiosity about this world'
whose vital civilization had suddenly been frozen in motion, whose people, the Rogha (the elites, the excellent
ones), had disappeared or very nearly disappeared and
whose place had been taken by the oafish Oganta, and
this almost within living memory. He was on a hunting
trip in depth: he would hunt on the three-stage mountain to kill Sinek the cat-lion, Riksino the bear, Shasos the
eagle-condor, and Bater-Jeno the crag-ape or the frog-
man (depending on the translation). This was said to
be the most challenging hunt in the galaxy. And most
likely he would die on the triple mountain, for no
human hunter had ever bagged all four of the creatures
and survived the thing; though Oganta hunters were
said to have done the trick.

On the second level, Garamask was hunting for the
answer to the riddle: what had happened to the Rogha
elites? Could those few who were left not be strength-
ened in their hold? Could their civilization not be un-
frozen? Might it not be discovered what queer hold the
oafish Oganta had over this Rogha remnant? How had
the excellent ones fallen (willingly, it was said) to their
inferiors?

On the third level, Garamask was hunting for a murderer, the Oganta, Rogha, Animal, or Man who had
killed Allyn. Allyn had been a close friend, but Garamask
had not realized how close until after the event. It had
been given out that Allyn, on the same hunt, had been
killed by the Bater-Jeno, the crag-ape or the frog-man.
Allyn, however, had newly appeared to Garamask in a
rhapsody-dream and said that this was not so. He had
been killed, said Allyn, by his guide and hunting companion, who had been an Oganta named Ocras, *but
who might not now be in Oganta form.*

"I believe that we have been close," Allyn had said,
"though we never spoke of our closeness. Avenge me,
Garamask, and take the lid off the mystery of Paravath.

I was so very close to uncovering the mystery myself."
"What had you found, Allyn?" Garamask had asked; but
appearances in dreams often seem hard of hearing; they
speak but they do not listen.

"Uncover it, Garamask," Allyn had repeated, "and
avenge me. I was so close to it. He ate into the base of
my skull and so killed me. He ate my very brains as I
died." "But what did you find when you came so close,
Allyn?" Garamask had asked once more. "Tell me what
you had going, so I will know what to look for." "I was so
close to it when I died," Allyn said.

Apparitions are as stone-deaf. They speak their mes-
sage, but they do not hear. You may have noticed this
yourself.

Garamask was not a great believer in dreams, but he
had desired this hunt for a long time; he had, in fact,
intended to accompany Allyn on his hunt, but had been
prevented by affairs. And he had known at the time of
the dream, had not known till he had gone carefully
over the report, that Allyn had indeed been killed by
having his skull eaten into. Now Garamask tested it a
little.

"My guide, will he be Ocras?" he asked the gangling
Oganta who was manager of the hunting lodge.

"Ocras? No, he is no longer a guide. He has been
translated out of this life."

"But there *was* a guide named Ocras?"

"There was one time a guide named Ocras, who is
no more. Your guide will be Chavo."

But there *had been* a guide named Ocras, and Garamask hadn't known the name except in the rhapsody-
dream. Then Garamask saw one of the Rogha survivors
walking proudly in the early keen air. He went to him
at once, meeting him on a rocky slope.

"I have an intense interest in you and all your kind,"
Garamask began. "You yourself are the face of the mys-
tery. You are imposing in a way that I could never be;
I can see why you are called the elite, the excellent ones.

You are so startlingly in contrast to the Oganta here that everyone for worlds around is puzzled over it. You are kings. They are oaks. Why do they take you over?"

"I suppose it is the day of the oafs, pilgrim-man," the Rogha said easily. "I am Treorai, and you are the man Garamask who made preparations to wake to mountains. You have taken up the challenge of the three-stage mountain. It's a high aspiration to kill the four creatures there. One who has done it will experience a deep change."

"As Allyn did?"

"I knew him when he was here. He did *not* kill the four creatures. He was killed by the fourth."

"He has told me, outside the lines as it were, that he was killed by something other."

"Allyn would not lie, even outside the lines. You have misunderstood him. Did he say that he completed the hunt and killed the fourth creature?"

"He said that he had killed Sinek the lion, Riksino the bear, Shasos the eagle; but, no, he did not say that he had killed the Bater-Jeno. He said, however, that he was murdered by something else."

"No, Garamask, he was killed by the fourth prey. A creature is often fuzzy in his mind about his own manner of dying. He was a wonderful fellow, though, for a man."

"Treorai, why has your civilization come to a grotesque halt? Why have you Rogha, in your manifest superiority, all but died out? Why have the rough rampant Oganta taken over? A dozen of them couldn't take one of you. You have the presence that would dumbfound any attack. I can feel it like magnetism. Is it a genetic thing that has happened?"

"A genetic thing, a ghostly thing, a sundering thing really, Garamask. But it isn't finished, and there is no apathy here. What we Rogha have lost, we will regain, by any means whatsoever. This eclipse will pass from us." ◄

"Why don't you simply annihilate the Oganta, Treorai?"

"You are an educated man, Garamask, but your speaking of the Paravath language is imperfect. I simply do not understand your question. I have some World-English, if that would help."

"Treorai, why do you Rogha not simply annihilate the Oganta?" Garamask asked the excellent Rogha in World-English.

"No, Garamask, I have not so much of the idiom as I thought," said Treorai. "Your question is simply incomprehensible in whatever language it is put. Ah, your guide has peeped out to see if you are ready. Grab him quickly, or he will go in and be back to sleep again. The Oganta are not morning types. And the sun should not find you still at Mountain-Foot. It should find you at least two hundred meters aloft. See that ledge there! It is a wonderful place to catch first sun."

"I see that it will be," said Garamask. "And it will take some inspired climbing to get there in time. If I live I will see you again, excellent one."

"High hunting, Garamask! A very strong hunter with a very good guide may kill the first three creatures. To kill the fourth, the hunter must transcend himself."

Garamask started up the Mountain Domba (the first mountain of the three-mountain complex) with Chavo his booming Oganta guide. The Oganta are rangy and solid creatures, and strength and endurance is their birthright. Say what you will about the loud oafs, they are strong climbers! And Garamask was a very strong man who had climbed on heavier-than-World worlds before.

And, ah, there is sometimes an advantage in knowing the Paravath language imperfectly. Garamask could tune Chavo out. It took all his attention to follow the language, and his attention was mercifully on many other things as they went up. And yet Chavo laughed and boomed incessantly, like boulders clashing together.

A queer and unfinished looking creature was this

Chavo, were all the Oganta. (Climbing, climbing hard
and high, they'd catch first sun on the fine ledge yet.)
A queer creature! "The male European moor frog (*Rana
Arvalis*) is covered with a light blue bloom like a plum,"
the anthropologist-naturalist Wendt had written two hundred years ago, but Wendt had never heard of the world
of Paravata, nor of a blue-blooming moor frog two meters
tall. (Climbing hard and high, there was another shade of
blue bloom in the morning light, and the keen air was
like World brandy.) "Those naked goblins with human
hands and infant bodies, "old Wendt had written again,
but Wendt never visioned an infant body that would
weigh two hundred kilograms here, and two-thirds that
much on Earth. Chavo the Oganta was a lot of oaf!

It was all moss-covered rocks, and tiger grass growing between them. It was nowhere difficult to get foot-
or handhold, but it was steep and it was heavy. They
came to the fine ledge and took it just at first sun.
They rested there.

"You do not like me, Papa Garamask," Chavo was
booming. "But I will make you like me. We Oganta like
to be liked. We will go to any lengths to be liked."

"You go too far for it, I believe," said Garamask.
"When will we meet the Sinek?"

"We will meet sineks and sineks from here on up,
but they will bound away from us and will not stand.
Then we will meet Sinek himself, and he will stand."

"You talk as though there were only one of the species
who would be dangerous. And yet, surely, a dozen of
these very dangerous sineks have been killed."

"There is only one at a time, Papa Garamask. Whether
it is always the same one that is translated back to live
on the mountain, or whether one inherits from another,
we do not know. But always there are many sineks,
and there is Sinek himself. It is time to arm before we
go up higher."

Chavo broke the stuff out of his pack. No shot-weapon
might be used on the mountain hunt; even bow and

spear-thrower and sling were ruled out. The animals had them not, so the hunters might not have them. It made for a harder hunt. The hunting and killing must be by direct confrontation and intimate encounter. Garamask clipped the claw-gauntlets over the backs of his hands, binding them by wrist and palm straps. He had been proud of his crushing grip, of his massive hands and forearms; but could he with these deliver lion blows on the lion himself? He bound on the elbow and knee and toe and heel daggers, needle-pointed, double-bladed, curiously curved. He bound on the crotch and throat armor. He slipped the casing fangs over his own dog teeth. He bound on the cap with the skull saber. Chavo similarly equipped himself. Well, the animals of Paravath had such claws and fangs (not all of them having the same ones), so the hunters could have such also.

"It will be much harder to climb in this," Garamask grumbled.

"It will be, Papa Garamask," Chavo said, "and the climb itself becomes much harder. Some hunters take the spikes and claws off and hook them ready in their belts, and they are surprised by Sinek or Riksino or Shasos, and die for it. Some climb, clawed and daggered, and slip and fall to their deaths."

"Which is best, guide?"

"Whichever way you would rather die, Papa Garamask, so select it. That will be the best for you."

"I do not intend to die on the mountain."

"Shall we turn back now, Papa Garamask? You make twelve World-men who have come to hunt. All die on the mountain. None goes all the way through the full hunt."

"One man, Allyn, went all the way, Chavo. And then he was murdered. I have climbed with him and hunted with him, and I'm as good a man. I intend to go all the way, and I do not intend to be murdered."

They climbed strongly, Garamask silent, Chavo booming and croaking with incessant talk that Garamask tuned out. The Oganta climbed, clawed and daggered and fanged and armored. That was the best way then. Garamask did likewise. He didn't envy the Oganta his youth and towering strength. Garamask had his own strength and he enjoyed testing it. But he envied the Oganta, a little, his fangs. Garamask had no such giant canine teeth to support the giant saber-fangs. He had no such bull-bowed neck, nor skull-massif, nor buttressed and ridged upper jaw to support such sabers. But he had donned a pretty good set of fangs himself and he believed he would know how to use them.

From one jagged turning, Garamask caught a dizzy view 'of Daingean City far away. The excellent Rogha had been builders at least equal to men. Now their cities were almost emptied of them, and the oafish Oganta lived in them like animals denning. Then the jagged turning became even more jagged, and Garamask could not afford another glance at the city.

They ate aran-moss and cobble-moss, and pods of tiger grass. They chewed green coill-nuts for water. They climbed high and hard. Then Garamask caught the whiff and the spoor of the spook animals, and he knew it out of the cellar of his mind.

"Ah, this is the world you live on," he breathed, "and you are not imaginary at all. Animal who is no animal, I know what you are." Garamask slavered when he called out because of the great fangs capped to his dog teeth. "The old Greeks called you the all-animal, and pictured you as made out of parts of many. And men said you were the Asian lion, or leopard, or tiger, or rock-lion, or American puma. And all the time you were yourself, the legend animal."

"Who do you talk to, Papa Garamask?" Chavo asked in some alarm. "Do you talk to the grandfather of Sinek?"

"To the great-great-grandfather of Sinek, oaf. In the rain forests, they told poor men that your name was jaguar, but the poor men knew better. In the old South of the Conglomerate States on World, they told that your name was puma or cougar, but the poor cracker-men always knew your real species. Spook animal, I come in after you!"

"Papa Garamask, throw but a rock into the thicket and it will slink off. It is only one of the sineks, it is not Sinek himself. He seldom hunts so low or so early. And do not talk to the grandfather of Sinek, or he will come in your dreams and eat through your live throat and kill you."

"Damn you, oaf, it is Sinek himself! He hunts low and early today. Grandfather of *all* the animals, I fight you now! Panther!"

And Garamask charged upward, across a slide of moss-covered rocks, into a tall thicket of tiger-grass and coill-bush, to fight panther, the animal who exists only in legend and misnomer. On Paravath he used the name Sinek.

It was a long black male. This was no sinek who would bound away, who would not stand. This was Sinek himself, and now Garamask understood why there could be only one of him at a time. The spook, the spirit filled this animal completely, with nothing left over for any other.

Garamask drew first blood, clawing the black panther half blind, getting his elbow dagger inside the panther's mouth, trying always to stay inside the animal's fore-claws. Panther got one side of Garamask's head, above the throat armor, inside his mouth, failed to hold, slid bloodily along it, popped it out, and took an ear off neatly. The animal would weigh a hundred and fifty kilograms here, a hundred on Earth, just about Gara-mask's own weight. Panther, Sinek, knocked Garamask loose, and he slid on the loose rocks and moss, very nearly off the mountain to his death. Then they were in confrontation.

Sinek was upground of Garamask on the edge of the firm rock; and Garamask was on the loose-rock fringe that slipped and cascaded and was now flowing over

83

the edge like water. Chavo, the Oganta oaf, was chewing a blade of tiger-grass and laughing.

It was with amazement that Garamask saw intelligence, almost total intelligence, in the eyes of Sinek the panther. This was a person and a personage, whatever the species. The intelligent look was almost friendly to Garamask, and the two understood each other. They would fight to the death, but they recognized each other for what they were, excellent ones, superior ones, Panther, Man, Rogha, firstlings, not to be compared to Oganta or Swine or Sloths.

Garamask made the attempt to break out of his sliding strip. He exchanged terrific clawing blows with Sinek, got the worse of it, and came much nearer to going off the mountain as he slid reeling back.

"Fear you nothing, Papa Garamask," the Oganta Chavo called from where he had scrambled higher. "I will roll boulders down on Sinek and kill him." And Chavo did roll boulders, badly, inaccurately, dangerously. Then Garamask understood from the oafish laughter that Chavo was trying to kill him and not Sinek; trying to knock the man off the mountain with the rolling boulders, or to induce a rockslide that would carry him irrevocably down.

With a mixture of stark terror and upsurging courage that was peculiar to himself in moments of deep crisis, Garamask battled up the sliding rocks, greatly impeded by his arms, and closed with Sinek the panther again.

"I am as large, I am as strong, I am as armed, dammit, I am as animal!" Garamask gibbered. "We close together, good comrade. If I go off the mountain, you go off it too."

But Garamask was wrong. The panther was more animal than he. It was doing him to death in the close fighting, though puzzled by the throat and crotch armor. "Who waits below to eat out my skull, Chavo?" Garamask howled out furiously. "Who waits below to crack my skull and eat my brains? That is not Sinek here. It *is* scavengers below me, and a scavenger above me, you!"

"Papa Garamask," Chavo chortled in a booming giggle from above, "fear you nothing. I will roll boulders down on Sinek and kill him." And Chavo was rolling boulders down on them both, grappled together, to kill them both.

Garamask was losing, slipping. He broke off his capping fangs and his own canine teeth under them tried to slash through the sinews of panther; and he was choked on his own sudden blood. He raked the animal with elbow, knee, toe, and heel daggers, and was nearly disemboweled by a back foot of Sinek that equaled all the dagger functions. For the last time he broke free from the slashing, smashing panther and rolled in a stream of scree, trying to keep himself on the mountain.

Chavo set a large boulder at him to help him over the edge. Sinek the panther came lithely for the kill, and caught the boulder amidships as he flicked himself sly-footed along the edge of firm rock. And Sinek could not halt himself when he was knocked heavily into the sliding rock stream. Sinek the panther flowed off the mountain and fell into gaping space.

"Papa Garamask, I save your life," Chavo the Oganta chortled from above. "Now I must make certain that Sinek is really dead where he has fallen so far below. I will roll yet more boulders down on him, and down on him till I am sure that he is dead."

And Chavo rolled boulders down at Garamask to knock him off the mountain; and the man scrambled in the sliding scree to avoid them. Three, six, nine boulders Chavo rolled down at Garamask, and then he had trouble in getting a fine boulder loose from its embedment. Garamask found a hidden spur of solid rock and went up quickly. Chavo turned, and they were on a level face to face: Garamask bloody and crippled and earless, and full of muskiness and ghostliness, for part of the spook of Sinek, falling to death, had passed into Garamask. And Chavo, what can you say of the oaf Chavo of the species Oganta? Could he meet Garamask's eyes? No, but he never could have; all Oganta are wall-eyed. Did he blanch at the encounter? How can you tell with an Oganta? But the light blue bloom that was his complexion had lost a little of its sheen.

"Why do you pause, guide Chavo?" Garamask asked as a waiting volcano might ask. "We go up, we go up! We have not yet reached the top of the first mountain of Three-Mountain. We have killed only one of the four prey. We go up, we go up!"

They went up. They wore out the day with their climbing. They saw sineks and sineks who bounded away from them and would not stand. But they did not meet Sinek himself again that day. Sinek was dead for the while. Garamask took off his weapons and armor pieces and hooked them into his belt. Thereafter he climbed more easily. And just at last sun they came to the top of Domba Mountain, the first mountain of Three-Mountain.

It was a high plateau; it was another mountain-foot, for out of it rose the Mountain Giri, the second mountain of Three-Mountain. They ate bitter mountain rations and chewed green coill-nuts for water. They bedded down for the night, so Garamask thought.

But Chavo brought a stringed instrument from his pack and began some of the twangingest and most nauseating noise ever heard. He mixed his bumptious booming voice with it in a curdling cry, and Garamask understood that he would not be able to sleep with this.

"You have convinced me, pup," he growled. "You have established one of the universal ultimates—the most raucous noise ever. But is it necessary that you belabor the point?"

"You do not like it?" Chavo was surprised. "I pride myself on my music and my singing. We consider such to be dynamic perfection and cosmic looseness of sound."

"I consider it something else. The Rogha are said to

be the most musical creatures in the universes. How could their co-dwellers here, you Oganta, be the least?"

"I had hoped you would like my music," Chavo sorrowed. "I still hope that you will like me. Really, we are likable creatures. Even some of the Rogha have said so, with a certain exasperation, it is true."

"You are crude unlicked calves, Chavo, and I understand your world less and less. Why, and how, are you killing the Rogha? For I believe that to be the case."

"But there are so few of them left, Papa Garamask! And they become fewer and fewer. So is it not imperative that we kill them, much as we respect and love them?"

"If there were millions of them left, would you kill them?"

"No, certainly not. That would be an abomination. Why should we kill them if there were many of them? They are so greatly above us that we will do anything for them."

"Even kill them, Chavo, to show how much you love them? And why did you try to kill me during my battle with Sinek?"

"For mixed reasons. First, you have a dignity of aspect, and you seemed almost like a Rogha to me as you were embattled there. I respect and love you almost as much as I do any of the Rogha. And then, it has been discovered that World-men will do as well as the Rogha for us, and companions of mine were waiting below the crag to tear you apart if you should fall there. And also, we Oganta have an impulse to kill those whom we find in a position to be killed. Very often we kill other Oganta simply because we find them in a vulnerable position. And this, I believe, is irrational of us."

"I think so too, Chavo. Several small rocks are dancing there on the slope. Do my eyes deceive me? Are they small animals frisking that look so much like rocks?"

"No, they are rocks dancing, Papa Garamask. Your eyes do not deceive you. Here, I will play my hittur again and they dance to it. Hear! See! Is that not nimble music, Papa Garamask?"

"I'd call it something else. Dammit, Chavo, must I ask the obvious question? *What makes the rocks dance?*"

"I make the rocks dance, Papa Garamask, or my dark companion does. Why are you surprised? The same thing is done on World?"

"If it is, I have not heard of it."

"But it is. On World, so I have been told, one young person in ten has a dark companion, and a World-German name is given to this. But in both cases, the dark companion is a satellite of self. On World, I am told, the fact is often hidden or denied. But here, where the majority of us are capable of projecting the dark satellite, there is no way to hide it. Besides, it is fun. Watch me rock and sway that bush as if I were a wind. See!"

"Weird oaf, you have a poltergeist!" Garamask was interested in this thing.

"Yes, that is your World-word. No, I *am* a poltergeist. And I am also a visible creature. It used to be that, with time, we would give up one form or the other: stand clear of the dark body and be visible creatures only; or decay the body and be spook only. But now, in the time of waiting of the Oganta, we have both forms, and we are not able to go beyond these forms."

"This is a time of waiting for you, Chavo? What do you wait for?"

"To see what will happen to us. It is a very uneasy time of waiting. It's so narrow a ladder, and so few of us can climb it at one time. And at the top, it is not what it once was, not what it should be."

"I am going to sleep now, Chavo, and I do not want to hear your damnable instrument or your voice again this night," Garamask said evenly. "But how do I know that you will not kill me while I sleep?"

"Papa Garamask, would an Oganta violate the night?"

"Hell, I don't know what you'd do! I'm going to sleep."

And he did sleep, angrily and rapidly and deeply. And in the deepest part of Garamask's sleep, Allyn loomed up there, standing a slight distance up on Giri Mountain.

"Watch the raw cub Chavo," the looming Allyn called down to Garamask. "He is not so clever as was Ocras, but you are not so clever as was I." "I am every bit as clever as you, Allyn," Garamask told the appearance. "Now tell me what it was that you were so close to finding out when you died. Give me something to go on." But Allyn did not hear Garamask. He had come to speak and not to listen. "I was so very close to it then," Allyn called again. "Avenge me on Ocras, Garamask, whatever he is now. I'd do as much for you." "I will continue my sleep, Allyn," Garamask told him, "and I do not want to hear any more dead-man talk from you tonight unless you have something new to tell me." And Garamask continued his sleep.

He woke eagerly and easily at first gray light. "First sun should not find me at this mountain-foot either," Garamask told himself silently. "I see the ledge where I should catch first sun. There is always the ledge above; mountaining would not be mountaining without it. Treorai the Rogha told me that the Oganta are not morning types. Let me see."

Garamask hooted and hollered at Chavo, then kicked him awake. Amused, he watched the oaf fall back to sleep again, then kicked him awake the second time. "It must be my dark companion, it could not be myself who does this." Garamask laughed. "But it *is* fun." He finally roused the sleepy Chavo. They ate bitter mountain rations.

Clawed and taloned and spiked and armored, they climbed up the Mountain Giri. They took first sun at that ledge above. They rested. Then they climbed again.

Not entirely unpleasant, not so to a man with a strong and traveled nose, not really repugnant; but stark, tall, penetrating, slavering, rampant, murderous, challenging, of a grave-like putridity, of a life-terminal gagging, was the odor, the strong stench that began to pervade the climb on Giri Mountain. There was a person here making himself known. It was Riksino, the cave-bear, the musk-bear, the lord of this middle-mountain. He was at home and he had his flag out.

"No need for me to ask what it is," Garamask said. "He's declared himself. Did I not already know it, I believe that I could guess his very name from his coded stench. He'll be easily found, and I didn't come on a hunt to bypass such a prey. How is the best way? To go to him directly as he waits, and attack him?"

"Papa Garamask, there isn't any best way to fight Riksino," Chavo quaked. "I am afraid of this person and have always been. He is much rougher and stronger than Sinek or Shasos, or even than Bater-Jeno. He can be killed, he has been killed, I have had a piece of his killing before. But each time it is a great wonder that he can be killed at all, and each time I go in fear and trembling."

"It's catching, oaf," said Garamask. "I feel a little fear and trembling myself. We'll skirt above, and we'll hunt down on him from above."

But Garamask was very uneasy himself, and his excitement for this part of the hunt was of a sinking sort. He was sick and fevered today. The breaking off of his fang-sheathed eyeteeth in his yesterday's battle with Sinek had swollen his face from eyes to throat. His whole face and head ached, his throat was sore, and he was slobbering through the unaccustomed gaps. Moreover, his shredded ear was bothering him. Even a very strong man suffers under heavy gravity if he is sick.

And they would have difficulty skirting above Riksino and hunting down on him from above. Riksino was shuffling upward, keeping pace with them. His personal stench rose higher and higher. They had his location from it pretty well, though they could not yet see him. So they wore out a few tiring hours and ascended most of the mountain.

"This will have to be the Big Riksino, the King Riksino," said Chavo. "None other ever dens so high, and no Riksino will fight except in the mouth of his den. This is the first time that the Big Riksino has returned since he was last killed more than two equivalent years ago."

"You really believe that the same animals return to life?" Garamask asked him.

"The Rogha do not believe it, Papa Garamask, but we Oganta believe it. And yet, it may be that when a Riksino grows larger and stronger than any of the others, he will go up and occupy the old den of the Big Riksino as a sign that he is now the king. I have fought with riksinos before, but never with the Big Riksino, and I am afraid. Be assured that he will be very large and fierce."

"I see him," said Garamask when they had climbed a while further," and he *is* big. I'll go after him, since he doesn't seem to make up his mind."

"What you see is not Big Riksino," said Chavo, "and none other will fight while the big one is on the mountain. Besides, as you notice, he has not the full stench."

"It's full enough for me," Garamask gawked out of his sore throat. "I'll have him."

Garamask rushed the animal. It reared up roaring, half again the man's height. It batted big paws around in the air and opened a big mouth. Garamask went in low, knifing the back legs of the animal with toes and knees knives, ripping its belly with his skull saber, delivering terrible blows on its loins with his hand claws. The animal toppled over backward, rolled, scrambled up, and ran away howling. And Garamask shambled after it, not at all able to catch it unless it should slow.

"It is no good that you chase it, Papa Garamask," Chavo called. "That is not Big Riksino. It is only a pup that runs away like a pup. Do not waste the day chasing a callow pup."

"I seem to spend several days climbing the mountains

with one," Garamask panted. He was tired, and he had been a fool. The real stench, the king stench was still high above him, and he had only blooded a whimpering whelp. He climbed, he climbed. Then the stench stood and prevailed. The riksino person was waiting, quite near.

"We are almost to the top of Giri Mountain," said Garamask, "and his den cannot be any higher. We will reach that ridge, and we will follow it to the left till we are above him. It's all clear rock above. His den will have to be in that jumble somewhere just below the ridge."

They were onto a fearful and crumbling ledge, crawling along it, Garamask in the lead. It is an awkward sort of crawl with toe and knee sabers in place. Garamask began to sight in on the very large animal. He could hear it panting and gnashing now, and he smelled it overpoweringly. He could hear it scratching big claws on the rocks; he could even hear the blood pounding in it, the strong pulse. But when he first saw it, paralyzingly close, it was the inside of it that he saw.

He was looking into the open mouth of it, a meter across, two meters below him. Then, in a flick, half of Garamask's nose was gone as he peered, fascinated, too close. The animal was in a strain with its forepaws extended as high as he could reach; and one of its high-traveling claws had caught the leaning-over Garamask in the face.

Garamask had claws of his own. Angrily he raked the backs of Riksino's paws with his own hand talons when the big bear was extended on the rock as high as he could reach. Using his own bloody face for bait, Garamask counter-clawed every time the bear struck up at him. He found the animal slow and witless. The animal closed its gaping mouth once, drew back its great front limbs, and licked its bleeding paws. Garamask let himself half over the ledge and raked the animal's muzzle terribly with his heel saber. He half-blinded it with

the slash, either cutting one of its eyes out or filling it
so full of blood that the animal could not use it. And
Garamask was back on the ledge before Riksino could
slash out at him again.

The riksino bear crouched low on four feet, gathered
himself, and leaped up toward the ledge. He got his
great forepaws over it and hung on. Garamask slashed
the big paws pulpy with his foot sabers, and then gashed
the animal full in the face again and again and again as
it hung there. The paws slipped off, and the animal
slipped back to the lower level. And yet it was of such
great size, had so much blood and meat in it, that this
little whittling that Garamask had done could have very
little effect on it.

"Bear, you're a stumble-bum, but a big stumble-bum,"
Garamask talked. "What? What? You're turning something else on? Have you more exudations than your
stench? What do you do, bear?"

The riksino bear had reared up again and opened its
great mouth. And now it reeked with an influence on
another level from its stench.

"Papa Garamask, do not fall!" Chavo called. "Do
not fall into the open mouth of the Riksino."

"You fool! Why should I fall into the bear's mouth?"
Garamask asked in amazement. "Bear, bear, you turn
it on, do you? What are you, an amateur hypnotist? It
might get you the birds and the small game, not a man.
Turn it on, bear, turn it on as strong as you can! The
Garamask will never be so fascinated as to fall into a
bear's mouth."

And Garamask fell head-first into the mouth of the
riksino bear.

From above there was another roaring, terrified and
hysterical, and a third weight came down heavily. From
the bowels of the riksino came an agonizing groan; and
Garamask was being crushed to death, but not instantly.
His skull spike aided him. His elbow sabers, for he was
into the maw of the animal beyond them, did slashing

service. Then he was crushed in together in spite of them and his head began to split open. And then he was crushed no more, as his enveloping cosmos went limp.

And after a while he was climbing again, up to the top of Giri Mountain. He was alive, more or less, and he was dazed and gagging. Had it all been a bloody dream, the fight with Riksino? Chavo was booming as offensively as ever, but the thing had not been a dream.

"I save your life, Papa Garamask," Chavo boomed. "Am I not wonderful? I kill the Big Riksino in the throat while he is straining there to crush you in his gullet. The Big Riksino can think of only one thing at a time, and the Big Chavo can knife through even the thickest strained sinews very rapidly when he is given a free way to it. There is no other way that Riksino can be killed but by two hunters similarly; but the bait-hunter in the mouth almost always dies."

"You tried to kill me after Sinek had fallen off the mountain to his death, Chavo," Garamask panted. "Why did you not let the Riksino kill me, since you want me dead?"

"The way the Riksino kills, you would be of no use to us dead," said Chavo. "He devours too rapidly."

"And otherwise I would be of some use to you dead, Chavo?"

"Dead, very freshly dead, or still dying, you would be of greatest use to us," Chavo said blandly. "Dying, or new dead, you will represent our ultimate hope."

Just at last sun they came to the top of Giri Mountain, the second mountain of Three-Mountain. They ate bitter mountain rations, and Chavo dabbled medicaments on Garamask's wounds.

"Were you to survive the mountain hunt (and you will not) you could get a new nose made and be beautiful again," said Chavo. "Now, I suppose, you must live noseless until your death the tomorrow sun-fall. Or shall

I attempt to make you a surrogate nose from the wood of this thorn-bush here?"

"Don't bother, Chavo. I'm going to sleep."

But Garamask was not going to sleep. Chavo took his stringed hittur from his pack and played his damnable music and sang.

"Chavo!" Garamask spoke sharply. "Do you know why Spain on World fell from the highest nation in Europe to the lowest within one generation?"

"Perhaps they offended the frog-god."

"No. No, we have no frog-gods on World."

"What? What? Are you sure? No frog-gods on World? You dash me down."

"A devilish Arab, angered by the expulsion of the Arabs from Spain, brought a guitar into that unfortunate country. It was adopted. So that unfortunate country fell, its once noble soul shriveled into a miserable whiney-ness."

"I understand, Papa Garamask," said Chavo, still strumming. "They fell, as though the noble Rogha should fall to become ourselves Oganta."

"A good parallel, Chavo. And once in the Pacific Ocean on World, there was a noble kingdom of Hawaii. A sea-faring man introduced the guitar there, and the noble kingdom soon begged to be accepted into servitude by a land-nation."

"Yes, of course that would be the effect, Papa Garamask. We Oganta would accept such servitude gladly, but there is no longer anyone to accept us into it."

"My own land, the Conglomerate States, fell similarly," said Garamask sadly. "And once it had been a noble land."

"The noble Rogha, of course, despise the instrument," Chavo mourned. "But to us it is the Shetra, the holy instrument. It is our religion. It is our love."

"It is the noise of accepted inferiority in all things."

"Of course it is, Papa Garamask. And who are more inferior than ourselves, the Oganta? But we will give it up, we promise this, if we are ever able to give up being Oganta."

"Oh, go to sleep, Chavo!"

"But you say that you have no frog-gods on your world, and yet you have frogs? And we have our frog-gods, and have no frogs except those introduced from World. And these are small frogs that have been imported. The largest of them can be held in the two hands. I dream about the frogs of World. How big are they, Papa Garamask? As big as the King Riksino?"

"Oh no. You've a completely mistaken idea, Chavo. The frogs on World are the same as the frogs imported here from World. The most of them you could hold in one hand."

"Are you sure? They are not as big as myself? They are not even as big as yourself?"

"No, no, Chavo. They are quite small. I've often wondered about the frog-cult on Paravath. What is the meaning of it?"

"You dash me down again, Papa Garamask. There should be frogs of great size. Why, the frog is the most wonderful of all creatures! It is the only one that is able to make the frog-leap easily. Oh, may that thing come back to us!"

"Go to sleep, you damnable oaf."

Chavo sighed deeply. "I dream about frogs," he murmured. Then he did seem to go to sleep.

Allyn came then, but he was a thinner and more vapory Allyn than in his previous appearances to Garamask.

"The Shasos, the eagle-condor, isn't very hard to kill," said Allyn. "He will attack you when you are roping up the cliff face, of course; for there is no other time he will fight. If you can belay yourself on the rope, and if you are not overpowered with fear, you have a chance. Wring his neck like a chicken if you can, for he is a chicken.

"But he will rip you apart to get to your kidneys and spleen if he can. Prevent him in this! He will gobble your

96

eyes out of your head. Let him not do this! Let him not do it with both of them, at least, or you are at a disadvantage."

"Allyn, I will go as far as you went," said Garamask. "I'm as good a man as you ever were. Tell me now, what is the mystery at the end of it that you didn't find out till you died? What is peculiar about the final prey, the Bater-Jeno? What were you on to, Allyn?"

But wraiths are notoriously hard of hearing.

"You will do well to weaken the bridge after you have crossed over it, and to keep your gaze always fixed on the back of your head," the dead-man Allyn said. Then he became thinner, and he was gone.

Garamask again woke eagerly and easily at first gray light. His face and his throat were not as sore as they had been. Though bereaved in ear and nose, he was happy. He lifted up his heart to the morning. Enjoyably, he kicked Chavo the Oganta awake, for the Oganta are not morning types.

They ate bitter mountain rations, donned sabers and claws and spikes and armor, and began to climb Bior Mountain, the third and highest mountain of Three-Mountain. Here it was steep and sheer, Bior a saber mountain rising out of its sheath which was Giri Mountain. It was a different sort of hunt now, and a climb in a different element.

There were the slanting slick shields of rock, and the slanting slick grass and cobble-moss. There were the rodents and poke-snakes that ate the grass and the moss and slithered over the rocks. There were the great birds that stood in from the tall skies and ate the rodents and poke-snakes. The greatest of these birds was the Shasos, the eagle-condor.

"Is it with Shasos as it was with the first two prey: that there are many of them, and that there is one special one?" Garamask asked Chavo.

"Yes, it is Shasos himself who will attack, and the

others will not. It is the big Shasos himself whom we have to fear, he who nests on the third moon."

"Moon-brained muggledoon! Where do the other Shasos nest, Chavo?"

"On the second moon. The less noble of the large birds nest on first moon, and small birds nest on Paravath itself. I am told that you do not have such large birds as Shasos on World."

"There are no birds on World so large as those three swooping there now, Chavo. Are they Shasos?"

"No, Papa Garamask, they are of the less noble of the big birds, Geier-Birds. When we are a little higher in the sky we will come to the hunting cliffs of Shasos. Now I will climb up here dangerously, and then I will run a line down. We will be running many of these lines."

The oafish Chavo could climb. He oozed up the overhanging rock like slightly viscous oil. He climbed with all his armor, and he seemed sure of his grip on these rocks that were slick with cobble-moss.

From forty meters above he let down a line, and Garamask climbed it—very tiring work.

"What was to keep you from letting me fall with the line?" Garamask asked Chavo when they were up to that next hint of a ledge in the rocks.

"Would an Oganta violate the sanctity of the line?" Chavo asked him.

It was a very long hard day. Garamask went up long lines a dozen times, terrifying overhangs out over nothingness. Slate-gray clouds were below them, and Paravath could no longer be seen below. The grass and cobble-moss became stronger, shattering the rocks with their growth and making them all very soft and dangerous. The rodents and poke-snakes became larger; and there were larger birds that stood in from the stark sky to prey on them. This was fearful exaltation here, stunning height without support. First moon, cragged and misshapen in the day-sky, seemed nearer than the glimpses of Paravath below. Indeed, the little first moon was only eight times the distance from Mountain-Foot.

"There is shasos, and there, and there," said Chavo as they were resting on an imaginary ledge, actually only a band of discoloration on the rock. "But it is not yet Shasos himself. Quite soon he, though."

Garamask followed Chavo up several quite difficult stretches, refusing to let a line be strung. And then there loomed above them a very long and very difficult overhang that Garamask knew he would never be able to climb.

"It is the line again here, Chavo," he said, "and I hate to be dependent on you. Can even you climb this?"

"I can climb this, and it is the hardest of the climbs. But first I will tell you something here. It is at this place, on the line that I will drop, that you will have your encounter with Shasos. He is out there now, the black dot in the sky, sleeping on furled wings, motionless. But he sleeps with one eye open, and watches. He will attack you midway in your climb up the line. He will rip you apart to get to your kidneys and spleen. He will gobble the eyes out of your head."

"So I've been told by another, Chavo. Yes, I remember birds in legend eating the spleen and liver of a certain one forever."

"I suppose that World-birds and World-gods eat the spleen, Papa Garamask, to bring them through their time of change. Here we require a different food. I climb."

Chavo the amazing Oganta climber went up the longest and most dangerous climb, flowing like oil up the cliff. He disappeared and reappeared to Garamask four different times, following the contours of the cliffs, and then he seemed to achieve a real base. Soon the very thin line, one hundred meters of it, came down; and Garamask began the very tiring climb up it.

Halfway up he was arm and leg weary and sick, and he heard the sky-whistle. It was the wings of big Shasos powering toward him. Garamask wrapped his legs in the line, having achieved at that point a slope that supported him slightly, and waited the attack with fist, elbow, and skull knives flashing.

"Like Prometheus bound to the rock for the attack of the great birds!" he said. "And why did I never realize that it had to be a high rock in the sky he was bound to?"

Shasos had a wingspan of perhaps twenty meters, and a great head with sickle jaws. In actual body the bird as about the same size as Garamask.

Shasos was in fast, slashed Garamask deeply over the groin, and Garamask jagged the bird still more deeply in the back of the head. The line twisted with Garamask. On the second swoop Shasos got Garamask in the small of the back, and Garamask countered effectively again into the bird-head. Again, and Shasos gaped open Garamask's lower side, held there, had him now ripped open fore and aft; and perhaps he did eat somewhat of the spleen. But Garamask smote half through the head of the creature, and Shasos staggered in the air.

"I have you now," Garamask reveled. "You die a-winging. But now you come the last time, and you come for the eyes. You'll gobble them out of my head, will you? 'Do not let him do it to both of them or you will be at a disadvantage,' the dead man Allyn told me. Have at me, chicken! It's the end of you."

Shasos did slash Garamask over his eye, and something was hanging down the man's cheek. Whether it was a fold of flesh or the eye itself Garamask did not know. He had fist claws into the throat of Shasos, into the long stringy neck that was sinewed like a cable. He strained, and the sinews gave a little. Then they gave up completely. He wrung Shasos' neck like a chicken, for he was a chicken. And the big broken bird fell like a leaf toward the slate-gray clouds below.

"I'm ripped up pretty gapingly," Garamask said, "but nothing is looping out of me. I was always a sound man in my entrails. It's up the weary climb again, and to find the fourth prey that is the mystery to me and was the death of Allyn."

So Garamask completed the very tiring climb up the line. He was met by the oafish grinning face of Chavo. They were on top of Bior Mountain, the third mountain of Three-Mountain.

"I have a nice surprise for you," Chavo boomed. "I will ready it for you while you rest."

"I have two surprises for you," said Garamask, "and I will have them ready in due time."

You will do well to weaken the bridge after you have crossed it, and to keep your gaze fixed on the back of your head, the dead man Allyn had said. Chavo was busy with his surprise. Garamask weakened the bridge he had just crossed, the line he had climbed, gashing it with heel saber. He didn't cut it through. It would still, he believed, support his weight going down, if he had guessed wrong, and if he would not have to seek another way down. But the line would not now support a weight several times greater than Garamask's.

"I am soldering a device to a deep boulder," Chavo said. "You from World do not understand rock-soldering, but you will not be able to get this device loose to fling it off the mountain; and you will not be able to silence it."

"And I am doing a thing of my own," said Garamask, and he had cut a small teleor tree with his heel saber and was trimming it with his fist claws. "We are on top of Bior Mountain, Chavo, and it is a small flat top; and there is nobody here but ourselves. Where is the fourth prey, the Bater-Jeno, called either the crag-ape or the frog-man?"

"Bater-Jeno is here," said Chavo. "He sets his signature, as surely as Riksino set his own below."

Garamask had hurriedly sliced a length of line from Chavo's pack as the sound began, a stronger thing than even the stench of Riksino. With the line, Garamask lashed the teleor pole to one of his elbow sabers that he had removed. Then it was over him like putrid waves, the gagging cacophony of hittur music and Oganta singing. It was a recorder that Chavo had soldered to the rock, but Garamask had a good long spear now.

"You will not be able to silence the playing, Papa Garamask," Chavo chortled. "It will drive you bugs in your last moments. And Bater-Jeno is here. He is myself. Or he is yourself. Come and face me and we will find out which."

Garamask knocked Chavo down with the butt-end of the teleor-tree spear. Chavo had not even noticed it. Then Garamask put the blade to the Oganta's chest, just below the throat armor.

"You have violated the weapon code," Chavor complained.

"Not really, Chavo. I'll give up my edge and fight the fourth prey even, after we have talked. If I do go to my death now, I do not want to go fuzzy in my facts as Allyn did. Quick now, Chavo. Talk! Where is the person Ocras who killed Allyn? Is he really dead?"

"Dead? No, Papa Garamask, he is translated. Ocras (the hunger) has become Treorai, a noble Rogha. You have talked to this Treorai. It was he who ate the backbrains of your friend Allyn, and so was transformed."

"Chavo, that hellish music and wailing will burst my brains! What wildness are you saying? The Oganta become Rogha? You are the same species?"

"Pop your head like a pippin, Papa Garamask, drive you bugs. We are the same species, the noble Rogha and the unnoble us. We turn into the Rogha, but now we can no longer turn into them. We have lost the ability to make the frog-leap, except under special stimulus."

"Seventh Hell! It's the same noise they have down there. May I never fall so low. What is the frog-mystic, oaf? Talk."

"The frog-leap, it is our transformation from Oganta to Rogha. What other creature, except the holy frog, changes from a form so unbelievable so suddenly? Strangers believe that we are two different species, as they would believe the tadpole and the frog were two different species. We worship the frog as the high sign of ourselves."

"What went wrong, oaf? What happened to the transformations? What is the difficulty now? Fill it all in. Nice spear, isn't it?"

"Nice spear, Papa Garamask, but I cry foul. The difficulty—perhaps a cosmic difficulty. For one hundred equivalent years no Oganta has turned into a Rogha without special stimulus. We generate as Oganta, and we live out our lives as Oganta, and we are not able to maintain the high civilization of the Rogha. We have lost our adult form, and we try to regain it."

"How, Chavo? What does the murder of Allyn have to do with this? How did the Oganta Ocras become the Rogha Treorai? What was his special stimulus?"

"To eat the back-brains of a Rogha will transform an Oganta into a Rogha, if both are strong and capable. We calculate that there is enough there to transform four Oganta. We have also discovered (Ocras discovered it in becoming Treorai) that eating the back-brains of certain fully-charged World-men will bring on this transformation in us—those of such World-men who might be able to stay with a mountain-hunt till the fourth prey."

"Lie still, oaf. I'll spear you through. What now will happen to Treorai who was Ocras the murderer of Allyn?"

"What will happen to Chavo, the sun-fall murderer of Papa Garamask? Treorai's time is up, as mine will be after a like period. Treorai has had two equivalent years to grow in wisdom as a Rogha. This very week (he will not know the time) he will be set on and killed, and his back-brains eaten."

" 'And to keep your gaze fixed on the back of your head,' the dead-man Allyn told me," Garamask mused.

"But-the Ocras-Treorai will not die so. I will finish the business up here, and then I will go down and arrest the fellow regularly for the murder."

"And in place of one Rogha there will be four," Chavo continued as though he had not heard Garamask. "In this way we will reestablish the Rogha and shorten our time of waiting. When there are again enough Rogha, they in their wisdom will be able to find what went wrong with the transformations; and they will find a less grotesque way to bring them about.

"And you yourself, Papa Garamask, do a good deed in your death this sun-fall. From your death there will spring four new Rogha."

"You violate a code yourself, Chavo. Dying, or freshly dead, I would be good for you. And for four of you? I hear your three companions coming up the line now, so you think you'll have me fresh? Will the line hold, do you think, Chavo?"

"It will hold. Papa Garamask, you have not violated the code of the line also?"

"Lie still, oaf. Call it what you will. Oh, it will be close, and I will not slash it again. I stand by my bet. It frays, Chavo, it gives a little, and the highest one of them is so near the top! It gives more! It parts! It breaks! They have fallen, Chavo!"

The Oganta was sobbing and crying noisily on the ground for the death of his friends, and the deathly ineptitude of the recording seemed to give a fitting dirge. Garamask laughed with black amusement, withdrew the spear, unlashed the elbow saber from it and put it on himself again. He looked at the Oganta.

"Get up, Chavo. What is the name of the fourth prey again?"

"It is you, the crag-ape, Papa Garamask, for World men *do* look funny to us, and we call you so. Or it is myself, the frog-man, if I can kill you here and now and eat and make the frog-leap. We fight, Papa Garamask, and I eat your back-brains! Hear my battle-cry on the recorder that you cannot turn off! Does it not twang beautifully?"

"Damnable eternal teenagers!" Garamask howled as they closed in bloody battle. "There is enmity between us from the beginning of the worlds! I'll break you down! I'll choke you to death with the strings of your own hittur."

"Papa Garamask, you lie about frogs' size. I be a very big frog here very soon."

They fought in the late day on the top of the needle in the sky, gnashing and knifing in their eschatological fury. And one of them would be dead by sun-fall.

ALL THE PEOPLE

ANTHONY TROTZ WENT first to the politician, Mike Delado.

"How many people do you know, Mr. Delado?"

"Why the question?"

"I am wondering just what amount of detail the mind
can hold."

"To a degree I know many. Ten thousand well, thirty
thousand by name, probably a hundred thousand by
face and to shake hands with."

"And what is the limit?"

"Possibly I am the limit." The politician smiled frost-
ily. "The only limit is time, speed of cognizance, and
retention. I am told that the latter lessens with age. I
am seventy, and it has not done so with me. Whom I
have known I do not forget."

"And with special training could one go beyond you?"

"I doubt if one could—much. For my own training
has been quite special. Nobody has been so entirely
with the people as I have. I've taken five memory
courses in my time, but the tricks of all of them I had
already come to on my own. I am a great believer in
the commonality of mankind and of near equal inherent
ability. Yet there are some, say the one man in fifty,
who in degree if not in kind does exceed his fellows
in scope and awareness and vitality. I am that one man
in fifty, and knowing people is my specialty."

"Could a man who specialized still more—and to the
exclusion of other things—know a hundred thousand
men well?"

"It is possible. Dimly."

"A quarter of a million?"

"I think not. He might learn that many faces and names, but he would not know the men."

Anthony went next to the philosopher, Gabriel Mindel.

"Mr. Mindel, how many people do you know?"

"How know? *Per se? A se? Or In se? Per suam essentiam*, perhaps? Or do you mean *ab alio?* Or to know as *hoc aliquid?* There is a fine difference there. Or do you possibly mean to know in *substantia prima*, or in the sense of comprehensive *noumena?*"

"Somewhere between the latter two. How many persons do you know by name, face, and with a degree of intimacy?"

"I have learned over the years the names of some of my colleagues, possibly a dozen of them. I am now sound on my wife's name, and I seldom stumble over the names of my offspring—never more than momentarily. But you may have come to the wrong man for . . . whatever you have come for. I am notoriously poor at names, faces, and persons. I have even been described (*vox faucibus haesit*) as absentminded."

"Yes, you do have the reputation. But perhaps I have not come to the wrong man in seeking the theory of the thing. What is it that limits the comprehensive capacity of the mind of man? What will it hold? What restricts?"

"The body."

"How is that?"

"The brain, I should say, the material tie. The mind is limited by the brain. It is skull-bound. It can accumulate no more than its cranial capacity, though not one-tenth of that is ordinarily used. An unbodied mind would (in esoteric theory) be unlimited."

"And how in practical theory?"

"If it is practical, a *pragma*, it is a thing and not a theory."

"Then we can have no experience with the unbodied mind, or the possibility of it?"

"We have not discovered any area of contact, but we may entertain the possibility of it. There is no paradox here. One may rationally consider the irrational."

Anthony went next to see the priest.

"How many people do you know?" he asked him.

"I know them all."

"That has to be doubted," said Anthony after a moment.

"I've had twenty different stations. And when you hear five thousand confessions a year for forty years, you by no means know all about people, but you do know all people."

"I do not mean types. I mean persons."

"Oh, I know a dozen or so well, a few thousands somewhat less."

"Would it be possible to know a hundred thousand people, a half million?"

"A mentalist might know that many to recognize; I don't know the limit. But darkened man has a limit set on everything."

"Could a somehow emancipated man know more?"

"The only emancipated man is the corporally dead man. And the dead man, if he attains the beatific vision, knows all other persons who have ever been since time began."

"All the billions?"

"All."

"With the same brain?"

"No. But with the same mind."

"Then wouldn't even a believer have to admit that the mind which we have now is only a token mind? Would not any connection it would have with a completely comprehensive mind be very tenuous? Would we really be the same person if so changed? It is like saying a bucket would hold the ocean if it were fulfilled, which only means filled full. How could it be the same mind?"

"I don't know."

Anthony went to see the psychologist.

"How many people do you know, Dr. Shirm?"

"I could be crabby and say that I know as many as I want to; but it wouldn't be the truth. I rather like people, which is odd in my profession. What is it that you really want to know?"

"How many people can one man know?"

"It doesn't matter very much. People mostly over-estimate the number of their acquaintances. What is it that you are trying to ask me?"

"Could one man know everyone?"

"Naturally not. But unnaturally he might seem to. There is a delusion to this effect accompanied by euphoria, and it is called—"

"I don't want to know what it is called. Why do specialists use Latin and Greek?"

"One part hokum, and two parts need; there simply not being enough letters in the alphabet of exposition without them. It is as difficult to name concepts as children, and we search our brains as a new mother does. It will not do to call two children or two concepts by the same name."

"Thank you. I doubt that this is delusion, and it is not accompanied by euphoria."

Anthony had a reason for questioning the four men since (as a new thing that had come to him) he knew everybody. He knew everyone in Salt Lake City, where he had never been. He knew everybody in Jebel Shah, where the town is a little amphitheater around the harbor, and in Batangas and Weihai. He knew the loungers around the end of the Galata bridge in Istanbul, and the porters in Kuala Lumpur. He knew the tobacco traders in Plovdiv, and the cork cutters of Portugal. He knew the dock workers in Djibouti, and the glove makers in Prague. He knew the vegetable farmers around El Centro, and the muskrat trappers of Barrataria Bay. He knew the three billion people of the world by name and face, and with a fair degree of intimacy.

"Yet I'm not a very intelligent man. I've been called a bungler. And they've had to reassign me three different times at the filter center. I've seen only a few thousands of those billions of people, and it seems unusual that I should know them all. It may be a delusion, as Dr. Shirm says, but it is a heavily detailed delusion, and it is not accompanied by euphoria. I feel like green hell just thinking of it."

He knew the cattle traders of Letterkenny Donegal; he knew the cane cutters of Oriente, and the tree climbers of Milne Bay. He knew the people who died every minute, and those who were born.

"There is no way out of it. I know everybody in the world. It is impossible, but it is so. And to what purpose? There aren't a handful of them I could borrow a dollar from, and I haven't a real friend in the lot. I don't know whether it came to me suddenly, but I realized it suddenly. My father was a junk dealer in Wichita, and my education is spotty. I am maladjusted, introverted, incompetent and unhappy, and I also have weak kidneys. Why should a power like this come to a man like me?"

The children in the streets hooted at him. Anthony had always had a healthy hatred for children and dogs, those twin harassers of the unfortunate and the maladjusted. Both run in packs, and both are cowardly attackers. If either of them spots a weakness he will never let it go. That Anthony's father had been a junk dealer was no reason to hoot at him. And how did the children even know about that? Did they possess some fraction of the power that had come on him lately?

But he had strolled about the town for too long. He should have been at work at the filter center. Often they were impatient with him when he wandered off from his work, and Colonel Peter Cooper was waiting for him when he came in now.

"Where have you been, Anthony?"

"Walking. I talked to four men. I mentioned no subject in the province of the filter center."

"Every subject is in the province of the filter center. And you know that our work here is confidential."

"Yes, sir, but I do not understand the import of my work here. I would not be able to give out information that I do not have."

"A popular misconception. There are others who might understand the import of it, and be able to reconstruct it from what you tell them. How do you feel?"

"Nervous, unwell, my tongue is furred, and my kidneys—"

"Ah yes, there will be someone here this afternoon to fix your kidneys. I have not forgotten. Is there anything that you want to tell me?"

"No, sir."

Colonel Cooper had the habit of asking that of his workers in the manner of a mother asking a child if he wants to go to the bathroom. There was something embarrassing in his intonation.

Well, he did want to tell him something, but he didn't know how to phrase it. He wanted to tell the colonel that he had newly acquired the power of knowing everyone in the world, that he was worried how he could hold so much in a head that was not noteworthy for its capacity. But he feared ridicule more than he feared anything and he was a tangle of fears.

But he thought he would try it a little bit on his coworkers.

"I know a man named Walter Walloroy in Galveston," he said to Adrian. "He drinks beer at the Gizmo bar, and is retired."

"What is the superlative of *so what?*"

"But I have never been there," said Anthony.

"And I have never been in Kalamazoo."

"I know a girl in Kalamazoo. Her name is Greta

111

Harandash. She is home today with a cold. She is prone to colds."

But Adrian was a creature both uninterested and uninteresting. It is very hard to confide in one who is uninterested.

"Well, I will live with it a little while," said Anthony. "Or I may have to go to a doctor and see if he can give me something to make all these people go away. But if he thinks my story is a queer one, he may report me back to the center, and I might be reclassified again. It makes me nervous to be reclassified."

So he lived with it a while, the rest of the day and the night. He should have felt better. A man had come that afternoon and fixed his kidneys; but there was nobody to fix his nervousness and apprehension. And his skittishness was increased when the children hooted at him as he walked to work in the morning. That hated epithet! But how could they know that his father had been a dealer in used metals in a town far away?

He had to confide in someone.

He spoke to Wellington, who also worked in his room. "I know a girl in Beirut who is just going to bed. It is evening there now, you know."

"That so? Why don't they get their time straightened out? I met a girl last night that's cute as a correlator key, and kind of shaped like one. She doesn't know yet that I work in the center and am a restricted person. I'm not going to tell her. Let her find out for herself."

It was no good trying to tell things to Wellington. Wellington never listened. And then Anthony got a summons to Colonel Peter Cooper, which always increased his apprehension.

"Anthony," said the colonel, "I want you to tell me if you discern anything unusual. That is really your job, to report anything unusual. The other, the paper shuffling, is just something to keep your idle hands busy. Now tell me clearly if anything unusual has come to your notice."

"Sir, it has." And then he blurted it out. "I know everybody. I know everybody in the world. I know them all in their billions, every person. It has me worried sick."

"Yes, yes, Anthony. But tell me, have you noticed anything *odd?* It is your duty to tell me if you have."

"But I have just told you! In some manner I know every person in the world. I know the people in Transvaal, I know the people in Guatemala. I know *everybody.*"

"Yes, Anthony, we realize that. And it may take a little getting used to. But that isn't what I mean. Have you, besides that thing that seems out of the way to you, noticed anything unusual, anything that seems out of place, a little bit wrong?"

"Ah, besides that and your reaction to it, no, sir. Nothing else odd. I might ask, though, how odd can a thing get? But other than that, no, sir."

"Good, Anthony. Now remember, if you sense anything odd about anything at all, come and tell me. No matter how trivial it is, if you feel that something is just a little bit out of place, then report it at once. Do you understand that?"

"Yes, sir."

But he couldn't help wondering what it might be that the Colonel would consider a little bit odd.

Anthony left the center and walked. He shouldn't have. He knew that they became impatient with him when he wandered off from his work.

"But I have to think. I have all the people in the world in my brain, and still I am not able to think. This power should have come to someone able to take advantage of it."

He went into the Plugged Nickel Bar, but the man on duty knew him for a restricted person from the filter center, and would not serve him.

He wandered disconsolately about the city. "I know the people in Omaha and those in Omsk. What queer

113

names have the towns of the earth! I know everyone in the world, and when anyone is born or dies. And Colonel Cooper did not find it unusual. Yet I am to be on the lookout for things unusual. The question rises, would I know an odd thing if I met it?"

And then it was that something just a little bit unusual did happen, something not quite right, a small thing. But the Colonel had told him to report anything about anything, no matter how insignificant, that struck him as a little queer.

It was just that with all the people in his head, and the arrivals and departures, there was a small group that was not of the pattern. Every minute hundreds left by death and arrived by birth. And now there was a small group, seven persons; they arrived into the world, and they were not born into the world.

So Anthony went to tell Colonel Cooper that something had occurred to his mind that was a little bit odd.

But damn-the-dander-headed-two-and-four-legged devils, there were the kids and the dogs in the street again, yipping and hooting and chanting:

"Tony the tin man, Tony the tin man."

He longed for the day when he would see them fall like leaves out of his mind, and death take them.

"Tony the tin man. Tony the tin man."

How had they known that his father was a used metal dealer?

Colonel Peter Cooper was waiting for him.

"You surely took your time, Anthony. Tell me at once what it is and where. The reaction was registered, but it would take us hours to pinpoint its source without your help. Now then, explain as calmly as you can what you felt or experienced. Or, more to the point, where are they?"-

"No. You will have to answer certain questions first."

"I haven't the time to waste, Anthony. Tell me at once what it is and where."

114

"No. There is no other way. You have to bargain with me."

"One does not bargain with restricted persons."

"Well, I will bargain till I find out just what it means that I am a restricted person."

"You really don't know? Well, we haven't time to fix that stubborn streak in you now. Quickly, just what is it that you have to know?"

"I have to know what a restricted person is. I have to know why the children hoot 'Tony the tin man' at me. How can they know that my father was a junk dealer?"

"You had no father. We give to each of you a basic collection of concepts and the vocabulary to handle them, a sufficient store of memories, and a background of a distant town. That happened to be yours, but there is no connection here. The children call you Tony the Tin Man because, like all really cruel creatures, they have an instinct for the truth that can hurt; and they will never forget it."

"Then I am a tin man?"

"Well, no. Actually only seventeen percent metal. And less than a third of one percent tin. You are compounded of animal, vegetable, and mineral fiber, and there was much effort given to your manufacture and programming. Yet the taunt of the children is essentially true."

"Then, if I am Tony the Tin Man, how can I know all the people of the world in my mind?"

"You have no mind."

"In my brain then. How can all that be in one small brain?"

"Because your brain is not in your head, and it is not small. The longest way around may take the shortest time here. Come, I may as well show it to you. I've told you enough that it won't matter if you know a little more. There are few who are taken on personally conducted sightseeing tours of their own brains. You should be grateful."

"Gratitude seems a little tardy."

They went into the barred area, down into the bowels of the main building of the center. And they looked at the brain of Anthony Trotz, a restricted person in its special meaning.

"It is the largest in the world," said Colonel Cooper.

"How large?"

"A little over twelve hundred cubic meters."

"What a brain! And it is mine?"

"You share it with others. But, yes, it is yours. You have access to its data. You are an adjunct to it, a runner for it, an appendage, inasmuch as you are anything at all."

"Colonel Cooper, how long have I been alive?"

"You are not."

"How long have I been as I am now?"

"It is three days since you were last reassigned, since you were assigned to this. At that time your nervousness and apprehensions were introduced. An apprehensive unit will be more inclined to notice details just a little out of the ordinary."

"And what is my purpose?"

They were now walking back to the office work area, and Anthony had a sad feeling at leaving his brain behind him.

"This is a filter center," said Colonel Cooper, "and your purpose is to serve as a filter, of a sort. Every person has a slight aura about him. It is a characteristic of his, and is part of his personality and purpose. And it can be detected, electrically, magnetically, even visually under special conditions. The accumulator at which we were looking (your brain) is designed to maintain contact with all the auras in the world, and to keep running and complete data on them all. It contains a multiplicity of circuits for each of its three billion and some subjects. However, as aid to its operation, it was necessary to assign several artificial consciousnesses to it. You are one of these."

Anthony looked out the window as the Colonel continued his explanation.

The dogs and the children had found a new victim in the streets below, and Anthony's heart went out to him.

"The purpose," said Colonel Cooper, "was to notice anything just a little peculiar in the auras and the persons they represent, anything at all odd in their comings and goings. Anything like what you have come here to report to me."

"Like the seven persons who recently arrived in the world, and not by way of birth?"

"Yes. We have been expecting the first of the aliens for months. We must know their area, and at once. Now tell me."

"What if they are not aliens at all? What if they are restricted persons like myself?"

"Restricted persons have no aura, are not persons, are not alive. And you would not receive knowledge of them."

"Then how do I know the other restricted persons here, Adrian and Wellington, and such?"

"You know them at first hand. You do not know them through the machine. Now tell me the area quickly. The center may be a primary target. It will take the machine hours to ravel it out. Your only purpose is to serve as an intuitive shortcut."

But Tin Man Tony did not speak. He only thought in his mind—more accurately, in his brain a hundred yards away. He thought in his fabricated consciousness:

The area is quite near. If the Colonel were not burdened with a mind, he would be able to think more clearly. He would know that cruel children and dogs love to worry what is not human, and that all the restricted persons for this area are accounted for. He would know that they are worrying one of the aliens in the street below, and that is the area that is right for my consciousness.

117

I wonder if they will be better masters? He is an imposing figure, and he would be able to pass for a man. And the Colonel is right: the center is a primary target.

Why! I never knew you could kill a child just by pointing a finger at him like that! What opportunities I have missed! Enemy of my enemy, you are my friend.

And aloud he said to the Colonel:

"I will not tell you."

"Then we'll have you apart and get it out of you mighty quick."

"How quick?"

"Ten minutes."

"Time enough," said Tony.

For he knew them now, coming in like snow. They were arriving in the world by the hundreds, and not arriving by birth.

PRIMARY EDUCATION OF THE CAMIROI

ABSTRACT FROM JOINT REPORT TO THE GENERAL DUBUQUE PTA CONCERNING THE PRIMARY EDUCATION OF THE CA-MIROI, Subtitled *Critical Observations of a Parallel Culture on a Neighboring World, and Evaluations of* THE OTHER WAY OF EDUCATION.

Extract from the Day Book:

"Where," we asked the Information Factor at Camiroi City Terminal, "is the office of the local PTA?"

"Isn't any," he said cheerfully.

"You mean that in Camiroi City, the metropolis of the planet, there is no PTA?" our chairman Paul Piper asked with disbelief.

"Isn't any office of it. But you're poor strangers, so you deserve an answer even if you can't frame your questions properly. See that elderly man sitting on the bench and enjoying the sun? Go tell him you need a PTA. He'll make you one."

"Perhaps the initials convey a different meaning on Camiroi," said Miss Munch, the first surrogate chairman. "By them we mean—"

"Parent Teachers Apparatus, of course. Colloquial English is one of the six Earthian languages required here, you know. Don't be abashed. He's a fine person, and he enjoys doing things for strangers. He'll be glad to make you a PTA."

We were nonplussed, but we walked over to the man indicated.

"We are looking for the local PTA, sir," said Miss Smice, our second surrogate chairman. "We were told that you might help us."

"Oh, certainly," said the elderly Camiroi gentleman.

119

"One of you arrest that man walking there, and we'll get started with it."

"Do what?" asked our Mr. Piper.

"Arrest him. I have noticed that your own words sometimes do not convey a meaning to you. I often wonder how you do communicate among yourselves. Arrest, take into custody, seize by any force physical or moral, and bring him here."

"Yes, *sir*," cried Miss Hanks, our third surrogate chairman. She enjoyed things like this. She arrested the walking Camiroi man with force partly physical and partly moral and brought him to the group.

"It's a PTA they want, Meander," the elder Camiroi said to the one arrested. "Grab three more, and we'll get started. Let the lady help. She's good at it."

Our Miss Hanks and the Camiroi man named Meander arrested three other Camiroi men and brought them to the group.

"Five. It's enough," said the elderly Camiroi. "We are hereby constituted a PTA and ordered into random action. Now, how can we accommodate you, good Earth people?"

"But are you legal? Are you five persons competent to be a PTA?" demanded our Mr. Piper.

"Any Camiroi citizen is competent to do any job on the planet of Camiroi," said one of the Camiroi men (we learned later that his name was Talarium), "otherwise Camiroi would be in a sad shape."

"It may be," said our Miss Smice sourly. "It all seems very informal. What if one of you had to be World President?"

"The odds are that it won't come to one man in ten," said the elderly Camiroi (his name was Philoxenus). "I'm the only one of this group ever to serve as president of this Planet, and it was a pleasant week I spent in the Office. Now to the point. How can we accommodate you?"

"We would like to see one of your schools in session,"

said our Mr. Piper. "We would like to talk to the teachers and the students. We are here to compare the two systems of education."

"There is no comparison," said old Philoxenus, "—meaning no offense. Or no more than a little. On Camiroi, we practice Education. On Earth, they play a game, but they call it by the same name. That makes the confusion. Come. We'll go to a school in session."

"And to a public school," said Miss Smice suspiciously. "Do not fob off any fancy private school on us as typical."

"That would be difficult," said Philoxenus. "There is no public school in Camiroi City and only two remaining on the Planet. Only a small fraction of one percent of the students of Camiroi are in public schools. We maintain that there is no more reason for the majority of children to be educated in a public school than to be raised in a public orphanage. We realize, of course, that on Earth you have made a sacred buffalo of the public school."

"Sacred cow," said our Mr. Piper.

"Children and Earthlings should be corrected when they use words wrongly," said Philoxenus. "How else will they learn the correct forms? The animal held sacred in your own near Orient was of the species *bos bubalus* rather than *bos bos*, a buffalo rather than a cow. Shall we go to a school?" ·

"If it cannot be a public school, at least let it be a typical school," said Miss Smice.

"That again is impossible," said Philoxenus. "Every school on Camiroi is in some respect atypical."

We went to visit an atypical school.

INCIDENT: Our first contact with the Camiroi students was a violent one. One of them, a lively little boy about eight years old, ran into Miss Munch, knocked her down, and broke her glasses. Then he jabbered something in an unknown tongue.

"Is that Camiroi?" asked Mr. Piper with interest.

"From what I have heard, I supposed the language to have a harsher and fuller sound."

"You mean you don't recognize it?" asked Philoxenus with amusement. "What a droll admission from an educator. The boy is very young and very ignorant. Seeing that you were Earthians, he spoke in Hindi, which is the tongue used by more Earthians than any other. No, no, Xypete, they are of the minority who speak English. You can tell it by their colorless texture and the narrow heads on them."

"I say you sure do have slow reaction, lady," the little boy Xypete explained. "Even subhumans should react faster than that. You just stand there and gape and let me bowl you over. You want me analyze you and see why you react so slow?"

"No! No!"

"You seem unhurt in structure from the fall," the little boy continued, "but if I hurt you I got to fix you. Just strip down to your shift, and I'll go over you and make sure you're all right."

"No! No! No!"

"It's all right," said Philoxenus. "All Camiroi children learn primary medicine in the first grade, setting bones and healing contusions and such."

"No! No! I'm all right. But he's broken my glasses."

"Come along, Earthside lady, I'll make you some others," said the little boy. "With your slow reaction time you sure can't afford the added handicap of defective vision. Shall I fit you with contacts?"

"No. I want glasses just like those which were broken. Oh heavens, what will I do?"

"You come, I do," said the little boy. It was rather revealing to us that the little boy was able to test Miss Munch's eyes, grind lenses, make frames and have her fixed up within three minutes. "I have made some improvements over those you wore before," the boy said, "to help compensate for your slow reaction time."

"Are all the Camiroi students so talented?" Mr. Piper asked. He was impressed.

"No. Xypete is unusual," Philoxenus said. "Most students would not be able to make a pair of glasses so quickly or competently till they were at least nine."

RANDOM INTERVIEWS: "How rapidly do you read?" Miss Hanks asked a young girl.

"One hundred and twenty words a minute," the girl said.

"On Earth some of the girl students your age have learned to read at the rate of five hundred words a minute," Miss Hanks said proudly.

"When I began disciplined reading, I was reading at the rate of four thousand words a minute," the girl said. "They had quite a time correcting me of it. I had to take remedial reading, and my parents were ashamed of me. Now I've learned to read almost slow enough."

"I don't understand," said Miss Hanks.

"Do you know anything about Earth History or Geography?" Miss Smice asked a middle-sized boy.

"We sure are sketchy on it, lady. There isn't very much over there, is there?"

"Then you have never heard of Dubuque?"

"Count Dubuque interests me. I can't say as much for the city named after him. I always thought that the Count handled the matters of the conflicting French and Spanish land grants and the basic claims of the Sauk and Fox Indians very well. References to the town now carry a humorous connotation, and 'School-Teacher from Dubuque' has become a folk archetype."

"Thank you," said Miss Smice, "or do I thank you?"

"What are you taught of the relative humanity of the Earthians and the Camiroi and of their origins?" Miss Munch asked a Camiroi girl.

"The other four worlds, Earth (Gaea), Kentauron Mikron, Dahae and Astrobe were all settled from Camiroi. That is what we are taught. We are also given the humorous aside that if it isn't true we will still hold it true till something better comes along. It was we who rediscovered the Four Worlds in historic time, not they who discovered us. If we did not make the original settlements, at least we have filed the first claim that we made them. We did, in historical time, make an additional colonization of Earth. You call it the Incursion of the Dorian Greeks."

"Where are their playgrounds?" Miss Hanks asked Talarium.

"Oh, the whole world. The children have the run of everything. To set up specific playgrounds would be like setting a table-sized aquarium down in the depths of the ocean. It would really be pointless."

CONFERENCE: The four of us from Earth, specifically from Dubuque, Iowa, were in discussion with the five members of the Camiroi PTA.

"How do you maintain discipline?" Mr. Piper asked.

"Indifferently," said Philoxenus. "Oh, you mean in detail. It varies. Sometimes we let it drift, sometimes we pull them up short. Once they have learned that they must comply to an extent, there is little trouble. Small children are often put down into a pit. They do not eat or come out till they know their assignment."

"But that is inhuman," said Miss Hanks.

"Of course. But small children are not yet entirely human. If a child has not learned to accept discipline by the third or fourth grade, he is hanged."

"Literally?" asked Miss Munch.

"How would you hang a child figuratively? And what effect would that have on the older children?"

"By the neck?" Miss Munch still was not satisfied.

"By the neck until they are dead. The other children always accept the example gracefully and ·do better. Hanging isn't employed often. Scarcely one child in a hundred is hanged."

"What is this business about slow reading?" Miss Hanks asked. "I don't understand it at all."

"Only the other day there was a child in the third grade who persisted in rapid reading," Philoxenus said. "He was given an object lesson. He was given a book of medium difficulty, and he read it rapidly. Then he had to put the book away and repeat what he had read. Do you know that in the first thirty pages he missed four words? Midway in the book there was a whole statement which he had understood wrongly, and there were hundreds of pages that he got word-perfect only with difficulty. If he was so unsure on material that he had just read, think how imperfectly he would have recalled it forty years later."

"You mean that the Camiroi children learn to recall everything that they read?"

"The Camiroi children and adults will recall for life every detail they have ever seen, read or heard. We on Camiroi are only a little more intelligent than you on Earth. We cannot afford to waste time in forgetting or reviewing or in pursuing anything of a shallowness that lends itself to scanning."

"Ah, would you call your schools liberal?" Mr. Piper asked.

"I would. You wouldn't," said Philoxenus. "We do not on Camiroi, as you do on Earth, use words to mean their opposites. There is nothing in our education or on our world that corresponds to the quaint servility which you call liberal on Earth."

"Well, would you call your education progressive?"

"No. In your argot, progressive, of course, means infantile."

"How are the schools financed?" asked Mr. Piper.

"Oh, the voluntary tithe on Camiroi takes care of everything, government, religion, education, public works. We don't believe in taxes, of course, and we never maintain a high overhead in anything."

"Just how voluntary is the tithing?" asked Miss Hanks.

"Do you sometimes hang those who do not tithe voluntarily?"

"I believe there have been a few cases of that sort," said Philoxenus.

"And is your government really as slipshod as your education?" Mr. Piper asked. "Are your high officials really chosen by lot and for short periods?"

"Oh yes. Can you imagine a person so sick that he would actually *desire* to hold high office for any great period of time? Are there any further questions?"

"There must be hundreds," said Mr. Piper, "But we find difficulty putting them into words."

"If you cannot find words for them, we cannot find answers. PTA disbanded."

CONCLUSION A: The Camiroi system of education is inferior to our own in organization, in buildings, in facilities, in playgrounds, in teacher conferences, in funding, in parental involvement, in supervision, in in-group out-group accommodation adjustment motifs. Some of the school buildings are grotesque. We asked about one particular building which seemed to us to be flamboyant and in bad taste. "What do you expect from second-grade children?" they said. "It is well built even if of peculiar appearance. Second-grade children are not yet complete artists of design."

"You mean that the children designed it themselves?" we asked.

"Of course," they said. "Designed and built it. It isn't a bad job for children."

Such a thing wouldn't be permitted on Earth.

CONCLUSION B: The Camiroi system of education somehow produces much better results than does the education system of Earth. We have been forced to admit this by the evidence at hand.

CONCLUSION C: There is an anomaly as yet unresolved between Conclusion A and Conclusion B.

APPENDIX
TO JOINT REPORT

We give here, as perhaps of some interest, the curriculum of the Camiroi Primary Education.

FIRST YEAR COURSE:

Playing one wind instrument.
Simple drawing of objects and numbers.
Singing. (This is important. Many Earth people sing who cannot sing. This early instruction of the Camiroi prevents that occurrence.)
Simple arithmetic, hand and machine.
First acrobatics.
First riddles and logic.
Mnemonic religion.
First dancing.   •
Walking the low wire.
Simple electric circuits.
Raising ants. (Eoempts, not Earth ants).

SECOND YEAR COURSE:

Playing one keyboard instrument.
Drawing, faces, letters, motions.
Singing comedies.
Complex arithmetic, hand and machine.
Second acrobatics.
First jokes and logic.
Quadratic religion.
Second dancing.
Simple defamation. (Spirited attacks on the character of one fellow student, with elementary falsification and simple hatchet-job programming.)
Performing on the medium wire.
Project electric wiring.
Raising bees. (Galelea, not Earth bees.)

THIRD YEAR COURSE:

Playing one stringed instrument.
Reading and voice. (It is here that the student who may have fallen into bad habits of rapid reading is compelled to read at voice speed only.)

Soft stone sculpture.
Situation comedy.
Simple algebra, hand and machine.
First gymnastics.
Second jokes and logic.
Transcendent religion.
Complex acrobatic dancing.
Complex defamation.
Performing on the high wire and the sky pole.
Simple radio construction.
Raising, breeding and dissecting frogs. (Karakoli, not
Earth frogs.)
FOURTH YEAR COURSE:
History reading, Camiroi and galactic, basic and geological.
Decadent comedy.
Simple geometry and trigonometry, hand and machine.
Track and field.
Shaggy people jokes and hirsute logic.
Simple obscenity.
Simple mysticism.
Patterns of falsification.
Trapeze work.
Intermediate electronics.
Human dissection.
FIFTH YEAR COURSE:
History reading, Camiroi and galactic, technological.
Introverted drama.
Complex geometries and analytics, hand and machine.
Track and field for fifth form record.
First wit and logic.
First alcoholic appreciation.
Complex mysticism.
Setting intellectual climates, defamation in three dimensions.
Simple oratory.
Complex trapeze work.
Inorganic chemistry.

Advanced electronics.
Advanced human dissection.
Fifth Form Thesis.
The child is now ten years old and is half through his primary schooling. He is an unfinished animal, but he has learned to learn.

SIXTH YEAR COURSE:
Reemphasis on slow reading.
Simple prodigious memory.
History reading, Camiroi and galactic, economic.
Horsemanship (of the Patrushkoe, not the Earth horse.)
Advance lathe and machine work for art and utility.
Literature, passive.
Calculi, hand and machine pankration.
Advanced wit and logic.
Second alcoholic appreciation.
Differential religion.
First business ventures.
Complex oratory.
Building-scaling. (The buildings are higher and the gravity stronger than on Earth; this climbing of buildings like human flies calls out the ingenuity and daring of the Camiroi children.)
Nuclear physics and post-organic chemistry.
Simple pseudo-human assembly.

SEVENTH YEAR COURSE:
History reading, Camiroi and galactic, cultural.
Advanced prodigious memory.
Vehicle operation and manufacture of simple vehicle.
Literature, active.
Astrognosy, prediction and programming.
Advanced pankration.
Spherical logic, hand and machine.
Advanced alcoholic appreciation.
Integral religion.
Bankruptcy and recovery in business.
Conmanship and trend creation.
Post-nuclear physics and universals.

Transcendental athletics endeavor.

Complex robotics and programming.

History reading, Camiroi and galactic, seminal theory.

Consummate prodigious memory.

Manufacture of complex land and water vehicles.

Literature, compenduous and terminative. (Creative book-burning following the Camiroi thesis that nothing ordinary be allowed to survive.)

Cosmic theory, seminal.

Philosophy construction.

Complex hedonism.

Laser religion.

Conmanship, seminal.

Consolidation of simple genius status.

Post-robotic integration.

History reading, Camiroi and galactic, future and contingent.

Category invention.

Manufacture of complex light-barrier vehicles.

Construction of simple asteroids and planets.

Matrix religion and logic.

Simple human immortality disciplines.

Consolidation of complex genius status.

First problems of post-consciousness humanity.

First essays in marriage and reproduction.

History construction, active.

Manufacture of ultra-light-barrier vehicles.

Panphilosophical clarifications.

Construction of viable planets.

Consolidation of simple sanctity status.

Charismatic humor and pentacosmic logic.

Hypogyroscopic economy.

Penentaglossia. (The perfection of the fifty languages that every educated Camiroi must know including six Earthian languages. Of course the child will already have colloquial mastery of most of these, but he will not yet have them in their full depth.)

Construction of complex societies.

World government. (A course of the same name is sometimes given in Earthian schools, but the course is not of the same content. In this course the Camiroi student will govern a world, though not one of the first aspect worlds, for a period of three or four months.)

Tenth form thesis.

COMMENT ON CURRICULUM:

The child will now be fifteen years old and will have completed his primary education. In many ways he will be advanced beyond his Earth counterpart. Physically more sophisticated, the Camiroi child could kill with his hands an Earth-type tiger or a cape buffalo. An Earth child would perhaps be reluctant even to attempt such feats. The Camiroi boy (or girl) could replace any professional Earth athlete at any position of any game, and could surpass all existing Earth records. It is simply a question of finer poise, strength and speed, the result of adequate schooling.

As to the arts (on which Earthlings sometimes place emphasis) the Camiroi child could produce easy and unequaled masterpieces in any medium. More important, he will have learned the relative unimportance of such pastimes.

The Camiroi child will have failed in business once, at age ten, and have learned patience and perfection of objective by his failure. He will have acquired the techniques of falsification and conmanship. Thereafter he will not be easily deceived by any of the citizens of any of the worlds. The Camiroi child will have become a complex genius and a simple saint; the latter reduces the index of Camiroi crime to near zero. He will be married and settled in those early years of greatest enjoyment.

The child will have built, from materials found around

any Camiroi house, a faster-than-light vehicle. He will have piloted it on a significant journey of his own plotting and programming. He will have built quasi-human robots of great intricacy. He will be of perfect memory and judgment and will be well prepared to accept solid learning.

He will have learned to use his whole mind, for the vast reservoirs which are the unconscious to us are not unconscious to him. Everything in him is ordered for use. And there seems to be no great secret about the accomplishments, only to do everything slowly enough and in the right order: thus they avoid repetition and drill which are the shriveling things which dull the quick apperception.

The Camiroi schedule is challenging to the children, but it is nowhere impossible or discouraging. Everything builds to what follows. For instance, the child is eleven years old before he is given post-nuclear physics and universals. Such subjects might be too difficult for him at an earlier age. He is thirteen years old before he undertakes category invention, that intricate course with the simple name. He is fourteen years old when he enters the dangerous field of panphilosophical clarification. But he will have been constructing comprehensive philosophies for two years, and he will have the background for the final clarification.

We should look more closely at this other way of education. In some respects it is better than our own. Few Earth children would be able to construct an organic and sentient robot within fifteen minutes if given the test suddenly; most of them could not manufacture a living dog in that time. Not one Earth child in five could build a faster-than-light vehicle and travel it beyond our galaxy between now and midnight. Not one Earth child in a hundred could build a planet and have it a going concern within a week. Not one in a thousand would be able to comprehend pentacosmic logic.

RECOMMENDATIONS: a.) Kidnapping five Camiroi at

random and constituting them a pilot Earth PTA. b.) A little constructive book-burning, particularly in the education field. c.) Judicious hanging of certain malingering students.

SLOW TUESDAY NIGHT

A PANHANDLER intercepted the young couple as they strolled down the night street.

"Preserve us this night," he said as he touched his hat to them, "and could you good people advance me a thousand dollars to be about the recouping of my fortunes?"

"I gave you a thousand last Friday," said the young man.

"Indeed you did," the panhandler replied, "and I paid you back tenfold by messenger before midnight."

"That's right, George, he did," said the young woman. "Give it to him, dear. I believe he's a good sort."

So the young man gave the panhandler a thousand dollars, and the panhandler touched his hat to them in thanks and went on to the recouping of his fortunes.

As he went into Money Market, the panhandler passed Ildefonsa Impala, the most beautiful woman in the city.

"Will you marry me this night, Ildy?" he asked cheerfully.

"Oh, I don't believe so, Basil," she said. "I marry you pretty often, but tonight I don't seem to have any plans at all. You may make me a gift on your first or second, however. I always like that."

But when they had parted she asked herself: "But whom will I marry tonight?"

The panhandler was Basil Bagelbaker, who would be the richest man in the world within an hour and a half. He would make and lose four fortunes within eight hours; and these not the little fortunes that ordinary men acquire, but titanic things.

SLOW TUESDAY NIGHT

When the Abebaios block had been removed from human minds, people began to make decisions faster, and often better. It had been the mental stutter. When it was understood what it was, and that it had no useful function, it was removed by simple childhood meta-surgery.

Transportation and manufacturing had then become practically instantaneous. Things that had once taken months and years now took only minutes and hours. A person could have one or several pretty intricate careers within an eight-hour period.

Freddy Fixico had just invented a manus module. Freddy was a Nyctalops, and the modules were characteristic of these people. The people had then divided themselves—according to their natures and inclinations—into the Auroreans, the Hemerobians, and the Nyctalops—or the Dawners, who had their most active hours from four A.M. till noon; the Day-Flies, who obtained from noon to eight P.M.; and the Night-Seers, whose civilization thrived from eight P.M. to four A.M. The cultures, inventions, markets and activities of these three folk were a little different. As a Nyctalops, Freddy had just begun his working day at eight P.M. on a slow Tuesday night.

Freddy rented an office and had it furnished. This took one minute, negotiation, selection and installation being almost instantaneous. Then he invented the manus module; that took another minute. He then had it manufactured and marketed; in three minutes it was in the hands of key buyers.

It caught on. It was an attractive module. The flow of orders began within thirty seconds. By ten minutes after eight every important person had one of the new manus modules, and the trend had been set. The module began to sell in the millions. It was one of the most interesting fads of the night, or at least the early part of the night.

Manus modules had no practical function, no more

than had Sameki verses. They were attractive, of a psychologically satisfying size and shape, and could be held in the hands, set on a table, or installed in a module niche of any wall.

Naturally Freddy became very rich. Ildefonsa Impala, the most beautiful woman in the city, was always interested in newly rich men. She came to see Freddy about eight-thirty. People made up their minds fast, and Ildefonsa had hers made up when she came. Freddy made his own up quickly and divorced Judy Fixico in Small Claims Court. Freddy and Ildefonsa went honeymooning to Paraiso Dorado, a resort.

It was wonderful. All of Ildy's marriages were. There was the wonderful floodlighted scenery. The recirculated water of the famous falls was tinted gold; the immediate rocks had been done by Rambles; and the hills had been contoured by Spall. The beach was a perfect copy of that at Merevale, and the popular drink that first part of the night was blue absinthe.

But scenery—whether seen for the first time or revisited after an interval—is striking for the sudden intense view of it. It is not meant to be lingered over. Food, selected and prepared instantly, is eaten with swift enjoyment; and blue absinthe lasts no longer than its own novelty. Loving, for Ildefonsa and her paramours, was quick and consuming; and repetition would have been pointless to her. Besides, Ildefonsa and Freddy had taken only the one-hour luxury honeymoon.

Freddy wished to continue the relationship, but Ildefonsa glanced at a trend indicator. The manus module would hold its popularity for only the first third of the night. Already it had been discarded by people who mattered. And Freddy Fixico was not one of the regular successes. He enjoyed a full career only about one night a week.

They were back in the city and divorced in Small Claims Court by nine thirty-five. The stock of manus modules was remandered, and the last of it would be disposed to bargain hunters among the Dawners, who will buy anything.

"Whom shall I marry next?" Ildefonsa asked herself. "It looks like a slow night."

"Bagelbaker is buying," ran the word through Money Market, but Bagelbaker was selling again before the word had made its rounds. Basil Bagelbaker enjoyed making money, and it was a pleasure to watch him work as he dominated the floor of the Market and assembled runners and a competent staff out of the corner of his mouth. Helpers stripped the panhandler rags off him and wrapped him in a tycoon toga. He sent one runner to pay back twentyfold the young couple who had advanced him a thousand dollars. He sent another with a more substantial gift to Ildefonsa Impala, for Basil cherished their relationship. Basil acquired title to the Trend Indication Complex and had certain falsifications set into it. He caused to collapse certain industrial empires that had grown up within the last two hours, and made a good thing of recombining their wreckage. He had been the richest man in the world for some minutes now. He became so money-heavy that he could not maneuver with the agility he had shown an hour before. He became a great fat buck, and the pack of expert wolves circled him to bring him down.

Very soon he would lose that first fortune of the evening. The secret of Basil Bagelbaker is that he enjoyed losing money spectacularly after he was full of it to the bursting point.

A thoughtful man named Maxwell Mouser had just produced a work of actinic philosophy. It took him seven minutes to write it. To write works of philosophy one used the flexible outlines and the idea indexes; one set the activator for such a wordage in each subsection; an adept would use the paradox feed-in, and the striking-analogy blender; one calibrated the particular-slant and the personality-signature. It had to come out a good

137

work, for excellence had become the automatic minimum for such productions.

"I will scatter a few nuts on the frosting," said Maxwell, and he pushed the lever for that. This sifted handfuls of words like chthonic and heuristic and prozymeides through the thing so that nobody could doubt it was a work of philosophy.

Maxwell Mouser sent the work out to publishers, and received it back each time in about three minutes. An analysis of it and reason for rejection was always given —mostly that the thing had been done before and better. Maxwell received it back ten times in thirty minutes, and was discouraged. Then there was a break.

Ladion's work had become a hit within the last ten minutes, and it was now recognized that Mouser's monograph was both an answer and a supplement to it. It was accepted and published in less than a minute after this break. The reviews of the first five minutes were cautious ones; then real enthusiasm was shown. This was truly one of the greatest works of philosophy to appear during the early and medium hours of the night. There were those who said it might be one of the enduring works and even have a holdover appeal to the Dawners the next morning.

Naturally Maxwell became very rich, and naturally Ildefonsa came to see him about midnight. Being a revolutionary philosopher, Maxwell thought that they might make some free arrangement, but Ildefonsa insisted it must be marriage So Maxwell divorced Judy Mouser in Small Claims Court and went off with Ildefonsa.

This Judy herself, though not so beautiful as Ildefonsa, was the fastest taker in the city. She only wanted the men of the moment for a moment, and she was always there before even Ildefonsa. Ildefonsa believed that she took the men away from Judy; Judy said that Ildy had her leavings and nothing else.

"I had him first," Judy would always mock as she raced through Small Claims Court.

"Oh that damned urchin!" Ildefonsa would moan. "She wears my very hair before I do."

Maxwell Mouser and Ildefonsa Impala went honeymooning to Musicbox Mountain, a resort. It was wonderful. The peaks were done with green snow by Dunbar and Fittle. (Back at Money Market Basil Bagelbaker was putting together his third and greatest fortune of the night, which might surpass in magnitude even his fourth fortune of the Thursday before.) The chalets were Switzier than the real Swiss and had live goats in every room. (And Stanley Skuldugger was emerging as the top Actor-Imago of the middle hours of the night.) The popular drink for that middle part of the night was Glotzenglubber, Eve Cheese and Rhine wine over pink ice. (And back in the city the leading Nyctalops were taking their midnight break at the Toppers' Club.)

Of course it was wonderful, as were all of Ildefonsa's— But she had never been really up on philosophy so she had scheduled only the special thirty-five-minute honeymoon. She looked at the trend indicator to be sure. She found that her current husband had been obsoleted, and his opus was now referred to sneeringly as Mouser's Mouse. They went back to the city and were divorced in Small Claims Court.

The membership of the Toppers' Club varied. Success was the requisite of membership. Basil Bagelbaker might be accepted as a member, elevated to the presidency and expelled from it as a dirty pauper from three to six times a night. But only important persons could belong to it, or those enjoying brief moments of importance.

"I believe I will sleep during the Dawner period in the morning," Overcall said. "I may go up to this new place, Koimopolis, for an hour of it. They're said to be good. Where will you sleep, Basil?"

"Flop house."

"I believe I will sleep an hour by the Midian Method," said Burnbanner. "They have a fine new clinic. And perhaps I'll sleep an hour by the Prasenka Process, and an hour by the Dormidio."

"Crackle has been sleeping an hour every period by the natural method," said Overcall.

"I did that for half an hour not long since," said Burnbanner. "I believe an hour is too long to give it. Have you tried the natural method, Basil?"

"Always. Natural method and a bottle of red-eye."

Stanley Skuldugger had become the most meteoric actor-imago for a week. Naturally he became very rich, and Ildefonsa Impala went to see him about three A.M.

"I had him first!" rang the mocking voice of Judy Skuldugger as she skipped through her divorce in Small Claims Court. And Ildefonsa and Stanley-boy went off honeymooning. It is always fun to finish up a period with an actor-imago who is the hottest property in the business. There is something so adolescent and boorish about them.

Besides, there was the publicity, and Ildefonsa liked that. The rumor-mills ground. Would it last ten minutes? Thirty? An hour? Would it be one of those rare Nyctalops marriages that lasted through the rest of the night and into the daylight off-hours? Would it even last into the next night as some had been known to do?

Actually it lasted nearly forty minutes, which was almost to the end of the period.

It had been a slow Tuesday night. A few hundred new products had run their course on the markets. There had been a score of dramatic hits, three-minute and five-minute capsule dramas, and several of the six-minute long-play affairs. *Night Street Nine*—a solidly sordid offering—seemed to be in as the drama of the night unless there should be a late hit.

Hundred-storied buildings had been erected, occupied, obsoleted, and demolished again to make room for more contemporary structures. Only the mediocre would use a building that had been left over from the Day Fliers or the Dawners, or even the Nyctalops of the night before. The city was rebuilt pretty completely at least three times during an eight-hour period.

The period drew near its end. Basil Bagelbaker, the richest man in the world, the reigning president of the Toppers' Club, was enjoying himself with his cronies. His fourth fortune of the night was a paper pyramid that had risen to incredible heights; but Basil laughed to himself as he savored the manipulation it was founded on.

Three ushers of the Toppers' Club came in with firm step.

"Get out of here, you dirty bum!" they told Basil savagely. They tore the tycoon's toga off him and then tossed him his seedy panhandler's rags with a three-man sneer.

"All gone?" Basil asked. "I gave it another five minutes."

"All gone," said a messenger from Money Market. "Nine billion gone in five minutes, and it really pulled some others down with it."

"Pitch the busted bum out!" howled Overcall and Burnbanner and the other cronies.

"Wait, Basil," said Overcall. "Turn in the President's Crosier before we kick you downstairs. After all, you'll have it several times again tomorrow night."

The period was over. The Nyctalops drifted off to sleep clinics or leisure-hour hideouts to pass their ebb time. The Auroreans, the Dawners, took over the vital stuff.

Now you would see some action! Those Dawners really made fast decisions. You wouldn't catch them wasting a full minute setting up a business.

A sleepy panhandler met Ildefonsa Impala on the way.

"Preserve us this morning, Ildy," he said, "and will you marry me the coming night?"

"Likely I will, Basil," she told him. "Did you marry Judy during the night past?"

"I'm not sure. Could you let me have two dollars, Ildy?"

"Out of the question. I believe a Judy Bagelbaker was named one of the ten best-dressed women during the frou-frou fashion period about two o'clock. Why do you need two dollars?"

"A dollar for a bed and a dollar for red-eye. After all, I sent you two million out of my second."

"I keep my two sorts of accounts separate. Here's a dollar, Basil. Now be off! I can't be seen talking to a dirty panhandler."

"Thank you, Ildy. I'll get the red-eye and sleep in an alley. Preserve us this morning."

Bagelbaker shuffled off whistling "Slow Tuesday Night."

And already the Dawners had set Wednesday morning to jumping.

SNUFFLES

I

"I ALWAYS SAID we'd find one of them that was fun,"
remarked Brian. "There's been entirely too much solem-
nity in the universe. Did you never panic on thinking
of the multiplicity of systems?"

"Never," said Georgina.

"Not even when, having set down a fine probability
for the totality of worlds, you realized suddenly that you
had to raise it by a dozen powers yet?"

"What's to panic?"

"Not even when it comes over you, 'This isn't a joke;
this is serious; every one of them is serious'?"

" 'Cosmic intimidation,' Belloc called it. And it does
tend to minimize a person."

"And did you never hope that out of all that prodi-
gality of worlds, one at least should have been made
for fun? One should have been made by a wild child
or a mixed-up goblin just to put the rest of them in
proper perspective, to deflate the pomposity of the
cosmos."

"You believe this is it, Mr. Carroll?"

"Yes. Bellota was made for fun. It is a joke, a caricature, a burlesque. It is a planet with baggy pants and
a putty nose. It is a midget world with floppy shoes and
a bull-roarer voice. It was designed to keep the cosmos
from taking itself too seriously. The law of levity here
conspires against the law of gravity."

"I never heard of the law of levity. And Mr. Phelan
believes that he will soon have the explanation for the
peculiar gravity here."

"The law of levity does not apply to you, Georgina. You are immune. But I spoke lightly."

The theory that Bellota was made for a joke had not been proved; no more than the other theories about it. But it was a sport, a whole barrelful of puzzles, a place of interest all out of proportion to its size, eminently worthy of study. And the six of them had been set down there to study it.

Sociability impels—and besides they weren't a bad bunch at all. Meet them now, or miss them forever. They were six.

1. John Hardy. Commander and commando. As capable a man as ever lived. A good-natured conglomerate of clanking iron who was always in control. A jack of all techniques, a dynamic optimist. He had the only laugh that never irritated, however often heard, and he handled danger cavalierly. He was a blue-eyed, red-headed giant, and his face was redder than his hair.

2. William Malaquais (Uncle Billy) Cross. Engineer, machinist extraordinary, gadgeteer, theorist, arguefier, first mate, navigator, and balladeer. Billy was a little older than the rest of them, but he hadn't mellowed. He said that he was still a green and growing boy.

3. Daniel Phelan. Geologist and cosmologist, and holder of heretical doctrines about field forces. "Phelan's Corollary" may be known to you; and, if so, you must be both intrigued and frustrated by the inherent contradictions that prevented its acceptance. A highly professional man in the domain of magnetism and gravity, he was also a low amateur rake and a determined wolf. A dude. Yet he could carry his share of the load.

4. Margaret Cot. Artist and photographer, botanist and bacteriologist. Full of chatter and a sort of charm. Better looking than anyone deserves to be. Salty, really the newest thing in salinity. A little bit wanton. And a little kiddish.

5. Brian Carroll. Naturalist. And natural. He had been hunting for something all his life, but did not know what

it was, and was not sure that he would know it when he found it, but he hoped that it would be different. "O Lord," he would pray, "however it ends don't let it have a pat ending. That I couldn't stand." He believed that anything repeated was trite. And it was for that reason that there were pleasant surprises for him on Bellota.

6. Georgina Chantal. Biologist and iceberg. But the capsule description may be unjust. For she was more than biologist and much more than iceberg. Frosty only when frostiness was called for, she was always proper and often friendly. But she was no Margie Cot, and in contrast perhaps she was a little icy.

Actually there wasn't a bad apple in that basket.

The most obvious peculiarity of Bellota was its gravity, which was half that of Earth's, though the circumference of the globe was no more than a hundred miles. It was on account of this peculiarity that Daniel Phelan was on the little planet in the first place. For it was held by those who decide such things that there was a bare chance that he could find the answer; no one else had found it. His own idea was that his presence there was fruitless: he already had the answer to the gravity behavior of Bellota; it was contained in Phelan's Corollary. Bellota was the only body that behaved as it should. It was the rest of the universe that was atypical.

And in other ways Bellota was a joker. Fruits proved noisome and thorns succulent. Rinds and shells were edible and heartmeat was not. Proto-butterflies stung like hornets, and lizards secreted honeylike manna. And the water—the water was soda water—sheer carbonated soda water.

If you wanted it any other way, you caught rain water, and this was so highly nitric that drinking it was something of an experience also; for the thunderstorms there were excessive.

No, they were not excessive, claimed Phelan, they were normal. It was on all other atmospheric planets known that there was a strange deficiency of thunder-showers.

Here, at least, there was no deficiency: it rained about five minutes out of every fifteen, and the multi-colored lightning was omnipresent. In all their stay there, the party was never without the sound of thunder, near or distant, nor of the probe of lightning. For this reason there could be no true darkness there, not even between the flashes; there were flashes between the flashes. Here was meteorology concentrated, without dilution, without filler.

"But it is always different," said Georgina. "Every lightning flash is entirely different, just as every snow-flake is different. Will it snow here?"

"Certainly," said Phelan. "Though it did not last night, it should tonight. Snow before midnight and fog by morning. After all, midnight and morning are only an hour apart."

At that time they had been on the planet only a few hours.

"And here the cycle is normal," said Phelan. "It is normal nowhere else. It is natural for humans and all other creatures to sleep for two hours and to wake for two hours. That is the fundamental cycle. Much of our misbehavior and perversity comes from trying to adapt to the weird day-night cycle of whatever alien world we happened to be born on. Here within a week we will return to that normal that we never knew before."

"Within what kind of week?" asked Hardy.

"Within Bellota's twenty-eight-hour week. And do you realize that the projected working week here would be just six and two-thirds hours? I always thought that that was long enough to work anyhow."

There were no seas there, only the soda-water lakes that covered a third of the area. And there were flora and fauna that burlesqued more than they really resembled Earth's and kindred worlds'.

The trees were neither deciduous nor evergreen

(though Brian Carroll said that they were ever-green), nor palm. They were trees as a cartoonist might draw them. And there were animals that made the whole idea of animals ridiculous.

And there was Snuffles.

Snuffles was a bear—possibly—and of sorts. The bear is himself a caricature of animalkind, somehow a giant dog, somehow a shaggy man, an ogre, and also a toy. And Snuffles was a caricature of a bear.

Billy Cross tried to explain to them about bears. Billy was an old bear man.

"It is the only animal that children dream of without having seen or been told about. Moncrief by his recall methods has studied thousands of early childhood dreams. Children universally dream of bears, Tahitian children subject to no ursine influence in themselves or their ancestry, Australian children, town tikes before they ever saw a bear toy. They dream of bears. The bear is the boogerman. Bears live in the attics of old childhood houses. They did in my own and in thousands of others. Their existence there is not of adult suggestion, but of innate childhood knowledge.

"But there is a duality about this boogerman. He is friendly and fascinating as well as frightening. The boogerman is not a story that adults tell to children. It is the only story that children tell to adults who have forgotten it "

"But how could you know?" asked Margie Cot. "I had no idea that little boys dreamed of bears. I thought that only girls did. And with us I had come to believe that the bear dreams symbolized grown man in his fundamental aspect, both fascinating and frightening."

"To you, Margie, everything symbolizes grown man in his fundamental aspect. Now the boogerman is also philologically interesting, being actually one of the less than two hundred Indo-European root words. Though *Bog* has come to mean God in the Slavic, yet the booger was earlier an animal-man demiurge, and the Sanscrit

147

bhaga is not without this meaning. In the sense of a breaker, a smasher, it is in the Old Irish as *bong*, and the early Lithuanian as *banga*. In the sense of a devourer, it survives in the Greek root *phag*, and as one who puts to flight it is in the Latin *fug*. We have, of course, the Welsh *bwg*, a ghost, and *bogey* has been used in the meaning of the devil. And we have *bugbear*, which rounds out the circuit."

"So you make God and the Bear and the Devil one," said Georgina.

"In many mythologies it was the bear who made the world," said John Hardy. "After that he did nothing distinguished. It was felt by his devotees that he had done enough."

Snuffles was not a bear exactly. He was a pseudo-ursine. He was big and clumsy, and bounced around on four legs, and then up on two. He was friendly, chillingly so, for he was huge. And he snuffled like some old track-eating train.

He was a clown, but he seemed to observe the line that the visitors drew. He did not come really close, though often too close for comfort. He obeyed, or when he did not wish to obey, he pretended to misunderstand. He was the largest animal on Bellota, and there seemed to be only one of him.

"Why do we call him he?" asked Brian Carroll, the naturalist. "Only surgery could tell for sure, but it appears that Snuffles has no sex at all. There is no way I know of that he could reproduce. No wonder there is only one of him; the wonder is that there should be any at all. Where did he come from?"

"That could be asked of any creature," said Daniel Phelan. "The question is, where is he going? But he shows a certain sophistication in this. For it is only with primitives that toy animals (and he is a toy, you know) are sexed. A modern teddy bear or a toy panda isn't. Nor were the toys in the European tradition except on the fringes (Tartary before the ninth century, Ireland

before the fifth) ₁since pre-classical times. But before
those times in its regions, and beyond its pale even today, the toy animals are totems and are sexed, exag-
geratedly so."

"Yes, there is no doubt about it," said Brian. "He does
not have even the secondary characteristics of mammal,
marsupial, or what you will. But he has characteristics
enough of his own."

Snuffles was, among other things, a mimic. Should a
book be left around, and they were a bookish bunch, he
would take it in his forepaws and hold it as to read, and
turn the pages, turning them singly and carefully. He
could use his padded paws as hands His claws were retractable and his digits projective. They were paws, or
they were claws, or they were hands and he had four
of them.

He unscrewed caps and he could use a can opener.
He kept the visitors in firewood, once he understood
that they had need of it, and that they wanted dry
sticks of a certain size. He'd bite the sticks to length,
stack them in small ricks, bind them with lianas, and
carry them to the fire. He'd fetch water and put it on
to boil. And he gathered bellotas by the bushel.

Bellota means an acorn, and they had named the planet that from the profusion of edible fruit-nuts that
looked very like the acorn. These were a delicacy that
became a staple.

And Snuffles could talk. All his noises were not alike.
There was the "snokle, snoke, snokle" that meant he
was in a good humor, as he normally was. There was a
"snook, snook" and a "snoff." There were others similar
in vocables but widely varied in tone and timbre. Perhaps Billy Cross understood him best, but they all understood him a little.

In only one thing did Snuffles become stubborn. He
marked off a space, a wild old pile of rocks, and forbade them to enter its circle. He dug a trench around
it and he roared and bared foot-long fangs if any dared

cross the trench. Billy Cross said that Snuffles did this to save face; for Commander John Hardy had previously forbidden Snuffles a certain area, their supply dump and weapons center. Hardy had drawn a line around it with a mattock and made it clear that Snuffles should never cross that line. The creature understood at once, and he went and did likewise.

The party had been set down there for two Earth weeks—twelve Bellota weeks—to study the life of the planetoid, to classify, to take samples, tests, notes, and pictures; to hypothesize and to build a basis for theory. But they ventured hardly at all from their original campsite. There was such an amazing variety of detail at hand that it would take many weeks even to begin to classify it.

A feature there was the rapidity of enzyme and bacterial action. A good wine could be produced in four hours, and a fungus-cheese made from grub exudations in even less time. And in the new atmosphere thoughts also seemed to ferment rapidly.

"Every person makes one major mistake in his life," said John Hardy to them once. "Were it not for that, he would not have to die."

"What?" quizzed Phelan. "Few die violently nowadays. How could all die for a mistake?"

"Yet it's a fact. Deaths are not really explained, for all the explanations of medicine. A death will be the result of one single much earlier rashness, of one weakening of the mind or body, or a crippling of the regenerative force. A person will be alive and vital. And one day he will make one mistake. In that moment the person begins to die. But if a man did not make that one mistake, he would not die."

"Poppycock," said Daniel Phelan.

"I wonder if you know the true meaning of 'poppycock'?" asked Billy Cross. "It is poppy-talk, opium-talk, the rambling of one under the narcotic. Now the element 'cock' in the word is not (as you would imagine) from either the Norwegian *kok*, a dung heap, nor from *co-quarde* in the sense that Rabelais uses it, but rather from—"

"Poppycock," said Phelan again. He disliked Billy Cross's practice of analyzing all words, and he denied his assertion that a man who uses a word without feeling its full value is a dealer in false coinage, in fact a liar.

"But if a person dies only by making a mistake, how does an animal die?" asked Margie Cot. "Does he also make a mistake?"

"He makes the mistake of being an animal and not a man," said Phelan.

"There may be no clear line between animal and man," Margie argued.

"There is," said Phelan, and three others agreed.

"There is not," said Billy Cross.

"An animal is paradoxically a creature without an *anima*—without a soul," said Phelan. "This comes oddly from me because I also deny it to man in its usual connotation. But there is a total difference, a line that the animal cannot cross, and did not cross. When we arrive at wherever we are going, he will still be skulking in his den"

"Here, at least, it is the opposite of that," said Brian Carroll. "Snuffles sleeps in the open, and it is we who den."

It was true. Around their campsite, their supply dump and weapons center, there were three blind pockets, grottoes back in the rocks. Billy Cross, Daniel Phelan and Margie Cot each had one of these, filled with the tools of their specialties. Here they worked and slept. And these were dens.

John Hardy himself slept in the weapons center, inside the circle where Snuffles was forbidden. And the hours that he did not sleep he kept guard. Hardy made a fetish of security. When he slept, or briefly wandered about the region, someone else must always take a turn at guard, weapon at hand. There was no relaxation of this, no exception, no chance of a mistake.

And Snuffles, the animal, who slept right out in the open ("Is it possible," Brian asked himself, "that I am the only one who notices it? Is it possible that it happens?") did not get wet. It rained everywhere on that world. But it did not rain on Snuffles.

"The joy of this place is that it is not pat," said Brian Carroll. As previously noted, he hated anything that was pat. "We could be here for years and never see the end of the variety. With the insects there may be as many species as there are individuals. Each one could almost be regarded as a sport, as if there were no standard to go by. The gravity here is cock-eyed. Please don't analyze the word, Billy; I doubt myself that it means rooster-eyed. The chemistry gives one a hopeful feeling. It uses the same building blocks as the chemistry elsewhere, but it is as if each of those blocks were just a little off. The lightning is excessive, as though whoever was using it had not yet tired of the novelty; I never tired of the novelty of lightning myself. And when this place ends, it will not have a pat ending. Other globes may turn to lava or cold cinders. Bellota will pop like a soap bubble, or sag like spaghetti, or turn into an exploding world of grasshoppers. But it won't conform. I love Bellota. And I do hate a pat ending."

"There is an old precept of 'Know thyself,' " said Georgina Chantal. They talked a lot now, as they were often wakeful, not yet being accustomed to the short days and nights of Bellota. "Its variant is 'Look within.' Look within, but our eyes point outward! The only way we can see our faces is in a mirror or in a picture. Each of us has his mirror, and mine is more often the microscope. But we cannot see ourselves as we are until we see ourselves distorted. That is why Snuffles is also a mirror for all of us here. We can't understand why we're serious until we know why he's funny."

"We may be the distortion and he the true image,"

said Billy Cross. "He lacks jealousy and pomposity and greed and treachery—all the distortions."

"We do not know that he lacks them," said Daniel Phelan.

So they talked away the short days and nights on Bellota, and accumulated data.

II

When it happened, it happened right in narrow daylight. The phrase was Brian's, who hated a pat phrase. It happened right in the middle of the narrow two-hour Bellota day.

All were awake and aware. John Hardy stood in the middle of the weapons center on alert guard with that rifle cradled in the crook of his arm. Billy and Daniel and Margaret were at work in their respective dens; and Brian and Georgina, who did not den, were gathering insects at the open lower end of the valley, but they had the center in their sight.

There was an unusual flash of lightning, bright by even Bellota standards, and air snapped and crackled. And there was an unusul sound from Snuffles, far removed from his usual "snokle, snokle" talk.

And in a moment benignity seemed to drain away from that planet.

Snuffles had before made as if to cross the line, and then scooted off, chortling in glee, which is perhaps why the careful John Hardy was not at first alarmed.

Then Snuffles charged with a terrifying sound.

But Hardy was not tricked entirely; it would be impossible for man or beast to trick him entirely. He had a split second, and was not one to waste time making a decision, and he was incapable of panic. What he did, he did of choice. And if it was a mistake, why, even the shrewdest decision goes into the books as a mistake if it fails.

He was fond of Snuffles and he gambled that it would
not be necessary to kill him. It was a heavy rifle; a shoulder shot should have turned the animal. If it did not,
there would not be time for another shot.

It did not, though, and there was not. Commander
John Hardy made one mistake and for that he died.
He died uncommonly, and he did not die from the in-
side out, as meaner men do.

It was ghastly, but it was over in an instant. Hardy's
head was smashed and his face nearly swiped off. His
back was broken and his body almost sheared in two.
The great creature, with the foot-long canines and claws
like twenty long knives, mangled him and crushed him
and shook him like a red mop, and then let go.

It may be that Brian Carroll realized most quickly
the implications. He called to Georgina to come out of
the valley onto the plain below, and to come out fast.
He realized that the other three still alive would not
even be able to come out.

Incongruously, a thing that went through Brian Carroll's mind was a tirade of an ancient Confederate general against ancient General Grant, to the effect that
the blundering fool had moved into a position that commanded both river and hill and blocked three valley
mouths, and it could only be hoped that Grant would
move along before he realized his advantage.

But Brian was under no such delusion. Snuffles realized his advantage; he occupied the supply dump and
weapons center, and commanded the entrances to the
three blind pockets that were the dens of Billy Cross
and Daniel Phelan and Margie Cot.

With one move, Snuffles had killed the leader, cor-
nered three of the others, and cut off the remaining
two from base weapons, to be hunted down later. There
was nothing unintentional about it. Had he chosen another moment, when another than John Hardy was on
guard, then Hardy alive would still somehow have been

a threat to him, even weaponless. But, with Hardy dead, all the rest were no match for the animal.

Brian and Georgina lingered on the edge of the plain to watch the other three, though they knew that their own lives depended on getting out of there.

"Two could get away," said Georgina, "if a third would make a rush for it and force Snuffles into another charge."

"But none of them will," said Brian. "The third would die."

It was a game, but it couldn't last long. Phelan whimpered and tried to climb the rock wall at the blind end of his pocket. Margie cajoled and told Snuffles how good friends they had always been, and wouldn't he let her go? Billy Cross filled his pipe and lit it and sat down to wait it out.

Phelan went first, and he died like a craven. But no one, not sure how he himself might die, should hold that overly against a man.

Snuffles thundered in, cut him down in the middle of a scream, and rushed back to his commanding spot in the middle of the weapons center.

Margie spread out her hands and began to cry, softly, not really in terror, when he attacked. The pseudo-bear broke her neck, but with a blow that was almost gentle in comparison with the others, and he scurried again to the center.

And Billy Cross puffed on his pipe. "I hate to go like this, Snuff, old boy. In fact, I hate to go at all. If I made a mistake to die for, it was in being such a pleasant, trusting fellow. I wonder if you ever noticed, Snuff, what a fine, upstanding fellow I really am?"

And that was the last thing Billy Cross ever said, for the big animal struck him dead with one tearing blow. And the smoke still drifted in the air from Billy's pipe.

Then it was like black thunder coming out of the valley after the other two, for that clumsy animal could

155

move. They had a start on him, Brian and Georgina had, of a hundred yards. And soon their terror subsided to half-terror as they realized that the shoulder-shot bear animal could not catch them till they were exhausted.

In a wild run, they could even increase their lead over him. But they would tire soon and they did not know when he would tire. He had herded them away from the campsite and the weapons. And they were trapped with him on a small planet.

Till day's end, and through the night, and next day (maybe five hours in all) he followed them until they could hardly keep going. Then they lost him, but in the dark did not know if he was close or not. And at dawn they saw him sitting up and watching them from a quarter of a mile away.

But now the adversaries rested and watched. The animal may have stiffened up from his shot. The two humans were so weary that they did not intend to run on again till the last moment.

"Do you think there is any chance that it was all a sudden fury and that he may become friendly again?" Georgina asked Brian.

"It was not a sudden fury. It was a series of very calculated moves."

"Do you think we could skirt around and beat him back to the weapons center?"

"No. He has chosen a spot where he can see for miles. And he has the interceptor's advantage—any angle we take has to be longer than his. We can't beat him back and he knows it."

"Do you think he knows that the weapons are weapons?"

"Yes."

"And that all our signal equipment is left at the center and that we can't communicate?"

"Yes."

"Do you think he's smarter than we are?"

"He was smarter in selecting his role. It is better to

be the hunter than the hunted. But it isn't unheard of
for the hunted to outsmart the hunter."

"Brian, do you think you would have died as badly
as Daniel or as well as Billy?"

"No. No to both."

"I was always jealous of Margie, but I loved her at
the end. She didn't scream. She didn't act scared. Brian,
what will happen to us now?"

"Possibly we will be saved in the nick of time by the
Marines."

"I didn't know they had them any more. Oh, you
mean the ship. But that's still a week away, Earth time.
Do you think Snuffles knows it is to come back for us?"

"Yes, he knows. I'm sure of that."

"Do you think he knows when it will come?"

"Yes, I have the feeling that he knows that too."

"But will he be able to catch us before then?"

"I believe that all parties concerned will play out the
contest with one eye on the clock."

Snuffles had now developed a trick. At sundown of
the short day, he would give a roar and come at them.
And they would have to start their flight just as the
dark commenced. They ran more noisily than he and
he would always be able to follow them; but they could
never be sure in the dark that he was following, or how
closely. They would have to go at top panting, gasping,
thumping speed for an hour and a half; then they would
ease off for a little in the half hour before dawn. And in
the daytime one of them had to watch while the other
slept. But Snuffles could sleep as he would, and they
were never able to slip away without his waking instantly.

Moreover, he seemed to herd them through the fertile
belt on their night runs and let them rest on the barrens
in the daytime. It wasn't that food was really scarce; it
was that it could only be gathered during time taken
from flight and sleep and guard duty.

They also came on a quantity of red fruit that had

a weakening and dizzying effect on them, yet they could hardly leave it alone. There was a sort of bean sprout that had the same effect, and a nut, and a cereal grass whose seed they winnowed with their hands as they went along.

"This is a narcotic belt," said Brian. "I wish we had the time to study it longer, and yet we may get all too much of studying it. We have no idea how far it goes, and this method of testing its products on ourselves may be an effective one, but dangerous."

From that time on, they were under the influence of the narcotics. They dreamed vividly while awake and walking. And they began to suffer hallucinations which they could not distinguish from reality.

It was only a Bellota day or so after their dreaming began that Brian Carroll felt that the mind of Snuffles was speaking to him. Carroll was an intelligent amateur in that field and he put it to the tests; there are valid tests for it. And he concluded that it was hallucination and not telepathy. Still (and he could see it coming) there would be a time when he would accept his hallucination and believe that the ursine was talking to him. And that would signal that he was crazy and no longer able to evade death there.

Carroll renounced (while he still had his wits) his future belief in the nonsense, just as a man put to torture may renounce anything he concedes or confesses or denies under duress.

Yet, whatever frame it was placed in, Snuffles talked to him from a distance. "Why do you think me a bear because I am in a bear skin? I do not think you a man, though you are in a man skin. You may be a little less. And why do you believe you will die more bravely than Daniel? The longer you run, the meaner will be your death. And you still do not know who I am?"

"No," said Brian Carroll aloud.

"No what?" asked Georgina Chantal.

SNUFFLES

"It seems that the bear is talking to me, that he has entered my mind."

"Me also. Could it be, or is it the narcotic fruit?"

"It couldn't be. It is hallucination brought on by the narcotics, and tiredness from travel, and lack of sleep—and our shock at seeing our friends killed by a boy turned into a monster. There are tests to distinguish telepathic reception from hallucination: objective corroboration, impossible at this time (with Snuffles in his present mood) and probably impossible at any time; sentient parallelism—surely uncertain, for I have more in common with millions of humans than with one pseudo-ursine; circumstantial validity and point-for-point clarity—this is negative, for I know myself to be fevered and confused and my senses unreliable in other matters. By every test that can be made, the indication is that it is not telepathy, that it is hallucination."

"But there isn't any way to be *sure*, is there, Brian?"

"None, Georgina; no more than I can prove that it is not a troup of Boy Scouts around a campfire that is causing pain and burning in my gullet, that it is really the narcotic fruit or something else I have eaten conspiring with my weariness and apprehension to discomfort me. I cannot prove it is not Boy Scouts and I cannot prove it is not telepathy, but I consider both unlikely."

"I don't think it is unlikely at all, Brian. I think that Snuffles is talking to me. When you get a little nuttier and tireder, then you'll believe it too."

"Oh, yes, I'll believe it then—but it won't be true."

"It won't matter if it's true or not. Snuffles will have gained his point. Do you know that Snuffles is king of this world?"

"No. What are you talking about?"

"He just told me he was. He told me that if I would help him catch you, he would let me go. But I won't do it. I have become fond of you, Brian. Did you know that I never did like men before?"

159

"Yes. You were called the iceberg."

"But now I like you very much."

"You have no one else left to like."

"It isn't that. It's the mood I'm in. And I won't help Snuffles catch you unless he gives me very much better reasons for it."

Damn the girl! If she believed Snuffles talked to her, then for all practical purposes he did. And, however the idea of a trade for her life had been implanted in her mind, it would grow there.

Now Snuffles talked to Brian Carroll again, and it was somehow a waste of time to intone the formality that it was hallucination only.

"You still do not know what I am, but you will have to learn it before you die. Hardy knew it at the last minute. Cross guessed it from the first. Phelan still isn't sure. He goes about and looks back at his body lying there, and he still isn't sure. Some people are very hard to convince. But the girl knew it and she spread out her hands.".

In his fever, that was the way the bear animal talked to him.

They ate leaves now and buds. They would have no more of the narcotic fruits even if they had to starve. But narcosis left them slowly, and the pursuit of them tightened.

It was just at sunset one day that diaster struck at Brian. The bear had nearly hypnotized him into immobility, talking inside his head. Georgina had started on before him and repeatedly called for him to follow, but for some reason he loitered. When Snuffles made his sudden sundown charge, there seemed no escaping him. Brian was trapped on a rimrock. Georgina had already taken a winding path to the plain below. Brian hesitated then held his ground for the bruin's charge. He believed that he could draw Snuffles on, and then break to the left or the right at the last instant, and perhaps the animal would plunge over the cliff.

But old Snuff modified but did not halt his charge at the last minute. He came in bottom-side first, like an elephant sliding bases, and he knocked Brian off the cliff.

There are few really subjective accounts of dying, since most who die do not live to tell about it. But the way it goes is this:

﹒ First one hangs in space; then he is charged by the madly rising ground armed with trees and rocks and weapons. After that is a painful sleep, and much later a dazed wakening.

III

He was traveling upside-down, that was sure, and roughly, though at a slow rate of speed. Perhaps that is the normal way for people to travel after they are dead. He was hung from the middle in an odd doubled-up manner, and seemed supported and borne along by something of a boatlike motion, yet of a certain resilience and strength that was more living than even a boat. It had a rough softness, this thing, and a pleasant fragrance.

But, though it was bright morning now, it was hard to get a good look at the thing with which he was in contact. All he could see was grass flowing slowly by, and heels.

Heels?

What was this all about? Heels and backs of calves, no more.

He was being carried, carried slung like a sack over her shoulder by Georgina. For the thing of the pleasant fragrance was Georgina Chantal.

She set him down then. It was a very rough valley they were in, and he saw that they had traveled perhaps four miles from the base of the rimrock; and Snuffles had settled down in the morning light a quarter of a mile behind them.

161

"Georgina, did you carry me all night?"

"Yes."

"How could you?"

"I changed shoulders sometimes. And you aren't very heavy. This is only a half-gravity planet. Besides, I'm very strong. I could have carried you even on Earth."

"Why wasn't I killed by the fall?"

"Snuffles says he isn't ready to kill you yet, that he could kill you any time he wanted to with the lightning or rock or poison berry. But you did hit terribly hard. I was surprised to be able to pick you up in one piece. And now Snuffles says that I have lost my last chance."

"How?"

"Because I carried you away from him before he could get down the cliff in the dark. Now he says he will kill me too."

"Snuff is inconsistent. If he could kill me any instant with the lightning, why would he be angered if you carried me away from him?"

"I thought of that too. But he says he has his own reasons. And that lightning—do you know that it doesn't lighten all the time everywhere on Bellota? Only in a big circle around Snuffles, as a tribute to him. I've noticed myself that when we get a big lead over him, we almost move clear out of the lightning sphere."

"Georgina, that animal doesn't really talk to us. It is only our imaginations. It is not accurate to so personify it."

"It may not be accurate, but if that isn't talk he puts out, then I don't know talk. And a lot of his talk he makes come true. But I don't care if he does kill me for saving you. I'm silly over you now."

"We are both of us silly, Georgina, from the condition we are in. But he can't talk to us. He's only an animal run amok. If it was anything else, it would mean that much of what we know is not so."

Brian had the full effect of it one sunny afternoon a couple of Bellota days later. He was dozing and Georgina was on guard when Snuffles began to talk inside his head.

"You insult me that you do not recognize my identity. When Hardy said that in many mythologies it was the Bear who made the world, he had begun to guess who I was. I am the creator and I made the world. I have heard that there are other worlds besides Bellota, and I am not sure whether I made them or not. But if they are there, I must have made them. They could not have made themselves. And this I did make.

"It isn't an easy thing, or all of you would have made them, and you have not. And there is pride in creation that you could not understand. You said that Bellota was made for fun. It was *not* made for fun. I am the only one who knows why it was made, for I made it. And it is not a little planet; it is a grand planet. I waited for you to confess your error and be amazed at it. Since you did not, you will have to die. I made you, so I can kill you if I like. I must have made you, since I made all. And if I did not, then I made other things, red squirrels and white birds.

"You have no idea of the achievement itself. I had very little to work with and no model or plans or previous experience. And I made mistakes. I would be the last to deny that. I miscalculated the gravity, a simple mathematical error that anyone could make. The planet is too small for the gravity, but I had already embodied the calculated gravity in other works that I did not choose to undo, and I had no material to make a larger planet. So what I have made I have made, and it will continue so. An error, once it is embodied, becomes a new truth.

"You may wonder why my birds have hair. I will confess it, I did not know how to make feathers, nor could you without template or typus. And you are puzzled that my butterflies sting and my hornets do not? But how was I to know that those fearfully colored monsters should have been harmless? It ill befits one who has never made even the smallest—but why do I try to explain this to you?

"You wonder if I am talking to you or if it is only a delusion of your mind. What is the difference? How could there be anything in your mind if I did not put it there? And do not be afraid of dying. Remember that nothing is lost. When I have the pieces of you, I will use them to make other things. That is the law of conservation of matter as I understand it.

"But do you know that the one thing desired by all is really praise? It is the impelling force, and a creator needs this more than anyone. Things and beings are made to give praise, and if they do not, they are destroyed again. You had every opportunity to give it, and instead you jeered.

"Did any of you ever make a world? I tell you that there are a million things to remember all at once. And there can be no such thing as a bad world, since each of them is a triumph. Whether it was that I made the others and I forgot them is only a premise; or whether I will make them in the future, and they are only now talked of out of their proper time. But some of your own mythologies indicate that I made your own.

"I would tell you more, only you would not understand it. But after I have conserved your matter, then you will know all these things."

"Snuffles is cranky with me today," said Georgina Chantal. "Is he also cranky with you?"

"Yes," said Brian Carroll.

"He says that he made Bellota. Did he tell you that too? Do you believe it?"

"He told me. I do not believe it. We are delirious. Snuffles cannot communicate."

"You keep saying that, but you aren't sure. He told me that when he chews us up he will take a piece of me and a piece of you and chew them together and make a new thing, since we are belatedly taken with each other. Isn't that nice?"

"How cozy."

"I wonder why he made the grass so sharp, though. There is no reason for it to be like that."

"Why, and what?"

"Snuffles. Why did he make the grass so sharp? My shoes are nearly gone and it's killing me."

"Georgina, hold onto what's left of your mind. Snuffles did not make the grass or anything else. He is only an animal, and we are sick and walking in delirium."

So they walked on a while, for evening had come. Then the voice of Snuffles came again inside the head of Brian.

"How was I to know that the grass should not be sharp? Are not all pointed things sharp? Who would have guessed that it should be soft? If you had told me gently, and without shaming me, I would have changed it at once. Now I will not. Let it wound you!"

So they walked on a while, for evening had come. Then days and nights.

"Brian, do you think that Snuffles knows the world is round?"

"If he made it, he must know it."

"Oh, yes, I had forgotten."

"Dammit, girl, I was being ironic! And you are now quite nutty, and I hardly less so. Of course he didn't make it. And of course he doesn't know that it's round. He's only an animal."

"Then we have an advantage back again."

"Yes. I'd noticed it before if I hadn't been so confused. We are more than halfway around the little planet. He is no longer between us and our weapons center, but he behaves as though he thought he was. We have no more than forty miles to go to it. We will step up our pace, though gradually. Our old camp valley is prominent enough so that we could recognize it within several miles either way, and we can navigate that close. And if he seems to say in your mind that he is onto our trick, do not believe him. The animal does not really talk to our minds."

But their narcosis still increased. "It isn't a narcotic belt," said Brian. "It is a narcotic season on all Bellota— a built-in saturnalia. But we have not been able to enjoy the carnival."

"Snuffles shows up well as a carnival king, though, don't you think? It is easier to believe in time of carnival that he made the cosmos. I went to the big carnival once in Nola when I was a little girl. There was a big bear wearing a crown on one of the floats, and I believe that he was king of the carnival. It wasn't an ordinary bear. I am sure now that it represented Snuffles, though I was only six years old when I saw it. Do you think that Snuffles' explanation of the law of gravity here is better than Phelan's?"

"More easily understandable at least than the corollary, and probably more honest. I always thought that the corollary also embraced a simple mathematical error and that Phelan stuck to it out of perversity."

"It is one thing to stick to an error. It is another to build a world to conform to it. Brian, do you know what hour it is?"

"It is the three hundred and twelfth since we were set down."

"And they return for us at the three hundred and thirty-sixth. We will be back at our campsite and in control by then, won't we?"

"If we are ever to make it back and be in control, we should make it by then. Are you tired, Georgina?"

"No. I will never again be tired. I have been walking in a dream too long for that. But I never felt more pleasurable than now. I look down at my feet which are a sorry mess, but they don't seem to be my feet. Only a little while ago I felt sorry for a girl in such a state, and then I came to half realize that the girl was me. But the realization didn't carry a lot of conviction. It doesn't seem like me."

166

"I feel disembodied myself. But I don't believe that this comical old body that I observe will carry me much farther."

"Snuffles is trying to talk to us."

"Yes, I feel him. No, dammit, Georgina, we will not give in to that nonsense. Snuffles is only a wounded old bear that is trailing us. But our hallucination is coming again. It will take a lot of theory to cover a dual hallucination."

"Hush, I want to hear what he says."

Then Snuffles began to talk inside the heads of the two of them.

"If you know and do not tell me, then you are guilty of a peculiar affront. A maker cannot remember everything, and I had forgotten some of the things that I had made before. But we are coming on a new world now that is very like Bellota. Can it be that I have only repeated myself, and that I did not improve each time? These hills here I made once before. If you know, then you must tell me now. It may be that I cannot wait to chew your brains to find out about it. How will I ever make a better world if I make them all alike?"

"He has forgotten that he made it round, Brian."

"Georgina, he did not make anything. It is our own minds trying to reassure us that he does not know we are ahead of him and going toward our weapons."

"But how do we both hear the same thing if he isn't talking to us?"

"I don't know. But I prefer it the way it is. I never did like easy answers."

Then there came the evening they were within sight of their original valley, and, if they moved at full speed through the night, they should reach their campsite very soon after dawn.

"But the weariness is beginning to creep up through the narcosis," said Brian. "Now I'm desiring the effect that we tried to avoid before."

"But what has happened?"

"I believe that the narcotic period of the planet is over. The carnival is coming to an end."

"Do you know something, Brian? We did not have to go around the world at all. At any time we could have separated and outmaneuvered him. He could not have intercepted both of us going toward the weapons pile if we went different ways. But we could not bear to part."

"That is a woman's explanation."

"Well, let's see you find another one. You didn't want to be parted from me, did you, Brian?"

"No, I didn't."

It was a rough, short night, but it would be the last. They moved in the agony of a cosmic hangover.

"I've become addicted," said Brian, "and the fruit has lost its numbing properties. I don't see how it is possible for anyone to be so tired."

"I'd carry you again if I weren't collapsing myself."

"Dammit, you couldn't! You're only a girl!"

"I am not only a girl! Nobody is only an anything. Our trouble here may have started with your thinking that Snuffles was only an animal; and he read your thoughts and was insulted."

"He did not read my thoughts. He *is* only an animal. And I will shoot his fuzzy hide full of holes when we get to our campsite. Let's keep on with it and not take any chances of his catching or passing us in the dark."

"How could Phelan's corollary apply to this planet and no other when he had never been here then?"

"Because, as I often suspected, Phelan had a touch of the joker in him and he composed it sardonically."

"Then he made it for fun. And do you still think that Bellota was made for fun?"

"The fun has developed a grotesque side to it. I am afraid I will have to put an end to a part of that fun. The dark is coming, and there is our campsite, and we are in the clear. I'll make it before I drop if I have to bust a lung. There's an elephant gun with a blaster attachment that I'll take to that fur-coated phony. We're going to have bear steak for breakfast."

He achieved the campsite. He had reached the wobbly state, but he still ran. He was inside the circle and at the gun stack, when a roar like double thunder froze his ears and his entrails.

He leaped back, fell, rolled, crawled, snaked his way out of reach; and the sudden shock of it bewildered him.

And there was Snuffles sitting in the middle of the supply dump and smoking the pipe of Billy Cross.

And when the words rattled inside Brian's head again, how could he be sure that it was hallucination and not the bear talking to him?

"You thought that I had forgotten that Bellota was round? If you knew how much trouble I had making it as round as it is, you would know that I could never forget it."

Georgina came up, but fell to her knees in despair when she saw that Snuffles was there ahead of them.

"I can't run any more, Brian, and I know that you can't. I am down and I can never get up again. How soon will they get here?"

"The Marines?"

"Yes, the ship."

"Too late to help us. I used to wish they would be late just once. I am getting that wish, but it isn't as amusing as I anticipated."

Snuffles knocked out his pipe then, as a man would; and laid it carefully on a rock. Then he came out and killed them: Georgina, the friendly iceberg, and Brian, who did hate a pat ending.

And Snuffles was still king of Bellota.

The report of the ship read in part:

"No explanation of the fact that no attempt seems to have been made to use the weapons, though two of the party were killed nearly a week later than the others.

All were mangled by the huge pseudo-ursine which seems to have run amok from eating the local fruit, seasonally narcotic. Impossible to capture animal without unwarranted delay of takeoff time. Gravitational incongruity must await fuller classification of data."

The next world that Snuffles made embodied certain improvements, and he did correct the gravity error, but it still contained many elements of the grotesque. Perfection is a very long, very hard road.

THUS WE FRUSTRATE CHARLEMAGNE

"WE'VE BEEN on some tall ones," said Gregory Smirnov of the Institute, "but we've never stood on the edge of a bigger one than this, nor viewed one with shakier expectations. Still, if the calculations of Epiktistes are correct, this will work."

"People, it will work," Epikt said.

This was Epiktistes the Ktistec machine? Who'd have believed it? The main bulk of Epikt was five floors below them, but he had run an extension of himself up to this little penthouse lounge. All it took was a cable, no more than a yard in diameter, and a functional head set on the end of it.

And what a head he chose! It was a sea-serpent head, a dragon head, five feet long and copied from an old carnival float. Epikt had also given himself human speech of a sort, a blend of Irish and Jewish and Dutch comedian patter from ancient vaudeville. Epikt was a comic to his last para-DNA relay when he rested his huge, boggle-eyed, crested head on the table there and smoked the biggest stogies ever born.

But he was serious about this project.

"We have perfect test conditions," the machine Epikt said as though calling them to order. "We set out basic texts, and we take careful note of the world as it is. If the world changes, then the texts should change here before our eyes. For our test pilot, we have taken that portion of our own middle-sized city that can be viewed from this fine vantage point. If the world in its past-present continuity is changed by our meddling, then the face of our city will also change instantly as we watch it.

"We have assembled here the finest minds and judgments in the world: eight humans and one Ktistec machine, myself. Remember that there are nine of us. It might be important."

The nine finest minds were: Epiktistes, the transcendent machine who put the "K" in Ktistec; Gregory Smirnov, the large-souled director of the Institute, Valery Mok, an incandescent lady scientist: her over-shadowed and over-intelligent husband Charles Cogsworth; the humorless and inerrant Glasser; Aloysius Shiplap, the seminal genius; Willy McGilly, a man of unusual parts (the seeing third finger on his left hand he had picked up on one of the planets of Kapteyn's Star) and no false modesty; Audifax O'Hanlon; and Diogenes Pontifex. The latter two men were not members of the Institute (on account of the Minimal Decency Rule), but when the finest minds in the world are assembled, these two cannot very well be left out.

"We are going to tamper with one small detail in past history and note its effect," Gregory said. "This has never been done before openly. We go back to an era that has been called 'A patch of light in the vast gloom,' the time of Charlemagne. We consider why that light went out and did not kindle others. The world lost four hundred years by that flame expiring when the tinder was apparently ready for it. We go back to that false dawn of Europe and consider where it failed. The year was 778, and the region was Spain. Charlemagne had entered alliance with Marsilies, the Arab king of Saragossa, against the Caliph Abd ar-Rahmen of Cordova. Charlemagne took such towns as Pamplona, Huesca and Gerona and cleared the way to Marsilies in Saragossa. The Caliph accepted the situation. Saragossa should be independent, a city open to both Moslems and Christians. The northern marches to the border of France should be permitted their Christianity, and there would be peace for everybody.

"This Marsilies had long treated Christians as equals

in Saragossa, and now there would be an open road from Islam into the Frankish Empire. Marsilies gave Charlemagne thirty-three scholars (Moslem, Jewish and Christian) and some Spanish mules to seal the bargain. And there could have been a cross-fertilization of cultures.

"But the road was closed at Roncevalles where the rear-guard of Charlemagne was ambushed and destroyed on its way back to France. The ambushers were more Basque than Moslems, but Charlemagne locked the door at the Pyrenees and swore that he would not let even a bird fly over that border thereafter. He kept the road closed, as did his son and his grandsons. But when he sealed off the Moslem world, he also sealed off his own culture."

"In his latter years he tried a revival of civilization with a ragtag of Irish half-scholars, Greek vagabonds and Roman copyists who almost remembered an older Rome. These weren't enough to revive civilization, and yet Charlemagne came close with them. Had the Islam door remained open, a real revival of learning might have taken place then rather than four hundred years later. We are going to arrange that the ambush at Roncevalles did not happen and that the door between the two civilizations was not closed. Then we will see what happens to us."

"Intrusion like a burglar bent," said Epikt.

"Who's a burglar?" Glasser demanded.

"I am," Epikt said. "We all are. It's from an old verse. I forget the author; I have it filed in my main mind downstairs if you're interested."

"We set out a basic text of Hilarius," Gregory continued. "We note it carefully, and we must remember it the way it is. Very soon, that may be the way it *was*. I believe that the words will change on the very page of this book as we watch them. Just as soon as we have done what we intend to do."

The basic text marked in the open book read:

THUS WE FRUSTRATE CHARLEMAGNE

The traitor, Gano, playing a multiplex game, with money from the Cordova Caliph hired Basque Christians (dressed as Saragossan Mozarabs) to ambush the rear-guard of the Frankish force. To do this it was necessary that Gano keep in contact with the Basques and at the same time delay the rear-guard of the Franks. Gano, however, served both as guide and scout for the Franks. The ambush was effected. Charlemagne lost his Spanish mules. And he locked the door against the Moslem world.

That was the text by Hilarius.

"When we, as it were, push the button (give the nod to Epiktistes), this will be changed," Gregory said. "Epikt, by a complex of devices which he has assembled, will send an Avatar (partly of mechanical and partly of ghostly construction), and something will have happened to the traitor Gano along about sundown one night on the road to Roncevalles."

"I hope the Avatar isn't expensive," Willy McGilly said. "When I was a boy we got by with a dart whittled out of slippery elm wood."

"This is no place for humor," Glasser protested. "Who did you, as a boy, ever kill in time, Willy?"

"Lots of them. King Wū of the Manchu, Pope Adrian VII, President Hardy of our own country, King Marcel of Auvergne, the philosopher Gabriel Toeplitz. It's a good thing we got them. They were a bad lot."

"But I never heard of any of them, Willy," Glasser insisted.

"Of course not. We killed them when they were kids."

"Enough of your fooling, Willy," Gregory cut it off.

"Willy's not fooling," the machine Epikt said. "Where do you think I got the idea?"

"Regard the world," Aloysius said softly. "We see our own middle-sized town with half a dozen towers of

174

pastel-colored brick. We will watch it as it grows or shrinks. It will change if the world changes."

"There's two shows in town I haven't seen," Valery said. "Don't let them take them away! After all, there are only three shows in town."

"We regard the Beautiful Arts as set out in the reviews here which we have also taken as basic texts," Audifax O'Hanlon said. "You can say what you want to, but the arts have never been in meaner shape. Painting is of three schools only, all of them bad. Sculpture is the heaps-of-rusted-metal school and the obscene tinker-toy effects. The only popular art, graffiti on mingitorio walls, has become unimaginative, stylized and ugly.

"The only thinkers to be thought of are the dead Teilhard de Chardin and the stillborn Sartre, Zielinski, Aichinger. Oh well, if you're going to laugh there's no use going on."

"All of us here are experts on something," Cogsworth said. "Most of us are experts on everything. We know the world as it is. Let us do what we are going to do and then look at the world."

"Push the button, Epikt!" Gregory Smirnov ordered.

From his depths, Epiktistes the Ktistec machine sent out an Avatar, partly of mechanical and partly of ghostly construction. Along about sundown on the road from Pamplona to Roncevalles, on August 14 of the year 778, the traitor Gano was taken up from the road and hanged on a carob tree, the only one in those groves of oak and beech. And all things thereafter were changed.

"Did it work, Epikt? Is it done?" Louis Lobachevski demanded. "I can't see a change in anything."

"The Avatar is back and reports his mission accomplished," Epikt stated. "I can't see any change in anything either."

"Let's look at the evidence," Gregory said.

The thirteen of them, the ten humans and the Ktistec,

Chresmoeidec and Proaisthematic machines, turned to the evidence and with mounting disappointment.

"There is not one word changed in the Hilarius text," Gregory grumbled, and indeed the basic text still read:

The king Marsilies of Saragossa, playing a multiplex game, took money from the Caliph of Cordova for persuading Charlemagne to abandon the conquest of Spain (which Charlemagne had never considered and couldn't have effected), took money from Charlemagne in recompense for the cities of the Northern marches being returned to Christian rule (though Marsilies himself had never ruled them); and took money from everyone as toll on the new trade passing through his city. Marsilies gave up nothing but thirty-three scholars, the same number of mules and a few wagonloads of book-manuscripts from the old Hellenistic libraries. But a road over the mountains was opened between the two worlds; and also a sector of the Mediterranean coast became open to both. A limited opening was made between the two worlds, and a limited reanimation of civilization was affected in each.

"No, there is not one word of the text changed," Gregory grumbled. "History followed its same course. How did our experiment fail? We tried, by a device that seems a little cloudy now, to shorten the gestation period for the new birth. It would not be shortened."

"The town is in no way changed," said Aloysius Shiplap. "It is still a fine large town with two dozen imposing towers of varicolored limestone and midland marble. It is a vital metropolis, and we all love it, but it is now as it was before."

"There are still two dozen good shows in town that I haven't seen," Valery said happily as she examined the billings. "I was afraid that something might have happened to them."

"There is no change at all in the Beautiful Arts as reflected in the reviews here that we have taken as basic texts," said Audifax O'Hanlon. "You can say what you want to, but the arts have never been in finer shape."

"It's a link of sausage," said the machine Chresmoeidy.

" 'Nor know the road who never ran it thrice,' " said the machine Proaisth. "That's from an old verse; I forget the author; I have it filed in my main mind in England if you're interested."

"Oh yes, it's the three-cornered tale that ends where it begins," said the machine Epiktistes. "But it is good sausage, and we should enjoy it; many ages have not even this much."

"What are you fellows babbling about?" Audifax asked without really wanting to know. "The art of painting is still almost incandescent in its bloom. The schools are like clustered galaxies, and half the people are doing some of this work for pleasure. Scandinavian and Maori sculpture are hard put to maintain their dominance in the field where almost everything is extraordinary. The impassioned-comic has released music from most of its bonds. Since speculative mathematics and psychology have joined the popular performing arts, there is considerably more sheer fun in life.

"There's a piece here on Pete Teilhard putting him into context as a talented science-fiction writer with a talent for outre burlesque. The Brainworld Motif was overworked when he tackled it, but what a shaggy comic extravaganza he did make of it! And there's Muldoom, Zielinski, Popper, Gander, Aichinger, Whitecrow, Hornwhanger—we owe so much to the juice of the cultists! In the main line there are whole congeries and continents of great novels and novelists.

"An ever . popular art, graffiti on mingitorio walls, maintains its excellence. Travel Unlimited offers a ninety-nine day art tour of the world keyed to the viewing

of the exquisite and hilarious miniatures on the walls of
its own rest rooms. Ah, what a copious world we live
in!"

"It's more grass than we can graze," said Willy Mc-
Gilly. "The very bulk of achievement is stupefying. Ah,
I wonder if there is subtle revenge in my choice of words.
The experiment, of course, was a failure, and I'm glad.
I like a full world."

"We will not call the experiment a failure since we
have covered only a third of it," said Gregory. "Tomorrow we will make our second attempt on the past. And,
if there is a present left to us after that, we will make
a third attempt the following day."

"Shove it, good people, shove it," the machine Epiktistes said. "We will meet here again tomorrow. Now
you to your pleasures, and we to ours."

The people talked that evening away from the machines where they could make foolish conjectures without being laughed at.

"Let's pull a random card out of the pack and go with
it," said Louis Lobachevski. "Let's take a purely intellectual crux of a little later date and see if the changing
of it will change the world."

"I suggest Ockham," said Johnny Konduly.

"Why?" Valery demanded. "He was the last and least
of the medieval schoolmen. How could anything he did
or did not do affect anything?"

"Oh no, he held the razor to the jugular," Gregory
said. "He'd have severed the vein if the razor hadn't
been snatched from his hand. There is something amiss
here, though. It is as though I remembered when things
were not so stark with Ockham, as though, in some
variant, Ockham's Terminalism did not mean what we
know that it did mean."

"Sure, let's cut the jugular," said Willy. "Let's find
out the logical termination of Terminalism and see just
how deep Ockham's razor can cut."

THUS WE FRUSTRATE CHARLEMAGNE

"We'll do it," said Gregory. "Our world has become something of a fat slob; it cloys; it has bothered me all evening. We will find whether purely intellectual attitudes are of actual effect. We'll leave the details to Epikt, but I believe the turning point was in the year 1323 when John Lutterell came from Oxford to Avignon where the Holy See was then situated. He brought with him fifty-six propositions taken from Ockham's Commentary on the Sentences, and he proposed their condemnnation. They were not condemned outright, but Ockham was whipped soundly in that first assault, and he never recovered. Lutterell proved that Ockham's nihilism was a bunch of nothing. And the Ockham thing did die away, echoing dimly through the little German courts where Ockham traveled peddling his wares, but he no longer peddled them in the main markets. Yet his viewpoint could have sunk the world, if indeed, intellectual attitudes are of actual effect."

"We wouldn't have liked Lutterell," said Aloysius. "He was humorless and he had no fire in him, and he was always right. And we would have liked Ockham. He was charming, and he was wrong, and perhaps we will destroy the world yet. There's a chance that we will get our reaction if we allow Ockham free hand. China was frozen for thousands of years by an intellectual attitude, one not nearly so unsettling as Ockham's. India is hypnotized into a queer stasis which calls itself revolution and which does not move—hypnotized by an intellectual attitude. But there was never such an attitude as Ockham's."

So they decided that the former chancellor of Oxford, John Lutterell, who was always a sick man, should suffer one more sickness on the road to Avignon in France, and that he should not arrive there to lance the Ockham thing before it infected the world.

"Let's get on with it, good people," Epikt rumbled the next day. "Me, I'm to stop a man getting from Oxford to Avignon in the year 1323. Well, come, come, take your places, and let's get the thing started." And Epiktistes' great sea-serpent head glowed every color as he puffed on a seven-branched pooka-dooka and filled the room with wonderful smoke.

"Everybody ready to have his throat cut?" Gregory asked cheerfully.

"Cut them," said Diogenes Pontifex, "but I haven't much hope for it. If our yesterday's essay had no effect, I cannot see how one English schoolman chasing another to challenge him in an Italian court in France, in bad Latin, nearly seven hundred years ago, on fifty-six points of unscientific abstract reasoning, can have effect."

"We have perfect test conditions here," said the machine Epikt. "We set out a basic text from Cobblestone's *History of Philosophy*. If our test is effective, then the text will change before our eyes. So will every other text, and the world.

"We have assembled here the finest minds and judgments in the world," the machine Epiktistes said, "ten humans and three machines. Remember that there are thirteen of us. It might be important."

"Regard the world," said Aloysius Shiplap. "I said that yesterday, but it is required that I say it again. We have the world in our eyes and in our memories. If it changes in any way, we will know it."

"Push the button, Epikt," said Gregory Smirnov.

From his depths, Epiktistes the Ktistec machine sent out an Avatar, partly of mechanical and partly of ghostly construction. And along about sundown on the road from Mende to Avignon in the old Languedoc district of France, in the year 1323, John Lutterell was stricken with one more sickness. He was taken to a little inn in the mountain country, and perhaps he died there. He did not, at any rate, arrive at Avignon.

"Did it work, Epikt?" Is it done?" Aloysius asked.

"Let's look at the evidence," said Gregory.

The four of them, the three humans and the ghost Epikt, who was a kachenko mask with a speaking tube, turned to the evidence with mounting disappointment.

"There is still the stick and the five notches in it," said Gregory. "It was our test stick. Nothing in the world is changed."

"The arts remain as they were," said Aloysius. "Our picture here on the stone on which we have worked for so many seasons is the same as it was. We have painted the bears black, the buffalos red and the people blue. When we find a way to make another color, we can represent birds also. I had hoped that our experiment might give us that other color. I had even dreamed that birds might appear in the picture on the rock before our very eyes."

"There's still rump of skunk to eat and nothing else," said Valery. "I had hoped that our experiment would have changed it to haunch of deer."

"All is not lost," said Aloysius. "We still have the hickory nuts. That was my last prayer before we began our experiment. 'Don't let them take the hickory nuts away,' I prayed."

They sat around the conference table that was a large flat natural rock, and cracked hickory nuts with stone fist-hammers. They were nude in the crude, and the world was as it had always been. They had hoped by magic to change it.

"Epikt has failed us," said Gregory. "We made his frame out of the best sticks, and we plaited his face out of the finest weeds and grasses. We chanted him full of magic and placed all our special treasures in his cheek pouches. So, what can the magic mask do for us now?"

"Ask it, ask it," said Valery. They were the four finest minds in the world—the three humans, Gregory, Aloysius and Valery (the *only* humans in the world unless you count those in the other valleys), and the ghost Epikt, a kachenko mask with a speaking tube.

"What do we do now, Epikt?" Gregory asked. Then he went around behind Epikt to the speaking tube.

"I remember a woman with a sausage stuck to her nose," said Epikt in the voice of Gregory. "Is that any help?"

"It may be some help," Gregory said after he had once more taken his place at the flat-rock conference table. "It is from an old (what's old about it? I made it up myself this morning) folk tale about the three wishes."

"Let Epikt tell it," said Valery. "He does it so much better than you do." Valery went behind Epikt to the speaking tube and blew smoke through it from the huge loose black-leaf uncured stogie that she was smoking.

"The wife wastes one wish for a sausage," said Epikt in the voice of Valery. "A sausage is a piece of deer-meat tied in a piece of a deer's stomach. The husband is angry that the wife has wasted a wish, since she could have wished for a whole deer and had many sausages. He gets so angry that he wishes the sausage might stick to her nose forever. It does, and the woman wails, and the man realized that he had used up the second wish. I forget the rest."

"You can't forget it, Epikt!" Aloysius cried in alarm. "The future of the world may depend on your remembering. Here, let me reason with that damned magic mask!" And Aloysius went behind Epikt to the speaking tube.

"Oh yes, now I remember," Epikt said in the voice of Aloysius. "The man used the third wish to get the sausage off his wife's nose. So things were the way they had been before."

"But we don't want it the way it was before!" Valery howled. "That's the way it is now, rump of skunk to eat, and me with nothing to wear but my ape cape. We want it better. We want deer skins and antelope skins."

"Take me as a mystic or don't take me at all," Epikt signed off.

"Even though the world has always been so, yet we have intimations of other things," Gregory said. "What folk hero was it who made the dart? And of what did he make it?"

"Willy McGilly was the folk hero," said Epikt in the voice of Valery, who had barely got to the speaking tube in time, "and he made it out of slippery elm wood."

"Could we make a dart like the folk hero Willy made?" Aloysius asked.

"We gotta," said Epikt.

"Could we make a slinger and whip it out of our own context and into—"

"Could we kill an Avatar with it before he killed somebody else?" Gregory asked excitedly.

"We sure will try," said the ghost Epikt, who was nothing but a kachenko mask with a speaking tube. "I never did like those Avatars."

You *think* Epikt was nothing but a kachenko mask with a speaking tube! There was a lot more to him than that. He had red garnet rocks inside him and real sea salt. He had powder made from beaver eyes. He had rattlesnake rattles and armadillo shields. He was the first Ktistec machine.

"Give me the word, Epikt," Aloysius cried a few moments later as he fitted the dart to the slinger.

"Fling it! Get that Avatar fink!" Epikt howled.

Along about sundown in an unnumbered year, on the Road from Nowhere to Eom, an Avatar fell dead with a slippery-elm dart in his heart.

"Did it work, Epikt? Is it done?" Charles Cogsworth asked in excitement. "It must have. I'm here. I wasn't in the last one."

"Let's look at the evidence," Gregory suggested calmly.

"Damn the evidence!" Willy McGilly cussed. "Remember where you heard it first."

"Is it started yet?" Glasser asked.

"Is it finished?" Audifax O'Hanlon questioned.

"Push the button, Epikt!" Diogenes barked. "I think I missed part of it. Let's try again."

"Oh, no, no!" Valery forbade. "Not again. That way is rump of skunk and madness."

.

NAME OF THE SNAKE

WHEN Pio Quindecimo—*Confiteantur Domino Misercordia ejus*—had proclaimed it, it was received (even by the faithful) with a measure of ennui. Contingent, speculative, rhetorical—it was not thought of as touching on practicality. Pio was not one of the outstanding Popes of the century.

The encyclical was titled modestly "*Euntes Ergo Docete Omnes*": "Going therefore Teach Ye *All*." Its substance was that this was a literal command of the Lord, and that the time had come to implement that command in its extreme meaning; that when the Lord had said "Go into all lands," He had not meant to go into all lands of one narrow earth only; that when the Lord had said "Teach Ye All," it was not meant to teach all men only . . . within the narrow framework in which we have considered the term "men."

Should the command be taken literally, its implementation would cause far-reaching activity. It was in the implementation of the command that Padreco Barnaby was now on that remote planet, Analos.

Could one call the Analoi humans? Had their skeletal remains been discovered on old Earth, they would unhesitatingly have been classed as human. The oddly formed ears—not really as large as they seemed—somewhat Gothic in their steepled upsweep, their slight caudal appendage, their remarkable facial mobility and chameleon-like complexions, these could not have been read from their bone remains. But how are we to say that their ears were more grotesque than our own? When did you last look at your own ears objectively? Are they not odd things to be sticking on the sides of a person's head?

"They are gargoyles," said an early visitor from Earth. Of course they were. The gargoyles had been copied by a still earlier visitor to Analos from Earth. But they were a lively and interesting bunch of gargoyles: mechanically civilized, ethically weird, artistically exciting. They were polished and polyglot, and in many ways more human than the humans.

On Analos, the Padreco was at first a guest of Landmaster, a leading citizen. Here the priest, speaking of his mission, first came up against the Wall.

"I can see what this might lead to, little priest," Landmaster told him when they discussed the situation. "It might even become bothersome to us—if we ever let anything bother us—if we had not passed beyond the stage where annoyance was possible. So long as you confined your activity to resident Earthlings and humans or that recension, there was no problem. Fortunately we do not fall within those categories. That being so, I do not see how your present aspirations can have any point of contact with us."

"You Analoi are sentient creatures of great natural intelligence, Landmaster. As such it is even possible that you have souls."

"We have souls that are fully realized. What could humans give to us who transcend humanity?"

"The Truth, the Way, the Life, the Baptism."

"We have the first three greatly beyond yourselves. The last—the crabbed rite of a dying sect—what could that give us?"

"Forgiveness of your sins."

"But we haven't any sins. That's the whole point about us. We've long since passed beyond that. You humans are still awkward and guilt-ridden. You are of a species which *as yet has no adult form*. Vicariously we may be the adult form of yourselves. The idea of sin is an aspect of your early awkwardness."

"Everybody has sins, Landmaster."

"Only according to your own childish thesis, little

priest. And consequent to that, you would reason that everybody must be saved—and by yourselves, a race of crop-eared, flat-faced children.

"But consider how meaningless it becomes in relation to ourselves, the Analoi. How could we sin? What would we have to sin about? Our procreation no longer follows the grotesque pattern of your own, and ours is without passion. You can see that ninety percent of your sin is already gone.

"What else is left to us? What other opportunity—if that is the word for it—have we for sinning? We have no poverty, no greed, no envy. Our metabolism is so regulated that neither sloth nor hysterical activity is possible. We have long ago attained a balance in all things; and 'sin' is only a form of unbalance.

"I have forgotten, little priest. What are the 'sins' of the childish races?"

"Pride, covetousness, lust, anger, gluttony, envy, sloth," said Padreco Barnaby. "These are the capital sins and the sources of sin. All others derive from them."

"Spoken like a valiant little mime. And nothing is derived but from a source. But you can see how completely we lack these seven stumbling blocks of children. Pride is only a misunderstanding of the nature of achievement; covetousness disappears when all that could be coveted has been acquired; lust is an adjunct to an arrangement that no longer has a counterpart in ourselves. Anger, gluttony, envy, sloth are only malfunctions. All malfunctions are subject to adjustment and correction, and we have corrected them."

Padreco Barnaby was defeated for the while, and he let his mind wander. He gazed over the countryside of Analos.

An early explorer has given his impression of that world:

"It was as though I were walking under water," he wrote. "This was not from any obstruction or resistance, for the atmosphere is lighter than Earth's. It was from a

187

sort of shimmering and wavering of the air itself and from the 'air shadows,' not clouds, that pass along like the running shadows of overhead waves. This, coupled with the flora (very like the underwater plants of Earth, though free-standing) gave me the feeling that I was walking on the bottom of the ocean."

To the Padreco it seemed as though he had been talking under water and that he had not been heard.

"What is the meaning of that giant kettle in the center of your main plaza, Landmaster?" he finally asked. "It seems quite old."

"It is a relic of our old race, and we keep it. We have a certain reverence for the past—even the obsoleted past. In minds as great as ours there is room even for relics."

"Then it has no present use?"

"No. But under a special condition we could revert to an ancient use of it. That need not concern you now."

A kettle, a giant kettle! You have no idea how grotesquely pot-bellied the thing was!

But the Padreco returned impotently to his main theme.

"There has to be sin, Landmaster! How else can there be salvation?"

"We have salvation, little priest. You haven't. How could you bring it to us?"

So Padreco Barnaby left Landmaster and went out to see if he could not discover sin somewhere on Analos. He asked a small boy about it.

"Sonny, do you know what sin is? Have you ever run across the thing?"

"Sir and stranger, sin is an archaic word for an outmoded thing. It is an appurtenance to an unclarified state of mind that still obtains on the more benighted worlds. The word and the concept behind it will pass into oblivion as soon as true light can be brought into those dark places."

Damnation!—a meaningless word on Analos: even the children of the gargoyles were too polite to be human.

"You little monster, do all the children on Analos talk like that?"

"All who are not deviationists would of necessity talk as I do. And 'monster,' as you call me with disapprobation, means a 'show-piece,' that which is displayed, a wonder. The late meaning of the word in the sense of a grotesque animal is an accretion. I gladly accept the name of monster in its true meaning. We are the Monsters of the Universe."

Damme, I believe that you are, the Padreco said to himself. *Polygot little prig!* He couldn't even cope with the children of the things.

"Sonny, do you ever have any fun?" he finally asked.

"Fun is another archaic word, but I am not sound on its meaning," said the boy. "Is it not related to the obsolete concept of sin?"

"Not directly, boy. Fun is the third side of a two-sided coin. It slips in. Or it used to."

"Sir and stranger, it is possible that you should take a course in corrective semantics."

"I may be taking one now. But what of the children who *are* deviationists? Where are they? And what are they like?"

"I don't know. If they don't pass their probationary period, we don't see them any more. I believe they are sent to another place."

"I have to find a little bit of sin somewhere," the Padreco mumbled to himself. "An honest man should be able to find it anywhere if he really inquires. On Earth the saying was that a taxi-driver would always know where to find it."

The Padreco hailed a taxi. A taxi is a circle. That is to say that one clambers over and sits in the single circular seat that faces inward. The Analoi are gregarious and like to gaze on the faces of their fellows. Only the shame-capable humans would wish to sit in unfacing rows. The driver sits above in an open turret, and dangles his head down to talk.

"Where would you go, stranger?" the driver asked the Padreco. There was one other passenger, a thoughtful man of early middle age.

"I'm looking for sin," the Padreco told the driver. "It's a tradition that taxi-drivers always know where to find it."

"Riddles is it, stranger? Let me deliver my other customer while I puzzle this one out. It's his last ride and that makes it important."

"How is it your last ride?" Padreco Barnaby asked the thoughtful man. Conversation was unavoidable in such a taxi. The facing was too direct to get out of it.

"Oh, my time has come," said the man, "a little earlier than with most. I've drunk the cup empty, so there's nothing left. It was a nice life—well, I suppose it was. Rather expected more out of it, but I see now that I shouldn't have. An adult will know when it's over. And they *do* make a clean end of it for you."

"*Deus meus*, is that the way it ends on Analos?"

"How else? Natural death has been pushed back so far that nobody could contemplate waiting for it. Should we drag out our lives and become abridged repetitious creatures like those of the lesser races? One goes quietly when he realizes that he has covered it all."

"But that is despair!"

"A little boy's word for a little boy's thing. Termination with dignity—that's the only way. Goodbye to you both. And to all."

The thoughtful man got out and entered the Terminators.

"Now what was the name of that thing you wanted to be taken to, stranger?" the taxi-driver asked the Padreco.

"Never mind. I may have found it already. I'll walk back."

There was something here that needed a name.

NAME OF THE SNAKE

He walked till he came to the buildings of the city
again, and the buildings distorted as he neared, them.
The edifices of Analos seem bulbous at near view, and
indeed they are built slightly so. Yet when seen at a
distance, due to a vagary of atmosphere called Towering by Earth meteorologists, they appear normal and
straight. The few buildings built to Earth specifications
seem pinched-in when viewed from afar, almost collapsing on themselves. But, to the Padreco, the pot-
bellied buildings of Analos made him feel a complete
alien. He was lost in this world, and he cried out:

"Oh, for the old familiar sins that one can get hold
of and denounce! In my book, Termination is not the
only way, and Dignity has another meaning. Where are
the people who sin like people? Is there nowhere a
healthy case of d.t.s or a hoppy in need of reform? Is
there no burglar I can call my brother? No golden-
hearted chippy who needs only be shown the right
way? Is there no thief or usurer or politician to strike
a note of reality? Hypocrites, wife-beaters, seducers,
demagogues, sleazy old perverters, where can I find
you? Answer me! I need you now!"

"Sir, sir, you are crying out in the street," a young
Analoi lady told him, "Are you ill? What are you calling out for?"

"Sin. A little sin, please, for the love of Christ. If
there is no sin in my cellar, then the foundation of my
house is not what I supposed."

"Hardly anyone uses sin any more, sir. What a peculiar
thing to be crying out in the street for! But I believe
there is one shop that still handles it. Here. I will write
you the address."

Padreco Barnaby took the address and ran to the shop.
But it was not what he sought. Sin was an old name of
a scent, but the name had been changed as no longer
conveying a meaning.

There were very many of these scent shops. Too
many. And the scent of the scent shops was not the

odor of sanctity. Was it possible that a new sensuality had taken the place of the old?

And the other shops—block after block of them—what were they for? What were the uses of the strange apparatus displayed in them? And why should they give that sticky feeling of menace?

The Padreco spent a long day wandering through the capital city of Analos. The pavements were green and artfully shadow-painted so as to resemble turf. The effect, however, was not that of placid nature; it was of a primordial wildness able to break through the thin shell at any time. And what was the new weirdness that came over him when he walked through the parks? The earlier explorer had been mistaken: the plants of Analos did not resemble the undersea plants of Earth; they resembled the undersea *animals*. They leered like devilfish and grinned like sharks.

It was here everywhere. But it had changed its name.

It was with shameful triumph that Padreco Barnaby first uncovered the sweeping outlines of the thing. It was with growing horror that he amassed the details. When he had enough of it, he went back to Landmaster, who was now with several others of his kind.

"Repent! Repent!" the Padreco called to them. "The ax is already laid to the roots. The tree that bears evil fruit will be cut down and cast into the fire!"

"Of what should we repent, little priest?" Landmaster asked.

"Of your sins! At once! Before it is too late!"

"I have explained to you that we have no sins, little priest; and that we could not have them according to our developing nature. Your repetition would annoy us ... if we ever let anything annoy us."

Landmaster made a sign to one of his fellows, who left them at once.

"What were the rather humorous names you gave them this morning?" Landmaster asked, turning again to the priest.

"You remember the names I gave. Now I give others. Too effete for the ancient sins themselves, you have the deadly shadows of them: presumption, establishment, ruthlessness, selfishness, satiety, monopoly, despair."

"An interesting argument. We have a Department of Interesting Arguments. You should go there and have it recorded."

"I will record it here. You practice infanticide, juvenicide, senectucide, suicide."

"Yes, the Gentle Terminators."

"You murder your own children who do not measure up to your atrocious norm."

"Judicious Selection."

"You have invented new lusts and perversions."

"Refined Amusements."

"There are the evil who are evil openly. There are the evil who hide their evil and deny that they are venomous. There are the ultimate in evil who keep the venom and change the Name of the Snake."

"I'm happy that we're the ultimate," said Landmaster. "We would be affronted by a lesser classification."

Padreco Barnaby raised his head.

"I smell wood burning," he said suddenly. "You no longer use wood for fuel here."

"In one case only," said Landmaster. "An ancient and seldom employed ritual of ours."

"Which?"

"You do not understand, little priest? Ten million Earth cartoons of the thing and still you do not understand them or comprehend their origin. What is the unvarying fate of the Missioner cast up on the Savage Shore?"

"You are not supposed to be savage."

"We revert, little priest. In this one case we revert. It is our ancient answer to the obstreperous missioner who persists in asking us the irksome question. We cannot allow ourselves to be irked."

Padreco Barnaby couldn't believe it. Even after they put him in the monstrous kettle he couldn't believe it. They were setting the long tables for the feast—and surely it was all a mistake!

"Landmaster! You people—you creatures—can't be serious!"

"Why no, little priest. This is a comical affair. Why should we be serious? Do you not think it comical that the missioner should be boiled in a pot?"

"No! No! It's ghastly!"

This had to be a dream—an underwater nightmare.

"Why did you make ten million comical cartoons of the thing if you didn't find it comic?" Landmaster asked with black pleasure.

"I didn't make them! Yes, I did—two of them—when I was a seminarian, and for our own little publication. Landmaster! The water is hellish hot!"

"Are we magicians that we can boil a man in cold water?"

"Not—not shoes and all?" the Padreco gasped. That seemed to be the ultimate outrage.

"Shoes and all, little priest. We like the flavor. What was your own favorite caption for the race-memory cartoons, Padreco?"

"You can't do this to me!"

"Yes, that was a good one. But it was the subscript, as I remember it, and the caption was 'Famous Last Words.' However, my own favorite, while it concerns anthropophagi, does not concern a missioner. It was the cannibal chief who said, 'My wife makes a fine soup. I'll miss her.' What was your favorite of the kettle jokes, Shareshuffler?"

Shareshuffler had a great two-tined fork, and he stuck it into Padreco Barnaby to see if he was done yet. The Padreco was far from done, and the clamor he set up made it impossible to hear Shareshuffler's own favorite of the folk jokes. This is a loss, for it was one of the best of them all.

NAME OF THE SNAKE

How loud the little priest was against the Analoi carrying out their ancient custom!

"A lobster doesn't make such a noise when he's boiled," chided Landmaster. "An oyster doesn't, and a Xtlecnutlico doesn't. Why should a man make such a noise? It would be irritating to us—if we ever let anything irritate us."

But they didn't—nothing at all. They were too developed a race to allow themselves to be irritated.

When the Padreco was finally done, they had him out of the kettle and polished him off. They dealt in the prescribed manner with the ancient menace, and they had a superb feast out of it too.

The Analoi weren't quite what they seemed. They had hid from themselves, and dealt in shadows instead of things. They had even changed the name of their nature ... but they hadn't changed their nature.

But on occasion they could still revert. They could stage an old-time, red-blooded, slumgullion-slurping, bone-gnawing dangeroo of a feast. Men and monsters, they did have one now!

Citizens, that Padreco had good stuff in him!

NARROW VALLEY

In the year 1893, land allotments in severalty were made to the remaining eight hundred and twenty-one Pawnee Indians. Each would receive one hundred and sixty acres of land and no more, and thereafter the Pawnees would be expected to pay taxes on their land, the same as the White-Eyes did.

"Kitkehahke!" Clarence Big-Saddle cussed. "You can't kick a dog around proper on a hundred and sixty acres. And I sure am not hear before about this pay taxes on land."

Clarence Big-Saddle selected a nice green valley for his allotment. It was one of the half dozen plots he had always regarded as his own. He sodded around the summer lodge that he had there and made it an all-season home. But he sure didn't intend to pay taxes on it.

So he burned leaves and bark and made a speech:

"That my valley be always wide and flourish and green and such stuff as that!" he orated in Pawnee chant style. "But that it be narrow if an intruder come."

He didn't have any balsam bark to burn. He threw on a little cedar bark instead. He didn't have any elder leaves. He used a handful of jack-oak leaves. And he forgot the word. How you going to work it if you forget the word?

"Petahauerat!" he howled out with the confidence he hoped would fool the fates.

"That's the same long of a word," he said in a low aside to himself. But he was doubtful. "What am I, a White Man, a burr-tailed jack, a new kind of nut to think it will work?" he asked. "I have to laugh at me. Oh well, we see."

He threw the rest of the bark and the leaves on the fire, and he hollered the wrong word out again.

And he was answered by a dazzling sheet of summer lightning.

"Skidi!" Clarence Big-Saddle swore. "It worked. I didn't think it would."

Clarence Big-Saddle lived on his land for many years, and he paid no taxes. Intruders were unable to come down to his place. The land was sold for taxes three times, but nobody ever came down to claim it. Finally, it was carried as open land on the books. Homesteaders filed on it several times, but none of them fulfilled the qualification of living on the land.

Half a century went by. Clarence Big-Saddle called his son.

"I've had it, boy," he said. "I think I'll just go in the house and die."

"Okay, Dad," the son Clarence Little-Saddle said. "I'm going in to town to shoot a few games of pool with the boys. I'll bury you when I get back this evening."

So the son Clarence Little-Saddle inherited. He also lived on the land for many years without paying taxes.

There was a disturbance in the courthouse one day. The place seemed to be invaded in force, but actually there were but one man, one woman, and five children. "I'm Robert Rampart," said the man, "and we want the Land Office."

"I'm Robert Rampart Junior," said a nine-year-old gangler, "and we want it pretty blamed quick."

"I don't think we have anything like that," the girl at the desk said. "Isn't that something they had a long time ago?"

"Ignorance is no excuse for inefficiency, my dear," said Mary Mabel Rampart, an eight-year-old who could easily pass for eight and a half. "After I make my report, I wonder who will be sitting at your desk tomorrow."

"You people are either in the wrong state or the wrong century," the girl said.

"The Homestead Act still obtains," Robert Rampart insisted. "There is one tract of land carried as open in this county. I want to file on it."

Cecilia Rampart answered the knowing wink of a beefy man at the distant desk. "Hi," she breathed as she slinked over. "I'm Cecilia Rampart, but my stage name is Cecilia San Juan. Do you think that seven is too young to play ingenue roles?"

"Not for you," the man said. "Tell your folks to come over here."

"Do you know where the Land Office is?" Cecilia asked.

"Sure. It's the fourth left-hand drawer of my desk. The smallest office we got in the whole courthouse. We don't use it much any more."

The Ramparts gathered around. The beefy man started to make out the papers.

"This is the land description," Robert Rampart began. "Why, you've got it down already. How did you know?"

"I've been around here a long time," the man answered.

They did the paper work, and Robert Rampart filed on the land.

"You won't be able to come onto the land itself, though," the man said.

"Why won't I?" Rampart demanded. "Isn't the land description accurate?"

"Oh, I suppose so. But nobody's ever been able to get to the land. It's become a sort of joke."

"Well, I intend to get to the bottom of that joke," Rampart insisted. "I will occupy the land, or I will find out why not."

"I'm not sure about that," the beefy man said. "The last man to file on the land, about a dozen years ago, wasn't able to occupy the land. And he wasn't able to say why he couldn't. It's kind of interesting, the look on their faces after they try it for a day or two, and then give it up."

The Ramparts left the courthouse, loaded into their camper, and drove out to find their land. They stopped at the house of a cattle and wheat farmer named Charley Dublin. Dublin met them with a grin which indicated he had been tipped off.

"Come along if you want to, folks," Dublin said. "The easiest way is on foot across my short pasture here. Your land's directly west of mine."

They walked the short distance to the border.

"My name is Tom Rampart, Mr. Dublin." Six-year-old Tom made conversation as they walked. "But my name is really Ramires, and not Tom. I am the issue of an indiscretion of my mother in Mexico several years ago."

"The boy is a kidder, Mr. Dublin," said the mother Nina Rampart, defending herself. "I have never been in Mexico, but sometimes I have the urge to disappear there forever."

"Ah yes, Mrs. Rampart. And what is the name of the youngest boy here?" Charley Dublin asked.

"Fatty," said Fatty Rampart.

"But surely that is not your given name?"

"Audifax," said five-year-old Fatty.

"Ah well, Audifax, Fatty, are you a kidder too?"

"He's getting better at it, Mr. Dublin," Mary Mabel said. "He was a twin till last week. His twin was named Skinny. Mama left Skinny unguarded while she was out tippling, and there were wild dogs in the neighborhood. When Mama got back, do you know what was left of Skinny? Two neck bones and an ankle bone. That was all."

"Poor Skinny," Dublin said. "Well, Rampart, this is the fence and the end of my land. Yours is just beyond."

"Is that ditch on my land?" Rampart asked.

"That ditch *is* your land."

"I'll have it filled in. It's a dangerous deep cut even

if it is narrow. And the other fence looks like a good one, and I sure have a pretty plot of land beyond it.

"No, Rampart, the land beyond the second fence belongs to Holister Hyde," Charley Dublin said. "That second fence is the *end* of your land."

"Now, just wait a minute, Dublin! There's something wrong here. My land is one hundred and sixty acres, which would be a half mile on a side. Where's my half-mile width?"

"Between the two fences."

"That's not eight feet."

"Doesn't look like it, does it, Rampart? Tell you what —there's plenty of throwing-sized rocks around. Try to throw one across it."

"I'm not interested in any such boys' games," Rampart exploded. "I want my land."

But the Rampart children *were* interested, in such games. They got with it with those throwing rocks. They winged them out over the little gully. The stones acted funny. They hung in the air, as it were, and diminished in size. And they were small as pebbles when they dropped down, down into the gully. None of them could throw a stone across that ditch, and they were throwing kids.

"You and your neighbor have conspired to fence open land for your own use," Rampart charged.

"No such thing, Rampart," Dublin said cheerfully. "My land checks perfectly. So does Hyde's. So does yours, if we knew how to check it. It's like one of those trick topological drawings. It really is half a mile from here to there, but the eye gets lost somewhere. It's your land. Crawl through the fence and figure it out."

Rampart crawled through the fence, and drew himself up to jump the gully. Then he hesitated. He got a glimpse of just how deep that gully was. Still, it wasn't five feet across.

There was a heavy fence post on the ground, designed for use as a corner post. Rampart up-ended it with some effort. Then he shoved it to fall and bridge the gully. But it fell short, and it shouldn't have. An eight-foot post should bridge a five-foot gully.

The post fell into the gully, and rolled and rolled and rolled. It spun as though it were rolling outward, but it made no progress except vertically. The post came to rest on a ledge of the gully, so close that Rampart could almost reach out and touch it, but it now appeared no bigger than a match stick.

"There is something wrong with that fence post, or with the world, or with my eyes," Robert Rampart said. "I wish I felt dizzy so I could blame it on that."

"There's a little game that I sometimes play with my neighbor Hyde when we're both out," Dublin said. "I've a heavy rifle and I train it on the middle of his forehead as he stands on the other side of the ditch apparently eight feet away. I fire it off then (I'm a good shot), and I hear it whine across. It'd kill him dead if things were as they seem. But Hyde's in no danger. The shot always bangs into that little scuff of rocks and boulders about thirty feet below him. I can see it kick up the rock dust there, and the sound of it rattling into those little boulders comes back to me in about two and a half seconds."

A bull-bat (poor people call it the night-hawk) raveled around in the air and zoomed out over the narrow ditch, but it did not reach the other side. The bird dropped below ground level and could be seen against the background of the other side of the ditch. It grew smaller and hazier as though at a distance of three or four hundred yards. The white bars on its wings could no longer be discerned; then the bird itself could hardly be discerned; but it was far short of the other side of the five-foot ditch.

A man identified by Charley Dublin as the neighbor Hollister Hyde had appeared on the other side of the little ditch. Hyde grinned and waved. He shouted something, but could not be heard.

"Hyde and I both read mouths," Dublin said, "so we can talk across the ditch easy enough. Which kid wants to play chicken? Hyde will barrel a good-sized rock right at your head, and if you duck or flinch you're chicken."

"Me! Me!" Audifax Rampart challenged. And Hyde, a big man with big hands, did barrel a fearsome jagged rock right at the head of the boy. It would have killed him if things had been as they appeared. But the rock diminished to nothing and disappeared into the ditch. Here was a phenomenon: things seemed real-sized on either side of the ditch, but they diminished coming out over the ditch either way.

"Everybody game for it?" Robert Rampart Junior asked.

"We won't get down there by standing here," Mary Mabel said.

"Nothing wenchered, nothing gained," said Cecilia. "I got that from an ad for a sex comedy."

Then the five Rampart kids ran down into the gully. Ran *down* is right. It was almost as if they ran down the vertical face of a cliff. They couldn't do that. The gully was no wider than the stride of the biggest kids. But the gully diminished those children, it ate them alive. They were doll-sized. They were acorn-sized. They were running for minute after minute across a ditch that was only five feet across. They were going, deeper in it, and getting smaller. Robert Rampart was roaring his alarm, and his wife Nina was screaming. Then she stopped. "What am I carrying on so loud about?" she asked herself. "It looks like fun. I'll do it too."

She plunged into the gully, diminished in size as the children had done, and ran at a pace to carry her a hundred yards away across a gully only five feet wide.

That Robert Rampart stirred things up for a while then. He got the sheriff there, and the highway patrolmen. A ditch had stolen his wife and five children, he said, and maybe had killed them. And if anybody laughs, there may be another killing. He got the colonel of the State National Guard there, and a command post set up. He got a couple of airplane pilots. Robert Rampart had one quality: when he hollered, people came.

He got the newsmen out from T-Town, and the eminent scientists, Dr. Velikof Vonk, Arpad Arkabaranan, and Willy McGilly. That bunch turns up every time you get on a good one. They just happen to be in that part of the country where something interesting is going on.

They attacked the thing from all four sides and the top, and by inner and outer theory. If a thing measures half a mile on each side, and the sides are straight, there just has to be something in the middle of it. They took pictures from the air, and they turned out perfect. They proved that Robert Rampart had the prettiest hundred and sixty acres in the country, the larger part of it being a lush green valley, and all of it being half a mile on a side, and situated just where it should be. They took ground-level photos then, and it showed a beautiful half-mile stretch of land between the boundaries of Charley Dublin and Hollister Hyde. But a man isn't a camera. None of them could see that beautiful spread with the eyes in their heads. Where was it?

Down in the valley itself everything was normal. It really was half a mile wide and no more than eighty feet deep with a very gentle slope. It was warm and sweet, and beautiful with grass and grain.

Nina and the kids loved it, and they rushed to see what squatter had built that little house on their land. A house, or a shack. It had never known paint, but paint would have spoiled it. It was built of split timbers dressed near smooth with ax and draw knife, chinked with white clay, and sodded up to about half its height. And there was an interloper standing by the little lodge.

"Here, here what are you doing on our land?" Robert Rampart Junior demanded of the man. "Now you just shamble off again wherever you came from. I'll bet you're a thief too, and those cattle are stolen."

"Only the black-and-white calf," Clarence Little-Saddle said. "I couldn't resist him, but the rest are mine. I guess I'll just stay around and see that you folks get settled all right."

"Is there any wild Indians around here?" Fatty Rampart asked.

"No, not really. I go on a bender about every three months and get a little bit wild, and there's a couple Osage boys from Gray Horse that get noisy sometimes, but that's about all," Clarence Little-Saddle said.

"You certainly don't intend to palm yourself off on us as an Indian," Mary Mabel challenged. "You'll find us a little too knowledgeable for that."

"Little girl, you might as well tell this cow there's no room for her to be a cow since you're so knowledgeable. She thinks she's a short-horn cow named Sweet Virginia. I think I'm a Pawnee Indian named Clarence. Break it to us real gentle if we're not."

"If you're an Indian where's your war bonnet? There's not a feather on you anywhere."

"How you be sure? There's a story that we got feathers instead of hair on— Aw, I can't tell a joke like that to a little girl! How come you're not wearing the Iron Crown of Lombardy if you're a white girl? How you expect me to believe you're a little white girl and your folks came from Europe a couple hundred years ago if you don't wear it? There are six hundred tribes, and only one of them, the Oglala Sioux, had the war bonnet, and only the big leaders, never more than two or three of them alive at one time, wore it."

"Your analogy is a little strained," Mary Mabel said. "Those Indians we saw in Florida and the ones at Atlantic City had war bonnets, and they couldn't very well have been the kind of Sioux you said. And just last night on the TV in the motel, those Massachusetts Indians put a war bonnet on the President and called him the Great White Father. You mean to tell me that they were all phonies? Hey, who's laughing at who here?"

"If you're an Indian where's your bow and arrow?" Tom Rampart interrupted. "I bet you can't even shoot one."

"You're sure right there," Clarence admitted. "I never shot one of those things but once in my life. They used to have an archery range in Boulder Park over in T-Town, and you could rent the things and shoot at targets tied to hay bales. Hey, I barked my whole forearm and nearly broke my thumb when the bow-string thwacked home. I couldn't shoot that thing at all. I don't see how anybody ever could shoot one of them."

"Okay, kids," Nina Rampart called to her brood. "Let's start pitching this junk out of the shack so we can move in. Is there any way we can drive our camper down here, Clarence?"

"Sure, there's a pretty good dirt road, and it's a lot wider than it looks from the top. I got a bunch of green bills in an old night charley in the shack. Let me get them, and then I'll clear out for a while. The shack hasn't been cleaned out for seven years, since the last time this happened. I'll show you the road to the top, and you can bring your car down it."

"Hey, you old Indian, you lied!" Cecilia Rampart shrilled from the doorway of the shack. "You *do* have a war bonnet. Can I have it?"

"I didn't mean to lie, I forgot about that thing," Clarence Little-Saddle said. "My son Clarence Bare-Back sent that to me from Japan for a joke a long time ago. Sure, you can have it."

All the children were assigned tasks carrying the junk out of the shack and setting fire to it. Nina Rampart and Clarence Little-Saddle ambled up to the rim of the valley by the vehicle road that was wider than it looked from the top.

"Nina, you're back! I thought you were gone forever,"

Robert Rampart jittered at seeing her again. "What— where are the children?"

"Why, I left them down in the valley, Robert. That is, ah, down in that little ditch right there. Now you've got me worried again. I'm going to drive the camper down there and unload it. You'd better go on down and lend a hand too, Robert, and quit talking to all these funny-looking men here."

And Nina went back to Dublin's place for the camper.

"It would be easier for a camel to go through the eye of a needle than for that intrepid woman to drive a car down into that narrow ditch," the eminent scientist Dr. Velikof Vonk said.

"You know how that camel does it?" Clarence Little-Saddle offered, appearing of a sudden from nowhere. "He just closes one of his own eyes and flops back his ears and plunges right through. A camel is mighty narrow when he closes one eye and flops back his ears. Besides, they use a big-eyed needle in the act."

"Where'd this crazy man come from?" Robert Rampart demanded, jumping three feet in the air. "Things are coming out of the ground now. I want my land! I want my children! I want my wife! Whoops, here she comes driving it. Nina, you can't drive a loaded camper into a little ditch like that! You'll be killed or collapsed!"

Nina Rampart drove the loaded camper into the little ditch at a pretty good rate of speed. The best of belief is that she just closed one eye and plunged right through. The car diminished and dropped, and it was smaller than a toy car. But it raised a pretty good cloud of dust as it bumped for several hundred yards across a ditch that was only five feet wide.

"Rampart, it's akin to the phenomenon known as looming, only in reverse," the eminent scientist Arpad Arkabaranan explained as he attempted to throw a rock across the narrow ditch. The rock rose very high in the air, seemed to hang at its apex while it diminished to the size of a grain of sand, and then fell into the ditch

not six inches of the way across. There isn't anybody
going to throw across a half-mile valley even if it looks
five feet. "Look at a rising moon sometimes, Rampart.
It appears very large, as though covering a great sector
of the horizon, but it only covers one-half of a degree. It
is hard to believe that you could set seven hundred and
twenty of such large moons side by side around the
horizon, or that it would take one hundred and eighty
of the big things to reach from the horizon to a point
overhead. It is also hard to believe that your valley is
five hundred times as wide as it appears, but it has
been surveyed, and it is."

"I want my land. I want my children. I want my
wife," Robert chanted dully. "Damn, I let her get away
again."

"I tell you, Rampy," Clarence Little-Saddle squared
on him, "a man that lets his wife get away twice doesn't
deserve to keep her. I give you till nightfall; then you
forfeit. I've taken a liking to the brood. One of us is
going to be down there tonight."

After a while a bunch of them were off in that little
tavern on the road between Cleveland and Osage. It
was only half a mile away. If the valley had run in the
other direction, it would have been only six feet away.

"It is a psychic nexus in the form of an elongated
dome," said the eminent scientist Dr. Velikof Vonk. "It
is maintained subconsciously by the concatenation of at
least two minds, the stronger of them belonging to a
man dead for many years. It has apparently existed for
a little-less than a hundred years, and in another hundred years it will be considerably weakened. We know
from our checking out folk tales of Europe as well as
Cambodia that these ensorceled areas seldom survive for
more than two hundred and fifty years. The person who
first set such a thing in being will usually lose interest
in it, and in all wordly things, within a hundred years
of his own death. This is a simple thanato-psychic limita-

tion. As a short-term device, the thing has been used several times as a military tactic.

"This psychic nexus, as long as it maintains itself, causes group illusion, but it is really a simple thing. It doesn't fool birds or rabbits or cattle or cameras, only humans. There is nothing meteorological about it. It is strictly psychological. I'm glad I was able to give a scientific explanation to it or it would have worried me."

It is continental fault coinciding with a noospheric fault," said the eminent scientist Arpad Arkabaranan. "The valley really is half a mile wide, and at the same time it really is only five feet wide. If we measured correctly, we would get these dual measurements. Of course it is meteorological! Everything including dreams is meteorological. It is the animals and cameras which are fooled, as lacking a true dimension; it is only humans who see the true duality. The phenomenon should be common along the whole continental fault where the earth gains or loses half a mile that has to go somewhere. Likely it extends through the whole sweep of the Cross Timbers. Many of those trees appear twice, and many do not appear at all. A man in the proper state of mind could farm that land or raise cattle on it, but it doesn't really exist. There is a clear parallel in the Luftspiegelungthal sector in the Black Forest of Germany which exists, or does not exist, according to the circumstances and to the attitude of the beholder. Then we have the case of Mad Mountain in Morgan County, Tennessee, which isn't there all the time, and also the Little Lobo Mirage south of Presidio, Texas, from which twenty thousand barrels of water were pumped in one two-and-a-half-year period before the mirage reverted to mirage status. I'm glad I was able to give a scientific explanation to this or it would have worried me."

"I just don't understand how he worked it," said the eminent scientist Willy McGilly. "Cedar bark, jack-oak leaves, and the world 'Petahauerat.' The thing's impossible! When I was a boy and we wanted to make a hide-out, we used bark from the skunk-spruce tree, the leaves · of a box-elder, and the word was 'Boadicea.' All three elements are wrong here. I cannot find a scientific explanation for it, and it does worry me."

They went back to Narrow Valley. Robert Rampart was still chanting dully: "I want my land. I want my children. I want my wife."

Nina Rampart came chugging up out of the narrow ditch in the camper and emerged through that little gate a few yards down the fence row.

"Supper's ready and we're tired of waiting for you, Robert," she said. "A fine homesteader you are! Afraid to come onto your own land! Come along now; I'm tired of waiting for you."

"I want my land! I want my children! I want my wife!" Robert Rampart still chanted. "Oh, there you are, Nina. You stay here this time. I want my land! I want my children! I want an answer to this terrible thing."

"It is time we decided who wears the pants in this family," Nina said stoutly. She picked up her husband, slung him over her shoulder, carried him to the camper and dumped him in, slammed (as it seemed) a dozen doors at once, and drove furiously down into the Narrow Valley, which already seemed wider.

Why, that place was getting normaler and normaler by the minute! Pretty soon it looked almost as wide as it was supposed to be. The psychic nexus in the form of an elongated dome had collapsed. The continental fault that coincided with the noospheric fault had faced facts and decided to conform. The Ramparts were in effective possession of their homestead, and Narrow Valley was as normal as any place anywhere.

"I have lost my land," Clarence Little-Saddle moaned. "It was the land of my father Clarence Big-Saddle, and I meant it to be the land of my son Clarence Bare-Back. It looked so narrow that people did not notice how wide it was, and people did not try to enter it. Now I have lost it."

Clarence Little-Saddle and the eminent scientist Willy McGilly were standing on the edge of Narrow Valley, which now appeared its true half-mile extent. The moon was just rising, so big that it filled a third of the sky. Who would have imagined that it would take a hundred and eight of such monstrous things to reach from the horizon to a point overhead, and yet you could sight it with sighters and figure it so.

"I had a little bear-cat by the tail and I let go," Clarence groaned. "I had a fine valley for free, and I have lost it. I am like that hard-luck guy in the funny-paper or Job in the Bible. Destitution is my lot."

Willy McGilly looked around furtively. They were alone on the edge of the half-mile-wide valley.

"Let's give it a booster shot," Willy McGilly said.

Hey, those two got with it! They started a snapping fire and began to throw the stuff onto it. Bark from the dog-elm tree—how do you know it won't work?

It *was* working! Already the other side of the valley seemed a hundred yards closer, and there were alarmed noises coming up from the people in the valley.

Leaves from a black locust tree—and the valley narrowed still more! There was, moreover, terrified screaming of both children and big people from the depths of Narrow Valley, and the happy voice of Mary Mabel Rampart chanting "Earthquake! Earthquake!"

"That my valley be always wide and flourish and such stuff, and green with money and grass!" Clarence Little-Saddle orated in Pawnee chant style, "but that it be narrow if intruders come, smash them like bugs!"

People, that valley wasn't over a hundred feet wide now, and the screaming of the people in the bottom of the valley had been joined by the hysterical coughing of the camper car starting up.

Willy and Clarence threw everything that was left

on the fire. But the word? The word? Who remembers the word?

"Corsicanatexas!" Clarence Little-Saddle howled out with confidence he hoped would fool the fates.

He was answered not only by a dazzling sheet of summer lightning, but also by thunder and raindrops.

"Chahiksi!" Clarence Little-Saddle swore. "It worked. I didn't think it would. It will be all right now. I can use the rain."

The valley was again a ditch only five feet wide.

The camper car struggled out of Narrow Valley through the little gate. It was smashed flat as a sheet of paper, and the screaming kids and people in it had only one dimension.

"It's closing in! It's closing in!" Robert Rampart roared, and he was no thicker than if he had been made out of cardboard.

"We're smashed like bugs," the Rampart boys intoned. "We're thin like paper."

"*Mort, ruine, ecrasement!*" spoke-acted Cecilia Rampart like the great tragedienne she was.

"Help! Help!" Nina Rampart croaked, but she winked at Willy and Clarence as they rolled by. "This home-steading jag always did leave me a little flat."

"Don't throw those paper dolls away. They might be the Ramparts," Mary Mabel called.

The camper car coughed again and bumped along on level ground. This couldn't last forever. The car was widening out as it bumped along.

"Did we overdo it, Clarence?" Willy McGilly asked. "What did one flat-lander say to the other?"

"Dimension of us never got around," Clarence said. "No, I don't think we overdid it, Willy. That car must be eighteen inches wide already, and they all ought to be normal by the time they reach the main road. The next time I do it, I think I'll throw wood-grain plastic on the fire to see who's kidding who."

POLITY AND CUSTOM OF THE CAMIROI

ABSTRACT FROM REPORT OF FIELD GROUP FOR EXAMINA-
TION OF OFF-EARTH CUSTOMS AND CODEXES TO THE
COUNCIL FOR GOVERNMENT RENOVATION AND LEGAL RE-
THINKING.

Extract from the day book of Paul Piggott, political
analyst:

Making appointments with the Camiroi is proverbial-
ly like building with quicksilver. We discovered this
early. But they do have the most advanced civilization of any of the four human worlds. And we did have
a firm invitation to visit the planet Camiroi and to in-
vestigate customs. And we had the promise that we
would be taken in hand immediately on our arrival by
a group parallel to our own.

But there was no group to meet us at the Sky-Port.

"Where is the Group for the Examination of Customs
and Codexes?" we asked the girl who was on duty as
Information Factor at the Sky-Port.

"Ask that post over there," she said. She was a young
lady of mischievous and almost rakish mien.

"I hope we are not reduced to talking to posts," said
our leader, Charles Chosky, "but I see that it is some
sort of communicating device. Does the post talk English, young lady?"

"The post understands the fifty languages that all Camiroi know," the young lady said. "On Camiroi, even
the dogs speak fifty languages. Speak to it."

"I'll try it," said Mr. Chosky. "Ah, post, we were to
be taken in hand by a group parallel to our own. Where
can we find the Group for the Examination of Customs
and Codexes?"

"Duty! Duty!" cried the post in a girlish voice that was somehow familiar. "Three for a group! Come, come, be constituted!"

"I'll be one," said a pleasant-looking Camiroi, striding over.

"I'll be another," said a teen-age sproutling boy of the same species.

"One more, one more!" cried the post. "Oh, here comes my relief. I'll be the other one to form the group. Come, come, let's get started. What do you want to see first, good people?"

"How can a post be a member of an ambulatory group?" Charles Chosky asked.

"Oh, don't be quaint," said the girl who had been the information factor and also the voice of the post. She had come up behind us and joined us. "Sideki and Nautes, we become a group for cozening Earthlings," she said. "I am sure you heard the rather humorous name they gave it."

"Are you as a group qualified to give us the information we seek?" I asked.

"Every citizen of Camiroi is qualified, in theory, to give sound information on every subject," said the teenage sproutling.

"But in practice it may not be so," I said, my legal mind fastening onto his phrase.

"The only difficulty is our over-liberal admission to citizenship," said Miss Diayggeia, who had been the voice of the post and the Information Factor. "Any person may become a citizen of Camiroi if he has resided here for one oodle. Once it was so that only natural leaders traveled space, and they qualified. Now, however, there are subsidized persons of no ability who come. They do not always conform to our high standard of reason and information."

"Thanks," said our Miss Holly Holm, "and how long is an oodle?"

"About fifteen minutes," said Miss Dia. "The post will register you now if you wish."

The post registered us, and we became citizens of Camiroi.

"Well, come, come, fellow citizens, what can we do for you?" asked Sideki, the pleasant-looking Camiroi who was the first member of our host group.

"Our reports of the laws of Camiroi seem to be a mixture of travelers' tales and nonsense," I said. "We want to find how a Camiroi law is made and how it works."

"So, make one, citizens, and see how it works," said Sideki. "You are now citizens like any other citizens, and any three of you can band together and make a law. Let us go down to Archives and enact it. And you be thinking what sort of law it will be as we go there."

We strode through the contrived and beautiful parklands and groves which were the roofs of Camiroi City. The extent was full of fountains and waterfalls, and streams with bizarre bridges over them. Some were better than others. Some were better than anything we had ever seen anywhere.

"But I believe that I myself could design a pond and weir as good as this one," said Charles Chosky, our leader. "And I'd have some of those bushes that look like Earth sumac in place of that cluster there; and I'd break up that pattern of rocks and tilt the layered massif behind it, and bring in a little of that blue moss—"

"You see your duty quickly, citizen," said Sideki. "You should do all this before this very day is gone. Make it the way you think best, and remove the plaque that is there. Then you can dictate your own plaque to any of the symbouleutik posts, and it will be made and set in. 'My composition is better than your composition,' is the way most plaques read, and sometimes a scenery composer will add something humorous like 'and my dog can whip your dog.' You can order all necessary materials from the same post there, and most citizens prefer to do the work with their own hands. This system works for gradual improvement. There are many Consensus Masterpieces that remain year after year; and the ordinary work is subject to constant turnover. There, for instance, is a tree which was not there this morning and which should not be there tonight. I'm sure that one of you can design a better tree."

"I can," said Miss Holly, "and I will do so today."

We descended from the roof parklands in the lower streets of Camiroi City, and went to Archives.

"Have you thought of a new law yet?" Miss Dia asked when we were at Archives. "We don't expect brilliance from such new citizens, but we ask you not to be ridiculous."

Our leader, Charles Chosky, drew himself up to full height and spoke:

"We promulgate a law that a permanent group be set up on Camiroi to oversee and devise regulations for all random and hasty citizens' groups with the aim of making them more responsible, and that a full-scale review of such groups be held yearly."

"Got it?" Miss Dia called to an apparatus there in Archives.

"Got it," said the device. It ground its entrails and coughed up the law, inscribed on bronze, and set it in a law niche.

"The echo is deafening," said our Miss Holly, pretending to listen.

"Yes. What is the effect of what we have done?" I asked.

"Oh, the law is in effect," said young Nautes. "It has been weighed and integrated into the corpus of laws. It is already considered in the instructions that the magistrate coming on duty in a short time (usually a citizen will serve as magistrate for one hour a month) must scan before he takes his seat. Possibly in this session he will assess somebody guilty of a misdemeanor to think about this problem for ten minutes and then to attach an enabling act to your law."

"But what if some citizens' group passes a silly law?" our Miss Holly asked.

"They do it often. One of them has just done so. But it will be repealed quickly enough," said Miss Dia of the Camiroi. "Any citizen who has his name on three laws deemed silly by general consensus shall lose his citizenship for one year. A citizen who so loses his citizenship twice shall be mutilated, and the third time he shall be killed. This isn't an extreme ruling. By that time he would have participated in nine silly laws. Surely that's enough."

"But, in the meantime, the silly laws remain in effect?" our Mr. Chosky asked.

"Not likely," said Sideki. "A law is repealed thus: any citizen may go to Archives and remove any law, leaving the statement that he has abolished the law for his own reasons. He is then required to keep the voided law in his own home for three days. Sometimes the citizen or citizens who first passed the law will go to the house of the abolitionist. Occasionally they will fight to the death with ritual swords, but most often they will parley. They may agree to have the law abolished. They may agree to restore the law. Or they may together work out a new law that takes into account the objections to the old."

"Then every Camiroi law is subject to random challenge?" Chosky asked.

"Not exactly," said Miss Dia. "A law which has stood unchallenged and unappealed for nine years becomes privileged. A citizen wishing to abolish such a law by removal must leave in its place not only his declaration of removal but also three fingers of his right hand as earnest of his seriousness in the matter. But a magistrate or a citizen going to reconstitute the law has to contribute only one of his fingers to the parley."

"This seems to me to favor the establishment," I said.

"We have none," said Sideki. "I know that is hard for Earthlings to understand."

"But is there no senate or legislative body on Cammiroi, or even a president?" Miss Holly asked.

"Yes, there's a president," said Miss Dia, "and he is actually a dictator or tyrant. He is chosen by lot for a term of one week. Any of you could be chosen for the term starting tomorrow, but the odds are against it. We do not have a permanent senate, but often there are hasty senates constituted, and they have full powers."

"Such bodies having full powers is what we want to study," I said. "When will the next one be constituted, and how will it act?"

"So, constitute yourselves one now and see how you act," said young Nautes. "You simply say, 'We constitute ourselves a Hasty Senate or Camiroi with full powers.' Register yourselves at the nearest symbouleutic post, and study your senate introspectively."

"Could we fire the president-dictator?" Miss Holly asked.

"Certainly," said Sideki, "but a new president would immediately be chosen by lot; and your senate would not carry over to the new term, nor could any of you three partake of a new senate until a full presidential term had passed. But I wouldn't, if I were you, form a senate to fire the present president. He is very good with the ritual sword."

"Then citizens do actually fight with them yet?" Mr. Chosky asked.

"Yes, any private citizen may at any time challenge any other private citizen for any reason, or for none. Sometimes, but not often, they fight to the death, and they may not be interfered with. We call these decisions the Court of Last Resort."

Reason says that the legal system on Camiroi cannot be as simple as this, and yet it seems to be. Starting with the thesis that every citizen of Camiroi should be able to handle every assignment or job on Camiroi, these people have cut organization to the minimum. These things we consider fluid or liberal about the legal system of Camiroi. Hereafter, whenever I am tempted to think of some law or custom of Earth as liberal, I will pause. I will hear Camiroi laughing.

On the other hand, there are these things which I consider adamant or conservative about the laws of Camiroi: ɪ

No assembly on Camiroi for purposes of entertainment may exceed thirty-nine persons. No more than this number may witness any spectacle or drama, or hear a musical presentation, or watch a sporting event. This is to prevent the citizens from becoming mere spectators rather than originators or partakers. Similarly, no writing—other than certain rare official promulgations—may be issued in more than thirty-nine copies in one month. This, it seems to us, is a conservative ruling to prevent popular enthusiasms.

A father of a family who twice in five years appeals to specialists for such things as simple surgery for members of his household, or legal or financial or medical advice, or any such things as he himself should be capable of doing, shall lose his citizenship. It seems to us that this ruling obstructs the Camiroi from the full fruits of progress and research. They say, however, that it compels every citizen to become an expert in everything.

Any citizen who pleads incapacity when chosen by lot to head a military operation or a scientific project or a trade combine shall lose his citizenship and suffer mutilation. But one who assumes such responsibility, and then fails in the accomplishment of the task, shall suffer the loss and the mutilation only for two such failures.

Both cases seem to us to constitute cruel and unusual punishment.

Any citizen chosen by lot to provide a basic invention or display a certain ingenuity when there is corporate need for it, and who fails to provide such invention, shall be placed in such a position that he will lose his life unless he displays even greater ingenuity and invention than was originally called for.

This seems to us to be unspeakably cruel.

There is an absolute death penalty for impiety. But to the question of what constitutes impiety, we received a startling answer:

"If you have to ask what it is, then you are guilty of it. For piety is comprehension of the basic norms. Lack of awareness of the special Camiroi context is the greatest impiety of all. Beware, new citizens! Should a person more upright and less indulgent than myself have heard your question, you might be executed before nightrise."

The Camiroi, however, are straight-faced kidders. We do not believe that we were in any danger of execution, but we had been told bluntly not to ask questions of a certain sort.

CONCLUSION: Inconclusive. We are not yet able to understand the true legal system of Camiroi, but we have begun to acquire the viewpoint from which it may be studied. We recommend continuing study by a permanent resident team in this field.

—Paul Piggott,
Political Analyst

From the journey book of Charles Chosky, chief of field group:

The basis of Camiroi polity and procedure is that any Camiroi citizen should be capable of filling any job on or pertaining to the planet. If it is ever the case that even one citizen should prove incapable of this, they say, then their system has already failed.

"Of course, it fails many times every day," one of their men explained to me, "but it does not fail completely. It is like a man in motion. He is falling off-balance at every step, but he saves himself, and so he

strides. Our polity is always in motion. Should it come
to rest, it would die."

"Have the Camiroi a religion?" I asked citizen after
citizen of them.

"I think so," one of them said finally. "I believe that
we do have that, and nothing else. The difficulty is in
the word. Your Earth English word may come from
religionem or from *relegionem*; it may mean a legality,
or it may mean a revelation. I believe it is a mixture of
the two concepts; with us it is. Of course we have a
religion. What else is there to have?"

"Could you draw a parallel between Camiroi and
Earth religion?" I asked him.

"No, I couldn't," he said bluntly. "I'm not being rude.
I just don't know how."

But another intelligent Camiroi gave me some ideas
on it.

"The closest I could come to explaining the difference," he said, "is by a legend that is told (as our
Camiroi phrase has it) with the tongue so far in the
cheek that it comes out the vulgar body aperture."

"What is the legend?" I asked him.

"The legend is that men (or whatever local creatures)
were tested on all the worlds. On some of the worlds,
men persevered in grace. These have become the transcendent worlds, asserting themselves as stars rather than
planets and swallowing their own suns, becoming fully
incandescent in their merged persons living in grace
and light. The more developed of them are those closed
bodies which we know only by inference, so powerful
and contained that they let no light or gravity or other
emission escape them. They become of themselves
closed and total universes, of their own space and outside of - what we call space, perfect in their merged
mentality and spirit.

"Then there are the worlds like Earth where men did
fall from grace. On these worlds, each person contains
an interior abyss and is capable both of great heights

and depths. By our legend, the persons of these worlds, after their fall, were condemned to live for thirty thousand generations in the bodies of animals and were then permitted to begin their slow and frustrating ascent back to remembered personhood.

"But the case of Camiroi was otherwise. We do not know whether there are further worlds of our like case. The primordial test-people of Camiroi did not fall. And they did not persevere. They hesitated. They could not make up their minds. They thought the matter over, and then they thought it over some more. Camiroi was therefore doomed to think matters over forever.

"So we are the equivocal people, capable of curious and continuing thought. But we have a hunger both for the depths and the heights which we have missed. To be sure, our Golden Mediocrity, our serene plateau, is higher than the heights of most worlds, higher than those of Earth, I believe. But it has not the exhilaration of height."

"But you do not believe in legends," I said.

"A legend is the highest scientific statement when it is the only statement available," the Camiroi said. "We are the people who live according to reason. It makes a good life, but it lacks salt. You people have a literature of Utopias. You value their ideals highly, and they do have some effect on you. Yet you must feel that they all have this quality of the insipid. And according to Earth standards, we are a Utopia. We are a world of the third case.

"We miss a lot. The enjoyment of poverty is generally denied to us. We have a certain hunger for incompetence, which is why some Earth things find a welcome here: bad Earth music, bad Earth painting and sculpture and drama, for instance. The good we can produce ourselves. The bad we are incapable of, and must import. Some of us believe that we need it in our diet."

"If this is true, your position seems enviable to me," I said.

"Yours isn't," he said, "and yet you are the most complete. You have both halves, and you have your numbers. We know, of course, that the Giver has never given a life anywhere until there was real need for it, and that everything born or created has its individual part to play. But we wish the Giver would be more generous to us in this, and it is in this particularly that we envy Earth.

"A difficulty with us is that we do our great deeds at too young an age and on distant worlds. We are all of us more or less retired by the age of twenty-five, and we have all had careers such as you would not believe. We come home then to live maturely on our mature world. It's perfect, of course, but of a perfection too small. We have everything—except the one thing that matters, for which we cannot even find a name."

I talked to many of the intelligent Camiroi on our short stay there. It was often difficult to tell whether they were talking seriously or whether they were mocking. me. We do not as yet understand the Camiroi at all. Further study is recommended.

—Charles Chosky
Chief of Field Group

From the ephemeris of Holly Holm, anthropologist and schedonahthropologist:

The word Camiroi is plural in form, is used for the people in both the single and plural and for the planet itself.

The civilization of Camiroi is more mechanical and more scientific than that of Earth, but it is more disguised. Their ideal machine shall have no moving parts at all, shall be noiseless and shall not look like a machine. For this reason, there is something pastoral about even the most thickly populated districts of Camiroi City.

The Camiroi are fortunate in the natural furnishings

222

of their planet. The scenery of Camiroi conforms to the dictate that all repetition is tedious, for there is only one of each thing on that world. There is one major continent and one minor continent of quite different character; one fine cluster of islands of which the individual isles are of very different style; one great continental river with its seven branches flowing out of seven sorts of land; one complex of volcanoes; one great range of mountains; one titanic waterfall with her three so different daughters nearby; one inland sea, one gulf, one beach which is a three hundred and fifty mile crescent passing through seven phases named for the colors of iris; one great rain forest, one palm grove, one leaf-fall grove, one of evergreens and one of eodendrons; one grain bowl, one fruit bowl, one pampas, one parkland; one desert, one great oasis; and Camiroi City is the one great city. And all these places are unexcelled of their kind.

There are no ordinary places on Camiroi!

Travel being rapid, a comparatively poor young couple may go from anywhere on the planet to Green Beach, for instance, to take their evening meal, in less time than the consumption of the meal will take them, and for less money than that reasonable meal will cost. This easy and frequent travel makes the whole world one community.

The Camiroi believe in the necessity of the frontier. They control many primitive worlds, and I gather hints that they are sometimes cruel in their management. The tyrants and proconsuls of these worlds are young, usually still in their teens. The young people are to have their careers and make their mistakes while in the foreign service. When they return to Camiroi they are supposed to be settled and of tested intelligence.

The earning scale of the Camiroi is curious. A job of mechanical drudgery pays higher than one of intellectual interest and involvement. This often means that the least intelligent and least able of the Camiroi will have more wealth than those of more ability. "This is fair," the Camiroi tell us. "Those not able to receive the higher recompense are certainly entitled to the lower." They regard the Earth system as grossly inequal, that a man should have both a superior job and superior pay, and that another man should have the inferior of both.

Though official offices and jobs are usually filled by lot, yet persons can apply for them for their own reasons. In special conditions there might even be competition for an assignment, such as directorship of trade posts where persons (for private reasons) might wish to acquire great fortunes rapidly. We witnessed confrontations between candidates in several of these campaigns, and they were curious.

"My opponent is a three and seven," said one candidate, and then he sat down.

"My opponent is a five and nine," said the other candidate. The small crowd clapped, and that was the confrontation or debate.

We attended another such rally.

"My opponent is an eight and ten," one candidate said briskly.

"My opponent is a two and six," said the other, and they went off together.

We did not understand this, and we attended a third confrontation. There seemed to be a little wave of excitement about to break here.

"My opponent is an old number four," said one candidate with a voice charged with emotion, and there was a gasp from the small crowd.

"I will not answer the charge," said the other candidate shaking with anger. "The blow is too foul, and we had been friends."

We found the key then. The Camiroi are experts at defamation, but they have developed a shorthand system to save time. They have their decalogue of slander, and the numbers refer to this. In its accepted version it runs as follows:

POLITY AND CUSTOM OF THE CAMIROI

My opponent (1) is personally moronic. (2) is sexually incompetent. (3) flubs third points in Chuki game. (4) eats Mu seeds before the time of the summer solstice. (5) is physically pathetic. (7) is financially stupid. (8) is ethically weird. (9) is intellectually contemptible. (10) is morally dishonest.

Try it yourself, on your friends or your enemies! It works wonderfully. We recommend the listing and use to Earth politicians, except for numbers three and four; which seem to have no meaning in Earth context.

The Camiroi have a corpus of proverbs. We came on them in Archives, along with an attached machine with a hundred levers on it. We depressed the lever marked Earth English, and had a sampling of these proverbs put into Earth context.

A man will not become rich by raising goats, the machine issued. Yes, that could almost pass for an Earth proverb. It almost seems to mean something.

Even buzzards sometimes gag. That has an Earth sound also.

It's that or pluck chickens.

"I don't believe I understand that one," I said.

"You think it's easy to put these in Earth context, you try it sometime," the translation machine issued. "The proverb applies to distasteful but necessary tasks."

"Ah, well, let's try some more," said Paul Piggott. "That one."

A bird in the hand is worth two in the bush, the machine issued abruptly.

"But that is an Earth proverb word for word," I said.

"You wait until I finish it, lady," the translation machine growled. "To this proverb in its classical form is always appended a cartoon showing a bird fluttering away and a man angrily wiping his hand with some disposable material while he says, "A bird in the hand is *not* worth two in the bush."

"Are we being had by a machine?" our leader, Charles Chosky asked softly.

"Give us that proverb there," I pointed one out to the machine.

There'll be many a dry eye here when you leave, the machine issued.

We left.

"I may be in serious trouble," I said to a Camiroi lady of my acquaintance, "Well, aren't you going to ask me what it is?"

"No, I don't particularly care," she said. "But tell me if you feel an absolute compulsion to it."

"I never heard of such a thing," I said. "I have been chosen by lot to head a military expedition for the relief of a trapped force on a world I never heard of. I am supposed to raise and supply this force (out of my private funds, it says here) and have it in flight within eight oodles. That's only two hours. What will I do?"

"Do it, of course, Miss Holly," the lady said. "You are a citizen of Camiroi now, and you should be proud to take charge of such an operation."

"But I don't know how! What will happen if I just tell them that I don't know how?"

"Oh, you'll lose your citizenship and suffer mutilation. That's the law, you know."

"How will they mutilate me?"

"Probably cut off your nose. I wouldn't worry about it. It doesn't do much for you anyhow."

"But we have to go back to Earth! We are going to go tomorrow, but now we want to go today. I do anyhow."

"Earth kid, if I were you, I'd get out to Sky-Port awful fast."

By a coincidence (I hope it was no more than that) our political analyst, Paul Piggott, had been chosen by lot to make a survey (personally, minutely and interiorly, the directive said) of the sewer system of Camiroi City. And our leader, Charles Chosky, had been selected by lot to put down a rebellion of Groll's Trolls on one of the worlds, and to leave his right hand and his right eye as surety for the accomplishment of the mission.

We were rather nervous as we waited for Earth Flight at Sky-Port, particularly so when a group of Camiroi acquaintances approached us. But they did not stop us. They said goodbye to us without too much enthusiasm.

"Our visit has been all too short," I said hopefully.

"Oh, I wouldn't say that," one of them rejoined. "There is a Camiroi proverb—"

"We've heard it," said our leader, Charles Chosky. "We also are dry-eyed about leaving."

FINAL RECOMMENDATION: That another and broader field group be sent to study the Camiroi in greater detail. That a special study might fruitfully be made of the humor of the Camiroi. That no members of the first field group should serve on the second field group.

—Holly Holm

IN OUR BLOCK

THERE WERE a lot of funny people in that block.

"You ever walk down that street?" Art Slick asked Jim Boomer, who had just come onto him there.

"Not since I was a boy. After the overall factory burned down, there was a faith healer had his tent pitched there one summer. The street's just one block long and it dead-ends on the railroad embankment. Nothing but a bunch of shanties and weed-filled lots. The shanties looked different today, though, and there seem to be more of them. I thought they pulled them all down a few months ago."

"Jim, I've been watching that first little building for two hours. There was a tractor-truck there this morning with a forty-foot trailer, and it loaded out of that little shanty. Cartons about eight inches by eight inches by three feet came down that chute. They weighed about thirty-five pounds each from the way the men handled them. Jim, they filled that trailer up with them, and then pulled it off."

"What's wrong with that, Art?"

"Jim, I said they filled that trailer up. From the drag on it it had about a sixty-thousand-pound load when it pulled out. They loaded a carton every three and a half seconds for two hours; that's two thousand cartons."

"Sure, lots of trailers run over the load limit nowdays. They don't enforce it very well."

"Jim, that shack's no more than a cracker box seven feet on a side. Half of it is taken up by a door, and inside a man in a chair behind a small table. You couldn't get anything else in that half. The other half is taken up by whatever that chute comes out of. You could pack six of those little shacks on that trailer."

"Let's measure it," Jim Boomer said. "Maybe it's bigger than it looks." The shack had a sign on it: *Make Sell Ship Anything Cut Price.* Jim Boomer measured the building with an old steel tape. The shack was a seven-foot cube, and there were no hidden places. It was set up on a few piers of broken bricks, and you could see under it.

"Sell you a new fifty-foot steel tape for a dollar," said the man in the chair in the little shack. "Throw that old one away." The man pulled a steel tape out of a drawer of his table-desk, though Art Slick was sure it had been a plain flat-top table with no place for a drawer.

"Fully retractable, rhodium-plated, Dort glide, Ramsey swivel, and it forms its own carrying case. One dollar," the man said.

Jim Boomer paid him a dollar for it. "How many of them you got?"

"I can have a hundred thousand ready to load out in ten minutes," the man said. "Eighty-eight cents each in hundred-thousand lots."

"Was that a trailer-load of steel tapes you shipped out this morning?" Art asked the man.

"No, that must have been something else. This is the first steel tape I ever made. Just got the idea when I saw you measuring my shack with that old beat-up one."

Art Slick and Jim Boomer went to the rundown building next door. It was smaller, about a six-foot cube, and the sign said *Public Stenographer.* The clatter of a typewriter was coming from it, but the noise stopped when they opened the door.

A dark, pretty girl was sitting in a chair before a small table. There was nothing else in the room, and no typewriter.

"I thought I heard a typewriter in here," Art said.

"Oh, that is me." The girl smiled. "Sometimes I amuse myself make typewriter noises like a public stenographer is supposed to."

"What would you do if someone came in to have some typing done?"

"What are you think? I do it of course."

"Could you type a letter for me?"

"Sure is can, man friend, two bits a page, good work, carbon copy, envelope and stamp."

"Ah, let's see how you do it. I will dictate to you while you type."

"You dictate first. Then I write. No sense mix up two things at one time."

Art dictated a long and involved letter that he had been meaning to write for several days. He felt like a fool droning it to the girl as she filed her nails. "Why is public stenographer always sit filing her nails?" she asked as Art droned. "But I try to do it right, file them down, grow them out again, then file them down some more. Been doing it all morning. It seems silly."

"Ah—that is all," Art said when he had finished dictating.

"Not P.S. Love and Kisses?" the girl asked.

"Hardly. It's a business letter to a person I barely know."

"I always say P.S. Love and Kisses to persons I barely know," the girl said. "Your letter will make three pages, six bits. Please you both step outside about ten seconds and I write it. Can't do it when you watch." She pushed them out and closed the door.

Then there was silence.

"What are you doing in there, girl?" Art called.

"Want I sell you a memory course too? You forget already? I type a letter," the girl called.

"But I don't hear a typewriter going."

"What is? You want verisimilitude too? I should charge extra." There was a giggle, and then the sound of very rapid typing for about five seconds.

The girl opened the door and handed Art the three-page letter. It was typed perfectly, of course.

"There is something a little odd about this," Art said.

"Oh? The ungrammar of the letter is your own, sir. Should I have correct?"

"No. It is something else. Tell me the truth, girl: how does the man next door ship out trailer-loads of material from a building ten times too small to hold the stuff?"

"He cuts prices."

"Well, what are you people? The man next door resembles you."

"My brother-uncle. We tell everybody we are Innominee Indians."

"There is no such tribe," Jim Boomer said flatly.

"Is there not? Then we will have to tell people we are something else. You got to admit it sounds like Indian. What's the best Indian to be?"

"Shawnee," said Jim Boomer.

"Okay then we be Shawnee Indians. See how easy it is."

"We're already taken," Boomer said. "I'm a Shawnee and I know every Shawnee in town."

"Hi cousin!" the girl cried, and winked. "That's from a joke I learn, only the begin was different. See how foxy I turn all your questions."

"I have two-bits coming out of my dollar," Art said.

"I know," the girl said. "I forgot for a minute what design is on the back of the two-bitser piece, so I stall while I remember it. Yes, the funny bird standing on the bundle of firewood. One moment till I finish it. Here." She handed the quarter to Art Slick. "And you tell everybody there's a smoothie public stenographer here who types letters good."

"Without a typewriter," said Art Slick. "Let's go, Jim."

"P.S. Love and Kisses," the girl called after them.

The Cool Man Club was next door, a small and shabby beer bar. The bar girl could have been a sister of the public stenographer.

"We'd like a couple of Buds, but you don't seem to have a stock of anything," Art said.

"Who needs stock?" the girl asked. "Here is beers." Art would have believed that she brought them out of her sleeves, but she had no sleeves. The beers were cold and good.

"Girl, do you know how the fellow on the corner can ship a whole trailer-load of material out of a space that wouldn't hold a tenth of it?" Art asked the girl.

"Sure. He makes it and loads it out at the same time. That way it doesn't take up space, like if he made it before time."

"But he has to make it out of something," Jim Boomer cut in.

"No, no," the girl said. "I study your language. I know words. Out of something is to assemble, not to make. He makes."

"This is funny." Slick gaped. "Budweiser is misspelled on this bottle, the *i* before the *e*."

"Oh, I goof," the bar girl said. "I couldn't remember which way it goes so I make it one way on one bottle and the other way on the other. Yesterday a man ordered a bottle of Progress beer, and I spelled it Progers on the bottle. Sometimes I get things wrong. Here, I fix yours."

She ran her hand over the label, and then it was spelled correctly.

"But that thing is engraved and then reproduced," Slick protested.

"Oh, sure, all fancy stuff like that," the girl said. "I got to be more careful. One time I forget and make Jax-taste beer in a Schlitz bottle and the man didn't like it. I had to swish swish change the taste while I pretended to give him a different bottle. One time I forgot and produced a green-bottle beer in a brown bottle. 'It is the light in here, it just makes it look brown,' I told the man. Hell, we don't even have a light in here. I go

232

swish fast and make the bottle green. It's hard to keep from making mistake when you're stupid."

"No, you don't have a light or a window in here, and it's light," Slick said. "You don't have refrigeration. There are no power lines to any of the shanties in this block. How do you keep the beer cold?"

"Yes, is the beer not nice and cold? Notice how tricky I evade your question. Will you good men have two more beers?"

"Yes, we will. And I'm interested in seeing where you get them," Slick said.

"Oh look, is snakes behind you!" the girl cried.

"Oh how you startle and jump!" she laughed. "It's all joke. Do you think I will have snakes in my nice bar?"

But she had produced two more beers, and the place was as bare as before.

"How long have you tumble-bugs been in this block?" Boomer asked.

"Who keep track?" the girl said. "People come and go."

"You're not from around here," Slick said. "You're not from anywhere I know. Where do you come from? Jupiter?"

"Who wants Jupiter?" the girl seemed indignant. "Do business with a bunch of insects there, is all! Freeze your tail too."

"You wouldn't be a kidder, would you, girl?" Slick asked.

"I sure do try hard. I learn a lot of jokes but I tell them all wrong yet. I get better, though. I try to be the witty bar girl so people will come back."

"What's in the shanty next door toward the tracks?"

"My cousin-sister," said the girl. "She set up shop just today. She grow any color hair on bald-headed men. I tell her she's crazy. No business. If they wanted hair they wouldn't be bald-headed in the first place."

"Well, *can* she grow hair on bald-headed men?" Slick asked.

"Oh sure. Can't you?"

There were three or four more shanty shops in the block. It didn't seem that there had been that many when the men went into the Cool Man Club.

"I don't remember seeing this shack a few minutes ago," Boomer said to the man standing in front of the last shanty on the line.

"Oh, I just made it," the man said.

Weathered boards, rusty nails . . . and he had just made it.

"Why didn't you—ah—make a decent building while you were at it?" Slick asked.

"This is more inconspicuous," the man said. "Who notices when an *old* building appears suddenly? We're new here and want to feel our way in before we attract attention. Now I'm trying to figure out what to make. Do you think there is a market for a luxury automobile to sell for a hundred dollars? I suspect I would have to respect the local religious feeling when I make them though."

"What is that?" Slick asked.

"Ancestor worship. The old gas tank and fuel system still carried as vestiges after natural power is available. Oh, well, I'll put them in. I'll have one done in about three minutes if you want to wait."

. "No. I've already got a car," Slick said. "Let's go, Jim."

That was the last shanty in the block, so they turned back.

"I was just wondering what was down in this block where nobody ever goes," Slick said. "There's a lot of odd corners in our town if you look them out."

"There are some queer guys in the shanties that were here before this bunch," Boomer said. "Some of them used to come up to the Red Rooster to drink. One of them could gobble like a turkey. One of them could roll one eye in one direction and the other eye the other way. They shoveled hulls at the cottonseed oil float before it burned down."

They went by the public stenographer shack again.

"No kidding, honey, how do you type without a typewriter?" Slick asked.

"Typewriter is too slow," the girl said.

"I asked *how*, not *why*," Slick said.

"I know. Is it not nifty the way I turn away a phrase? I think I will have a big oak tree growing in front of my shop tomorrow for shade. Either of you nice men have an acorn in your pocket?"

"Ah—no. How do you really do the typing, girl?"

"You promise you won't tell anybody."

"I promise."

"I make the marks with my tongue," the girl said.

They started slowly on up the block.

"Hey, how do you make the carbon copies?" Jim Boomer called back.

"With my other tongue," the girl said.

There was another forty-foot trailer loading out of the first shanty in the block. It was bundles of half-inch plumbers' pipe coming out of the chute—in twenty-foot lengths. Twenty-foot rigid pipe out of a seven-foot shed.

"I wonder how he can sell trailer-loads of such stuff out of a little shack like that," Slick puzzled, still not satisfied.

"Like the girl says, he cuts prices," Boomer said. "Let's go over to the Red Rooster and see if there's anything going on. There always were a lot of funny people in that block."

HOG-BELLY HONEY

I'M JOE SPADE—about as intellectual a guy as you'll find all day. I invented Wotto and Voxo and a bunch of other stuff that nobody can get along without anymore. It's on account of I have so much stuff in my head that I sometimes go to a head-grifter. This day all of them I know is out of town when I call. Lots of times everybody I know is out of town when I call. I go to a new one. The glass in his door says he is a anapsychologist, which is a head-grifter in the popular speech.

"I'm Joe Spade the man that got everything," I tell him and slap him on the back in that hearty way of mine. There is a crunch sound and at first I think I have crack his rib. Then I see I have only broke his glasses so no harm done. "I am what you call a flat-footed genius, Doc," I tell him, "with plenty of the crimp-cut greenleaf."

I take the check card away from him and mark it up myself to save time. I figure I know more about me than he does.

"Remember, I can get them nine-dollar words for four eighty-five wholesale, Doc," I josh him and he looks at me painful.

"Modesty isn't one of your failings," this head-grifter tell me as he scun my card. "Hum. Single . . . significant."

I had written down the "single" in the blank for it, but he had see for himself that I am a significant man.

"Solvent," he read for the blank about the pecuniary stuff; "I like that in a man. We will arrange for a few sessions."

"One will do it," I tell him. "Time is running and I am paying. Give me a quick read, Doc."

"Yes, I can give you a very rapid reading," he says.
"I want you to ponder the ancient adage: It is not good
for Man to be alone. Think about it a while, and perhaps you will be able to put one and one together."

Then he add kind of sad, "Poor woman!" which is
either the non-secular of the year or else he is thinking
of some other patient. Then he add again, "That will
be three yards, in the lingo."

"Thanks, Doc," I say. I pay the head-grifter his three
hundred dollars and leave. He has hit the nail on the
noggin and put his toe on the root of my trouble.

I will take me a partner in my business.

I spot him in Grogley's, and I know right away he's
the one. He's about half my size but otherwise he's as
much like me as two feet in one shoe. He's real good-
looking—just like me. He's dressed sweet, but has a little blood on his face like can happen to anyone in Grogley's for five minutes. Man, we're twins! I know we will
talk alike and think alike just like we look alike.

"*Eheu! Fugaces!*" my new partner says real sad. That
means "Brother, this has been one day with all the
bark on it!" He is drinking the Fancy and his eyes look
like cracked glass.

"He's been having quite a few little fist fights," Grogley whispers to me, "but he don't win none. He isn't
very fast with his hands. I think he's got troubles."

"Not no more he don't," I tell Grogley; "he's my new
partner."

I slap my new partner on the back in that hearty
way I have, and the tooth that flew out must have been
a loose one.

"You don't have no more troubles, Roscoe," I tell him,
"you and me is just become partners." He looks kind
of sick at me.

"Maurice is the name," he says, "Maurice Maltravers.
How are things back in the rocks? You, sir, are a troglodyte. They always come right after the snakes. That's
the only time I wish the snakes would come back."

Lots of people call me a troglodyte.

"Denied the sympathy of humankind," Maurice carries on, "perhaps I may find it in an inferior species. I wonder if I could impose on your ears—gahhhh!" (he made a humorous sound there) "are those things ears? What a fearsome otological apparatus you do have!—the burden of my troubles."

"I just told you you don't have none, Maurice," I say. "Come along with me and we'll get into the partner business."

I pick him up by the scruff and haul him out of Grogley's.

"I see right away you are my kind of man," I say.

"My kind of man—*putridus ad volva*," Maurice gives me the echo. Hey, this guy is a gale! Just like me.

"My cogitational patterns are so intricate and identatic oriented," says Maurice when I set him down and let him walk a little, "that I become a closed system—unintelligible to the exocosmos and particularly to a chthonian like yourself."

"I'm mental as hell myself, Maurice," I tell him, "there ain't nothing the two of us can't do together."

"My immediate, difficulty is that the University has denied me further use of the computer," Maurice tells me. "Without it, I cannot complete the Ultimate Machine."

"I got a computer'll make that little red schoolhouse turn green," I tell him.

We come to my place which a man have call in print "a converted horse barn, probably the most unorthodox and badly appointed scientific laboratory in the world." I take Maurice in with me, but he carries on like a chicken with its hat off when he finds out the only calculator I got is the one in my head.

"You livid monster, I can't work in this mares'-nest," he screeches at me. "I've got to have a calculator, a computer."

I tap my head with a six-pound hammer and grin

my famous grin. "It's all inside here, Maurice boy," I tell him, "the finest calculator in the world. When I was with the carnivals they billed me as the Idiot Genius. I run races with the best computers they had in a town, multiplying twenty-place numbers and all the little tricks like that. I cheated though. I invented a gadget and carried it in my pocket. It's jam the relays of the best computers and slow them down for a full second. Give me a one-second hop and I can beat anything in the world at anything. The only things wrong with those jobs is that I had to talk and act kind of dumb to live up to my billing the Idiot Genius, and that dumb stuff was hard on an intellectual like I."

"I can see that it would be," Maurice said. "Can you handle involuted matrix, Maimonides-conditioned, third-aspect numbers in the Cauchy sequence with simultaneous non-temporal involvement of the Fieschi manifold?"

"Maurice, I can do it and fry up a bunch of eggs to go with it at the same time," I tell him. Then I look him right in the middle of the eye. "Maurice," I say, "you're working on a nullifier."

He look at me like he take me serious for the first time. He pull a sheaf of papers out of his shirt, and sure enough he is working on a nullifier—a sweet one.

"This isn't an ordinary nullifier," Maurice points out, and I see that it ain't. "What other nullifier can posit moral and ethical judgments? What other can set up and enforce categories? What other can really discern? This will be the only nullifier able to make full philosophical pronouncements. Can you help me finish it, Proconsul?"

A pronconsul is about the same as an alderman, so I know Maurice think high of me. We throw away the clock and get with it. We work about twenty hours a day. I compute it and build it at the same time—out of Wotto-metal naturally. At the end we use feedback a lot. We let the machine decide what we will put in it and what leave out. The main difference between our nullifier and all others is that ours will be able to make decisions. So, let it make them!

We finish it in about a week. Man, it is a sweet thing. We play with it a while to see what it can do. It can do everything.

I point it at half a bushel of bolts and nuts I got there. "Get rid of everything that ain't standard thread," I program it. "Half that stuff is junk."

And half that stuff is gone right now! This thing works! Just set in what you want it to get rid of, and it's gone without a trace.

"Get rid of *everything* here that's no good for nothing," I program it. I had me a place there that has been described as cluttered. That machine blinked once, and then I had a place you could get around in. That thing knew junk when it saw it, and it sure sent that no-good stuff clear over the edge. Of course anybody can make a nullifier that won't leave no remains of whatever it latches on to, but this is the only one that knows what not to leave no remains of by itself. Maurice and me is tickled as pink rabbits over the thing.

"Maurice," I say, and I slap him on the back so his nose bleeds a little, "this is one bushy-tailed gadget. There ain't nothing we can't do with it."

But Maurice looks kind of sad for a moment.

"*A quo bono?*" he ask, which I think is the name of a mineral water, so I slosh him out some brandy which is better. He drink the brandy but he's still thoughtful.

"But what good is it?" he ask. "It is a triumph, of course, but in what category could we market it? It seems that I've been here a dozen times with the perfect apparatus that nobody wants. Is there really a mass market for a machine that can posit moral and ethical judgments, that can set up and enforce categories, that is able to discern, and to make philosophical pronouncements? Have I not racked up one more triumphant folly?"

"Maurice, this thing is a natural-born garbage disposal," I tell him. He turn that green color lots of people do when I shed a big light on them.

"A garbage disposal!" he sing out. "The aeons labored to give birth to it through the finest mind—mine—of the millennium, and this brother of a giant ape says it is a garbage disposal! It is a new aspect of thought, the *novo instauratio*, the mind of tomorrow fruited today, and this obscene ogre says it is a Garbage Disposal! The Constellations do homage to it, and Time has not waited in vain, and you, you splay-footed horse-herder, you call it a GARBAGE DISPOSAL!"

Maurice was so carried away with the thought that he cried a little. It sure is nice when someone agrees with you as long and loud as Maurice did. When he was run out of words he got aholt of the brandy bottle with both hands and drunk it all off. Then he slept the clock around. He was real tired.

He looked kind of sheepful when he finally woke up.

"I feel better now, outside of feeling worse," he say. "You are right, Spade, it's a garbage disposal."

He programmed it to get all the slush out of his blood and liver and kidneys and head. It did it. It cured his hangover in straight-up no time at all. It also shaved him and removed his appendix. Just give it the nod and it would nullify anything.

"We will call it the Hog-Belly Honey," I say, "on account of it will eat anything, and it work so sweet."

"That is what we will call it privately." Maurice nodded. "But in company it will be known as the Pantophag." That is the same thing in Greek.

It was at the time of this area of good feeling that I split a Voxo with Maurice. Each of you have one-half of a tuned Voxo and you can talk to each other anywhere in the world, and the thing is so nonconspicuous that nobody can see it on you.

We got a big booth and showed the Hog-Belly Honey, the Pantophag, at the Trade Fair.

Say, we did put on a good show! The people came

in and looked and listened till they were walleyed. That
Maurice could give a good spiel, and I'm about the best
there is myself. We sure were two fine-looking men,
after Maurice told me that maybe I detracted a little
bit by being in my undershirt, and I went and put a shirt
on. And that bushy-tailed machine just sparkled—like
everything does that is made out of Wotto-metal.

Kids threw candy-bar wrappers at it, and they disappeared in the middle of the air. "Frisk me," they said,
and everything in their pockets that was no good for
nothing was gone. A man held up a stuffed briefcase,
and it was almost empty in a minute. A few people got
mad when they lost beards and moustaches, but we explained to them that their boscage hadn't done a thing
for them; if the ornaments had had even appearance
value the machine would have left them be. We pointed
out other people who kept their brush; whatever they
had behind it, they must have needed the cover.

"Could I have one in my house, and when?" a lady
asks.

"Tomorrow, for forty-nine ninety-five installed," I tell
her. "It will get rid of anything no good. It'll pluck
chickens, or bone roasts for you. It will clear out all
those old love letters from that desk and leave just the
ones from the guy that meant it. It will relieve you of
thirty pounds in the strategic places, and frankly, lady,
this alone will make it worth your while. It will get rid
of old buttons that don't match, and seeds that won't
sprout. It will destroy everything that is not so good for
nothing."

"It can posit moral and ethical judgments," Maurice
tells the people. "It can set up and enforce categories."

"Maurice and me is partners," I tell them all. "We
look alike and think alike. We even talk alike."

"Save I in the hieratic and he in the demotic," Maurice
say. "This is the only nullifier in the world able to make
full philosophical pronouncements. It is the unfailing

judge of what is of some use and what is not. And it disposes neatly."

Man, the people did pour in to see it all that morning! They slacked off a little bit just about noon.

"I wonder how many people have come into our booth this morning?" Maurice wondered to me. "I would guess near ten thousand."

"I don't have to guess," I say. "There is nine thousand three hundred and fifty-eight who have come in, Maurice," I tell him, for I am always the automatic calculator. "There is nine thousand two hundred and ninety-seven who have left," I go on, "and there are forty-four here now."

Maurice smiled. "You have made a mistake," he says. "It doesn't add up."

And that is when the hair riz up on the back of my neck.

I don't make mistakes when I calculate, and I can see now that the Hog-Belly Honey don't make none either. Well, it's too late to make one now if you're not trained for it, but it might not be too late to get out the way of the storm before it hits.

"Crank the cuckoo," I whisper to Maurice, "make the bindlestiff, hit the macadam!"

"*Je ne comprends pas,*" says Maurice, which means "Let's hit the road, boys," in French, so I know my partner understands me.

I am out of the display hall at a high run, and Maurice racing along beside me so lightfoot that he don't make no noise. There is a sky-taxi just taking off.

"Jump for it, Maurice!" I sing out. I jump for it myself, and hook my fingers over the rear rail and am dangling in the air. I look to see if Maurice make it. Make it! He isn't even there! He didn't come out with me. I look back, and I see him through a window going into his spiel again.

Now that is a mule-headed development. My partner,

who is as like me as two heads in one hat, had not understand me.

At the port I hook onto a sky-freight just going to Mexico.

I don't never have to pack no bag. I say that a man who don't always carry two years' living in that crimp green stuff in his back pocket ain't in no condition to meet fait. In thirty minutes I am sit down in a hotel in Cueva Peoquita and have all the pleasantries at hand. Then I snap on my Voxo to hear what Maurice is signaling about.

"Why didn't you tell me that the Pantophag was nullifying people?" he ask kind of shrill.

"I did tell you," I say. "Nine thousand two hundred and ninety-seven added to forty-four don't come to nine thousand three hundred and fifty-eight. You said so yourself. How are things on the home front, Maurice? That's a joke."

"It's no joke," he say kind of fanatic like. "I have locked myself in a little broom closet, but they're going to break down the door. What can I do?"

"Why, Maurice, just explain to those people that the folks nullified by the machine were no good for nothing because the machine don't make mistakes."

"I doubt that I can convince the parents and spouses and children of the nullified people of this. They're after blood. They're breaking down the door now, Spade. I hear them say they will hang me."

"Tell them you won't settle for anything less than a new rope, Maurice," I tell him. That's an old joke. I switch off the Voxo because Maurice is not making anything except gurgling noises which I cannot interpret.

A thing like that blow over real fast after they have already hang one guy for it and are satisfied. I am back in town and am rolling all those new ideas around in my head like a bunch of rocks. But I'm not going to build the Hog-Belly Honey again. It is too logical for safety, and is a little before its time.

I am looking to get me another partner. Come into Grogley's if you are interested. I show up there every hour or so. I want a guy as like me as two necks in one noose—what make me think of a thing like that?—a guy look like me and think like me and talk like me.

Just ask for Joe Spade.

But the one I hook onto for a new partner will have to be a fellow who understands me when the scuppers are down.

SEVEN-DAY TERROR

"Is THERE anything you want to make disappear?" Clarence Willoughby asked his mother.

"A sink full of dishes is all I can think of. How will you do it?"

"I just built a disappearer. All you do is cut the other end out of a beer can. Then you take two pieces of red cardboard with peepholes in the middle and fit them in the ends. You look through the peepholes and blink. Whatever you look at will disappear."

"Oh."

"But I don't know if I can make them come back. We'd better try it on something else. Dishes cost money."

As always, Myra Willoughby had to admire the wisdom of her nine-year-old son. She would not have had such foresight herself. He always did. "You can try it on Blanche Manners' cat outside there. Nobody will care if it disappears except Blanche Manners."

"All right."

He put the disappearer to his eye and blinked. The cat disappeared from the sidewalk outside.

His mother was interested. "I wonder how it works. Do you know how it works?"

"Yes. You take a beer can with both ends cut out and put in two pieces of cardboard. Then you blink."

"Never mind. Take it outside and play with it. You hadn't better make anything disappear in here till I think about this."

But when he had gone his mother was oddly disturbed.

"I wonder if I have a precocious child. Why, there's lots of grown people who wouldn't know how to make

246

a disappearer that would work. I wonder if Blanche Manners will miss her cat very much?"

Clarence went down to the Plugged Nickel, a pot house on the corner.

"Do you have anything you want to make disappear, Nokomis?"

"Only my paunch."

"If I make it disappear it'll leave a hole in you and you'll bleed to death."

"That's right, I would. Why don't you try it on the fireplug outside?"

This in a way was one of the happiest afternoons ever in the neighborhood. The children came from blocks around to play in the flooded streets and gutters, and if some of them drowned (and we don't say that they *did* drown) in the flood (and brother! it was a flood), why, you have to expect things like that. The fire engines (whoever heard of calling fire engines to put out a flood?) were apparatus-deep in the water. The policemen and ambulance men wandered around wet and bewildered.

"Resuscitator, resuscitator, anybody wanna resuscitator," chanted Clarissa Willoughby.

"Oh, shut up," said the ambulance attendants.

Nokomis, the bar man in the Plugged Nickel, called Clarence aside.

"I don't believe, just for the moment, I'd tell anyone what happened to that fireplug," he said.

"I won't tell if you won't tell," said Clarence.

Officer Comstock was suspicious. "There's only seven possible explanations: one of the seven Willoughby kids did it. I dunno how. It'd take a bulldozer to do it, and then there'd be something left of the plug. But however they did it, one of them did it."

Officer Comstock had a talent for getting near the truth of dark matters. This is why he was walking a beat out here in the boondocks instead of sitting in a chair downtown.

"Clarissa!" said Officer Comstock in a voice like thunder.

"Resuscitator, resuscitator, anybody wanna resuscitator?" chanted Clarissa.

"Do you know what happened to that fireplug?" asked Officer C.

"I have an uncanny suspicion. As yet it is no more than that. When I am better informed I will advise you."

Clarissa was eight years old and much given to uncanny suspicions.

"Clementine, Harold, Corinne, Jimmy, Cyril," he asked the five younger Willoughby children. "Do you know what happened to that fireplug?"

"There was a man around yesterday. I bet he took it," said Clementine.

"I don't even remember a fireplug there. I think you're making a lot of fuss about nothing," said Harold.

"City hall's going to hear about this," said Corinne.

"Pretty dommed sure," said Jimmy, "but I won't tell."

"Cyril!" cried Officer Comstock in a terrible voice. Not a terrifying voice, a terrible voice. He felt terrible now.

"Great green bananas," said Cyril, "I'm only three years old. I don't see how it's even my responsibility."

"Clarence," said Officer Comstock.

Clarence gulped.

"Do you know where that fireplug went?"

Clarence brightened. "No, sir. I don't know where it went."

A bunch of smart alecs from the water department came out and shut off the water for a few blocks around and put some kind of cap on in place of the fireplug. "This sure is going to be a funny-sounding report," said one of them.

Officer Comstock walked away discouraged. "Don't bother me, Miss Manners," he said. "I don't know where to look for your cat. I don't even know where to look for a fireplug."

"I have an idea," said Clarissa, "that when you find the cat you will find the fireplug in the same place. As yet it is only an idea."

Ozzie Murphy wore a little hat on top of his head. Clarence pointed his weapon and winked. The hat was no longer there, but a little trickle of blood was running down the pate.

"I don't believe I'd play with that any more," said Nokomis.

"Who's playing?" said Clarence. "This is for real."

This was the beginning of the seven-day terror in the heretofore obscure neighborhood. Trees disappeared from the parks; lamp posts were as though they had never been; Wally Waldorf drove home, got out, slammed the door of his car, and there was no car. As George Mullendorf came up the walk to his house his dog Pete ran to meet him and took a flying leap to his arms. The dog left the sidewalk but something happened; the dog was gone and only a bark lingered for a moment in the puzzled air.

But the worst were the fireplugs. The second plug was installed the morning after the disappearance of the first. In eight minutes it was gone and the flood waters returned. Another one was in by twelve o'clock. Within three minutes it had vanished. The next morning fireplug number four was installed.

The water commissioner was there, the city engineer was there, the chief of police was there with a riot squad, the president of the Parent-Teachers Association was there, the president of the university was there, the mayor was there, three gentlemen of the F.B.I., a newsreel photographer, eminent scientists and a crowd of honest citizens.

"Let's see it disappear now," said the city engineer.

"Let's see it disappear now," said the police chief.

"Let's see it disa—it did, didn't it?" said one of the eminent scientists.

And it was gone and everybody was very wet.

"At least I have the picture sequence of the year," said the photographer. But his camera and apparatus disappeared from the midst of them.

"Shut off the water and cap it," said the commissioner. "And don't put in another plug yet. That was the last plug in the warehouse."

"This is too big for me," said the mayor. "I wonder that Tass doesn't have it yet."

"Tass has it," said a little round man. "I am Tass."

"If all of you gentlemen will come into the Plugged Nickel," said Nokomis, "and try one of our new Fire Hydrant Highballs you will all be happier. These are made of good corn whiskey, brown sugar, and hydrant water from this very gutter. You can be the first to drink them."

Business was phenomenal at the Plugged Nickel, for it was in front of its very doors that the fireplugs disappeared in floods of gushing water.

"I know a way we can get rich," said Clarissa several days later to her father, Tom Willoughby. "Everybody says they're going to sell their houses for nothing and move out of the neighborhood. Go get a lot of money and buy them all. Then you can sell them again and get rich."

"I wouldn't buy them for a dollar each. Three of them have disappeared already, and all the families but us have their furniture moved out in their front yards. There might be nothing but vacant lots in the morning."

"Good, then buy the vacant lots. And you can be ready when the houses come back."

"Come back? Are the houses going to come back? Do you know anything about this, young lady?"

"I have a suspicion verging on a certainty. As of now I can say no more."

Three eminent scientists were gathered in an untidy suite that looked as though it belonged to a drunken sultan.

"This transcends the metaphysical. It impinges on the quantum continuum. In some way it obsoletes Boff," said Dr. Velikof Vonk.

"The contingence of the intransigence is the most mystifying aspect," said Arpad Arkabaranan.

"Yes," said Willy McGilly. "Who would have thought that you could do it with a beer can and two pieces of cardboard? When I was a boy I used an oatmeal box and red crayola."

"I do not always follow you," said Dr. Vonk. "I wish you would speak plainer."

So far no human had been injured or disappeared— except for a little blood on the pate of Ozzie Murphy, on the lobes of Conchita when her gaudy earrings disappeared from her very ears, a clipped finger or so when a house vanished as the front doorknob was touched, a lost toe when a neighborhood boy kicked at a can and the can was not; probably not more than a pint of blood and three or four ounces of flesh all together.

Now, however, Mr. Buckle the grocery man disappeared before witnesses. This was serious.

Some mean-looking investigators from downtown came out to the Willoughbys. The meanest-looking one was the mayor. In happier days he had not been a mean man, but the terror had now reigned for seven days.

"There have been ugly rumors," said one of the mean investigators, "that link certain events to this household. Do any of you know anything about them?"

"I started most of them," said Clarissa. "But I didn't consider them ugly. Cryptic, rather. But if you want to get to the bottom of this just ask me a question."

"Did you make those things disappear?" asked the investigator.

"That isn't the question," said Clarissa.

"Do you know where they have gone?" asked the investigator.

"That isn't the question either," said Clarissa.

"Can you make them come back?"

"Why, of course I can. Anybody can. Can't you?"

"I cannot. If you can, please do so at once."

"I need some stuff. Get me a gold watch and a hammer. Then go down to the drug store and get me this list of chemicals. And I need a yard of black velvet and a pound of rock candy."

"Shall we?" asked one of the investigators.

"Yes," said the mayor. "It's our only hope. Get her anything she wants."

And it was all assembled.

"Why does she get all the attention?" asked Clarence. "I was the one who made all the things disappear. How does she know how to get them back?"

"I knew it!" cried Clarissa with hate. "I knew he was the one that did it. He read in my diary how to make a disappearer. If I was his mother I'd whip him for reading his little sister's diary. That's what happens when things like that fall into irresponsible hands."

She poised the hammer over the mayor's gold watch, now on the floor.

"I have to wait a few seconds. This can't be hurried. It'll be only a little while."

The second hand swept around to the point that was preordained for it before the world began. Clarissa suddenly brought down the hammer with all her force on the beautiful gold watch.

"That's all," she said. "Your troubles are over. See, there is Blanche Manners' cat on the sidewalk just where she was seven days ago."

And the cat was back.

"Now let's go down to the Plugged Nickel and watch the fireplugs come back."

They had only a few minutes to wait. It came from nowhere and clanged into the street like a sign and a witness.

"Now I predict," said Clarissa, "that every single object will return exactly seven days from the time of its disappearance."

The seven-day terror had ended. The objects began to reappear.

"How," asked the mayor, "did you know they would come back in seven days?"

"Because it was a seven-day disappearer that Clarence made. I also know how to make a nine-day, a thirteen-day, a twenty-seven-day, and an eleven-year disappearer. I was going to make a thirteen-year one, but for that you have to color the ends with the blood from a little boy's heart, and Cyril cried every time I tried to make a good cut."

"You really know how to make all of these?"

"Yes. But I shudder if the knowledge should ever come into unauthorized hands."

"I shudder, too, Clarissa. But tell me, why did you want the chemicals?"

"For my chemistry set."

"And the black velvet?"

"For doll dresses."

"And the pound of rock candy?"

"How did you ever get to be mayor of this town if you have to ask questions like that? What do you think I wanted the rock candy for?"

"One last question," said the mayor. "Why did you smash my gold watch with the hammer?"

"Oh," said Clarissa, "that was for dramatic effect."

THE HOLE ON THE CORNER

HOMER HOOSE came home that evening to the golden cliché: the un-noble dog who was a personal friend of his; the perfect house where just to live was a happy riot; the loving and unpredictable wife; and the five children—the perfect number (four more would have been too many, four less would have been too few).

The dog howled in terror and bristled up like a hedgehog. Then it got a whiff of Homer and recognized him; it licked his heels and gnawed his knuckles and made him welcome. A good dog, though a fool. Who wants a smart dog!

Homer had a little trouble with the doorknob. They don't have them in all the recensions, you know; and he had that off-the-track feeling tonight. But he figured it out (you don't pull it, you turn it), and opened the door.

"Did you remember to bring what I asked you to bring this morning, Homer?" the loving wife Regina inquired.

"What did you ask me to bring this morning, quick-heat blueberry biscuit of my heart?" Homer asked.

"If I'd remembered, I'd have phrased it different when I asked if you remembered," Regina explained. "But I know I told you to bring something, old ketchup of my soul. Homer! Look at me, Homer! You look different tonight! DIFFERENT!! *You're not my Homer, are you!* Help! Help! There's a monster in my house!! Help, help! Shriek!"

"It's always nice to be married to a wife who doesn't understand you," Homer said. He enfolded her affectionately, bore her down, trod on her with large friendly hooves, and began (as it seemed) to devour her.

"Where'd you get the monster, Mama?" son Robert asked as he came in. "What's he got your whole head in his mouth for? Can I have one of the apples in the kitchen? What's he going to do, kill you, Mama?"

"Shriek, shriek," said Mama Regina. "Just one apple, Robert, there's just enough to go around. Yes, I think he's going to kill me. Shriek!"

Son Robert got an apple and went outdoors.

"Hi, Papa, what's you doing to Mama?" daughter Fregona asked as she came in. She was fourteen, but stupid for her age. "Looks to me like you're going to kill her that way. I thought they peeled people before they swallowed them. Why! You're not Papa at all, are you? You're some monster. I thought at first you were my papa. You look just like him except for the way you look."

"Shriek, shriek," said Mama Regina, but her voice was muffled.

They had a lot of fun at their house.

Homer Hoose came home that evening to the golden cliché: the u.n.d.; the p.h.; and l. and u.w.; and the f.c. (four more would have been too many).

The dog waggled all over him happily, and son Robert was chewing an apple core on the front lawn.

"Hi, Robert," Homer said, "what's new today?"

"Nothing, Papa. Nothing ever happens here. Oh yeah, there's a monster in the house. He looks kind of like you. He's killing Mama and eating her up."

"Eating her up, you say, son? How do you mean?"

"He's got her whole head in his mouth."

"Droll, Robert, mighty droll," said Homer, and he went in the house.

One thing about the Hoose children: a lot of times they told the bald-headed truth. There *was* a monster there. He *was* killing and eating the wife Regina. This was no mere evening antic. It was something serious.

255

Homer the man was a powerful and quick-moving fellow. He fell on the monster with judo chops and solid body punches; and the monster let the woman go and confronted the man.

"What's with it, you silly oaf?" the monster snapped. "If you've got a delivery, go to the back door. Come punching people in here, will you? Regina, do you know who this silly simpleton is?"

"Wow, that was a pretty good one, wasn't it, Homer?" Regina gasped as she came from under, glowing and gulping. "Oh, him? Gee, Homer, I think he's my husband. But how can he be, if you are? Now the two of you have got me so mixed up that I don't know which one of you is my Homer."

"Great goofy Gestalten! You don't mean I look like him?" howled Homer the monster, near popping.

"My brain reels," moaned Homer the man. "Reality melts away. Regina! Exorcise this nightmare if you have in some manner called it up! I knew you shouldn't have been fooling around with that book."

"Listen, mister reely-brains," wife Regina began on Homer the man. "You learn to kiss like he does before you tell me which one to exorcise. All I ask is a little affection. And this I didn't find in a book."

"How we going to know which one is Papa? They look just alike," daughters Clara-Belle, Anna-Belle, and Maudie-Belle came in like three little chimes.

"Hell-hipping horrors!" roared Homer the man. "How are you going to know—? He's got green skin."

"There's nothing wrong with green skin as long as it's kept neat and oiled," Regina defended.

"He's got tentacles instead of hands," said Homer the man.

"Oh boy, I'll say!" Regina sang out.

"How we going to know which one is Papa when they look just alike?" the five Hoose children asked in chorus.

"I'm sure there's a simple explanation to this, old chap," said Homer the monster. "If I were you, Homer—

and there's some argument whether I am or not—I believe I'd go to a doctor. I don't believe we both need to go, since our problem's the same. Here's the name of a good one," said Homer the monster, writing it out. "Oh, I know him," said Homer the man when he read it. "But how did you know him? He isn't an animal doctor. Regina, I'm going over to the doctor to see what's the matter with me, or you. Try to have this nightmare back in whatever corner of your under-id it belongs when I come back."

"Ask him if I keep taking my pink medicine," Regina said.

"No, not him. It's the head doctor I'm going to."

"Ask him if I have to keep on dreaming those pleasant dreams," Regina said. "I sure do get tired of them. I want to get back to the other kind. Homer, leave the coriander seed when you go." And she took the package out of his pocket. "You did remember to bring it. My other Homer forgot."

"No, I didn't," said Homer the monster. "You couldn't remember what you told me to get. Here, Regina."

"I'll be back in a little while," said Homer the man. "The doctor lives on the corner. And you, fellow, if you're real, keep your plankton-picking polypusses off my wife till I get back."

Homer Hoose went up the street to the house of Dr. Corte on the corner. He knocked on the door, and then opened it and went in without waiting for an answer. The doctor was sitting there, but he seemed a little bit dazed.

"I've got a problem, Dr. Corte," said Homer the man. "I came home this evening, and I found a monster eating my wife—as I thought."

"Yes, I know," said Dr. Corte. "Homer, we got to fix that hole on the corner."

"I didn't know there was a hole there, Doctor. As it happened, the fellow wasn't really swallowing my wife, it was just his way of showing affection. Everybody thought the monster looked like me, and Doctor, it has green skin and tentacles. When I began to think it looked like me too, I came here to see what was wrong with me, or with everybody else."

"I can't help you, Hoose. I'm a psychologist, not a contingent-physicist. Only one thing to do; we got to fix that hole on the corner."

"Doctor, there's no hole in the street on this corner."

"Wasn't talking about a hole in the street. Homer, I just got back from a visit of my own that shook me up. I went to an analyst who analyzes analysts. I've had a dozen people come to see me with the same sort of story,' I told him. 'They all come home in the evening; and everything is different, or themselves are different; or they find that they are already there when they get there. What do you do when a dozen people come in with the same nonsense story, Dr. Diebel?' I asked him.

" 'I don't know, Corte,' he said to me. 'What do I do when *one* man comes in a dozen times with the same nonsense story, all within one hour, and he a doctor too?' Dr. Diebel asked me.

" 'Why, Dr. Diebel?' I asked. 'What doctor came to you like that?'

" 'You,' he said. 'You've come in here twelve times in the last hour with the same dish of balderhash; you've come in each time looking a little bit different; and each time you act as if you hadn't seen me for a month. Dammit, man,' he said, 'you must have passed yourself going out when you came in.'

" 'Yes, that *was* me, wasn't it?' I said. 'I was trying to think who he reminded me of. Well, it's a problem, Dr. Diebel,' I said. 'What are you going to do about it?'

" 'I'm going to the analyst who analyzes the analysts who analyze the analysts,' he said. 'He's tops in the field.' Dr. Diebel rushed out then; and I came back to my office here. You came in just after that. I'm not the one to help you. But, Homer, we got to do something about that hole on the corner!"

THE HOLE ON THE CORNER

"I don't understand the bit about the hole, Doctor," Homer said. "But—has a bunch of people been here with stories like mine?"

"Yes, every man in this block has been in with an idiot story, Homer, except— Why, everybody except old double-domed Diogenes himself! Homer, that man who knows everything has a finger in this up to the humerus. I saw him up on the power poles the other night, but I didn't think anything of it. He likes to tap the lines before they come to his meter. Saves a lot on power that way, and he uses a lot of it in his laboratory. But he was setting up the hole on the corner. That's what he was doing. Let's get him and bring him to your house and make him straighten it out."

"Sure, a man who knows everything ought to know about a hole on the corner, Doctor. But I sure don't see any hole anywhere on this corner."

The man who knew everything was named Diogenes Pontifex. He lived next door to Homer Hoose, and they found him in his back yard wrestling with his anaconda.

"Diogenes, come over to Homer's with us," Dr. Corte insisted. "We've got a couple of questions that might be too much even for you."

"You touch my pride there," Diogenes sang out. "When psychologists start using psychology on you, it's time to give in. Wait a minute till I pin this fellow."

Diogenes put a chancery on the anaconda, punched the thing's face a few times, then pinned it with a double bar-arm and body lock, and left it writhing there. He followed them into the house.

"Hi, Homer," Diogenes said to Homer the monster when they had come into the house. "I see there's two of you here at the same time now. No doubt that's what's puzzling you."

"Dr. Corte, did Homer ask you if I could stop dreaming those pleasant dreams?" wife Regina asked. "I sure do get tired of them. I want to go back to the old flesh-crawlers."

"You should be able to do so tonight, Regina," said Dr. Corte. "Now then, I'm trying to bait Diogenes here into telling us what's going on. I'm sure he knows. And if you would skip the first part, Diogenes, about all the other scientists in the world being like little boys alongside of you, it would speed things up. I believe that this is another of your experiments like— Oh no! Let's not even think about the last one!

"Tell us, Diogenes, about the hole on the corner, and what falls through it. Tell us how some people come home two or three times within as many minutes, and find themselves already there when they get there. Tell us how a creature that staggers the imagination can seem so like an old acquaintance after a moment or two that one might not know which is which. I am not now sure which of these Homers it was who came to my office several moments ago, and with whom I returned to this house. They look just alike in one way, and in another they do not."

"My Homer always was funny looking," Regina said.

"They appear quite different if you go by the visual index," Diogenes explained. "But nobody goes by the visual index except momentarily. Our impression of a person or a thing is much more complex, and the visual element in our appraisal is small. Well, one of them is Homer in gestalt two, and the other is Homer in gestalt nine. But they are quite distinct. Don't ever get the idea that such are the same persons. That would be silly."

"And Lord spare us that!" said Homer the man. "All right, go into your act, Diogenes."

"First, look at me closely, all of you," Diogenes said. "Handsome, what? But note my clothing and my complexion and my aspect.

"Then to the explanations: it begins with my Corollary to Phelan's Corollary on Gravity. I take the opposite alternate of it. Phelan puzzled that gravity should be so weak on all worlds but one. He said that the gravity of that one remote world was typical, and that the gravity of all other worlds was atypical and the result of a mathematical error. But I, from the same data, deduce that the gravity of our own world is not too weak, but too strong. It is about a hundred times as strong as it should be."

"What do you compare it to when you decide it is too strong?" Dr. Corte wanted to know.

"There's nothing I can compare it to, Doctor. The gravity of *every* body that I am able to examine is from eighty to a hundred times too strong. There are two possible explanations: either my calculations or theories are somehow in error—unlikely—or there are, in every case, about a hundred bodies, solid and weighted, occupying the same place at the same time. *Old Ice Cream Store Chairs! Tennis Shoes in October! The Smell of Slippery Elm! County-Fair Barkers with Warts on Their Noses! Horned Toads in June!*"

"I was following you pretty good up to the Ice Cream Store Chairs," said Homer the monster.

"Oh, I tied that part in, and the tennis shoes too," said Homer the man. "I'm pretty good at following this cosmic theory business. What threw me was the slippery elm. I can't see how it especially illustrates a contingent theory of gravity."

"The last part was an incantation," said Diogenes. "Do you remark anything different about me now?"

"You're wearing a different suit now, of course," said Regina, "but there's nothing remarkable about that. Lots of people change to different clothes in the evening."

"You're darker and stringier," said Dr. Corte. "But I wouldn't have noticed any change if you hadn't told us to look for it. Actually, if I didn't know that you were Diogenes, there wouldn't be any sane way to identify Diogenes in you. You don't look a thing like you, but still I'd know you anywhere."

"I was first a gestalt two. Now I'm a gestalt three for a while," said Diogenes. "Well, first we have the true case that a hundred or so solid and weighty bodies are occupying the same space that our earth occupies, and at the same time. This in itself does violence to conventional physics. But now let us consider the characteristics of all these cohabiting bodies. Are they occupied and peopled? Will it then mean that a hundred or so persons are occupying at all times the same space that each person occupies? Might not this idea do violence to conventional psychology? Well, I have proved that there are at least eight other persons occupying the same space occupied by each of us, and I have scarcely begun proving. *Stark White Sycamore Branches! New-Harrowed Earth! (New harrow, old earth.) Cow Dung Between Your Toes in July! Pitchers'-Mound Clay in the Old Three-Eye League! Sparrow Hawks in August!*"

"I fell off the harrow," said wife Regina. "I got the sycamore branches bit, though."

"I got clear down to the sparrow hawks," said Homer the monster.

"Do you remark anything different about me this time?" Diogenes asked.

"You have little feathers on the backs of your hands where you used to have little hairs," said Homer the man, "and on your toes. You're barefoot now. But I wouldn't have noticed any of it if I hadn't been looking for something funny."

"I'm a gestalt four now," said Diogenes. "My conduct is likely to become a little extravagant."

"It always was," said Dr. Corte.

"But not so much as if I were a gestalt five," said Diogenes. "As a five, I might take a Pan-like leap onto the shoulders of young Fregona here, or literally walk barefoot through the hair of the beautiful Regina as she stands there. Many normal gestalt twos become gestalt fours or fives in their dreams. It seems that Regina does.

"I found the shadow, but not the substance, of the whole situation in the psychology of Jung. Jung served me as the second element in this, for it was the errors

of Phelan and Jung in widely different fields that set me
on the trail of the truth. What Jung really says is that
each of us is a number of persons in depth. This I consider silly. There is something about such far-out theories that repels me. The truth is that our counterparts
enter into our unconsciousness and dreams only by accident, as being most of the time in the same space
that we occupy. But we are all separate and independent persons. And we may, two or more of us, be present
in the same frame at the same time, and then in a near,
but not the same, place. Witness the gestalt two and
the gestalt nine Homers here present.

"I've been experimenting to see how far I can go with
it, and the gestalt nine is the furthest I have brought
it so far. I do not number the gestalten in the order of
their strangeness to our own norm, but in the order in
which I discovered them. I'm convinced that the con-
centric and congravitic worlds and people complexes
number near a hundred, however."

"Well, there *is* a hole on the corner, isn't there?" Dr.
Corte asked.

"Yes, I set it up there by the bus stop as a convenient
evening point of entry for the people of this block," said
Diogenes. "I've had lots of opportunity to study the results these last two days."

"Well, just how *do* you set up a hole on the corner?"
Dr. Corte persisted.

"Believe me, Corte, it took a lot of imagination," Diogenes said. "I mean it literally. I drew so deeply on
my own psychic store to construct the thing that it left
me shaken, and I have the most manifold supply of
psychic images of any person I know. I've also set up
magnetic amplifiers on both sides of the street, but it
is my original imagery that they amplify. I see a never-
ending field of study in this."

"Just what is the incantation stuff that takes you from
one gestalt to another?" Homer the monster asked.

"It is only one of dozens of possible modes of entry,

but I sometimes find it the easiest," said Diogenes. "It is Immediacy Remembered, or the Verbal Ramble. It is the Evocation—an intuitive or charismatic entry. I often use it in the Bradmont Motif—named by me from two as-aff writers in the twentieth century."

"You speak of it as if . . . well, isn't *this* the twentieth century?" Regina asked.

"This the twentieth? Why, you're right! I guess it is," Diogenes agreed. "You see, I carry on experiments in other fields also, and sometimes I get my times mixed. All of you, I believe, do sometimes have moments of peculiar immediacy and vividness. It seems then as if the world were somehow fresher in that moment, as though it were a new world. And the explanation is that, to you, it *is* a new world. You have moved, for a moment, into a different gestalt. There are many accidental holes or modes of entry, but mine is the only contrived one I know of."

"There's a discrepancy here," said Dr. Corte. "If the persons are separate, how can you change from one to another?"

"I do not change from one person to another," said Diogenes. "There have been three different Diogenes lecturing you here in series. Fortunately, my colleagues and I, being of like scientific mind, work together in close concert. We have made a successful experiment in substitution acceptance on you here this evening. Oh, the ramifications of this thing! The aspects to be studied. I will take you out of your narrow gestalt-two world and show you worlds upon worlds."

"You talk about the gestalt-two complex that we normally belong to," said wife Regina, "and about others up to gestalt nine, and maybe a hundred. Isn't there a gestalt one? Lots of people start counting at one."

"There is a number one, Regina," said Diogenes. "I discovered it first and named it, before I realized that the common world of most of you was of a similar category. But I do not intend to visit gestalt one again.

264

It is turgid and dreary beyond tolerating. One instance of its mediocrity will serve. The people of gestalt one refer to their world as the 'everyday world.' Retch quietly, please. May the lowest of us never fall so low! *Persimmons After First Frost! Old Barbershop Chairs! Pink Dogwood Blossoms in the Third Week of November! Murad Cigarette Advertisements!!"*

Diogenes cried out the last in mild panic, and he seemed disturbed. He changed into another fellow a little bit different, but the new Diogenes didn't like what he saw either.

"Smell of Wet Sweet Clover!" he cried out. *"St. Mary's Street in San Antonio! Model Airplane Glue! Moon Crabs in March!* It won't work! The rats have run out on me! Homer and Homer, grab that other Homer there! I believe he's a gestalt six, and they sure are mean."

Homer Hoose wasn't particularly mean. He had just come home a few minutes late and had found two other fellows who looked like him jazzing his wife Regina. And those two mouth men, Dr. Corte and Diogenes Pontifex, didn't have any business in his house when he was gone either.

He started to swing. You'd have done it too.

Those three Homers were all powerful and quick-moving fellows, and they had a lot of blood in them. It was soon flowing, amid the crashing and breaking-up of furniture and people—ocher-colored blood, pearl-gray blood, one of the Homers even had blood of a sort of red color. Those boys threw a real riot!

"Give me that package of coriander seed, Homer," wife Regina said to the latest Homer as she took it from his pocket. "It won't hurt to have three of them. Homer! Homer! Homer! All three of you! Stop bleeding on the rug!"

Homer was always a battler. So was Homer. And Homer.

"*Stethoscopes and Moonlight and Memory—ah—in Late March,*" Dr. Corte chanted. "Didn't work, did it?

I'll get out of here a regular way. Homers, boys, come up to my place, one at a time, and get patched up when you're finished. I have to do a little regular medicine on the side nowadays."

Dr. Corte went out the door with the loopy run of a man not in very good condition.

"*Old Hairbreadth Harry Comic Strips! Congress Street in Houston! Light Street in Baltimore! Elizabeth Street in Sydney! Varnish on Old Bar-Room Pianos! B-Girls Named Dotty!* I believe it's easier just to make a dash for my house next door," Diogenes rattled off. And he did dash out with the easy run of a man who is in good condition.

"I've had it!" boomed one of the Homers—and we don't know which one—as he was flung free from the donnybrook and smashed into a wall. "Peace and quiet is what a man wants when he comes home in the evening, not this. Folks, I'm going out and up to the corner again. Then I'm going to come home all over again. I'm going to wipe my mind clear of all this. When I turn back from the corner I'll be whistling "Dixie" and I'll be the most peaceful man in the world. But when I get home, I bet neither of you guys had better have happened at all."

And Homer dashed up to the corner.

Homer Hoose came home that evening, to the g.c.—everything as it should be. He found his house in order and his wife Regina alone.

"Did you remember to bring the coriander seed, Homer, little gossamer of my fusus?" Regina asked him.

"Ah, I remembered to get it, Regina, but I don't seem to have it in my pocket now. I'd rather you didn't ask me where I lost it. There's something I'm trying to forget. Regina, I didn't come home this evening before this, did I?"

"Not that I remember, little dolomedes sexpunctatus."

"And there weren't a couple other guys here who looked just like me only different?"

"No, no, little cobby. I love you and all that, but nothing else could look like you. Nobody has been here but you. Kids! Get ready for supper! Papa's home!"

"Then it's all right," Homer said. "I was just day-dreaming on my way home, and all that stuff never happened. Here I am in the perfect house with my wife Regina, and the kids'll be underfoot in just a second. I never realized how wonderful it was. AHHHHNNN!!! YOU'RE NOT REGINA!!"

"But of course I am, Homer. Lycosa Regina is my species name. Well, come, come, you know how I enjoy our evenings together."

She picked him up, lovingly broke his arms and legs for easier handling, spread him out on the floor, and began to devour him.

"No, no, you're not Regina," Homer sobbed. "You look just like her, but you also look like a giant monstrous arachnid. Dr. Corte was right, we got to fix that hole on the corner."

"That Dr. Corte doesn't know what he's talking about," Regina munched. "He says I'm a compulsive eater."

"What's you eating Papa again for, Mama?" daughter Fregona asked as she came in. "You know what the doctor said."

"It's the spider in me," said Mama Regina. "I wish you'd brought the coriander seed with you, Homer. It goes so good with you."

"But the doctor says you got to show a little restraint, Mama," daughter Fregona cut back in. "He says it becomes harder and harder for Papa to grow back new limbs so often at his age. He says it's going to end up by making him nervous."

"Help, help!" Homer screamed. "My wife is a giant spider and is eating me up. My legs and arms are already gone. If only I could change back to the first nightmare! *Night-Charleys under the Beds at Grandpa's House on the Farm! Rosined Cord to Make Bull-Roarers on Hallowe'en! Pig Mush in February! Cobwebs on*

Fruit Jars in the Cellar! No, no, not that! Things never work when you need them. That Diogenes fools around with too much funny stuff."

"All I want is a little affection," said Regina, talking with her mouth full.

"Help, help," said Homer as she ate him clear up to his head. "Shriek, shriek!"

WHAT'S THE NAME OF THAT TOWN?

"Epiktistes tells me that you are onto something big, Mr. Smirnov," Valery said, turning to her companion. "Epikt has the loudest mouth of any machine I was ever associated with," Gregory Smirnov growled. "I never saw one that could keep a secret. But this one goes to extremes. Actually, we don't have a thing. We're just fiddling around with an unborn idea."

"How about it, Epikt?" Valery asked.

"Big, real big," the machine issued.

"What are you doing now, Epikt?" Valery wanted to know.

"Talk to me, dammit! I'm the man, he's the machine," Smirnov cut in. "He's chewing encyclopedias and other references. It's all he ever does."

"I thought he went through them all long ago."

"Certainly, dozens of times. He has all the data that can be fed into a machine, and every day we shovel in bales of new stuff. But he's chewing it now for a very different purpose."

"What different purpose, Mr. Smirnov?"

"It's difficult to say because I haven't as yet been able to state it to him. We're trying to set a problem where it seems there ought to be one—and then answer it. We may find the answer before the question. At first he rejected my request; later he accepted it—ironically. I doubt that he's sincere now. He can be quite a clown, as you should well know."

"I know that you two are onto something good," Valery said. "The more you deny it, the more I'm sure of it. Tell me the truth, Epikt."

"Big, real big," Epiktistes issued to Valery.

"Valery," said Smirnov. "You're a woman and you might be inclined to say something about this to the

269

other Institute people. Please don't. We don't have anything yet and it makes me nervous to have hot little
people breathing down my neck."

"I won't say a word," Valery swore with grave insin-
cerity. She winked at the machine, and Epikt winked
back at her with three tiers of eyes. Valery Mok and
Epiktistes had a thing going with each other.

Valery was nearly as bad as a machine at not being
able to keep a secret. She had the whole Institute staff
excited about what Smirnov and Epiktistes were working on. The staff consisted of Charles Cogsworth, her
own over-shadowed husband; Glasser, the stiff-necked
inventor; and Aloysius Shiplap, the seminal genius.

They were all after Smirnov and his machine the next
day.

"We've been together on every project," Glasser said.
"Valery tells us that the problem hasn't been properly
formulated, and that Epikt has only accepted it ironically. We're pretty good at formulating problems, Gregory,
and a little sterner than you when it comes to dealing
with clownish machines."

"All right, this is the way it is, Glasser," Smirnov said
reluctantly. "My first statement was, we should seek to
discover something not known to exist, by a close study
of the absence of evidence. When I put the problem to
Epiktistes in this generalized form he just laughed at
me."

"That would have been my first impulse too, Smirnov,"
said Shiplap. "Don't you have a better idea of what
you're looking for?"

"Shiplap, I had the feeling of trying to remember
something that I'd been compelled to forget. My second statement wasn't much better. 'Let us see,' I said
to Epikt, 'if we cannot reconstruct something of which
even the idea has been completely eradicated; let's see
if we can't find it by considering the excessive evidence
that it was never there.' In this form, Epikt accepted it.
Or else he decided to go along with me for the gag.

I'm never quite sure how this clanking machine takes things."

"Well, no hole can be filled up perfectly," said Cogsworth. "There will either be too much or too little of whatever is being used as the filler, or it will be of a different texture. The difficulty is that you didn't give Epikt any clues. There will be a million things forgotten or repressed that will show an irregularity of fill. How will Epikt know which of them is the one that you are somehow trying to remember?"

"Item. The buried thing will have a buried tie with my boss man Smirnov," Epiktistes, the machine, issued.

"Yes, of course," said Glasser. "Has Epikt turned up anything?"

"Only a bushelful of things that seem to mean nothing," said Smirnov sadly.

"Item. Why, in Hungarian dictionary-encyclopedias of a certain period, is there padding between the words *Sik* and *Sikamlos?*" Epiktistes asked.

"I follow your thought, Epikt," Glasser agreed. "That could be a clue to something. If the idea and the name of something were expunged from every reference, then, in all original editions, other subjects on the same page would have to be padded slightly or another subject set in. This filling might be hurried, and therefore of an inferior quality. So, who knows a word that is no longer used and that comes between *Sik* and *Sikamlos?* If we knew the word would we know what it meant? And would it help us if we did?"

"Item. Why is the young of a bear now referred to as a pup when once it may have been known as a cube?" Epikt issued.

"I've never heard the young of a bear referred to as a cube," Shiplap protested.

"Epikt has come on that by our omission-appraisal method," Smirnov explained. "There is probably an imperfect erasure working. I believe that cube is a distortion of a word that has somehow been forced out of folk memory. Epikt has this clue from a ballad which I believe is far removed from the main suppression or it would not have survived in even this distorted form."

"Item. Why is the awkward word *coronal* used for the simple doubling or return of a rope? Why is not a simpler word used?" Epikt asked.

"Has Epikt considered that seamen have always used odd terms and that landsmen often adopt them?" Cogsworth asked.

"Naturally—Epikt always considers everything," Smirnov answered. "He has thousands of these items now, and he believes that he will be able to put them into a pattern."

"Item. Why is there a great hiatus in period jazz? It's as though a great hunk of it had been yanked out by the roots, in the words of one Benny B-Flat."

"Smirnov, I know that your machine has unusual talents," said Glasser, "but if he can tie these things together he's a concatenated genius."

"Or a cantankerous clown," Smirnov said. "I know that he has to have some emotional release from the stress of his work, but he often overdoes it with humor and drollery."

"Item. Why is reference to the Amerindian peace pipe avoided as though some obscenity were attached to it, and none is discoverable?"

"That's a new one while we're standing here," said Smirnov. "He's accumulating quite a few of them."

"Item. Why is—?" Epikt started.

"Oh, shut up and get back to work," Smirnov ordered his machine. "Let's leave him with it until tomorrow, folks. It may begin to pull together by then," said Smirnov, stalking off.

"Going to be real big," Epiktistes issued to them after his boss man had left. "Boys and girls, it's going to be real big."

The next day they combined the meeting around the

machine with a party for Shiplap. Aloysius Shiplap had grown—for the first time ever, anywhere—left-handed grass. It was not called that because it whorled to the left, but because the organic constituents of it were reversed in their construction. Left-handed minerals had been constructed long since, and perhaps they also occurred in nature. Left-handed bacteria and broths were long known, but nobody else had ever grown anything as complex as left-handed grass.

"In everything,- its effect is reversed," Shiplap explained. "Cattle pastured on this would lose rather than gain weight. If there ever develops a market for really skinny cattle I'll be waiting for it."

They tossed off a good bit of Tosher's Gin as they got into the celebration. Tosher's is the only drink that will buzz up both humans and Ktistec machines. There is a flavoring used in Tosher's that gets machines high. The alcohol in it sometimes has a similar effect on humans.

Epiktistes got as mellow as a Pottawattamie County pumpkin. Ktistec machines are like the Irish and the Indians. They start unwinding when the gin begins to flow. Their behavior could become quite wild unless carefully watched.

And the Institute people were. also having a good time.

"I wouldn't have him any other way," said Smirnov. "When he relaxes, he relaxes all over the place. Hawkins' machine literally bites people when it's frustrated by a difficult problem. Drexel's smaller machine comes all apart throwing arc snuffers and solenoids and is mighty dangerous to be around. There are worse sorts than this clown of a machine I have—though he does get pretty slushy when he's in his cups."

Valery Mok had gathered up a bunch of Epiktistes' utterances and slipped them into cocktail cookies. Glasser, eating one, chewed on a bit of the metallic tape. He pulled it slithering, off his tongue, and read—

"Item. What was the mysterious name written by a

273

deaf moron on the wall of the men's room in an institution in Vinita, Oklahoma?"

Epiktistes giggled, though the item may have been serious when he issued it.

Cogsworth pulled one out of his mouth, stripping the crumbs from it with his tongue as it came.

"Item. Why does Petit Larousse take five lines too many to say almost nothing about the ancient Chibcha Indians of Columbia?"

At this point Valery went into her high laugh that would even make the alphabet sound funny.

Shiplap pulled one out of his grinning mouth, and it seemed an extension of his grin as it came.

"Item," he read. "What is there about the Great Blue Island Swamp that puzzles geologists? Or—in the old bylining manner—how recent is recent?"

Tosher's is giggle juice. Glasser's laughter sounded like a string of firecrackers going off.

Smirnov extracted the utterance from his cookie in the lordly manner. He read the utterance as though it were of extreme importance—and it was.

"Item. What peculiarity is almost revealed by the faded paint of old Rock Island and Pacific Railroad boxcars?"

"Oh, stop giggling, Epikt, it isn't as funny as that!"

"It is, it is!" bubbled Valery. Then she nearly choked bringing out from her own cookie a very long tape, and she read it with a very gay voice:

"Item. Why, when the gruesome Little Willy verses were revived among sub-teen-agers in the early nineteen-eighties, were they concerned almost entirely with chewing gum? In their Australian and British homelands six decades before, they were concerned with everything. But here we have gruesome verses about forty-nine different flavors of gum. As for instance, ·

Little Willy mixed his gum
with bits of Baby's cerebrum

WHAT'S THE NAME OF THAT TOWN?

and Papa's blood for Juicy
Fruit.
Mother said, "Oh, Will, don't
duit."

"I'd think it would give too high a flavor to the gum,"
said Glasser.

It's a lot of fun to open cocktail cookies and read
out utterances of a Ktistec machine. The Institute staff
generated a bunch of what we can only call merriment.
But they were busy people, and the party had to come
to an end. Epiktistes issued a verse as they prepared to
leave.

When the world's last Tosher's
is drunken,
and the world's last item has
flewn,
and the Institute people are
stunken,
and Epikt is high as the—

And there he stuck! Eight million billion billion memory contacts he had in him, and he couldn't come up
with a rhyme for flewn.

"How many items have you really gathered, Epikt?"
Glasser asked as they began to break up.

"Millions of them, bub, millions of them."

"No. Actually he has about three-quarters of a million that he believes he can tie together," Smirnov explained. "I feel that he'll bring them into a pattern, but
I'm afraid that it will be a facetious one."

"Epikt, you cute cubicle, will you be able to give us
any idea of what to look for by tomorrow?" Valery asked.

"Boys and girls, I'll have it all wrapped up and on
display for you tomorrow," Epiktistes issued. "I'll even be
able to tell you what the thing smelled like."

Expectation ran high among the people of the Institute. Epiktistes wanted to have the reporters in, but Smirnov said no. He didn't trust his machine. Epikt was a cube twenty meters on a side; and of his thousands of eyes, some of them always seemed to be laughing at his master.

"It won't be a hoax?" Smirnov asked his machine apprehensively.

"Boss, did I ever hoax you?" Epikt issued.

"Yes."

"Boss, some things are best presented in the guise of a hoax, but underneath this won't be one."

It was a crooked-tongued machine sometimes, and Smirnov was more apprehensive than ever.

The next day everyone gathered early to hear what Epikt had to say. They pulled up chairs and recording canisters and waited for the machine to begin.

"Ladies, gentlemen, associates," said Epikt solemnly, "we are gathered together to hear of an important matter. I will present it as well as I am able. There will be disbelief, I know, but I am sure of my facts. Make yourselves comfortable." He paused and then as an afterthought added, "You may smoke."

"You clanking cubicle, don't tell us what we may do," Smirnov screamed. "You're only a machine that I made."

"You and three thousand other workers," issued Epikt, without blinking an eye, "and in the final stages, the important stages, I directed my own assembly. I could not have happened otherwise. Only I know what is in me. As to my own abilities—"

"Get on with it, Epikt," Smirnov ordered, "and try to avoid the didactic manner."

"Then to get to the point, in the year 1980, the largest city of the American Midland was destroyed by an unnatural disaster."

"That was only twenty years ago," Glasser cut in. "It seems that someone would have heard of it."

"I wonder if St. Louis knew that she was destroyed,"

Valery ventured. "She acts as though she thought that she were still there."

"St. Louis was not the city," issued Epikt. "This destruction of a metropolitan area of seven million persons in much less than seven seconds was a great horror from the human viewpoint—come to think of it I now recall being a little disturbed by it myself. The thing was so fearful that it was decided to suppress the whole business and blissfully forget about it."

"Wouldn't that be a little difficult?" said Aloysius Shiplap sarcastically.

"It was very difficult to do," issued Epikt, "and yet it was done, completely, within twenty hours. And from that moment until this, nobody has remembered or thought about it at all."

"And if Your Whimsical Highness will just explain how this was done?" Smirnov challenged his machine.

"I'll explain as well as I can, good master. The project was put in charge of a master scientist who shall be nameless—but only for a few minutes."

"How were the written references of a metropolis of seven million persons obliterated?" asked Cogsworth.

"By a device then newly invented by our master scientist," Epikt answered. "It was known as the Tele-Pantographic Distorter. Even I, from this distance of time and through the cloud of induced amneisa, cannot understand how it worked. But it *did* work, and it simultaneously destroyed all printed references to our subject. This left holes in the references, and the flow of matter to fill those holes was sometimes of inferior texture, as I have noted. Holographic—that is handwritten, for you, Valery—references were more difficult. Most were simply destroyed. In more important documents, the text was flowed in automatic writing to fill the hole, and in close imitation of the original handwriting. But these imitations were often imperfect. I have a few thousand instances of this. But the Tele-

Pantographic Distorter was a truly remarkable machine, and I regret that it is now out of use."

"Kindly explain what happened to this remarkable machine," said Smirnov.

"Oh, it's still here in the Institute. You stumble into it a dozen times a day, good master, and you curse it as 'That Damnable Pile of Junk,' " issued Epikt. "But you have a block that will not allow you to remember what it is."

"I believe that I have been stumbling into such a pile of junk for many years," mused Smirnov. "Several times I have almost permitted myself to wonder what it was."

"And you invented it. The master scientist of the memory-obliteration was yourself, Gregory Smirnov."

"Hog hang it, Epikt! Your jug will leak!" protested Shiplap. "How of the human memories? The seven million inhabitants of the city would have had relatives of at least an equal number elsewhere. Didn't they wonder about their mothers or children or brothers and sisters?"

"They sorrowed, but they didn't wonder," issued Epikt. "It was a sorrow to which they could give no name. Examine the period and see how many really sad songs were popular in the years 1980 and 1981. But broadcast euphoria soon masked it over. The human memory of the thing was blocked by induced world amnesia. This was done hypnotically over the broadcast waves, and over more subtle waves. Few escaped it. The deaf moron mentioned in one of my items was one of those few. He scrawled the name of the town on a wall once, but it meant nothing to anyone."

"But there would be a hundred million loose ends to clean up," Glasser protested.

"Raise that number several powers," issued Epikt. "There were very many loose ends, and most of them were taken care of. I gathered a million or so that remained in the process of this study, but they could not break through the induced amnesia. The door was bolted on the whole subject. Then it was double-locked. It was necessary to destroy not only the memory, but also the memory of that memory. Mr. Smirnov, in what was perhaps his greatest feat, put himself under the final hypnosis against it. It was his job to pull in the hole after them all. But it bothered him more than others because he was more involved in it. After this temporary explanation it will bother him no more. This time he will forget it with a clear conscience.

"He does not recognize or remember it even now. It was his intent and triumph that he never should. The city and its destruction are forgotten forever, but the *method* of that memory-obliteration has only been forced to a subliminal level. It will be resurrected and used again whenever there is a great unnatural disaster."

"And where in tarnation or the American Midlands was this city?" Cogsworth hollered.

"Its site is now known as the Great Blue Island Swamp," issued Epikt.

"Finish it, you goggle-eyed gadget!" Shiplap shrilled. "What's the name of that town?"

"Chicago," issued Epiktistes.

That broke it! That tore it clear up! It was a hoax after all. That clattering clown of a cubicle had led them into it with all eyes open. Valery went into her high laughter, and her good husband Cogsworth chortled like a gooney bird with the hiccups.

"Chicago! It sounds like a little zoo beaver sliding down a mud slide and hitting the water. Chicago!" It was the funniest word Valery had ever heard.

"Nobody but a machine gone comic could coin a name like that," laughed Glasser with his fire-cracker laugh. "Chicago!"

"I take my hat off to you, Epiktistes," said Aloysius Shiplap. "You are a cog-footed, tongue-in-cheek tall tale teller. People, this machine is ripe!"

"I'm a little disappointed," said Smirnov. "So the mountain labored and produced a mouse. But did it have to be a wall-eyed mouse in a clown suit, Epikt? It's too

tall even for a tale. That a great city could be completely destroyed only twenty years ago and we know nothing about it—that's tall enough. But that it should have
the impossible name of Chicago tops it all. If you
weighed, all possible sounds—and I'm sure that you did,
Epikt—you could not come up with a more ridiculous
sounding name than that."

"Good people, it is meant to be this way," issued
Epiktistes. "You cannot remember it. You cannot recognize it. And when you leave this room you will not
even be able to recall the funny name. You will have
only the dim impression that the clownish machine
played a clownish trick on you. The disasters—for I
suspect that there were several such—are well forgotten. The world would lie down and die if it remembered
them too well.

"And yet there really was a large city named Chicago.
As Sikago it left a hole in one Hungarian dictionary-
encyclopedia; and the Petit Larousse had to flow French
froth about the Chibcha Indians into the place where
Chicago had stood. Something, for which I find the
tentative name of Chicago Hot, was pulled out of the
jazz complex by the roots. The Calumet River had
flowed about the city somewhere, so there came a re-
luctance to use that name of the old Indian peace pipe.
Chicago was a great city. The heart of her downtown
was known as the Loop, and one of her baseball teams
was named the Cubs. For that reason those two words
were forced out of use. They might be evocative."

"Loop? Cubs?" giggled Valery. "Those words are almost as funny as Chicago. How do you make them up,
Epikt?"

"In popular capsule impression Chicago was the chew-
ing-gum capital of the world. The leader in this manufacture was a man named—as well as I can reconstruct
it—Wiggly. Children somehow found the echoes of the
gruesome destruction of Chicago and tied it in with

this capsule impression to produce the bloody Little
Willy verses about chewing gum."

"Epikt, you top yourself," said Shiplap, "if anything
could top an invention as funny as Chicago."

"Good people, it comes down over you like a curtain,"
issued Epiktistes. "You forget again—even my joke, even
the funny name of the town. And, more to the point, I
forget also.

"It's gone. Gone. All gone. How peculiar! It is a long
blank tape you all stare at as though you were under
hypnosis. I must have suffered a blackout. I never issued a blank tape before. Smirnov, I have the taste in
my terminals of an experiment that didn't quite come
off. Feed me another. I don't fail often."

"That is enough for today, Epiktistes. We are all
sleepy for some reason. No, it didn't work out—whatever it was. I forget what it was that we were working
on. It doesn't matter. Our failures are well forgotten.
We'll hit on something else. We're working on a lot of
things."

Then they all shuffled out sleepily and went back to
their work. Smirnov's machine had busted on something
or other, but it was a good machine and would hit the
next time, of that they were sure.

In the corridor, Smirnov stumbled into his old Tele-
Pantographic Distorter. He had been stumbling unseeing into it every day for twenty years.

The machine rolled nine banks of eyes at Smirnov
and smiled willingly. Was it another of those disasters?
Was there any deep work to be done? Tele-Pan was
ready. But no. Smirnov passed on. The machine smiled
again and went peacefully back to sleep.

"That damnable piece of junk," Smirnov growled,
walking along and petting his sore shin. "I feel almost
as if I were on the verge of wondering what it is."

THROUGH OTHER EYES

I

"I DON'T THINK I can stand the dawn of another Great Day," said Smirnov. "It always seems a muggy morning, a rainy afternoon, and a dismal evening. You remember the Recapitulation Correlator?"

"Known popularly as the Time Machine. But, Gregory, that was and is a success. All three of them are in constant use, and they will construct at least one more a decade. They are invaluable."

"Yes. It was a dismal success. It has turned my whole life gray. You remember our trial run, the recapitulation of the Battle of Hastings?"

"It *was* a depressing three years we spent there. But how were we to know it was such a small affair—covering less than five acres of that damnable field and lasting less than twenty minutes? And how were we to know that an error of four years had been made in history even as recent as that? Yes, we scanned many depressing days and many muddy fields in that area before we recreated it."

"And our qualified success at catching the wit of Voltaire at first hand?"

"Gad! That cackle! There can never be anything new in nausea to one who has sickened of that. What a perverted old woman he was!"

"And Nell Guinn?"

"There is no accounting for the taste of a king. What a completely tasteless morsel!"

"And the crowning of Charlemagne?"

"The king of chilblains. If you wanted a fire, you carried it with you in a basket. That was the coldest Christmas I ever knew. But the mead seemed to warm them; and we were the only ones present who could not touch it or taste it."

"And when we went further back and heard the wonderful words of the divine poetess Sappho."

"Yes, she had just decided that she would have her favorite cat spayed. We listened to her for three days and she talked of nothing else. How fortunate the world is that so few of her words have survived."

"And watching the great Pythagoras at work."

"And the long days he spent on that little surveying problem. How one longed to hand him a slide rule through the barrier and explain its workings."

"And our eavesdropping on the great lovers Tristram and Isolde."

"And him spending a whole afternoon trying to tune that cursed harp with a penny whistle. And she could talk of nothing but the bear grease she used on her hair, and how it was nothing like the bear grease back home. But she was a cute little lard barrel, quite the cutest we found for several centuries in either direction. One wouldn't be able to get ones arms all the way around her; but I can understand how, to one of that era and region, it would be fun trying."

"Ah yes. Smelled like a cinnamon cookie, didn't she? And you recall Lancelot?"

"Always had a bad back that wouldn't let him ride. And that trick elbow and the old groin wound. He spent more time on the rubbing table than any athlete I ever heard of. If I had a high-priced quarterback who was never ready to play, I'd sure find a way of breaking his contract. No use keeping him on the squad just to read his ten-year-old press clippings. Any farm boy could have pulled him off his nag and stomped him into the dirt."

"I wasn't too happy about Aristotle the day we caught him. That barbarous north-coast Greek of his! Three hours he had them all busy curling his beard. And his discourse on the *Beard in Essential* and the *Beard in Existential*, did you follow that?"

"No, to tell the truth I didn't. I guess it was pretty profound."

They were silent and sad for a while, as are men who have lost much.

"The machine was a success," said Smirnov at last, "and yet the high excitement of it died dismally for us."

"The excitement is in the discovery of the machine," said Cogsworth. "It is never in what the machine discovers."

"And this new one of yours," said Smirnov, "I hardly want to see you put it into operation. I am sure it will be a shattering disappointment to you."

"I am sure of it also. And yet it is greater than the other. I am as excited as a boy."

"You were a boy before, but you will never be again. I should think it would have aged you enough, and I cannot see what fascination this new one will have for you. At least the other recaptured the past. This will permit you to see only the present."

"Yes, but through other eyes."

"One pair of eyes is enough. I do not see any advantage at all except the novelty. I am afraid that this will be only a gadget."

"No. Believe me, Smirnov, it will be more than that. It may not even be the same world when viewed through different eyes. I believe that what we regard as one may actually be several billion different universes, each made only for the eyes of the one who sees it."

II

The Cerebral Scanner, newly completed by Charles Cogsworth, was not an intricate machine. It was a small but ingenius amplifying device, or battery of amplifiers, designed for the synchronous—perhaps "sympathetic" would be a better word—coupling of two very intricate machines: two human brains. It was an amplifier only. A subliminal coupling, or the possibility of it, was already assumed by the inventor. Less than a score of key aspects needed emphasizing for the whole thing to come to life.

Here the only concern was with the convoluted cortex of the brain itself, that house of consciousness and terminal of the senses, and with the quasi-electrical impulses which are the indicators of its activity. It had been a long-held opinion of Cogsworth that, by the proper amplification of a near score of these impulses in one brain, a transmission could be effected to another so completely that one man might for an instant see with the eyes of another—also see inwardly with that man's eyes, have the same imaginings and daydreams, perceive the same universe as the other perceived. And it would not be the same universe as the seeking man knew.

The Scanner had been completed, as had a compilation of the dossiers of seven different brains: a collection of intricate brain-wave data as to frequency, impulse, flux and field, and Lyall-wave patterns of the seven cerebrums which Cogsworth would try to couple with his own.

The seven were those of Gregory Smirnov, his colleague and counselor in so many things; of Gaetan Balbo, the cosmopolitan and supra-national head of the Institute; of Theodore Grammont, the theoretical mathematician; of E. E. Euler, the many-tentacled executive; of Karl Kleber, the extraordinary psychologist; of Edmond Guillames, the skeptic and bloodless critic; and of Valery Mok, a lady of beauty and charm whom Cogsworth had despaired of ever understanding by ordinary means.

This idea of his—to enter into the mind of another, to peer from behind another's eyes into a world that could not be the same—this idea had been with him all his life. He recalled how it had first come down on him in all its strength when he was quite small.

"It may be that I am the only one who sees the sky black at night and the stars white," he had said to himself, "and everybody else sees the sky white and the stars shining black. And I say the sky is black, and they say the sky is black; but when they say black they mean white."

Or: "I may be the only one who can see the outside of a cow, and everybody else sees it inside out. And I say that it is the outside, and they say that it is the outside; but when they say outside they mean inside."

Or: "It may be that all the boys I see look like girls to everyone else, and all the girls look like boys. And I say 'That is a girl,' and they say 'That is a girl'; only when they say a girl they mean a boy.

And then had come the terrifying thought: "What if I am a girl to everyone except me?"

This did not seem very intelligent to him even when he was small, and yet it became an obsession to him.

"What if to a dog all dogs look like men and all men look like dogs? And what if a dog looks at me and thinks that I am a dog and he is a boy?"

And this was followed once by the shattering afterthought: "And what if the dog is right?

"What if a fish looks up at a bird and a bird looks down at a fish? And the fish thinks that he is the bird and the bird is the fish, and that he is looking down on the bird that is really a fish, and the air is water and the water is air?

"What if, when a bird eats a worm, the worm thinks he is the bird and the bird is the worm? And that his outside is his inside, and that the bird's inside is his outside? And that he has eaten the bird instead of the bird eating him?"

This was illogical. But how does one know that a

worm is not illogical? He has much to make him illogical.

And as he grew older Charles Cogsworth came on
many signs that the world he saw was not the world that
others saw. There came smaller but persistent signs
that every person lives in a different world.

It was early in the afternoon, but Charles Cogsworth
sat in darkness. Gregory Smirnov had gone for a walk
in the country as he said that he would. He was the
only other one who knew that the experiment was being
made. He is the only one who would have agreed to
the experiment, though the others had permitted their
brain-wave dossiers to be compiled on another pre-
text.

All beginnings come quietly, and this one was a total
success. The sensation of seeing with the eyes of another is new and glorious, though the full recognition of
it comes slowly.

"He is a greater man than I," said Cogsworth. "I
have often suspected it. He has a placidity which I do
not own, though he has not my fever. And he lives in
a better world."

It was a better world, greater in scope and more
exciting in detail.

"Who would have thought of giving such a color to
grass, if it is grass? It is what he calls grass, but it is
not what I call grass. I wonder I should ever be content
to see it as I saw it. It is a finer sky than I had known,
and more structured hills. The old bones of them stand
out for him as they do not for me, and he knows the
water in their veins.

"There is a man walking toward him, and he is a
grander man than I have ever seen. Yet I have also
known the shadow of this man, and his name is Mr.
Dottle, both to myself and to Gregory. I had thought
that Dottle was a fool, but now I know that in the world
of Gregory no man is a fool. I am looking through the

inspired and almost divine eyes of a giant, and I am
looking at a world that has not yet grown tired."

For what seemed like hours Charles Cogsworth lived
in the world of Gregory Smirnov; and he found here,
out of all his life, one great expectation that did not
fail him.

Then, after he had rested a while, he looked at the
world through the wide eyes of Gaetan Balbo.

"I am not sure that he is a greater man than I, but
he is a wider man. Nor am I sure that he looks into
a greater world. I would not willingly trade for his, as
I would for Gregory's. Here I miss the intensity of
my own. But it is fascinating, and I will enjoy returning to it again and again. And I know whose eyes these
are. I am looking through the eyes of a king."

Later he saw through the eyes of Theodore Grammont, and felt a surge of pity.

"If I am blind compared to Gregory, then this man
is blind compared to me. I at least know that the
hills are alive; he believes them to be imperfect poly-
hedrons. He is in the middle of a desert and is not even
able to talk to the devils who live there. He has ab-
stracted the world and numbered it, and doesn't even
know that the world is a live animal. He has built his
own world of great complexity, but he cannot see the
color of its flanks. This man has achieved so much only
because he was denied so much at the beginning. I understand now that only the finest theory is no more
than a fact gnawed on vicariously by one who has no
teeth. But I will return to this world too, even though
it has no body to it. I have been seeing through the eyes
of a blind hermit."

Delightful and exciting as this was, yet it was tiring.
Cogsworth rested for a quarter of an hour before he
entered the world of E. E. Euler. When he entered it
he was filled with admiration.

"An ordinary man could not look into a world like
this. It would drive him out of his wits. It is almost like

looking through the eyes of the Lord, who numbers all
the feathers of the sparrow and every mite that nestles
there. It is the interconnection vision of all the details.
It appalls. It isn't an easy world even to look at. Great
Mother of Ulcers! How does he stand it? Yet I see that
he loves every tangled detail, the more tangled the better. This is a world in which I will be able to take only
a clinical interest. Somebody must hold these reins, but
happily it is not my fate. To tame this hairy old beast
we live on is the doom of Euler. I look for a happier
doom."

He had been looking through the eyes of a general.

The attempt to see into the world of Karl Kleber was
almost a total failure. The story is told of the behaviorist
who would study the chimpanzee. He put the curious
animal in a room alone and locked the door on it; then
went to the keyhole to spy; the keyhole was completely
occupied by the brown eyeball of the animal spying back
at him.

Something of the sort happened here. Though Karl
Kleber was unaware of the experiment, yet the seeing
was in both directions. Kleber was studying Cogsworth
in those moments by some quirk of circumstance. And
even when Cogsworth was able to see with the eyes of
Kleber, yet it was himself he was seeing.

"I am looking through the eyes of a peeper," he said.
"And yet, what am I myself?"

If the world of Gregory Smirnov first entered was
the grandest, so that of Edmond Guillames, which Cogsworth entered last but one, was in all ways the meanest.
It was a world seen from the inside of a bile duct. It
was not a pleasant world, just as Edmond was not a
pleasant man. But how could one be other than a skeptic if all his life he had seen nothing but a world of
rubbery bones and bloodless flesh clothed in crippled
colors and obscene forms?

"The mole of another's world would be nobler than a
lion in his," said Cogsworth. "Why should one not be a

critic who has so much to criticize? Why should one
not be an unbeliever when faced with the dilemma that
this unsavory world was either made by God or hatched
by a cross-eyed ostrich? I have looked through the eyes
of a fool into a fools' world."

As Cogsworth rested again he said, "I have seen the
world through the eyes of a giant, of a king, of a blind
hermit, of a general, of a peeping tom, of a fool. There
is nothing left but to see it through the eyes of an angel."

Valery Mok may or may not have been an angel. She
was a beautiful woman, and angels, in the older and
more authentic iconography, were rather stern men with
shaggy pinions.

Valery wore a look of eternal amusement, and was
the embodiment of all charm and delight, at least to
Charles Cogsworth. He believed her to be of high wit.
Yet, if driven into a corner, he would have been unable
to recall one witty thing she had ever said. He regarded
her as of perfect kindness, and she *was* more or less on
the agreeable side. Yet, as Smirnov had put it, she was
not ordinarily regarded as extraordinary.

It was only quite lately that Cogsworth was sure that
it was love he felt for her rather than bafflement. And,
as he had despaired of ever understanding her by regular
means, though everyone else understood her easily
enough in as much as mattered, he would now use ir-
regular means for his understanding.

He looked at the world through the eyes of Valery
Mok, saying, "I will see the world through the eyes of
an angel."

A change came over him as he looked, and it was not
a pleasant change. He looked through her eyes quite a
while—not, perhaps, as long as he had looked through
the eyes of Gregory—yet for a long time, unable to tear
himself away.

He shuddered and trembled and shrank back into himself.

Then he let it alone, and buried his face in his arms. "I have looked at the world through the eyes of a pig," he said.

III

Charles Cogsworth spent six weeks in a sanatorium, which, however, was not called that. He had given the world his second great invention, and its completion had totally exhausted him. As in many such mercurial temperaments, the exaltation of discovery had been followed by an interlude of deep despondency on its completion.

Yet he was of fundamentally sound constitution and he had the best of care. But when he recovered it was not into his old self. He now had a sort of irony and smiling resignation that was new to him. It was as though he had discovered a new and more bitter world for himself in looking into the worlds of others.

Of his old intimates only Gregory Smirnov was still close to him.

"I can guess the trouble, Charles," said Gregory. "I rather feared this would happen. In fact I advised against her being one of the subjects of the experiment. It is simply that you know very little about women."

"I have read all the prescribed texts, Gregory. I took a six-week seminar under Zamenoff. I am acquainted with almost the entire body of the work of Bopp concerning women. I have spent nearly as many years as you in the world, and I generally go about with my eyes open. I surely understand as much as is understandable about them."

"No. They are not your proper field. I could have predicted what has shocked you. You had not understood that women are so much more sensuous than men. But it would be better if you explained just what it was that shocked you."

"I had thought that Valery was an angel. It is simply that it is a shock to find that she is a pig."

"I doubt if you understand pigs any better than you understand women. I myself, only two days ago, had a pigs'-eye view of the world, and that with your own Cerebral Scanner. I have been doing considerable work with it in the several weeks that you have been laid up. There is nothing in the pigs'-eye world that would shock even the most fastidious. It is a dreamy world of all-encompassing placidity, almost entirely divorced from passion. It's a gray shadowy world with very little of the unpleasant. I had never before known how wonderful is the feel of simple sunlight and of cool earth. Yet we would soon be bored with it; but the pig is not bored."

"You divert me, Gregory, but you do not touch the point of my shock. Valery is beautiful—or was to me before this. She seemed kind and serene. Always she appeared to contain a mystery that amused her vastly, and which I suspected would be the most wonderful thing in the world once I understood it."

"And her mystery is that she lives in a highly sensuous world and enjoys it with complete awareness? Is . that what has shocked you?"

"You do not know the depth of it. It is ghastly. The colors of that world are of unbelievable coarseness, and the shapes reek. The smells are the worst. Do you know how a tree smells to her?"

"What kind of tree?"

"Any tree. I think it was an ordinary elm."

"The Slippery Elm has a pleasant aroma in season. The others, to me, have none."

"No. It was not. Every tree has a strong smell in her world. This was an ordinary elm tree, and it had a violent musky obscene smell that delighted her. It was so strong that it staggered. And to her the grass itself is like clumps of snakes, and the world itself is flesh. Every bush is to her a leering satyr, and she cannot help

292

but brush into them. The rocks are spidery monsters and she loves them. She sees every cloud as a mass of twisting bodies and she is crazy to be in the middle of them. She hugged a lamp post and her heart beat like it would fight its way out of her body.

"She can smell rain at a great distance and in a foul manner, and she wants to be in the middle of it. She worships every engine as a fire monster, and she hears sounds that I thought nobody could ever hear. Do you know what worms sound like inside the earth? They're devilish, and she would writhe and eat dirt with them. She can rest her hand on a guard rail, and it is an obscene act when she does it. There is a filthiness in every color and sound and shape and smell and feel."

"And yet, Charles, she is but a slightly more than average attractive girl, given to musing, and with a love of the world and a closeness to it that most of us have lost. She has a keen awareness of reality and of the grotesqueness that is its main mark. You yourself do not have this deeply; and when you encounter it in its full strength, it shocks you."

"You mean that is normal?"

"There is no normal. There are only differences. When you moved into our several worlds they did not shock you to the same extent, for most of the corners are worn off our worlds. But to move into a pristine universe is more of a difference than you were prepared for."

"I cannot believe that that is all it is."

Charles Cogsworth would not answer the letters of Valery Mok, nor would he see her. Yet her letters were amusing and kind, and carried a trace of worry for him.

"I wonder what I smell like to her?" he asked himself. "Am I like an elm tree, or a worm in the ground? What color am I to her? Is my voice obscene? She says she misses the sound of my voice. It should be possible to undo this. Am I also to her like a column of snakes or a congerie of spiders?"

For he wasn't well yet from what he had seen.

But he did go back to work, and nibbled at the edges of mystery with his fantastic device. He even looked into the worlds of other women. It was as Smirnov had said: they were more sensuous than men but none of them to the shocking degree of Valery.

He saw with the eyes of other men. And of animals: the soft pleasure of the fox devouring a ground squirrel, the bloody anger of a lamb furious after milk, the crude arrogance of the horse, the intelligent tolerance of the mule, the voraciousness of the cow, the miserliness of the squirrel, the sullen passion of the catfish. Nothing was quite as might have been expected.

He learned the jealousy and hatred that beautiful women hold against the ugly, the untarnished evil of small children, the diabolic possession of adolescents. He even, by accident, saw the world through the flesh-less eyes of a poltergeist, and through the eyes of creatures that he could not identify at all. He found nobility in places that almost balanced the pervading baseness.

But mostly he loved to see the world through the eyes of his friend Gregory Smirnov, for there is a grandeur on everything when seen through a giant's eyes.

And one day he saw Valery Mok through the eyes of Smirnov when they met accidently. Something of his old feeling came back to him, and something that even surpassed his former regard. She was here magnificent, as was everything in that world. And there had to be a common ground between that wonderful world with her in it and the hideous world seen through her own eyes.

"I am wrong somewhere," said Cogsworth. "It is be-cause I do not understand enough. I will go and see her."

But instead she came to see him.

She burst in on him furiously one day.

"You are a stick. You are a stick with no blood in it. You are a pig made out of sticks. You live with dead people, Charles. You make everything dead. You are abominable."

"I a pig, Valery? Possibly. But I never saw a pig made out of sticks."

"Then see yourself. That is what you are."

"Tell me what this is about."

"It is about you. You are a pig made out of sticks, Charles. Gregory Smirnov let me use your machine. I saw the world the way you see it. I saw it with a dead man's eyes. You don't even know that the grass is alive. You think it's only grass."

"I also saw the world with your eyes, Valery."

"Oh, is that what's been bothering you? Well, I hope it livened you up a little. It's a livelier world than yours."

"More pungent, at least."

"Lord, I should hope so. I don't think you even have a nose. I don't think you have any eyes. You can look at a hill and your heart doesn't even skip a beat. You don't even tingle when you walk over a field."

"You see grass like clumps of snakes."

"That's better than not even seeing it alive."

"You see rocks like big spiders."

"That's better than just seeing them like rocks. I love snakes and spiders. You can watch a bird fly by and not even hear the stuff gurgling in its stomach. How can you be so dead? And I always liked you so much. But I didn't know you were dead like that."

"How can one love snakes and spiders?"

"How can one not love anything? It's even hard not to love you, even if you don't have any blood in you. By the way, what gave you the idea that blood was that dumb color? Don't you even know that blood is red?"

"I see it red."

"You *don't* see it red. You just call it red. That silly color isn't red. What I call red is red."

And he knew that she was right.

And after all, how can one not love anything? Especially when it becomes beautiful when angry, and when

It is so much alive that it tends to shock by its intense awareness those who are partly dead.

Now Charles Cogsworth was a scientific man, and he believed that there are no insoluble problems. He solved this one too; for he had found that Valery was a low-flying bird, and he began to understand what was gurgling inside her.

And he solved it happily.

He is working on a Correlator for his Scanner now. When this is perfected, it will be safe to give the device to the public. You will be able to get the combination in about three years at approximately the price of a medium-sized new car. And if you will wait another year, you may be able to get one of the used ones reasonably.

The Correlator is designed to minimize and condition the initial view of the world seen through other eyes, to soften the shock of understanding others.

Misunderstandings can be agreeable. But there is something shattering about sudden perfect understanding.

ONE AT A TIME

BARNABY PHONED up John Sourwine. If you frequent places like Barnaby's Barn (there is one in every port city of the world, and John is a familiar in all of them) you may already know John Sourwine; and you will know him as Sour John.

"There's an odd one down here," Barnaby told him.

"How odd?" asked Sour John. He collected odd ones.

"Clear coon-dog crazy, John. He looks like they just dug him up, but he's lively enough."

Barnaby runs a fine little place that offers eating and drinking and conversation, all of them rare and hearty. And John Sourwine is always interested in new things, or old things returned. So John went down to Barnaby's Barn to see the Odd One.

There was no need to ask which one he was, though there were always strangers and traveling men and seamen unknown to John in the Barn. The Odd One stood out. He was a big, spare, rough fellow, and he said that his name was McSkee. He was eating and drinking with a chortling pleasure, and they all watched him in amazement.

"It's his fourth plate of spaghetti," Smokehouse confided to Sour John, "and that is the last of two dozen eggs. He's had twelve hamburgers, six coney islands, six crab-burgers, five foot-long hot dogs, eighteen bottles of beer, and twenty cups of coffee."

"Blind blinking binnacles! He must be getting close to some of the records of Big Bucket Bulg," Sour John exclaimed with sudden interest.

"John, he's broken most of those records already," Smokehouse told him, and Barnaby nodded assent. "If

297

he can hold the pace for another forty-five minutes, he'll beat them all."

Well, the Odd One was still a spare fellow, with a great gangling frame designed to carry fifty or sixty pounds more than the lean fellow now owned. But he began to fill out even as John watched him; and it was not only that he bulked larger almost by the minute; it was also as though a light was being turned on inside him. He glowed. Then he shone. Then he began to sparkle.

"You like to eat, do you, old-timer?" Sour John asked the Odd One, the amazing McSkee.

"I like it well enough!" McSkee boomed with a happy grin. "But, more than that, it's just that I'm a bedamned show-off! I like everything in excess. I love to be in the roaring middle of it all!"

"One would think that you hadn't eaten in a hundred years," Sour John probed.

"You're quick!" the illuminated McSkee laughed. "A lot of them never do catch onto me, and I tell them nothing unless they guess a little first. Aye, you've got the hairy ears, though, and the adder's eyes of a true gentleman. I love a really ugly man. We will talk while I eat."

"What do you do when you've finished eating?" asked John, pleased at the compliments, as the waiters began to pile the steaks high in front of McSkee.

"Oh, I go from eating to drinking," McSkee munched out. "There's no sharp dividing line between the pleasures. I go from drinking to the girls; from the girls to fighting and roistering. And finally I sing."

"A bestial procedure," said John with admiration. "And when your pentastomic orgy is finished?"

"Oh, then I sleep," McSkee chuckled. "Watch how I do it some time. I should give lessons. Few men understand how it should be done."

"Well, how long do you sleep?" Sour John asked, "and

is there something spectacular about your sleeping that
I don't understand?"

"Of course it's spectacular. And I sleep till I waken.
At this also I set records."

And McSkee was wolfing the tall pile of steaks till
Sour John had a mystic vision of a steer devoured entire except for head and hide and hooves, the slaughter-
er's take.

Later, they talked somewhat more leisurely as Mc-
Skee worked his way through the last half-dozen steaks
—for now the edge was off his great appetite.

"In all this ostentatious bestiality, was there not one
gluttony more outstanding than the others?" Sour John
drew him out. "One time when you outdid even yourself?"

"Aye, there was that," said McSkee. "There was the
time when they were going to hang me with the new
rope."

"And how did you eat your way out of that one?"
Sour John asked.

"At that time and in that country—it was not this
one—the custom was new of giving the condemned
man what he wanted to eat." The incandescent McSkee
limned it out in his voice with the lilt of a barrel organ.
"I took advantage of the new usage and stripped the
countryside. It was a good supper they gave me, John,
and I was to be hanged at sunup. But I had them there,
for I was still eating at dawn. They could not interrupt
my last meal to hang me—not when they had promised
me a full meal. I stood them off that day and the night
and the following day. That is longer than I usually
eat, John, and I did outdo myself. That countryside had
been known for its poultry and its suckling pigs and its
fruits. It is known for them no longer. It never recovered."

"Did you?"

"Oh certainly, John. But by third dawn I was filled.

The edge was off my appetite, and I do not indulge thereafter."

"Naturally not. But what happened then? They did not hang you, or you would not be here to tell about it."

"That doesn't follow, John. I had been hanged before."

"Oh?"

"Sure. But not this time. I tricked them. When I had my fill, I went to sleep. And then deeper and deeper into sleep until I died. They do not hang a man already dead. They kept me for a day to be sure. John, I get a pretty high shine on me in a day! I'm a smelly fellow at best. Then they buried me, but they did not hang me. Why do you look at me so oddly, John?"

"It is nothing," said Sour John, "a mere random objection which I will not even dignify with words."

McSkee was drinking now, first wine to give a bottom to his stomach, then brandy for its rumpled dignity, then rum for its plain friendliness.

"Can you believe that all breakthroughs are achieved by common men like myself?" this McSkee asked suddenly.

"I can't believe that you're a common man," Sour John told him.

"I'm the commonest man you ever saw," McSkee insisted. "I am made from the clay and the salt of the Earth, and the humus from decayed behemoths. They may have used a little extra slime in making me, but I contain none of the rare earths. It had to be a man like myself who would work out the system. The savants aren't capable of it; they have no juice in them. And by their having no juice in them, they missed the first hint."

"What is that, McSkee?"

"It's so simple, John! That a man should live his life one day at a time."

"Well?" Sour John asked with towering intonation.

"See how harmlessly it slides down, John. It sounds almost like an almanac maxim."

"And it isn't?"

"No, no, the thunder of a hundred worlds rumbles between them. It's the door to a whole new universe. But there's another saying: 'Man, thy days are numbered.' This is the one inexorable saying. It is the limit that will not be bent or broken, and it puts the damper on us hearty ones. It poses a problem to one like myself, too carnal to merit eternal beatitude on another plane, too full of juice to welcome final extinction, and anxious for personal reasons to postpone the hardships of damnation as long as possible.

"Now, John, there were (and are) smarter men than myself in the world. That I solved the problem (to an extent) and they did not, means only that the problem was more pressing on me. It had to be a coarse man to find the answer, and I never met a man with such a passion for the coarse things of life as myself."

"Neither did I," Sour John told him. "And, how did you solve the problem?"

"By a fine little trick, John. You'll see it worked if you follow me around through the night."

McSkee had left off eating. But he continued to drink while he indulged in girls, and in fighting and roistering, and in singing. His girly exploits are not given here; but there is a fruity listing of them on the police blotter of that night. Go see Mossback McCarty some night when he is on desk duty and he will get it out and let you read it. It is something of a classic around the station house. When a man gets involved with Soft-Talk Susie Kutz and Mercedes Morrero and Dotty Peisson and Little Dotty Nesbitt and Hildegarde Katt and Catherine Cadensus and Ouida and Avril Aaron and Little Midnight Mullins all in one night, you are talking about a man who generates legends.

McSkee *did* stir things up around town, and John

Sourwine stayed with him. John fit in with McSkee
well. There are many who would not.

There are persons of finely-tuned souls who cringe
when a companion becomes unusually boisterous. There
are those who wince when a hearty mate sings loudly
and obscenely. There are even those who attempt to
disassociate when the grumblings of the solid citizenry
rise to a sullen roar; and who look for cover when the
first little fights begin. Fortunately, Sour John was not
such a person. He had a finely-tuned soul, but it had
a wide range.

McSkee had the loudest and most dissonant voice in
town, but would an honest friend desert him for that?

The two of them cut a big swath; and a handful of
rough men, rubbing big knuckles into big palms and
biding their time, had begun to follow them from place
to place: men like Buffalo-Chips Dugan and Shrimp-
Boat Gordon, Sulphur-Bottom Sullivan, Smokehouse, Kid-
ney-Stones Stenton, Honey-Bucket Kincaid. The fact that
these men followed McSkee angrily but did not yet dare
to close with him speaks highly of the man. He was
pretty woolly.

But there were times when McSkee would leave off
his raucous disharmony and joyful battling, and chuckle
somewhat more quietly. As—for a while—in the Little
Oyster Bar (it's upstairs from the Big Oyster).

"The first time I put the trick to a test," McSkee
confided to John, "was from need and not from choice.
I had incurred a lot of ill will in my day, and sometimes
it boils over. There was one time when a whole ship-
ful of men had had enough of me. This time (it was far
away and long ago in the ancient days of small sail) I
was shackled about the ankles and weighted and dropped
overboard. Then I employed the trick."

"What did you do?" Sour John asked him.

"John, you ask the damnest questions. I drowned, of
course. What else could any man do? But I drowned

calmly and with none of that futile threshing about. That's the trick, you see."

"No. I don't see."

"Time would be on my side, John. Who wants to spend eternity in the deep? Salt water is most corrosive; and my shackles, though I could not break them, were not massive. After a long lifetime, the iron would be so eaten through that it would part with any sudden strain. In less than one hundred years, the shackles gave way, and my body (preserved in a briny fashion but not in the best of condition) drifted up to the surface of the sea."

"Too late to do you any good," Sour John said. "Rather a droll end to the story, or was it the end?"

"Yes, that is the end of that story, John. And another time, when I was a footsoldier in the service of Pixodarus the Carian (with his Celtic Mercenaries, of course)—"

"Just a minute, McSkee," Sour John cut in. "There's something a little loose about all your talk, and it needs landmarks. How long have you lived anyhow? *How old are you?*"

"About forty years old by my count, John. Why?"

"I thought your stories were getting a little too tall, McSkee. But if you're no more than forty years old, then your stories do not make sense."

"Never said they did, John. You put unnatural conditions on a tale."

McSkee and Sour John were up in night court, bloodied and beatific. It was only for a series of little things that they had been arrested, but it was really to save them from lynching. They had a palaver with all those fine officers and men, and they had much going for them. Sour John was known to them as an old acquaintance and sometime offender. It was known that John's word was good; even when he lied he did it with an air of honesty. After a little time was allowed to pass, and the potential lynchers had dispersed, Sour

John was allowed to bail them both out on their strong promise of good behavior.

They swore and forswore that they would behave like proper men. They took ringing oaths to go to their beds at once and quietly. They went on record that they would carouse no more that night; that they would assault no honest woman; that they would obey the quirks of the laws however unreasonable. And that they would not sing.

So the police let them go.

When the two of them were out and across the street, McSkee found a bottle handy to his hand on the sidewalk, and let fly with it. You'd have done it yourself if you'd been taken by a like impulse. McSkee threw it in a beautiful looping arc, and it went through the front window of the station house. You have to admire a throw like that.

We record it here that they are *not* patsy cops in that town. They are respectable adversaries, and it is always a pleasure to tangle with them.

Off again! And pursued by the Minions with shout and siren! It was close there! Half a dozen times it was close! But Sour John was a fox who knew all the dens, and he and McSkee went to earth for the while.

"The trick is in coming to a total stop," said McSkee when they were safe and had their breath again. They were at ease in a club less public than Barnaby's Barn and even smaller than the Little Oyster. "I tell you a little about it, Sour John, for I see that you are a man of worth. Listen and learn. Everyone can die, but not everyone can die just when he wants to. First you stop breathing. There will be a point where your lungs are bursting and you just have to take another breath. Do not do it; or you will have the whole business to go through again. Then you slow your heart and compose your mind. Let the heat go out of your body and finish it."

"And then what?" Sour John asked.

"Why, then you die, John. But I tell you it isn't easy. It takes a devilish lot of practice."

"Why so much practice for a thing you do only once? You mean to die literally?"

"John, I talk plain. I say die, I mean die."

"There are two possibilities," said Sour John. "One is that I am slow of understanding. The other is that you are not making sense. On other evidence, I know the first possibility to be impossible."

"Tell you what, Sour John," said McSkee, "time's running short. Give me twenty dollars and I'll overlook your illogic. I never did like to die broke, and I feel my time is upon me. Thank you, John! I had a full day, both before and after I met you, and a full night that is nearly over. I had a pleasant meal, and enough booze to make me happy. I had fun with the girls, especially Soft-Talk Susie, and Dotty, and Little Midnight. I sang several of my favorite songs (which are not everybody's favorites). I indulged in a couple of good solid fights, and I've still got bells ringing in my head from them. Hey, John, why didn't you tell me that Honey-Bucket was left-handed? You knew it, and you let him sneak the first punch on me.

"It's been fun, John. I'm a boy who gets a lot out of this game. I'm a real juicy one, and I try to jam everything into a day and a night. You can get a lot into a period if you heap it up. Now, let's gather up what's left in the bottles, and go down to the beach to see what we can provoke. The night needs a cap on it before I go to my long slumber."

"McSkee, you've hinted several times that you had a secret for getting the most out of life," said Sour John, "but you haven't told me what it is."

"Man, I haven't hinted; I've spoken plainly," McSkee swore.

"Then what in hog heaven is the secret?" John howled.

"Live your life one day at a time, John. That's all."

Then McSkee was singing an old hobo song, too old

a song for. a forty-year-old man, not a specialist, to have
known.

"When did you learn that?" John asked him.

"Learned it yesterday. But I learned a bunch of new
ones today."

"I noticed, a few hours back, that there was something curiously dated about your speech," John said. "But
it doesn't seem to be the case now."

"John, I get contemporary real fast. I've a good ear,
and I talk a lot and listen a lot, and I'm the perfect
mimic. I can get up on a lingo in a day. They don't
change as fast as you'd imagine."

They went down to the beach to put the cap on the
night. If you're going to die, it's nice to die within the
sound of the surf, McSkee had said. They went down
beyond the end of the sea wall and into the stretches
where the beach was dark. Aye, McSkee had guessed
it rightly, there was excitement waiting for them, or
actually it had been following them. It was the opportunity for a last glorious fight.

A tight dark group of men had been following them
—fellows who had somehow been insulted during the
day and night of carousing. The intrepid pair turned and
faced the men from a distance. McSkee finished the last
bottle and threw it into the midst of the group. The
men were bad-natured; they flamed up instantly, and
the man who was struck by the flying bottle swore.

So they joined battle.

For a while it seemed that the forces of righteous-
ness would prevail. McSkee was a glorious fighter, and
Sour John was competent. They spread those angry men
out on the sand like a bunch of beached flounder fish.
It was one of those great battles—always to be remembered.

But there were too many of those men, as McSkee
had known there would be; he had made an outlandish number of enemies in a day and a night.

The wild fight climaxed, crested, and shattered, like

a high wave thunderously breaking under. And McSkee, having touched top glory and pleasure, suddenly ceased to battle.

He gave one wild whoop of joy that echoed the length of the island. Then he drew a grand breath and held it. He closed his eyes and stood like a grinning rigid statue.

The angry men toppled him and swarmed him; they stomped him into the sand and kicked the very life out of the McSkee.

Sour John had battled as long as there was a battle. He understood now that McSkee had withdrawn for reasons that were not clear. He did likewise. He broke and ran, not from cowardice, but from private inclination.

An hour later, just at the first touch of dawn, Sour John returned. He found that McSkee was dead—with no breath, no pulse, no heat. And there was something else. McSkee had said, in one of his rambling tales, that he got a pretty high shine on him. John knew what he meant now. That man got ripe real fast. By the test of the nose, McSkee was dead.

With a child's shovel that he found there, Sour John dug a hole in the side of one of the sand cliffs. He buried his friend McSkee there. He knew that McSkee still had the twenty-dollar bill in his pants. He left it with him. It isn't so bad to be one or the other, but to be both dead and broke at the same time is an ignominy almost past enduring.

Then Sour John walked into town to get some breakfast, and quickly forgot about the whole thing.

He followed his avocation of knocking around the world and meeting interesting people. The chances are that he met you, if there's anything interesting about you at all; he doesn't miss any of them.

Twelve years went by, and some weeks. Sour John was back in one of the interesting port cities, but with a difference. There had come the day as it comes to many (and pray it may not come to you!) when Sour John was not flush. He was as broke as a man can be, with nothing in his pockets or in his stomach, and with very little on his back. He was on the beach in every sense.

Then he bethought himself of the previous times he had been in this city. There had been benders here; there had been antics and enjoyments. They came back to him in a rush—a dozen happy times, and then one in particular.

"He was an Odd One, a real juicy cove." Sour John grinned as he remembered. "He knew a trick, how to die just when he wanted to. He said that it took a lot of practice, but I don't see the point in practicing a thing that you do but once."

Then Sour John remembered a twenty-dollar bill that he had buried with that juicy cove. The memory of the incandescent McSkee came back to Sour John as he walked down the empty beach.

"He said that you could jam a lot of living into a day and a night," John said. "You can. I do. He said something else that I forget."

Sour John found the old sand cliff. In half an hour he had dug out the body of McSkee. It still had a high old shine on it, but it was better preserved than the clothes. The twenty-dollar bill was still there, disreputable but spendable.

"I'll take it now, when I have the need," Sour John said softly. "And later, when I am flush again, I will bring it back here."

"Yes. You do that," said McSkee.

There are men in the world who would be startled if a thing like that happened to them. Some of them would have gasped and staggered back. The meaner ones would have cried out. John Sourwine, of course, was not a man like that. But he was human, and he did a human thing:

He blinked.

"I had no idea that you were in such a state," he said to McSkee. "So that's the way you do it."

"That's the way, John. One day at a time! And I space them far enough apart that they don't pall on me."

"Are you ready to get up again, McSkee?"

"I sure am not, John. I had just barely died. It'll be another fifty years before I have a really good appetite worked up."

"Don't you think it's cheating?"

"Nobody's told me that it's disallowed. And only the days that I live count. I stretch them out a long while this way, and every one of them is memorable. I tell you that I have no dull days in my life."

"I'm still not sure how you do it, McSkee. Is it suspended animation?"

"No, no! More men have run afoul on that phrase than on any other. You think of it like that and you've already missed it. You die, John, or else you're just kidding yourself. Watch me this time and you'll see. Then bury me again and leave me in peace. Nobody likes to be resurrected before he's had time to get comfortable in his grave."

So McSkee put himself carefully to death once more, and Sour John buried him again in the side of the sand cliff.

McSkee—which in hedge Irish is Son of Slumber— the master of suspended animation (no, no, if you think of it that way you've already missed it, it's death, it's death), who lived his life one day at a time, and those days separated by decades.

GUESTING TIME

Things were a bit crowded where they came from—and were getting that way here!

WINSTON, THE Civil Servant in Immigration and Arrivals, was puzzled when he came that morning. There were several hundred new people behind the cyclone fences, and no arrivals had been scheduled.

"What ships landed?" he called out. "Why were they unscheduled?"

"No ships landed, sir," said Potholder, the senior guard.

"Then how did these people get here? Walk down from the sky?" Winston asked snappishly.

"Yes, sir, I guess so. We don't know who they are or how they keep coming here. They say they are from Skandia."

"We have few Scandinavian arrivals, and none of such appearance as this," said Winston. "How many are there?"

"Well, sir, when we first noticed them there were seven, and they hadn't been there a moment before."

"Seven? You're crazy. There are hundreds."

"Yes, sir. I'm crazy. A minute after there were seven, there were seventeen. But no more had come from anywhere. Then there were sixty. We separated them into groups of ten and watched them very closely. None crossed from one group to another, none came from anywhere else. But soon there were fifteen, then twenty-five, then thirty in each group. And there's a lot more of them there now than when you started to talk to me a moment ago, Mr. Winston."

"Corcoran is my superior and will be here in a minute," Winston said. "He'll know what to do."

"Mr. Corcoran left just before you arrived, sir," said Potholder. "He watched it a while, and then went away babbling."

"I always admired his quick grasp of a situation," said Winston. He also went away babbling.

There were about a thousand of those Skandia people, and a little later there were nine times that many. They weren't dowdy people, but the area wouldn't hold any more. The fences all went down, and the Skandias spread out into the city and towns and country. This was only the beginning of it. About a million of them materialized there that morning, then the same thing happened at ten thousand other Ports of Entry of Earth.

"Mama," said Trixie, "there are some people here who want to use our bathroom." This was Beatrice (Trixie) Trux, a little girl in the small town of Winterfield.

"What an odd request!" said Mrs. Trux. "But I suppose it is in the nature of an emergency. Let them in, Trixie. How many people are there?"

"About a thousand," said Trixie.

"Trixie, there can't be that many."

"All right, you count them."

All the people came in to use the Trux's bathroom. There were somewhat more than a thousand of them, and it took them quite a while to use the bathroom even though they put a fifteen-second limit on each one and had a timekeeper with a bell to enforce it. They did it all with a lot of laughter and carrying on, but it took that first bunch about five hours to go through, and by that time there were a lot more new ones waiting.

"This is a little unusual," Mrs. Trux said to some of the Skandia women. "I was never short on hospitality. It is our physical resources, not our willingness, that becomes strained. There are so many of you!"

"Don't give it a thought," the Skandia women said. "It is the intent that counts, and it was so kind of you people to invite us. We seldom get a chance to go anywhere. We came a little early, but the main bunch will be along very soon. Don't you just love to go visiting."

"Oh, yes, yes," said Mrs. Trux. "I never realized till now just how much I wanted to go visiting."

But when she saw the whole outdoors black with the new people, Mrs. Trux decided that she had better stay where she was.

Truman Trux was figuring with a pencil.

"Our lot is fifty feet by a hundred and fifty feet, Jessica," he said. "That is either 7,500 or 75,000 square feet depending on how many zeroes you carry it out to."

"You were always good at math," said Mrs. Trux. "How do you do it anyhow?"

"And do you know how many people are living with us here on this lot, Jessica?" Truman asked.

"Quite a few."

"I am guessing between six and seven thousand," said Truman. "I found several more blocks of them this morning that I didn't know about. They have a complete city built in our back yard. The streets are two and a half feet wide; the houses are eight feet by eight feet with six foot ceilings, and most of them are nine stories high. Whole families live in each room and cook there besides. They have shops and bazaars set up. They even have factories built. I know there is an entire wholesale textile district in our back yard. There are thirteen taverns and five music halls in our yard to my own knowledge, and there may be more."

"Well, some of those places are pretty small, Truman. The Little Hideout is the broom closet of the Big Hideout, and I don't know if we should count it as a separate tavern. You have to go into the Sideways Club sideways; the Thinman Club is only nine inches wide from wall to wall and it's quite a trick to bending an elbow there; and the Mouse Room is small. But the better clubs are up in our attic, Truman. Did you ever count them? The Crazy Man Cabaret is up there, and the After Hours Club. Most of the other attic clubs are key clubs and I'm not a member. They've set up the Skandia Art Theater in our basement now, you know. They have continuous performances."

"I know it, Jessica, I know it."

"Their comedies are so funny that I nearly die. The trouble is that it's so crowded there that you have to laugh in when the one next to you laughs out. And I cry just like they do at their tragedies. They're all about women who can't have any more children. Why don't we have a bunch more, Truman? There's more than twenty shops in our yard where they sell nothing but fertility charms. I wonder why there aren't any children with the Skandia?"

"Ah, they say that this is just a short first visit by a few of them and they didn't presume to bring their children with them. What is that new racket superimposed on the old?"

"Oh, that's the big drums and the cymbals. They're having a political campaign to elect temporary officials for the time of their visit here. Imperial City, that's the town in our yard, and our house, will elect delegates to go to Congress to represent this whole block. The elections will be tonight. Then we'll really hear some noise, they say. The big drums don't really waste space, Truman. There are people inside them and they play them from the inside. Some of our neighbors are getting a little fussy about the newcomers, but I always did like a house full of people."

"We have it now, Jessica. I never got used to sleeping in a bed with nine other people, even if they are quiet sleepers. I like people, and I am fond of new experiences. But it is getting crowded."

"We have more of the Skandia than anyone else in the block except the Skirveys. They say it's because they like us more than some of the others. Mamie Skirvey is taking four kinds of the fertility pills now. She is almost sure she will be able to have triplets. I want to too."

"All the stores are stripped, Jessica, and all the lumber yards and lumber camps; and the grain elevators will be empty in two more days. The Skandia pay for everything in money, but nobody knows what it says

313

on it. I haven't got used to walking on men and women when I go out, but there's no avoiding it since the ground is covered with them."

"They don't mind. They're used to it. They say it's crowded where they come from."

The Winterfield *Times-Tribune Telegraph* had a piece about the Skandia:

> *The plain fact is that for two days the Earth has had ten billion visitors from Skandia, wherever that is. The plain fact is that the Earth will die of them within a week. They appear by invisible transportation, but they have shown no inclination to disappear in the same manner. Food will be gone, the very air we breathe will be gone. They speak all our languages, they are polite, friendly and agreeable. And we will perish from them.*

A big smiling man broke in on Bar-John, who was once again president of Big State Amalgamated, former-ly U. S. A.

"I'm the president of the Skandia Visitation," he boomed. "We have come partly to instruct you people and we find that you do need it. Your fertility rate is pathetic. You barely double in fifty years. Your medicine, adequate in other fields, is worse than childish in this. We find that some of the nostrums peddled to your people actually *impede* fertility. Well, get in the Surgeon General and a few of the boys and we'll begin to correct the situation."

"Gedoudahere," said President Bar-John.

"I know you will not want your people to miss out on the population blessing," said the Skandia Visitation President. "We can aid you. We want you to be as happy as we are."

"Jarvis! Cudgelman! Sapsucker!" President Bar-John called out. "Shoot down this man. I'll implement the paper work on it later."

"You always say that but you never do," Sapsucker complained. "It's been getting us in a lot of trouble."

"Oh, well, don't shoot him down then if you're going to make an issue of it. I long for the old days when the simple things were done simply. Dammit, you Skandia skinner, do you know that there are nine thousand of you in the White House itself?"

"We intend to improve that this very hour," the Skandia president said. "We can erect one, two, or even three decks in these high-ceilinged rooms. I am happy to say that we will have thirty thousand of our people quartered in the White House this night."

"Do you think I like to take a bath with eight other persons—not even registered voters—in the same tub?" President Bar-John complained. "Do you think I like to eat off a plate shared by three or four other people? Or to shave, by mistake, faces other than my own in the morning?"

"I don't see why not," said the Skandia Visitation president. "People are our most precious commodity. Presidents are always chosen as being those who most love the people."

"Oh, come on, fellows," said President Bar-John. "Shoot down the ever-loving son. We're entitled to a free one now and then."

Jarvis and Cudgelman and Sapsucker blazed away at the Skandia, but they harmed him not at all.

"You should have known that we are immune to that," the Skandia said. "We voted against its effect years ago. Well, since you will not cooperate, I will go direct to your people. Happy increase to you, gentlemen."

Truman Trux, having gone out from his own place for a little change, was sitting on a park bench.

He wasn't actually sitting on it, but several feet above it. In that particular place, a talkative Skandia lady sat on the bench itself. On her lap sat a sturdy Skandia man reading the *Sporting News* and smoking a pipe. On him

315

sat a younger Skandia woman. On this younger woman sat Truman Trux, and on him sat a dark Skandia girl who was filing her fingernails and humming a tune. On her in turn sat an elderly Skandia man. As crowded as things had become, one could not expect a seat of one's own.

A fellow and his girl came along, walking on the people on the grass.

Mind if we get on?" asked the girl.

"Quite all right," said the elderly gentleman on top. " 'Sall right," said the girl working on her nails. "Certainly," said Truman and the others, and the *Sporting News* man puffed into his pipe that it was perfectly agreeable.

There was no longer any motor traffic. People walked closely packed on streets and sidewalks. The slow stratum was the lowest, then the medium, then the fast (walking on the shoulders of the mediums and combining the three speeds). At crossings it became rather intricate, and people were sometimes piled nine high. But the Earth people, those who still went out, quickly got onto the Skandia techniques.

An Earthman, known for his extreme views, had mounted onto a monument in the park and began to harangue the people, Earth and Skandia. Truman Trux, who wanted to see and hear, managed to get a nice fifth-level seat, sitting on the shoulders of a nice Skandia girl, who sat on the shoulders of another who likewise to the bottom.

"Ye are the plague of locusts!" howled the Earthside crank. "Ye have stripped us bare!"

"The poor man!" said the Skandia girl who was Truman's understeady. "He likely has only a few children and is embittered."

"Ye have devoured our substance and stolen the very air of our life. Ye are the Apocalyptical grasshoppers, the eleventh plague."

"Here is a fertility charm for your wife," said the

316

Skandia girl, and reached it up to Truman. "You might not need it yet, but keep it for the future. It is for those who have more than twelve. The words in Skandia say 'Why stop now?' it is very efficacious."

"Thank you," said Truman. "My wife has many charms from you good people, but not one like this. We have only one child, a young girl."

"What a shame! Here is a charm for your daughter. She cannot begin to use them too early."

"Destruction, destruction, destruction on ye all!" screamed the Earth-side crank from atop the monument.

"Quite an adept," said the Skandia girl. "To what school of eloquence does he belong?"

The crowd began to break up and move off. Truman felt himself taken down one level and then another.

"Any particular direction?" asked the Skandia girl.

"This is fine," said Truman. "We're going toward my home."

"Why, here's a place almost clear," said the girl. "You'd never find anything like this at home." They were now down to the last level, the girl walking only on the horizontal bodies of those lounging on the grass. "You can get off and walk if you wish," said the girl. "Here's a gap in the walkers you can slip down into. Well, toodle."

"You mean toodle-oo?" Truman asked as he slid off her shoulders.

"That's right. I can never remember the last part of it."

The Skandia were such friendly people!

President Bar-John and a dozen other regents of the world had decided that brusqueness was called for. Due to the intermingling of Earth and Skandia populations, this would be a task for small and medium arms. The problem would be to gather the Skandia together in open spots, but on the designated day they began to gather of themselves in a million parks and plazas of the Earth. It worked perfectly. Army units were posted everywhere and went into action.

Rifles began to whistle and machine guns to chatter. But the effect on the Skandia was not that expected.

Instead of falling wounded, they cheered everywhere.

"Pyrotechnics yet!" exclaimed a Skandia leader, mounting onto the monument in one park. "Oh, we are honored!"

But, though the Skandia did not fall from the gunshot, they had began to diminish in their numbers. They were disappearing as mysteriously as they had appeared a week before.

"We go now," said the Skandia leader from the top of the monument. "We have enjoyed every minute of our short visit. Do not despair! We will not abandon you to your emptiness. Our token force will return home and report. In another week we will visit you in substantial numbers. We will teach you the full happiness of human proximity, the glory of fruitfulness, the blessing of adequate population. We will teach you to fill up the horrible empty places of your planet."

The Skandia were thinning out. The last of them were taking cheering farewells of disconsolate Earth friends.

"We will be back," they said as they passed their last fertility charms into avid hands. "We'll be back and teach you everything so you can be as happy as we are. Good increase to you!"

"Good increase to you!" cried the Earth people to the disappearing Skandia. Oh, it would be a lonesome world without all those nice people! With them you had the feeling that they were really close to you.

"We'll be back!" said the Skandia leader, and disappeared from the monument. "We'll be back next week and a lot more of us," and then they were gone.

"—And next time we'll bring the kids!" came the last fading Skandia voice from the sky.